R. I. P.

A Novel

Nigel Williams

corsair

For Suzan

CORSAIR

First published in Great Britain in 2015 by Corsair, an imprint of
Little, Brown Book Group

1 3 5 7 9 10 8 6 4 2

A CIP catalogue record for this book
is available from the British Library.

ISBN 978-1-47211-816-5 (hardback)
ISBN 978-1-47211-859-2 (ebook)

Typeset in by SX Composing DTP Ltd
Printed and bound in Great Britain by Clays Ltd, St Ives Plc

Corsair
An imprint of
Little, Brown Book Group
100 Victoria Embankment
London EC4Y 0DY

An Hachette UK Company
www.hachette.co.uk

www.littlebrown.co.uk

PART ONE

The Knight looked surprised…'What does it matter where my body happens to be?' he said. 'My mind goes on working all the same.'

Alice Through the Looking Glass, Lewis Carroll

Chapter One

'George!' said Esmeralda, in a more than usually irritable tone. 'Are you just going to lie there all day?'

It was true, George reflected, that since he'd retired from the bank he had been getting up later and later. Why not lie there all day? Was there anything, really, that made getting up a worthwhile proposition?

It had not always been like this. In the first few years after what his friend Porter had called the Great Escape (he had sent George a note on the day of his leaving party, which read, 'Don't stop running till you reach the perimeter fence'), he had found it impossible to stay asleep after eight a.m.

He had, after all, been getting up at eight a.m. for nearly thirty years. It was a wonder that he didn't shoot out of bed, struggle into his suit and find himself halfway down Putney Hill before he woke up to the fact that the NatWest bank had no further need of him.

For about eight years and six months, of course, he had had to get up in order to stop Partridge crapping on the floor. More positive-minded people than George might have put that another way. Why could he not tell himself he simply wanted to see the dog? To share the Irish wolfhound's simple joy in the world? To get out there on Putney Heath and watch him sniff his way through the heather? To try looking as if he hadn't noticed when the animal relieved itself of about half a kilo of intricately coiled faeces?

George, however, had never been positive-minded. His relationship with Partridge was one of Strindbergian complexity and awfulness. Somehow, George's role seemed to be to stop it doing any of the things it wanted to do – like eat the sofa and defecate on the floor – and in the process he had more or less ruined the dog's life.

It was, he decided, all Esmeralda's fault. It was Esmeralda who had kept up a vicious campaign against the animal for every minute of its increasingly narrow and wretched life.

'Don't let him into the kitchen with dirty paws.'

'Don't let him lick the dirty plates in the dishwasher.'

'Don't let him eat things off the sides.'

One of the few high points of Partridge's life had been the moment he'd realized he was large enough to eat things off the work surfaces; but after Esmeralda had screamed at him when he attempted to repeat the experience, he retired to his basket and spent most of the rest of his life staring glumly over his paws at the distant horizons of Esmeralda's kitchen floor.

And now he was dead. He had gone where the good doggies go. To a place where Esmeralda could not scream at him any more.

'Lying there!' she was saying. 'Like a toad! All I can see is bits of your hair poking out from under the duvet!'

She obviously thought he was asleep. If he carried on lying very, very still, she might continue to think that. And, possibly, shut the fuck up. Although the likelihood of Esmeralda ever shutting up about anything was – George had to admit – pretty remote.

She had a few more important criticisms to make before she was through.

'It's a quarter to nine. There are hundreds of people in the house. The whole of your fucking family. Your mother. Your brother. Your sister. Your mother's mad lesbian friends. And you are lying there like a toad.'

Why had she got it in for toads? Toads were nice. They crouched in the bushes, doing no one any harm.

'Barry and Maurice are here. Ella Bella is here. Bella Ella is here. Jojo is here. Ginny is here. You bloody asked them. And you're lying there like a toad.'

For a moment, George thought she was going to poke him. If she did, he didn't feel it. It seemed possible that running through a few of his deficiencies had made her feel better about the world in general.

She lowered her head slightly closer to the duvet as she remembered a few more. 'You're so vague. You never engage. You don't seem to live in the real world. You won't come to the book group. You were appallingly rude to that electrician. You sneer at the television. You're fat.'

This, George thought, was low of her. It was about the worst word in Esmeralda's vocabulary. It was, for her, the equivalent of someone accusing Hemingway of being a fruit.

She had obviously decided he was asleep. There was a confident, almost relaxed tone to her voice that suggested she knew that, for once, she was not likely to get any comeback. George was not usually a man to take an insult lying down. If you called him fat, he called you fat right back.

Yet this morning he seemed to be taking this lying down. Literally. Why? Was he losing his edge? Perhaps now, at the age of sixty-five, he had decided to retire, hurt, from the long sparring match that was his marriage.

'I'm going downstairs to tidy the kitchen,' Esmeralda was saying. 'As I did yesterday. And the day before. All you do is lie there. You are completely…irrelevant. You are a minor person of no importance.'

It was hard to find an answer to this. Perhaps because – at the moment anyway – it seemed to be pretty much on the money. Perhaps also because he had heard it all before. In forty years of marriage they had just about said everything they had to say to each other.

George heard her stomp off to the bathroom. There were women, he had heard, who spent hours perfecting their appearance before they went out to meet the world. Esmeralda was not one of them. It was into the bathroom, grab the bra off the radiator, peer at herself critically in the mirror, on with the tracksuit and the gigantic bracelet, then off downstairs to shout at people.

Once, her brassières had performed an important erotic function in his life. These days, they played the same role in his existence as did his socks in hers. She never wore knickers. This was not, as she had patiently explained to George, to do with sex. 'It's for myself!' she had barked, when he had asked her why she did this. 'I feel free without pants!' Free to do what?

She was now clomping down the stairs, to make life difficult for people other than George. If there were any brave enough to have ventured downstairs. George knew every timbre and half-tone of her footsteps and, from their texture and quality, he reckoned things were going to be pretty rough for anyone foolish enough to find themselves in the hall/kitchen-diner area.

'Ha!' he heard her say, as she reached the ground floor. 'Ha!'

This sounded, to George, like the kind of 'Ha!' that meant she had found new evidence of his failure to be a decent human being. A shoe, perhaps, abandoned before the long, slow trudge up the wooden stairs? A half-empty wine bottle? A cigarette – horror of horrors? Possibly all three. He had been drunk last night. He remembered that.

As she headed for the kitchen-diner, she kept up her monologue. Though it was still aimed, principally, at him, other people, like driftwood in the aftermath of a tsunami, floated past on the great sea of her contempt for the world and the people in it.

'...no thought for anyone and just *off* with the shoes and *fling* them on to the stairs as if some *butler* was going to pick them up, the butler being me, I suppose, and a fucking *cigarette*. I do not believe it! Was it that Mullins woman? I do not know why I have to put up with the long face from you and the "Is there any bacon?" rubbish when all you do is *waddle* around on your stumpy little legs and...'

This, thought George, really was not fair. He did not have stumpy little legs. His legs – most people thought – were his best feature. Even as he articulated the idea, however, he realized he had absolutely no evidence for its being true. Most people had no views, favourable or unfavourable, about George's legs. He had them. They got him down the hill to Waitrose and up the hill to the common, but they were of no interest to anyone apart from him and, so it seemed, Esmeralda.

But thinking things seemed to make them true. Why? George was wrestling with this deep philosophical conundrum when Esmeralda let out a scream of the kind usually reserved for housemaids discovering a dismembered body on the drawing-room carpet.

Perhaps she was just registering the fact that he had left a half-eaten sausage on one of the dining-room chairs, or, possibly, vomited all over her copy of *The Selected Poems of Carol Anne Duffy*. He was pretty sure he had chundered last night at some point in the proceedings. He had been hitting the parsnip wine pretty hard.

Had he possibly done a Partridge? Surely not. And yet…it was just conceivable that he had done a massive dump somewhere on the property. It had been a pretty uninhibited evening. It had been a night for saying what you thought of Ed Miliband. Or really getting down to brass tacks on the subject of Wagner and the Nazis.

Why not round it off by lowering the trousers and emptying the bowels in a quiet corner of the scullery?

'Oh, no! No! No! No!'

Whatever George had got up to in the early hours of the morning, he couldn't help thinking that Esmeralda was over-reacting. You would have thought he had strewn the remains of a full-on voodoo ritual all over the sideboard, or artfully inserted a severed human finger into the cutlery basket of the dishwasher.

'Oh, my God! My God! You must come! George! Stephen! Lulu? Did you stay? Oh, my God! It's Jessica! Jessica! Oh, my God! Jessica!'

Why was she shouting George's mother's name? George always felt peculiar when he heard her using it. 'Jessica – can I have the recipe for that wonderful chocolate cake you make?' 'Jessica – was George a competitive child?'

'Jessica' was a completely different person from George's mother. George's mother was 'Mum' or 'Ma' or 'The Old Lady' – or, if you were feeling annoyed with her, 'Mother'. If he was feeling even more annoyed with her she could become 'The Madwoman of Chaillot', 'The Old Bat' or 'The Witch of Endor' – but she was never, ever 'Jessica'. Jessica was who she had been before she embarked on the all-important task of being George's mother. Jessica was the name by which the Mullins woman, Sylvia Deakins and all those other women from her teacher-training college all those years ago used to call her. Jessica was the woman in the skiing photographs of the 1930s when she and other perfectly formed youngsters swanned around the Sud Tyrol trying not to look as if they sympathized with the Hitler Youth.

George was not entirely sure whether, if he had had the chance to meet his mother in 1936, he would have liked her.

'Oh, Jessica! Oh, my God, Jessica! Jessica! Jesus, Jessica! Jesus! Help! Oh, my God! Jessica! Help!'

George's mum had, presumably, fucked around with the coffee machine or something. Esmeralda hated anyone touching her coffee machine – almost as much as she disliked George spitting into her side of the basin when brushing his teeth. George felt he really ought to make some kind of response – even if it was only to turn over and pretend to be deeply asleep. Somehow he just couldn't seem to manage it. He was not up to even trying to earn the award of Esmeralda's favourite adjective – 'involved'. Someone from Wandsworth Council had rung him the other day to ask him how he thought the council were doing. He had answered, 'Don't know,' to all fifty-one questions. And these were about things that, normally, he cared about. Things like…dustbins and parking restrictions. He was getting old. Old and apathetic.

'Jessica! Come, someone! Please! Someone, help! Oh, Jessica! Jessica! Jessica! Oh, my God! Jessica! Jesus Christ! No! Jessica! What's happened to you, Jessica? Speak to me, Jessica!'

Perhaps she had broken the Venetian glasses. The ones they had brought back from Murano three years ago. As, somewhere on the upper floors of the house, people started to wake up in response to whatever it was that was making Esmeralda come on like a freshly crucified soprano, George found himself once more pondering his wife's inability to use his mother's Christian name without revealing the terrible inadequacy of their relationship. When Esmeralda said 'Jessica' – particularly when doing so to her face – she managed to make it sound as if they had only just met. Not only that. She also managed to suggest that she was about to uncover new and difficult truths about the woman almost everyone, in and out of her family, referred to as 'a marvel' and 'an astonishing old lady'.

She was ninety-nine today and, until whatever had happened a few seconds ago, she had shown no sign whatsoever of slowing up. Perhaps she had finally been a little too free and easy with the Zimmer frame. Perhaps she had done in the other hip. Perhaps—

'She's dead! Oh, my God! She's dead! Jessica is dead! Jesus Christ! Come, someone! Come! Come! Oh, God! Jessica's dead!'

This was sensational news. Unless this was an even more than usually elaborate attempt to gain attention, it looked as if George's mother was dead. He had better do something. Quickly. Other people seemed to be rising to the occasion. Stephen was clattering down the stairs at double-quick speed. Lulu, of course, had *not* stayed the night, but Barry and Maurice and Ginny and Jojo were here, as was, inevitably, Frigga. George could hear her familiar footsteps in the box room and then on the stairs. Could he hear the more masculine tread of the Mullins woman and the pad-pad of Beryl Vickers?

George heard Stephen's voice – manly, responsible and, as always, sounding very grown-up for a younger brother.

'George, mate! George! A serious situation here I'm afraid, mate!'

Well, thought George, I'd rather gathered that.

Then, above the babble of screaming, crying and vaguely

10

audible attempts at amateur medicine ('Try to sit her up!' 'Give her the kiss of life' 'Is she breathing or not, do we know?'), he heard the unmistakable sound of Frigga backing into the limelight of concern. Her high, wobbly voice and her habit of accentuating the wrong word in each sentence suggested she was auditioning for one of the small but impactful roles she so often played for the Putney Thespians – her Nurse in *Romeo and Juliet* or her (less successful) French Lady in Waiting in *Henry V*.

'Oh, *my* God! How can *this* be? Can *my* mother be dead?'

Frigga always talked like a character in a Victorian melodrama, and the sudden death of a close relative had not added any restraint to her performance.

'*We* must do something! We must hit *her* in the chest!' (Why?) 'I have some St John's wort in my *bag*! *Or* coltsfoot! *It* is very restorative! Or…' a slight pause before she added this clearly less attractive alternative '…we should *get* an ambulance! Or *a* doctor!'

Why not both, Frigga? Preferably at the same time! George still could not understand why he seemed unable to get out of bed. You would have thought that the death of one's mother, even at the ripe old age of ninety-nine, would elicit some more positive response than hiding under the duvet until it was all over.

He was under the duvet. Of that, he was absolutely sure. And yet, George found himself thinking, how did he *know* he was under the duvet? He could not feel the familiar sensation of high-thread White Company linen. He was not aware of the slight but comfortable pressure of the goose down on his chest or shoulders. Well, he knew he was under the duvet because Esmeralda had told him so. You knew things without necessarily experiencing them. That, thought George, was what being human was all about. The next time

11

Esmeralda – or someone like her – had a go at him for being vague, evasive and not in touch with things, he should point that out to her.

Downstairs, Esmeralda was saying, 'He's just asleep like a pig! He just lies there like a pig! Snoring! His mother is dead and he just lies there like a pig!'

For once George was prepared to admit that this might be a fair comment. He really ought to get up and join in more. There were people down there clearly in need of his unique blend of judicious self-interest and total indifference to the feelings of others. Someone needed to go down there and tell them all to get a grip on themselves. Stephen, as usual, was doing a lot of responsible acting, which, if past history was anything to go by, people were not taking at all seriously.

'What we need to do,' he was saying, in his best newsreader's voice, 'is get on to the police ASAP. And – obviously – a doctor. ASAP again. I'm happy to do that, Esmeralda. She is my mother, after all. It is your house but she is...er...my mother. Obviously.'

'George!'

Esmeralda was on her way. She made even more noise stomping up the stairs than she had done stomping down them. George made one more determined attempt to lever himself up from the prone position but, somehow, he did not seem to be making any more progress than he had in any of his earlier efforts. He just stayed right there under the duvet, aware, because she had told him so, that a tuft of his thick black hair was poking out on to the pillow, a guilty signpost to the trail that led inexorably to sixteen stone of Retired High Street Banker – a man so totally callous to human feeling that he could not be bothered to climb out from under the bedclothes and take a shufti at the freshly minted corpse of the woman who had given life to him, sent him to a minor public school and even managed to pretend to tolerate the small, muscular, irritable woman to whom he had been married for forty years.

'George! Have you no feelings at all? Are you dead to the world, George? Why are you just lying there like a toad when this terrible thing has happened?'

From downstairs, someone – the Mullins woman? – was saying something about the police but here, in the bedroom, things had gone suddenly very quiet indeed. Esmeralda had whipped off the duvet. George knew that she had done this because he was aware, somehow, that it was lying in a tangled heap on the floor, some two yards from the bed.

This was, in itself, unusual.

For him to be able to do this, he should, logically, have lifted his head at some kind of angle to the horizontal and yet, in so far as he was aware of anything at all, he would have said that he was still offering an angle of 180 degrees to the plane surface on which he seemed to be fixed. He might have insisted he was lying down but his field of vision seemed to be that of a standing man. 'Insisted' was the wrong word. He was just lying down. That was all there was to it. He did not seem to have any choice in the matter.

No. Not quite. Not quite that.

'George! George!'

Esmeralda seemed rather less assertive than usual. If George had not known her better, he might have said she was showing some concern for him. This was, he thought, very worrying. They had been married for an interminable length of time, but he had known her for much longer than that. They had met at St Jude's Church of England Primary School, Putney, at about the same time as the Suez crisis. George had been – or so he told people at dinner parties – seven and a half years old. Esmeralda was nearly nine. She had hit him with the handle of her skipping rope. George had burst into tears. 'It was all downhill after that...' George often said, adding his carefully worked-up 'boom' laugh to let people know that it was supposed to be funny. He had said it so often that Esmeralda was now occasionally heard to remark that if he did so one more time she would hit him with something a lot harder than a skipping-rope handle.

She never showed concern.

'George! Oh, my God! George! What is it? George! Oh, Jesus Christ! Oh, no! Oh, fuck! Oh, no! George! George! George!'

What was the matter with her this morning? She was leaving herself nowhere to go. If she carried on like this she was going to be in full hysterics by elevenses and as crazy as Ophelia in Act Four by lunchtime.

She seemed to be putting her hand to his face. She did this with the kind of caution that suggested he was about to lift his head from the pillow and bite off one of her fingers. This, thought George, was excessive. No – he did not like being woken up but he was a reasonable man. His mother was dead. He was – in the fullness of time – going to make a real effort to respond to this news.

Esmeralda's voice had dropped to a whisper.

'Speak to me, George! Say something, George! Tell me you're still there, George! Just let me know you're there! Oh, my God! Oh, darling!'

Darling! This was obviously very serious indeed.

'Darling! Tell me you're not dead!'

George pulled himself together. Or, at least, he had the illusion of doing some of the things associated with that course of action. He was pretty sure he had opened his mouth. He was almost positive he had lifted his left arm and even, perhaps, raised himself to a sitting position in order to let his wife know that, although he was sixty-five and then some, and not, admittedly, in superb physical shape, he was – in his opinion anyway – not actually dead yet.

'Oh, Jesus Christ! Oh, God! Oh, no! Oh, fuck! Oh, for God's sake! How can they do this? You can't be! Oh, George! Oh, no!'

She was in tears now. She was also leaning forwards and trying something she had not attempted for at least fifteen years – an early-morning embrace. It wasn't a very successful one because, as far as George could tell (although he was beginning to lose confidence in the reliability of his senses), he did not make any kind of response. That was almost the strangest thing to have happened so far in this unpleasantly eventful morning. He usually tried to make some kind of response to a direct physical approach – even if it was only to tell her he had a headache. You had to take it where you could find it at sixty-five.

His being dead might explain his lack of enthusiasm for a bit of pokey. Maybe he was dead. If he was, sex was liable to be out for the foreseeable future.

'Come! Come up here! Please! Come here now! It's George! This is unbelievable! I think George is dead too!'

Chapter Two

George was pretty sure he wasn't dead. If he were dead he wouldn't know about it. If he knew about it – he wasn't dead. *I think therefore I am.* The problem seemed to be that almost everyone else in the immediate vicinity seemed to think he *was* dead. They were pretty emphatic about it. Even if he had found a way of letting them know that he was still in there somewhere, he had the distinct impression that he would have been shouted down fairly rapidly. He became convinced, as the morning wore on, that some of them would have been prepared to whack him over the head with a length of lead piping in order to make their point. He was dead. That was the *on dit*.

There was a lot of stuff round his bedside of the 'How Can You Be Really Sure?' variety. Everyone seemed to have views – most of them, as far as George could tell, gleaned from extensive viewings of *CSI Miami* or the adventures of Hercule Poirot. Someone suggested getting a mirror and holding it over his mouth. Someone else (Frigga) obeyed and the thing was done, but the only reward seemed to be a spectacular view of George's molars. Esmeralda, who seemed alarmingly well up on techniques for establishing morbidity, put her index finger to a vein in his neck, listened intently for signs of activity in his chest and, at one stage, suggested

16

putting a thermometer up his rectum. Nobody – including George – thought this was a very good idea.

In the end it was Stephen, good old Stephen, who, with customary panache, took on the job of articulating the obvious. 'What we still need, basically,' he said, in the gravelly voice that had launched a thousand current-affairs programmes, 'is a doctor. And we need one fast. Does anyone here know a good, level-headed, reliable local doctor?'

Esmeralda had started crying again, perhaps out of pique that no one had favoured her thermometer-up-the-arse strategy, but she managed to get out the words 'Nathaniel' and 'Pinker'. Yes, Nathaniel Pinker was a doctor. That was true. He was level-headed to the point of being pretty uninterested in all forms of disease unless they were ones he himself seemed to have contracted. He was utterly, utterly local. But a 'good' doctor? No. A 'reliable' doctor? Definitely not.

'He's a family friend,' sobbed Esmeralda. 'I'm not sure he could take...you know...seeing poor George in this...in this...' She paused slightly, then went into a short burst of sobbing, moaning and rocking backwards and forwards that would not have disgraced Hecuba, on the walls of Troy, catching sight of her son's corpse being dragged backwards through the dust behind Achilles' chariot. '...in this...in this...condition!'

'He's a doctor,' said Stephen, who seemed now to have taken charge of the proceedings. 'He will have seen any number of dead bodies.'

He had indeed, thought George, and many of them had been put in that state by his own lack of diagnostic skills. That being said, he reflected grimly, this was one of the few occasions when Nat was not going to be able to do serious damage to either him or his mother. They were both, as far as George could make out, beyond the reach of clinical error.

17

As it turned out, of course, George could not have been more wrong.

The Mullins woman and Beryl Vickers had appeared on the landing, within striking distance of the bedroom door. They were both doing a lot of the anxious quivering George had often noticed as a feature of women of a certain age. Their anxiety was, however, at the moment anyway, of a rather general kind. They could have been fretting about catching a train or the non-arrival of their old-age pensions. Even the Mullins woman's large, knobbly features darted this way and that, giving her the look of a chicken searching the ground for uneaten seeds.

Neither of them liked George. Mullins had once asked him why he was so fat and he had, in return, asked her how she'd got her designer stubble looking so authentic. Vickers was a craftier number – but she had given George quite a few peculiar looks over the years.

'Somebody should be with Jessica,' Mullins was saying. 'I can't bear to think of her being all alone down there.'

How about *moi*? thought George. Do I have no need of company? And, if we're thinking along those lines, what difference does it make to either of us? You could play poker on our exposed bellies if you so cared, couldn't you? Aren't we…er…dead?

But Beryl Vickers and the Mullins woman were tiptoeing away to 'be with Jessica'. From the look of them, thought George, it would not be long before they were both even more completely with his mother in whatever place God had chosen for dead and blameless women. Where do you go when you die? It was a question that had often occurred to him. It had never seemed likely that the answer might be 22 Hornbeam Crescent, Putney.

Well, he had always told Esmeralda he didn't want to

move. 'They'll have to carry me out of Hornbeam Towers,' he used to say at dinner parties. It looked as if, for once, George's table talk had been bang on the money.

There now seemed to be two emerging factions among the unusually large number of people who had stopped over last night in the hope of celebrating Jessica's ninety-ninth birthday this afternoon. The Let's-Be-With-Jessica move-ment, spearheaded by Beryl Vickers and the Mullins woman, had an early recruit in the form of Frigga. Frigga had never been particularly keen on her older brother's company and trekking upstairs to be in the room with his corpse seemed a pretty low priority, as far as she was concerned.

'I'm going to see if Beryl's all right,' she called, from down-stairs, in her high, plaintive voice. 'I'm worried about them. They were so looking forward to Mummy's birthday. And I've made goulash.'

This news brought forth more tears all round – a particu-larly appropriate response to Frigga's goulash. His middle sister had no real aptitude for anything, apart from looking distressed, but 'lack of aptitude' didn't really begin to describe her cooking. The red peppers and onions looked as if they had been butchered by some vegetarian Jack the Ripper, while the paprika lay in wait in dark, dangerous clouds in the gravy, like mist from the Red Planet. Sometimes, George remembered, she put beetroot in it . . .

'I'll call Nathaniel!' Stephen was saying.

Where were his sons? Why were they not rushing in to get a good look at his corpse? He'd understand if the lads decided to give it a miss. George liked his sons. One of his main ambitions in life was to spare them trouble; he would like them to remember him as he was last night, well, perhaps in the earlier part of last night. Had he chundered? Had he been singing Irish songs?

'We're back, motherfuckers!' said Barry, down in the hall. The front door was opened and slammed, hard.

They must have been out, thought George. Buying cigarettes?

'Sssh! Please! Sssh! This is a House of Mourning!' said the Mullins woman.

'We know that, motherfucker,' said Maurice, who, like his brother and George, enjoyed making the Mullins woman feel uncomfortable. 'Which is why we come here as rarely as possible.'

'Except,' said Barry, 'when our granny – who can't even remember our motherfucking *names* – is being, like, ninety-nine! Hey!'

George heard the rapid footwork, double high-five and loud whoop associated with the Belly Bump. Both George's sons – who were about as close to twins as it was possible to be without actually being twins – were fat. George was fat. Barry was fat. Maurice was fat. Every male in his particular bit of the Pearmain family was fat. Not grotesquely or unpleasantly fat. Not wobbling or drooping fat. They were springily, energetically plump, a reminder of a time when people were not expected to look as if they were suffering from a wasting disease. There was a tautness in the Pearmain bellies that gave them the look of a highly sprung mattress, and when George's two thirty-something boys were, as they seemed to be at the moment, pleased with the world and their place in it, they bumped bellies.

George could hear one of his granddaughters, Bella, laugh. She liked the Belly Bump. The lads must have taken their girls round the corner.

'Your grandmother,' the Mullins woman was saying, in dramatic tones, 'is dead. She may have been murdered. Your father is also dead. He is dead in his bed. We don't yet know why he is dead.'

George heard her hissed aside to Beryl Vickers: 'He drank enough!'

Neither Barry nor Maurice seemed to have worked out any kind of response to this news. At least, unlike everyone else in the place, they were not sobbing or trying to dash up the stairs to give him a last embrace. Chips off the old block, he thought, with grim satisfaction. I raised them tough. They are tough. They are estate agents of whom I can be genuinely proud.

After a while he thought he heard Maurice say, 'Shit,' and emit a long, low whistle.

After an even longer while, Barry added, 'Bad call. Christ. Bad call.'

That's my boys! thought George.

Many of George's friends often asked, with an edge of malice, if his children were named after the Bee Gees. He would tell them that Maurice was named after the French singer who had given their father so much pleasure with the song 'Sank 'Eavern Fur Leedle Gurls' while Barry was named after the eponymous hero of Thackeray's master-piece. If they didn't know what 'eponymous' meant, or that George thought *Barry Lyndon* was Thackeray's best novel, they could, in George's view, just go and fuck themselves.

Barry Lyndon, George thought, had just the right combi-nation of greed, charm and misplaced ambition to serve as a role model for youth seeking to survive the modern world and, in fact, he was happy to see that both his sons had these qualities in spades.

Esmeralda had not deserted him, although George was beginning to wish she would find something to do other than sit by his cadaver looking miserable. She was still doing the rocking backwards and forwards but, to her credit, she had eased back on the sobbing and the sighing. 'Oh, darling

George,' she was saying, 'oh, darling, darling George. Oh, my darling. What has happened to you?'

'I am dead, motherfucker!' George wanted to say, but, of course, as a direct result of the validity of his intended response, found it impossible to get it out there in front of the public. What had happened to him happened to a lot of people. What was so unusual about it? He had been a bank manager. He had retired. He had drunk a lot. He had eaten even more. He had smoked the odd cigar. And now he was dead. Get with the programme.

She began to do something George instantly recognized as 'keening'. Wikipedia, which had, until recently, been George's sole source of knowledge about everything, described this as an improvised vocal lament, usually by a female, over a body awaiting burial. He wasn't, surely, quite at that point yet, was he? Wasn't Esmeralda getting a bit ahead of herself? She was, thank Christ, not yet at the stage of listing the genealogy of the deceased, praising his achievements or bemoaning the woeful state of those left behind – but she looked as if she might get around to that at any moment.

Women, thought George, were extraordinary. Only a few minutes ago she had been telling him he was a worthless sod who had no right to live and now here she was, carrying on as if the world had just lost a man who had had the edge on Mozart, Galileo or Charles Dickens. She was, he reflected, behaving not unlike his mum had behaved when confronted with the human remains of George Pearmain Senior in that side-room at Putney Hospital thirty-odd years ago. And Jessica – when her husband was alive – had been unstinting in her criticism of him. 'I packed a bag many a time,' she used to say. 'Many a time I packed a bag.'

Death, in the short term anyway, seemed to improve people's standing. Maybe George was about to look forward to a few weeks of universal praise. Certainly, from the way Esmeralda was behaving, you would have thought no one had ever stiffed before.

What was it the Mullins woman had said? George's mother had been murdered. That couldn't possibly be right. Who would want to murder Mrs Jessica Pearmain? Apart from Esmeralda. And Stephen. And George. And that bloke who was married to the woman who 'cleaned' for her.

'Mabel does so much more than clean,' the old bat used to say. 'She's a personal friend.'

Yeah. A personal friend who lifted her on and off the lavatory and listened to her endless attempts to explain the plot of *The Sound of Music* ('It's about this very nice Nazi aristocrat with lovely blond-haired children, who is being hunted by some *bad* Nazis!') and who, every third Saturday, lifted her off her sofa and let her stagger round the garden to look at the lovely birdies.

Mabel had been mentioned in Jessica's will, in all her wills, and there were a few of them. Mabel was a person, who, in George's view, would have had no compunction whatsoever about murdering an old lady in order to get her hands on a few thousand quid. How had they done it? Had she been stabbed? Strangled? Gassed? Poisoned? And why did Mullins seem so confident about the fact that George's mum had been illegally offed? She had always been pretty emphatic about the fact that Jessica was being done down by her family ('You never go to see her George. 'She loves you George. Show her you love her'). Perhaps Mullins's love for Mrs Pearmain Senior was so intense that she felt the need to deprive the world of a presence too exquisite to bear before the old bat got any closer to three figures.

'Old bat' was not a nice phrase to use about one's mother. She was dead. But, then, so was George, it seemed. They were, at long last, even. The living were the ones who had to respect the dead. He was relieved of responsibility.

As if she had intuited this, Esmeralda had started to use the kind of hushed tones adopted by English middle-class agnostics in French cathedrals. 'I'm going now, George. I'm going, darling. But I'm coming back. Oh, George. I can't believe this is happening. How does God let something like this happen?'

With remarkable ease, thought George. Sixty-five-year-old man dies in bed in Putney. So what? Teenage girls die of cancer every day. Thousands of men, women and children have been shot or blown up or tortured in Syria or Iraq. Any number of Jews in the Holocaust. God could do a lot better than one English pensioner if he really tried. He watched Esmeralda lift herself, heavily, from the bed and trudge off to the landing, presumably to get her sons up to speed on the body count at 22 Hornbeam Crescent, Putney. Her shoulders were bowed. Her big head drooped. She looked, as so often, like a refugee on her way out of a bombed city with all her worldly possessions packed into one shabby suitcase. That this bore no relation whatsoever to the real facts of Esmeralda's life – a reasonably comfortable childhood in the country as the only daughter of a GP and his neurotic wife (both now, thankfully, in the same position as George), an Oxford education and a successful career as a teacher – did not inhibit the curious compassion she seemed to provoke in her husband.

He felt sorry for her. Why was this? He was the one who was fucking dead.

There were other things to wonder at. In the literature dealing with souls that had left the body – at least, the bits of it George had encountered – those who had known the pleasure of out-of-body experiences recalled floating around on the ceiling looking down at themselves with detached compassion. There were a whole lot of other things involved as well – a great deal of white light, a feeling of deep peace and a general sense that the afterlife had been designed by the guys who had brought you Apple computers.

This did not seem to be happening to George. The things that made him what he was did not seem, at the moment, to be much in evidence at 22 Hornbeam Crescent – but he was pretty sure his soul was in the place where he usually looked for it (and usually failed to find it), i.e. inside George Pearmain. He did, however, have the uneasy feeling that it was not going to be there for much longer. At any moment, he told himself, he could be residing in thrilling regions of thick ribbed ice or rolling down a hill in some heavily spiked barrel towards a large bucket of shit.

Dante, thought George, grimly, what a tosser! If he'd had anything remotely right about what lay in store for mortals such as George Pearmain, the next few years were going to be tough.

In spite of the obvious dangers of his situation, though, he seemed to feel remarkably calm. He was ahead of the game. He was certainly much less anxious than he had been last night. Maybe he was still alive. Or, if he was dead, he was only technically dead. Maybe in a few minutes he would be up and about and annoying people. Although he had drunk nearly three bottles of Frigga's parsnip wine last night, *he did not have the slightest trace of a hangover.* This not being able to move business wasn't such a big deal. If he'd had a plan for the day, it had probably involved lying on his own in a darkened room for long periods. Which seemed to be what his family had in mind for him. *Death was a pretty sure fire way of dealing with a hangover.*

An American insurance proverb, first heard long ago,

floated across his mind: 'Death is Nature's way of telling us to slow down.' George found, to his surprise, that he was laughing. He did not have any of the usual symptoms associated with laughter – spasm, hiccup or sneeze; what he felt was the essence of laughter, an intense perception of the absurdity and impermanence of things that was, if anything, more pleasurable and easier to savour than any chuckle, grin or snigger he had known when alive.

His hearing was pin sharp, too. Downstairs he actually managed to hear Esmeralda whispering to Barry and Maurice, 'It's awful. Awful. Awful. First George's mother. Then George. What is happening?'

George wasn't sure how she could be so precise about the times of death. Maybe she was sticking to the order in which she had discovered the bodies. Barry, as usual, was asking for details. He always looked after the details at Pearmain and Pearmain. His brother took care of the bigger questions – like where they went for lunch.

'Someone broke into the house and attacked Granny savagely,' said Esmeralda.

'Was it Granny they were after?' said Barry. 'Were they…like…perverts with a thing about old people?'

'We think,' replied Esmeralda, 'that it was a burglary that went badly wrong. Someone has smashed a pane in the french windows. And, of course, George forgot to close the security grille.'

Aha! thought George. The honeymoon period is over. Not more than a few hours dead and my closing minutes on the planet are already being scrutinized for errors of judgement.

'Was Dad murdered?' Maurice was saying, in a smaller voice than George was accustomed to hearing from him. He felt something that was close to a pang as he heard his younger son sound something he very rarely was: serious.

'We don't think so,' George heard Stephen say, in his Refugees in Africa voice, compassionate but tough, as opposed to his Many Dead in Libya voice, angry and confused. 'We think your dad just died in the night. We have no idea why. It could be his heart. It could be his lungs. Or his brain. He may have had a massive stroke, a lesion in his brain that just whacked him out of court in seconds. As if a bomb hit him. I saw a guy hit by a bomb in Iraq. One minute he was there. Next minute he was quite definitely not. He was in thousands of pieces all over the walls of this mosque. It's a bit like that.'

George was pretty sure his brother had never been to Iraq or, if he had, it was for five minutes in the Green Zone, but so decisive and clipped was Stephen's voice that it was hard to believe he had not seen a great many things that made his older brother stiffing in the marital bed look pretty small beer.

'He wouldn't have known a thing about it,' went on Stephen, even more decisively, 'if he was asleep. Which he was. He was spark out. He was pissed. Last night he was pissed. I was pissed. We were all pissed. He went to bed. He passed out and, you know, wham, bam, thank you, ma'am. Kapow! Kerchunga! Cheerio!'

That was, thought George, supposed to comfort them. It did not seem to have that effect on Esmeralda, who sounded as if she was now gearing up for a full-scale musical account of George's lineage and achievements, whatever they might be. It was hard to tell what effect Stephen's latest piece-to-invisible-camera was having on Barry and Maurice.

They regarded their uncle with a kind of amused distrust that George had once thought normal in nephew/uncle relationships but now thought might be something to do with his own cautious but provisional affection for his younger and (admit it, George) more successful brother.

'Pinker knows his stuff,' Stephen was saying in crisp, purposeful tones. 'He's a good doctor. A capable man. I mean, I've never been treated by him but he always seems a level-headed bloke to me. Which is what we need right now. There's no sense in running round like headless chickens. Even if that's what we feel like doing.'

Esmeralda started to howl. Perhaps, thought George, as a form of protest at having to listen to a man she referred to – often to his face – as a pompous bastard. Her tears had absolutely no effect on Stephen but, then, for as long as they had known each other, nothing either said or did had any effect on the other.

'I know what you're going through, Esmeralda,' went on Stephen, dropping his voice slightly and sounding much as he did whenever he had to announce the news of a bomb blast or major road accident on the BBC. 'Lulu had a dodgy smear some years back. I went through hell.' He paused, very briefly. Then – in case there was any danger of interruption – added, 'Death is so final. It is the hardest thing we have to deal with. I went through this when my father died. I just couldn't believe I was never going to see him again but, of course, I didn't.'

Esmeralda was now, George felt, definitely keening.

'Today of all days,' Stephen was saying. 'Mother's birthday. My God! A day of celebration. A large-scale celebration. Of Mother's ninety-ninth. And not only is she dead but people are coming to the house, including Lulu, of course, who is, even as we speak, on her way to...' A note of genuine panic came into his voice: 'Lulu! Lulu's coming! Oh, my God! My God! I'd better phone her!'

Then, abandoning all pretence of having been in charge of the proceedings, George's younger brother started to prod furiously at his mobile. George could hear the ping of the

28

keys. Suddenly he stopped. 'No. I'd better email her. She prefers email. She hates voicemail. Email would be more appropriate. Email it is.'

George could not quite understand why there should be any etiquette about the way in which the news of his – and indeed his mother's – death should be circulated. Email. Text. Voicemail. The odd black-edged note. As far as he was concerned they were welcome to rush out into Hornbeam Crescent and scream it at the June sky. Still, Stephen's concern for his wife's feelings was touching. OK, he seemed to think her peace of mind was more important than his brother croaking or his mother being bludgeoned to death, but you had to get your priorities right, did you not?

George could hear his brother talking to his over-intelligent phone. Stephen's latest machine was too elaborate to be called a mobile and worthy of a far more laudatory adjective than 'smart'. It was a kind of Jeeves, coping with all of Stephen's many, many administrative requirements. Including the well-being of the very scary woman who had been George's sister-in-law for more than twenty years.

'Is Lulu free?' he heard Stephen say. 'Because my mother is dead!'

'Lulu is not dead,' said Stephen's phone, in tones as almost totally drained of emotion as its owner's. 'Lulu is in Basingstoke.'

'My mother,' said Stephen, slowly, 'is dead.'

'Your mother is not dead,' said Stephen's phone. 'It is her birthday. You must go there. Now.'

'Shut up, Jacqui!' said Stephen, in a voice that indicated, for the first time, some of the tension coiled within him. 'My mother is dead!'

'I am sorry for your loss,' said Stephen's phone. 'Would you like a list of reliable florists?'

'I want,' said Stephen, 'to send Lulu an email. I want you
to send her an email.'

'Email,' said Stephen's phone, 'is a method of exchanging
digital messages whose invention is sometimes credited to
Howard Proez of Boston in 1964, but in fact is—'

Before it could go any further into the controversy
surrounding this – to George anyway – no longer relevant
invention, the bell rang. Esmeralda thundered towards the
door and George heard the unmistakable tones of the man
who was his friend, his doctor, and now the person with
the task of letting the world know how, why and when G.
Pearmain had died.

Let's hope, he reflected, he's better with dead patients than
live ones.

Chapter Three

Nathaniel Pinker – or 'Dr Nat' as he was known in Putney – was, according to Sue Pankworth, Esmeralda's semi-friend from Roehampton, 'the handsomest doctor in SW15'. George had never had the opportunity to examine any of the other male doctors in his postal area – though Percy Lewens from the East Sheen borders was widely concerned fairly doable – but he was prepared to concede, and even to look a little proud, that he was on close terms with a hot sexual property.

Nat had the look of a man sculpted out of high-quality toilet soap. His dark, close-clustered curls suggested one of the racier Greek gods and his upper body was generally considered to be something into which any red blooded woman would be keen to sink her teeth.

'It's his lips,' Geraldine Fairclough-Henley had hissed to Esmeralda at her fortieth wedding anniversary party. 'They're sort of bee-sting lips. And when his little tongue peeps out between them you just want him to...' At which she waggled her behind in a way George had found disturbing in a sixty-two-year-old grandmother.

'I'm here,' George heard him say, in the deep, reassuring voice that had so confidently announced so many wrong diagnoses. 'I'm here.'

Esmeralda had stopped howling. George was never quite

sure how far she trusted Nat. If only because he had spent
so many hours watching her listen to his wife on the subject
of his many crimes. George didn't want to know most of
the things he had been told about a man he'd thought of
as a friend. Was it relevant to their relationship for George
to know that Dr Nat liked to be given a hand job in the
shower? Did he care that the man thought UKIP were 'the
party of the future'? Veronica Pinker was absolutely entitled
to consider her husband 'boring, boring, boring', but George
did not wish to know this. Or that Nat often pleasured her
in front of *Channel 4 News*.

Esmeralda had been known to use the B word about her
friend's husband, but that, as far as George could make out,
did not stop her fancying him or – on this occasion anyway
– accepting comfort from the man.

'I was shouting at him...' George heard her snuffle, '...and
calling him a toad...and the next thing he was dead...'

Let that be a lesson to you, thought George.

'One minute I was abusing him! A minute later he...'

'I know,' said Nat. 'It happens all the time.'

'It does,' sniffed Esmeralda. 'I'm always calling him a toad.'

'Death takes absolutely no account of our feelings,' Nat
was saying, in a low, soothing voice. George was almost
certain he was enfolding Esmeralda in his well-toned arms.
His voice was testament to the fact that what he lacked in
medical knowledge he more than made up for in bedside
manner. 'It just comes along and changes everything like
a...like a...' he hunted for a way to complete the simile
'...like a...rhinoceros barging into the furniture.'

There was a silence. Then—

'I understand,' said Nat, slowly and carefully, 'that some
bastard of a burglar broke in and battered George's mum to
death, then went upstairs and killed him in his bed.'

'That,' said Stephen, crisply, 'may be how it happened. I've called the police. They'll send whoever they think is appropriate. We know two people are dead. My mother was battered to death. There are signs of a break-in. George seems to have died in the night, as far as we can see. Is there any relationship between the two deaths? Why did they happen at the same time? *Did* they happen at the same time?'

He stopped. Stephen's pieces to camera had been famous for his way with rhetorical questions. It wasn't, however, just the questions that made you think he was in the middle of a filmed report for some long gone TV news programme. He started to pace up and down the hall, doing the slicing-the-air gesture with his right hand that had made him, about thirty years ago, almost famous. He finished the broadcast in fine style.

'We do not yet know. The police will have a view on that. As they do. And you will take a view from the medical perspective. Hopefully, at some stage, we will reach some kind of conclusion, although God alone knows what it will be!'

There was a long silence while Nat absorbed this information. Then he said, 'Which one would you like me to look at first?'

'I'm not sure it makes any difference,' said Stephen, in the sort of voice that gave the impression he would have enjoyed a full and democratic debate about whether it did. 'They're both dead. As far as we can tell. But we're not doctors. You are a doctor. We're in your hands, old boy.'

Another long pause. Then Nat replied, 'I think I'll take a look at George first. He was my friend. If there's any chance at all that he's not dead I'd like to, you know, give him the benefit of the doubt!'

'Thank you,' said Esmeralda. 'Thank you, darling Nat.'

Well, get a move on, thought George. Don't spend all day talking about it. I'm only one floor up, guys. And, while we're at it, what's with this 'darling Nat' business?

'George was sixty-five,' went on Nat, who still did not seem over-keen on establishing whether G. Pearmain was or was not clinically dead. 'Mrs Pearmain was ninety-nine. George had a few more years left. Or has, possibly. If he's still alive. Let's hope so. Let's hope to God that is the case. There are conditions that simulate death. Catalepsy, for example. It's a kind of trance.'

'George was quite often in a kind of trance,' said Esmeralda. 'For quite long periods he just used to sit there and stare at the wall. I was quite often critical of him because of it.' Suddenly she began to howl in a spectacular fashion.

'Edgar Allan Poe had it,' said Stephen, keen, as always, to show off his stock of cultural references.

'Sometimes,' said Nat, who had, George was fairly sure, never heard of Edgar Allan Poe, 'the lack of a pulse, or the apparent lack of a pulse, does not imply that death is present.'

Neither he nor Stephen nor, indeed, any of them seemed to be showing any sign of heading up to the first floor and trying a bit of emergency resuscitation. So far, George reflected bitterly, no one had even thought to whack him on the chest. What was needed here was a bit of action. He might have been better pegging out in the Putney Leisure Centre – a place well supplied with defibrillators – rather than the master bedroom at 22 Hornbeam Crescent.

Finally he heard the sound of Nat's expensive leather shoes hitting the staircase with almost grudging slowness. As he came closer and closer to where George was lying, he continued to improve the moment with snippets of medical knowledge. Snippets, thought George glumly, were about as far as Nat went, these days.

'Verifying death is not easy,' George heard him say, in his deep, evenly accented tones. 'In 1905, for example, a French doctor was so keen to be absolutely sure his patient was actually dead that he inserted a needle into the patient's heart. It turned out he was alive. Well, he *had* been alive until the doctor had stuck a needle in his heart but, you know, you have to admire the thoroughness.'

Esmeralda sobbed.

'But don't worry, darling...' *Darling!* '...I won't be doing any of that. There are tests I can do. It may be that George has had a stroke. He didn't take much exercise. He was a drinker. He smoked cigars. He was overweight. It's amazing he's got this far, really.'

If George had had a stroke – and he found this thought comforting because although having a stroke wasn't ideal it was, at least, a marginal improvement on being dead – they did not seem in a hurry to do anything about it. Weren't you supposed to try to walk a stroke sufferer round the room and get them to repeat favourite bits of poetry? No one had yet asked George to give them a chunk of Robert Browning or that limerick about the man who tried to bugger a tube train. Perhaps, even now, he was morphing seamlessly into being a vegetable. If he was, was Nat the man to bring him back into the animal kingdom?

They came round the bedroom door in the manner of a group of gunfighters entering a room in the Old West, Nat in front, Esmeralda at his shoulder and behind her Stephen and Frigga, who had clearly grown bored with looking at their mother's body and had decided to give her eldest son's corpse a little face time instead. If, of course, it was his corpse. Something in him was alive – even if nobody seemed able to see it. *No change there, then.*

As often in the past he found he was awaiting Nat's

diagnosis with almost light-headed eagerness. It was not unlike the moment when they had all been on holiday in Portugal in 1994 and George had asked him to look at that weird lump on his leg – or the time when he had done a spot of coughing for him behind the Earl Spencer in 2004. He had a sudden burst of confidence in his old friend. If George wasn't dead, Nat was the man to steer him away from the route other people seemed too keen to prescribe for him – the embalming, the coffin, the—

'My God...' Nat was saying. 'My God...'

He said this in the kind of quiet and serious tones that George thought did not bode well.

'This man,' went on Nat, 'is dead. I am afraid to say that I can see he's definitely dead. Even from this distance and I'm – what? Four feet away.'

Six feet, thought George, at least six.

'I can tell you, he's dead. Believe you me. He won't be drinking any more Young's Special. Ever.'

There was another long silence.

'I'd better examine him, though. We don't want any bad feedback on my decision here. Which can happen. I am in a bit of doo-doo with the Primary Care Trust over that Asian woman who fell down a manhole. Or womanhole, I suppose, in her case. And the business with the Siamese twins. If that was what they were, although...'

'We'll leave you alone with him,' said Stephen. 'You need to do your job. And we need to do ours. I've emailed Lulu. She may not be long now. Do you need anything? Hot water?'

Nat thought about this. George could see he was very tempted by the possibility, but he managed to control himself and, shaking his head, said, 'That will not be necessary, I'm afraid. This man is dead. Completely dead.'

George found himself wondering what he would have

used the hot water for if George had not been dead. Maybe hot water was just what he needed to bring him round – or, at least, to get him to the point when he could start telling people that they had got this wrong. Wasn't hot water usually used for home births as opposed to home deaths? He did not feel in the slightest dead. He felt fine.

'We'll go and stand by Mummy's body,' said Frigga. 'I've strewn some fresh herbs on the kitchen floor!'

'Why have you done that?' said Nat.

Frigga said something incoherent about St John's wort and burst into tears again. Stephen ushered out Esmeralda and George's sister, and George was left alone with the nearest thing he had to a friend in the suburb where he had lived for nearly all his life.

Things were often slow between him and Nat. If their wives had not been friends – and Esmeralda and Veronica were tied together in ways that George would never, could never understand – he would probably not have chosen to spend quite so much time with Nat Pinker as he had done over the last thirty years. He was fond of the guy. Nat had never done anyone any harm. He had tried, and clearly failed, to be a competent GP. He had sung, off-key, in the Putney Choir for the last ten years. He had built his own bicycle. His fish smoker was something of a legend in SW15.

He wasn't, however, a natural conversationalist. When alone with him in the pub – at least two or three times a week – George was often hard put to find words. Oh, he found *some* words – 'Fancy another pint?'; 'The Young's Special doesn't seem itself tonight!'; 'Is it my round? Really?' – but they were never, somehow, words that conveyed the deep feelings of his heart. Perhaps because George had no deep feelings in his heart. Or, at least, not where Nat was concerned.

That was not really true. It was much more that conversations with Nat proceeded like one of those complicated forms you were obliged to fill in when booking tickets on the internet. Just as you were about to proceed to the next level you discovered you had left out some mandatory detail and were obliged to go back to the beginning. And, like the man in Kafka's story, you never quite got the details right so you were always in transit, groping for but never reaching the consummation of conversational exchange.

There was, of course, now no onus on George to keep up his end of the conversation. He was dead. He was, clearly, not supposed to sparkle. He imagined, indeed, the whole business would take place in total silence but, to George's surprise, Nat was far more chatty than usual. Perhaps dead bodies coaxed hitherto untapped reserves of dialogue to make the long journey from the Pinker brain to the Pinker voice box. Or perhaps – George had the uncomfortable feeling he was about to find out a great many things about himself he might have been better off not knowing – he never let the poor bastard get a word in edgeways. Not when he was alive anyway.

'Well, George, my boy, this is a pretty kettle of fish!' said Nat, as he began to apply his fingers to George's ribcage. 'I must say, I thought you had a few more years in you yet! We were all looking forward to you finally bringing out that volume of poetry. There were a few more publishers to try, I gather. I mean – not many but, you know, a few!'

He put his thumb and forefinger up to George's eyelids and, with the practised assurance of someone who did this for a living, closed his wife's friend's husband's eyes for what he clearly imagined was the last time.

It didn't seem to stop George watching him do it. He'd read somewhere – in H. G. Wells, perhaps, the supreme

38

information scavenger of all time – that there is a pineal eye somewhere deep in the brain through which we may perceive visions. It did not feel as if it was this eye that was observing Dr Nat go about his final examination of George Pearmain, B. A. Oxon. In so far as George had a point of view, it still seemed to be coming from the area of his bonce. Perhaps this would change. He was not looking forward to the fairly prolonged spell in a pine box that was – if this was not an unfortunate way of putting it – *de rigueur* for the newly dead.

Best not to go down that route. What was the thing you were supposed to do with death? Accept it. You didn't have much fucking choice, thought George, grimly, but panicking wouldn't help. He did not, for the moment anyway, seem to have any means of letting people know that he was still on the scene; although this, he had to admit, was not a new experience for him as far as 22 Hornbeam Crescent was concerned. He would just have to grit his teeth, get on with it and accentuate the positive.

It was not easy to feel positive about Nat's build-up to awarding him his death certificate. The man gave him the medical equivalent of a quick polish – not even bothering (to George's relief) to lift his pyjama bottoms and see if anything ghastly had happened to his cock. Then he took out a pad from his big black bag and started scribbling.

'It was your heart, old boy,' he said. 'It just gave up on you, mate. It sort of said, "George, I don't want this any more. I don't want to live in a world run by Islamic terrorists."'

Not for the first time, George felt a sneaky urge to disagree with him but was unable to begin the complicated process of questioning what Nat clearly thought were shared assumptions.

'Romanians,' he went on, as he continued to prod at George's chest, 'swarming all over the place. Interest rates at rock bottom. England despised all over the world. Black newsreaders. I give up, mate. And so, obviously, have you. I see your point, Georgy. You've had a massive heart attack, old boy.'

This speech, thought George, was both politically and medically questionable. Was that all it took? A quick feel of his sternum, a rapid flick of the eyelids and off to the golf course? How did Nat know he'd had a heart attack? It had obviously stopped working – but why?

Nat seemed to think he was done. He stepped back from the bed and gave something that was halfway between a salute and a wave. 'Goodbye, George!' he said, in a suitably solemn fashion. He turned on his heel and headed for the door. When he got to it he peered out on to the landing to make sure no one was listening. Then, after closing it completely, he turned back into the room.

'I've never told anyone this,' he said, 'not even Veronica. And she gets pretty much everything out of me. In time. As you know. I've never told you this, George, but I'm telling you now. When it's, er, safe to do so, as it were.' He cleared his throat. 'A few years back…I can't remember quite when. Ten? Can't remember. Anyway. A good few years. I think the summer we all went to Sicily. My God! Sicily! What a dump! Anyway, Esmeralda and I…I don't quite know how to put this but…I imagine you have a pretty good idea of what I'm trying to say…'

George would not, he felt, even if he had not just been pronounced dead.

'But…I won't go into detail. You were a great bloke, George. A great bloke. You could be very funny, George. Very amusing. That time you put that bucket on your head in Nîmes. My God. I nearly died laughing. But you could be…which was why Esmeralda and I…you know…I mean there were times, George, when I could cheerfully have murdered you. And I think Esmeralda felt the same. Anyway. I had to get that off my chest. I think it's cleared things up. So...thanks. Thanks for everything. Especially that piece of advice you gave me in Dieppe in 1993. My God. Saved my life. Such wisdom. Such wisdom. Look...'nuff said. Cheerio...I'm...you know...'

For a moment George thought that Nat might be about to lower the general tone by bursting into tears, but he did not. He closed the door reverently, and tiptoed away down the stairs. Why were people always closing the door on dead bodies? They had done it, George remembered, when his father had finally conked out in that sad little side-room in the hospital. Was it that people were worried some passing stranger might blunder in and see the unmentionable? Or was it some primitive fear that the body was going to rise up from the bed and do a zombie? In George's case, he reflected, that seemed a distinct possibility.

Esmeralda and Nat, eh? What exactly had they got up to? As a confession, thought George, Nat's speech needed work. It lacked detail. It needed a little more than '...why Esmeralda and I, you know...' From what George could remember of that holiday in Sicily there was hardly any time for sexual intercourse – even between people who were supposed to be staying in the same room. That time they went shopping in La Malfatta di Stagione or whatever the place was called? She might just have had time to give him a gobble in the hire car when they were going up the mountain road and George and Veronica had got lost. But...

And while we were at it, what was the invaluable piece of advice George was supposed to have given Nat in Dieppe in 1993? To give up medicine, perhaps? Not to say, 'Shall we have the other half?' after they had consumed two pints each? George couldn't remember ever having gone anywhere near Dieppe. The whole of the nineties had been a bit of a blur, even while he was living through them, and now he was dead they were more or less totally impenetrable. Perhaps because there were things he really didn't care to remember.

Had she, somehow, found out about Julie Biskiborne? Had she discovered that letter? It wasn't a great letter – Ms Biskiborne was no great shakes as a prose stylist – but, at the time it had meant a great deal to George. Which was why he had hidden it under the water tank in the attic. There had been a difficult two or three days last year when Esmeralda had decided to clear 'all that rubbish in the loft so as we can move somewhere smaller'. George had refused to help and, after three days of humping, pulling and desperate screams from the murky corners where roof met wall, she had given up.

She had not said anything but he would not have put it past her to have recovered the letter, read it, photocopied it and put it back exactly where she had found it to use against him at a later date. George thought he knew most of her moves in the marital boxing ring but, even after forty years, she was still capable of surprising him.

He supposed he was going to have to get used to seeing a lot of the details of his life made public. The dead have absolutely no defence against snoopers. They cannot even sue for libel. A full-length biography was not very likely. Unless, by some freak chance, someone stumbled across his poems, published them and George became a sort of middle-aged male English equivalent of Emily Dickinson, the most he was going to get was a few lines in the local paper.

If there was a local paper. George had a feeling they did not exist any more. Maybe someone would blog. Or maybe they wouldn't.

Nevertheless, in the small circle of people who made up George's public – Esmeralda, Barry, Maurice, Barry's wife Ginny, Maurice's wife Jojo, Nat and Veronica, Stephen, Frigga and (God help us) Lulu – it was going to be open season on his life. God! Maybe they were going to find the suspender belt! He had the distinct, though unjustifiable, feeling that he was breaking out in a sweat.

It was curious. He could have sworn that, although he was clearly not drawing breath and his heart was no longer beating, he still did have physical sensation. He had read somewhere that people who had lost a leg or an arm sometimes had the illusion they could waggle their toes or develop an itch on their palms. Maybe he was suffering from a similar form of hallucination; he had lost the use of heart, brain and nervous system but was, somehow, still under the illusion they were working away on his behalf. Was he, perhaps, like one of those cartoon mice who, when pushed off a cliff, still seem to stand, pedalling furiously, on the empty air? At any second would his system crash and the light inside George Pearmain be switched off for ever?

Something was worrying him. It wasn't what Nat had said about Esmeralda in Sicily (which sounded like the title of a novel she might read) and it wasn't the advice he had or hadn't given his friend in Dieppe in 1993. What was it?

As he tried to remember, he had the distinct sensation that he was moving his left leg off the bed. So vivid was this delusion that he could have sworn he felt the White Company sheets brush against his thigh. With it came a sudden and quite pleasurable awareness of the day outside. He could see his garden. He could see the silver birch tree. He could see the clematis against the fence. The big lawn and the rough ground beyond it. The parakeets were screeching their way from tree to tree on the borders of George's ridiculously large

43

garden. It was sunny. Everything out there was blue and gold and deep green.

Had he decided to move his leg off the bed? Or had it been done for him? Was he, perhaps, in the control of some Higher Power? In fact, he realized, as soon as his left foot hit the floor he became involved with the decision to move the other after it. The right leg. It wasn't easy. It felt (no, 'felt' was the wrong word)…It reminded him of how it felt when you ungummed your eyelids after sleep. It was like pulling the leg out of a bath of treacle so that, for a moment, George had the idea that he was dripping on to Esmeralda's carefully polished floor.

Curiouser and curiouser.

When George set himself the task of getting his arms to follow his legs, things did not proceed according to the same pattern. For a moment it seemed as if his legs and feet were out there on their own, in the middle of the floor, ready for duty, like a pair of unclaimed prosthetic limbs abandoned in a hospital ward. He was, somehow or other, going to have to move the middle section, head, arms and groin, and bolt them on to the as yet unclaimed appendages parked in the centre of the bedroom.

He concentrated on his upper body – which he had never done enough when alive – and found, to his surprise, that it seemed to be floating, free of the flesh that was still lying on the bed. His shoulders, too, were drifting upwards, aimlessly at first, then settling, as lightly as a butterfly, above his chest. His midriff came next, tearing itself away from the thing on the bed and weaving through the air like some aerodynamic puppy until it locked itself in place alongside head, eyes, ears, nose and mouth, all twanging their way back home with the decisiveness of a snapped garter belt.

And now other pieces of phantom George were docking,

like spacecraft returning to the mother ship in deep, deep space, so that, soon, a new kind of body had been reassembled next to the old one. He did not, as yet, seem to have any control over it. It looked, somehow, wrong. Did he have two left feet? Was his right hand screwed on backwards? Was that hole in his neck his belly button? He had the idea that if he managed to smuggle the thinking bit of himself – the only bit that seemed to have survived – into this ramshackle assortment of body parts, it would all begin to make sense. It would have a human shape even if it wasn't quite him. Maybe he'd be able to make it move. Maybe he'd be able to make it walk. Perhaps, eventually, he could persuade it to communicate. The idea excited him and, with a supreme effort, he concentrated on trying to steer the thing that was still George Pearmain up into the air and away from the bed.

It was as he was doing this, and it seemed to take an age, that he realized what was worrying him. He couldn't have said why he thought this (had he overheard someone downstairs whisper it?) but he felt he knew that Nat had, as usual, got it completely wrong and that there was something not right about his death. The word that echoed in his head – and it was his head now, as he seemed to have parted company from the dead ex-bank manager who was still stretched out beneath his unmortgaged ceiling – was, to his surprise, 'murder'. Mur-der. Mur-der. Mur-der. It banged around his newly reoccupied skull, like the noise of a battering ram against the walls of a castle, like the noise of water pipes booming in some old, abandoned house. Mur-der. Mur-der. Mur-der.

Chapter Four

Had this new, rather alarming thought (for which he had no evidence whatsoever) done something serious to his powers of perception?

What was strange was that now George was inside his body or, at least, a body that had looked vaguely like the one still on the bed, he couldn't see it any more. When he looked down at his toes, they were nowhere in evidence. This, of course, had more or less been the case since his late forties, principally because his stomach was in the way, but now his paunch seemed also to have done a bunk.

George found this very worrying. He was fond of his paunch. It was, or had been, a reassuring presence. A proof that he was there. Even when he studied it, critically, in the mirror before getting into bed, he had to admit to himself that its shape, like a large, carefully drawn comma, decorated with a network of thick, curly black hairs, was something of which he was secretly proud. Now, when he peered down at his feet, and he had the illusion of being inside a body which enabled him to do precisely that, he saw absolutely nothing at all.

Nevertheless, because of the highly wrought mental manoeuvre that had got him off the bed, he did feel he was inside a functioning body, even if he couldn't see it. Indeed, now he was no longer aware if his knees were on backwards or his nose had developed the alarming habit of slipping off his face and into his lap, he felt a whole lot better. He felt completely real, even if he was, to himself anyway, invisible. He didn't alto- gether like the idea that the next person to come round the door might be able to see what he could not – for all he knew, he might look to the world like the Beast from the Swamp or, indeed, a fully kitted out angel, wraith or demon – but, for the first time that morning, he had the illusion of making progress.

He concentrated on moving his right foot forward and was rewarded with the sensation of covering a good yard of the highly polished floor. Then, more quickly now, he brought his left leg past the right, and then, almost without thinking, as his left foot (yes, he could feel his right foot!) passed its opposite number, the right ankle, knee, calf and thigh (though not quite in that order) were off again in a pattern familiar to him since childhood. He was walking!

George had been slow to walk. Even after he had learned to do it, he had, according to his mother, been suspicious of it. After a few steps, he would sink gracefully to the floor and sit, like a small Buddha, for minutes of contemplation, before attempting any more of the difficult art of movement.

That was not his mood now. Caution was a thing of the past. He was dead. What had he got to lose?

He found he was walking briskly in a circle round his bedroom. He could see things like underpants and discarded socks in his way, but he paid them no attention. His circles started small but, as he gained in confidence, they widened until he was jumping up on the marital bed, storming across the inert lump and even leaping, with ease, on to the chest of drawers on Esmeralda's side.

The phrase 'out of breath' occurred to him as he completed his tenth lap of the room. It struck him as comic. The mortal remains on the bed were out of breath, all right, but whatever had survived the events of the night appeared to be in first-class shape. In a mood of hectic self-confidence, the kind referred to by his grandmother as 'getting above himself', George practically ran for the door and reached for the handle.

He did not seem able to make contact with it.

He swiped feebly in the general direction of the brass knob but, perhaps unsurprisingly, it remained indifferent to his advances. He tried again. No dice. Then he allowed himself the illusion of sitting on the side of the bed and muttering, at a level that, had he had any vocal equipment, would have been clearly audible, the word 'fuck'.

It always made him feel better. Dead or alive. The fact that Esmeralda always winced when she heard him use it (even though she could quite often be free with it herself) made it an even more satisfactory form of therapy. If he was going to be a ghost – and it seemed possible that that was what he was – he would be the kind of ghost who said 'fuck' occasionally.

He said it again: 'Fuck!' Aloud and silently in the empty room. 'Fuck!'

He was dying, if that was not an inappropriate term, to be out and about and downstairs to see how and when and why his mum had been brutally murdered. If he was a ghost, surely he would be able to use a few traditional ghost techniques for getting from A to B and back again. Ghosts in Hollywood movies were always on the move. They were always pushing their upper bodies through brick walls, then dragging the rest of their shadowy selves after them. In one film he had seen, the bloke, although he had been brutally murdered only a few days before, was able without difficulty to join in his wife's pottery class.

He couldn't even open the bedroom door. This was bad. He was an English ghost. Was that the problem?

Neither – he was starting to get seriously annoyed now – had he been vouchsafed any harp music or white light nor discovered any powers more sensational than the ability to walk, at speed, round his own bedroom. Was he doomed to stay up here with his corpse until the men in black jackets lumbered up the stairs to prepare him for the wagon labelled 'PRIVATE AMBULANCE'?

Just as he was thinking this, the door opened and Frigga stole into the room. 'George,' she called, in a light, coaxing voice. 'Are you there?'

Where had she been for the last half-hour? He was dead, wasn't he? Or had his younger sister somehow acquired the ability to cotton on to the fact that George Pearmain was not entirely deceased? She had always had pretensions to being *au fait* with the spirit world.

She wasn't, as far as George could tell, looking at where he thought he was. She seemed to think the slowly stiffening five feet ten inches of lard parked on the bed was worth a few carefully chosen words. To confirm his suspicion, she began to advance, priest-like, towards the very spot where George liked to think he was sitting. Her long, lank white hair bounced listlessly about her pale, blemished face, and, as she got closer, she extended her two skinny arms in a gesture that was vaguely druidical. She looked, George thought, considerably more ghostly than he felt.

'Oh George,' she said, in her customary, high monotone, 'peace to your spirit. Be among the ancestors. Let the Great Mother heal you. Go placidly with Our Father and join with Jessica and Great Aunt Maud who have all gone before.'

So far, to his distinct relief, George had not caught a glimpse of any of his ancestors. The thought that he might bump into Great Aunt Maud at any moment in the near future brought him out in a strong, if notional, sweat. He had not been aware of the full extent of Frigga's New Age problems. Yes, she had gone on about echinacea (if that was how you spelt it) and the healing properties of Old Mother Riley's Root Tea (even to the extent of forcing George to drink it) but he'd had no idea that her interest in herbs had led her into a belief system even older and crazier than Christianity.

Before she could sit on him, George managed to nip out of her way and watched as she laid her long, cold fingers on his pale forehead.

'I am very, very troubled, George. I am not sure but I think it's possible I may bear some responsibility for your death. I haven't shared this with anyone else, George – but I'm sharing it with you.'

Uh? thought George. The people she needed to share this kind of information with were the Metropolitan Police. Anyway, what did she mean by 'some responsibility'? Was she trying to tell him she was part of a conspiracy?

'I don't know, George. That is the thing. I just do not know. I don't think I did anything wrong. But I do not know. And if I did – did I do it deliberately, George? I had hostile feelings towards you, George. I did. As did you for me. I know you found me embarrassing. I know you feel I moan. I do moan, George. At night I moan. I moan for my barren womb. I moan for that man I met on holiday, Kevin or whatever his name was. I am wicked, George. I have wicked feelings. I have feelings of hate. Did those feelings of hate make me deliberately careless? I am usually so careful with things like – like – you know what. It is possible, George. I do not know, George. I do not know. Am I responsible for your death?'

You tell me, bitch. I'd like to know.

For a moment she looked as if she was going to do just that, but the effort of even opening up this clearly painful subject was too much for her, and Frigga began to make a noise that recalled a fox having sexual intercourse. Her mouth imploded dramatically. Her ears seemed to tremble. Her eyes and nose began to cry real tears.

George took this opportunity to tiptoe towards the open door.

To what could she be referring? Frigga was a woman who enjoyed feeling guilty about all sorts of things. She had always, for example, carried on as if the Falklands War was her fault. When Barry failed his A levels she had come to George, weeping, to tell him she felt she had distracted him. When George mentioned this to Barry, Barry seemed to have some difficulty remembering who Auntie Frigga was.

Her much-publicized guilt was nearly always, in George's view, another way of gaining attention. This was a woman who had, in the past, put a tea towel on her head and howled like a dog if anyone was careless enough to smuggle meat on to her plate or light up within two hundred yards – even in the open air. It was pretty clear that claiming some responsibility for his heart attack was just another—

Hang on. Hang on. She might be aware of something she didn't wish to admit even to herself. It was possible. She had said what she had said to an audience incapable – as far as she was aware – of response. If something dodgy had gone on last night, it might explain why George had failed to complete his departure from the world. Didn't ghosts usually come back to avenge themselves on whoever it was who had ended their lives ahead of schedule? Was this his mission?

He wasn't yet aware that anyone had murdered him, but it was possible. Among the many possible candidates for the role (including that bloke from the Wandsworth Parking Office and the man who had bought George's last car but two), Frigga must be a prime contender.

He turned back, briefly, at the door to the landing and

tried a bit of the kind of thing ghosts usually used on persons who, in spite of their having committed unspeakable crimes against them, seemed to be still tickety-boo. He tried out the beginnings of a wail but, although he could have sworn some kind of noise emerged from what were clearly not his lungs, the sound did not register with Frigga Brunhilde Pearmain.

George's mother had been heavily into Wagner when she fell pregnant with Frigga. She had also been reading a very obscure Norse saga that made the Elder Edda look like Jane Austen. Cnut beheaded Glyf who smote Ocki who drowned Boldrum the son of Klog. That kind of thing.

George had a theory that people's characters were influenced by their given names. He had known four people called Philippa – only one of whom was trustworthy. All Alans were devious. People called Nigel were almost always homosexually inclined. Parents created forenames out of their hidden ambitions and dreams. If Jessica Pearmain had given her only daughter a moniker that suggested mists, mountains and large amounts of random violence, might it not be because she wanted her to turn into the kind of woman who was useful in a blood feud?

Frigga might well be a murderer, thought George. She was, now he thought about it, the kind of librarian who could all too easily run amok.

She was also, clearly, not about to reveal any more information about how and why she felt responsible for George's death. She was now making a noise that sounded a bit like someone opening and shutting a very squeaky gate. She seemed also to be pulling out chunks of her hair. He had things to do. There were people to see. He had to get downstairs for a last look at his mum before they shipped her off to the morgue in a black bin liner.

George had just got to the head of the stairs when he

somehow knew the front-door bell was about to ring. He didn't actually hear it but he was positive that that was what it was going to do.

Down below, in the hall, in various attitudes of grief, numbness and paralysis, were his immediate family. Ginny and Jojo had arrived from wherever they had been hiding. Ginny (Barry's wife) was holding eighteen-month Bella while Jojo (Maurice's wife) was standing over eighteen-month Ella, who seemed to be asking if her favourite cartoon character was anywhere about. Bella appeared to want to know where Ganpa was. A question no one, at the moment anyway, seemed inclined to answer.

Bella showed no sign of giving up her question. On the fifth time of asking, Ginny said, in a quiet, refined voice, 'We think Ganpa may be dead.'

'Dead,' repeated Bella, in a bright, cheery voice. 'Ganpa dead. Play oven?'

'I think,' Ginny was saying to Barry, 'it's important for them not to get upset about it. Or feel it's a bad thing.'

George had never got on with Ginny. This last remark, he felt, marked an even steeper downturn in their relationship than when she had told him her father wanted her to get married on a boat on the Thames and expected George to pay half.

'Bad thing!' said Bella.

Esmeralda burst into tears again. Barry started muttering something to Ginny, and Ginny looked at Esmeralda with the profound surprise that the sight of her mother-in-law always seemed to evoke in her. She showed every sign, George thought, of ticking her off for upsetting her granddaughter. Maurice, Jojo and Ella went off to find a room without a dead body in it and Barry, Ginny and Bella followed them.

The rest of them – Esmeralda, Stephen, the Mullins

woman and Beryl Vickers – all looked as if they were waiting for something. For one crazy moment, George wondered if they might be waiting for him. Perhaps – he seemed to be standing, now, at the head of the stairs – one of them would be able to see him in, at least, dim outline. A spectral fragment of his head, perhaps. Or, failing that, a vague sense that he was not entirely absent from the house for which he had only recently finished paying.

Perhaps one of his grandchildren might pick up on his presence. Weren't they more sensitive to the spirit world than adults? Ella was now in the front room, watching a rerun of a television show about a toad called, by some strange coincidence, George. She knew who he was, all right. She often referred to him as Gondid, and he had had the impression, the last time he had held her hand and walked her across Maurice's kitchen floor, that she had begun to clock him. Maybe her weirdly wonderful perceptions of a world in which teddy bears ate and drank, cats had fully human status and a journey to the fridge had the epic quality of a Tolkien narrative would allow her to perceive George.

He realized, with a pang of self pity, that he wanted someone to perceive him. Even if they were not quite two feet high.

Everything seemed to be taking an unconscionably long time. The doorbell had not yet rung – George thought – yet now the people in the hall seemed to have cottoned on to the fact that a visitor was on his or her way. They seemed to be standing staring at the front door, their faces buckled and distorted by something that was probably, George thought, the passing of time slowed to an almost painful pace. He himself was experiencing the sharp end of delay in action. His feet were sinking into the stair carpet and its fibres were folding over his naked toes, like warm mud in a tropical

R . I . P .

swamp. He saw that Stephen, moving now, like an athlete to the finishing line in filmed slow motion, was pulling the front door open. Whoever was out there must have been waiting ages. And yet they hadn't. What was happening was more peculiar than an event taking longer to fill the passing minutes than usual.

Quite often, in the afterlife, things seemed to happen before the occurrence that might logically be supposed to have caused them. *Ante hoc ergo propter hoc*. George could have sworn that his family were all goggling at the front door, that the front door opened and that then, and only then, did the bell ring, long and loud and harsh. The sort of imperious, no-nonsense application of forefinger to button of the kind practised by pretty serious policemen.

And, indeed, that was what was standing in George's hall. A man in a dark suit, large, black shoes, a white shirt, an anonymous tie, and a general demeanour that suggested "Ello, 'ello, 'ello.' Next to him, with the air of one who had been put there specifically to remind the world that there was nothing plain about her companion's plain clothes, was a small, fat female officer. She seemed to be doing the introductions.

'DC Barbara Purves,' she was saying, 'and this is DI Hobday.'

Hobday nodded slowly. 'DI Hobday,' he said thoughtfully.

George had the impression that the man was not altogether happy about the way his subordinate was handling things. Too much, his pale blue eyes seemed to suggest, had already been revealed. He also had the air of a man who would have preferred a more dramatic way of entering George's property. Just coming in through the front door was clearly tame, as far as Hobday was concerned.

He looked, George thought, like a man used to battering his way into people's places at the break of day, preceded, if possible, by a group of men in blue, wearing Perspex helmets, carrying shields of matching material and festooned with snub-nosed machine guns. He was not, as yet, clasping a Glock pistol in both hands and sweeping it to and fro across the field of fire immediately ahead of him but he looked as if he might resort to this mode of advance at any moment.

'I understand,' he said to Stephen, 'that there are two bodies on the premises.'

'There are,' said Stephen, crisply. 'Two bodies.'

'I,' said Nat, 'am a doctor!'

'Yes,' said Hobday. 'Indeed.'

'He is,' said Stephen, anxious not to abandon his status as Most Responsible Person Present, 'the family doctor. We called him in to examine my brother. Which he has done. Although he was too late. My brother is dead.'

'I'm sorry to hear that,' said DC Purves, who was, obviously, the member of the team in charge of the personal side of things.

Hobday went back to looking at the floor. 'Murder,' he said, 'is never pleasant. But the murder of a close family member is very hard to deal with. For another close family member.'

'My brother,' said Stephen, 'has not been murdered. It was my mother who was murdered. At least – I don't think my brother was murdered. Was he murdered, Nat?'

'He was not,' said Nat. 'At least, not as far as I can tell. I'll be issuing a death certificate. It was his heart.'

Hobday trained his eyes on Dr Nat. *Oh, was it indeed?* his pale blue eyes seemed to be saying. *Barging in here and telling me my job! We'll see about that, matey!*

George was, once again, staggered at the certainty of doctors. The man had squinted at him once or twice in a darkened room and he was pronouncing with the confidence of the Pope on the Virgin Birth. Nat's qualifications, however, were going to cut little ice with Hobday. He was evidently a man who suspected anyone and everyone; he was not going to be easily impressed by a few years at medical college and a good bedside manner.

'My mother,' Stephen was saying, 'is on the kitchen floor. We found her. It looks like a break-in. There is a pane of glass in the french windows. Smashed. By a burglar. The man broke the glass and opened the door. He broke in to burgle. And ... burgled. Or not. But he was probably interrupted. By my mother. Who was sleeping downstairs. She had a Zimmer frame but she could walk. With it. The Zimmer frame is also on the floor. Pushed there. By the burglar.'

DI Hobday looked Stephen up and down. Slowly. 'Perhaps,' he said, 'you'll let us be the judge of that!' He inclined his head, very slowly, in the direction of the kitchen-diner at the back of the house. Then, with an even briefer nod to DC Purves, he slid almost imperceptibly towards the door to the kitchen. The assorted members of the Pearmain family – though not Jessica's two friends – showed every sign of trying to follow him. DI Hobday held up his hand. 'I shall need the person who found the body,' he said. 'No one else. Who discovered the body?'

There was a slightly accusatory tone to this question. Perhaps this was why no one, at first, seemed very keen to answer it, but eventually, in a small voice, Esmeralda owned up: it was she who had stumbled across her mother-in-law first.

'And you are?' said Hobday.

'Her daughter-in-law,' said Esmeralda. 'Mrs Esmeralda Pearmain.'

Hobday studied her closely. It was clear, from his expression, that he thought being someone's daughter-in-law was a pretty good motive for murder. George, from his experience of this particular blood tie, could not help but agree with him. If Esmeralda had not topped his mother (and her surprise this morning had sounded fairly genuine) then Lulu was certainly in the running for prime suspect, as far as the killing of the ninety-nine-year-old ex-piano teacher was concerned. He would not have been surprised to learn that Lulu Belhatchett (she never, ever used her married name, and only soiled her mouth with George's family's handle once it had been carefully disinfected with inverted commas) had put the rubbing-out of Jessica in the hands of some reliable firm of assassins, while she gave herself an alibi by slithering off to Basingstoke early yesterday evening.

He was just thinking this when, this time in ordered sequence, the bell was rung, the front door was opened and his sister-in-law had appeared on the mat, bearing the aspect, as usual, of one who had just been teleported from some distant galaxy where terminal *sangfroid* was the norm. Lulu's clothes, as usual, were immaculate. Lulu's coiffure, as usual, suggested she had just been wheeled out of some exclusive salon in a weatherproof container. Lulu's shoes bore no trace of having been in contact with anything as vulgar as the pavement. Lulu's jewellery – the tiny budded golden earrings, the chunky gold bracelet, the discreetly expensive pearls – spoke to anyone with the insolence to examine it closely of but one thing. Insurance. Lulu's skin – if there was anything that corresponded to that word under the inches of anti-wrinkle cream, deep, pure cleansing oil and wholly natural essence of jojoba – glowed like virgin snow under arc lights. Lulu's manicured nails, tapping restlessly on her personal organizer, spoke of boundless ambition, impatience and hostility to those foolish enough not to understand the fundamental importance of Lulu Belhatchett.

And then, of course, there was the nose. It was built on a massive scale. In its day the nose had struck terror into the hearts of countless politicians and celebrities. Strong men had been known to run when they saw it coming round a corner; and yet, thought George, there was still something glamorous about it.

The effect on DI Hobday was sensational.

George had taken him for a man who was hard to impress. If Einstein himself had wandered into George's front hall, George felt that he would have been just another potential suspect. He was a man who had seen dead bodies and not blinked. He was a man who was capable of being unmoved by strong men crying for mercy or gorgeous women throwing their tits at him in order to escape a jail sentence.

At the sight of Lulu Belhatchett, however, his poise crumbled, like an old digestive biscuit in a cup of hot coffee. His jaw did what jaws are supposed to do when men register shock. It dropped. His eyes widened and, for a moment, he seemed to be less excited than usual at the thought of a freshly killed murder victim.

'My God,' he said. '*Come Sit On My Knee.*'

Lulu allowed herself a small smile. '*Come Sit On My Knee*,' she said, 'Indeed. *Come Sit On My Knee.*'

DI Hobday seemed unable to get his jaw up and running. His eyes remained glued to Lulu's face as he said, 'You are Lulu Belhatchett. You did *Come Sit On My Knee.*'

Now, and only now, when she was sure of her ground, and waking up to the possibility that she might be walking into the unquestioning loyalty of one of her many, many fans, Lulu allowed the persons in the hall the luxury of an uninterrupted view of dental work that was almost as expensive as her jewellery. 'Lulu Belhatchett.' She smirked. '*Come Sit On My Knee!*'

Chapter Five

Come Sit on My Knee had started life as a radio programme,
developed, or, some said, regressed, into a television programme and, at a certain point in the 1990s, become a
legend. It had originally been presented by a stout lesbian
called Maureen O'Reilly; there were those who said the
programme had been her idea, but there was little doubt in
anyone's mind that it had never really established itself with
the public until Lulu Belhatchett made the move from news
reporting into being the voice and, later, the face of the show.

'So…Tony Blair…' she would say, in low, controlled
tones, '…come…sit on my knee.' And the nation shivered
with anticipation.

Maureen O'Reilly, a motherly person, who had started
life as a nurse, had wanted to do an interview show, which,
as she put it, 'let people be themselves'. She had a natural
horror of the awkward question. When Colin Bleah, the
heavy-metal guitarist who had just been through a messy
divorce and a two-year jail sentence for possession of heroin,
was on the programme, Maureen had refused to ask him
about any subject other than gardening, of which he was
reported to be fond.

The original notion behind *Come Sit On My Knee*
was that guests would be encouraged to talk about their

childhood 'as if they were talking to their mothers' but, as the years went on, O'Reilly became more and more obsessed with the concept of the show and less and less interested in the celebrities who were hauled in front of her by her production team.

'So,' she would say, 'now you're on my knee, how does it feel? Did it seem a long way to clamber up there? Do you need the loo at all?'

There were some who found her line of questioning, with its constant harping on the issue of how, when and why the participants had got on and off her knee, a trifle distasteful. When she asked the permanent under-secretary for the Treasury if he felt he needed the potty, it was thought time for her to go.

Lulu Belhatchett dealt in hard news. She had covered no less than three wars. She had insulted Martin McGuinness and asked Gerry Adams what it felt like to have blood on his hands. She had received death threats from an obscure group of Serbian nationalists after she had described them, publicly, as 'loonies' and she was rumoured never to have shown fear in the presence of Margaret Thatcher.

Her real name was not, of course, Belhatchett. Her real voice – which no one had ever heard – was, George suspected, nothing like the precision-steel instrument with which she tortured all those unfortunate enough to be in the news. Some said she came from Glasgow. Others swore she was originally from Cardiff. 'Wherever she comes from,' Esmeralda always said, 'she did not learn to talk like that in our galaxy. Her elocution lessons must have happened on Mars.'

There was something extra-terrestrial about Lulu's voice. She formed her full and elegant lips into a perfect O when she needed to pronounce the fourth in the series of major vowels. She gave a kind of sideways gasp when negotiating the first letter of the alphabet, and though she had not, as yet, dared risk the *i* for *ou* substitution common among real toffs, her suspiciously emphatic consonants, the pristine purity of her *u* and the creaking purity of her vowels suggested that something horribly regional had been beaten out of her before she had appeared on national television.

But even if she had left vulgarity behind her, along with her first husband and her brief career as a children's television presenter, she still had something of the Glasgow head-banger about her. When she said, in those thrilling, bass tones, 'So…David Cameron…come sit on my knee,' you knew that the next thing she was going to do was to kick him in the balls.

DI Hobday, George suspected, was a fan.

He looked like a man who had suddenly forgotten all about dead bodies. He hadn't yet got round to asking the questions everyone usually wanted to ask ('Did David Bowie really try to bite you?', 'Did Nick Clegg actually belch?'). He was at the first stage of celebrity worship. The stage at which the sufferer simply wants to stare at his or her idol in order to try to match image to reality. He was warming both hands before the fire of fame.

Or was he? There was something George did not quite understand about the look Hobday was giving his sister-in-law. Was there an element of distrust, even hostility, in his expression? Whatever it was, when he finally spoke to her his voice was friendly and impartial, registering a tone that at once acknowledged her celebrity and, at the same time, managed to make light of it.

'It's a pleasure to meet you, Lulu,' he said.

'Mother is dead,' said Stephen to his wife. 'Did my email not get through? George is also dead.'

'Oh,' said Lulu, bridling slightly, as if someone had pinched her bottom. 'Oh.'

'We think,' Stephen went on, 'that a burglar attacked Mother and that George had a heart attack.'

'Was he watching?' said Lulu. 'Was it the shock?'

Lulu was always prepared to think the worst of George. Even so, George reflected, a scenario in which he watched some lout beat his mother to death and fought back by staging a cardiac arrest was, even by her standards, a serious underestimation of her brother-in-law's worth. They had never liked each other. George had always found the sight of her stepping backwards into the limelight a dispiriting business.

DI Hobday shook himself awake. 'I think,' he said slowly, 'I would now like Mrs Esmeralda Pearmain to accompany myself and DC Purves while we examine the body.'

'If I can be of any help, Officer...' said Stephen. 'I was not, obviously, first on the scene but I was there pretty quickly. I was the first in after my sister-in-law. I heard her scream. And I came down the stairs. Two at a time. If you asked me whether I was first on the scene I would have to say, "No. No. I wasn't." But I was there pretty promptly. I thought you should know that.'

'Thank you, Mr Pearmain,' said Hobday, as, holding out one arm, he indicated to Esmeralda that she should follow him into the kitchen. As she passed him he turned to the rest of the group in the hall. 'We shall want to talk to all of you,' he said, 'so we would be grateful if you could wait for a while and we will do some interviews.'

The Mullins woman clearly felt it was time to show proper respect for the boys in blue. 'Can we get you a cup of tea, Officer?' she said. 'And some biscuits?'

Esmeralda was clearly unimpressed by the retired

63

headmistress's attempts to make free with her kitchen. This, her brief glance in the ninety-four-year-old's direction seemed to suggest, was no time for tea or biscuits.

George followed her and the two detectives into the kitchen. Somehow or other, he seemed to get there before they did. He wasn't quite sure how he had managed this. He was pretty sure he had started out just as DC Purves's large behind disappeared round the kitchen door; and yet, as she waddled smartly forward across the quarry-tiled floor, with the June sunlight pouring in across the big, scrubbed wooden table, the dressers, sparkling with immaculate glasses and the sideboards still strewn with the remains of last night's meal, George seemed to find himself, already, over by the french windows, the untended garden behind him, looking at a dead body that, for a change, was not his.

Jessica Pearmain was flat on her back, with her feet pointed towards the dishwasher. Her right hand was flung out behind her head. Her left arm lay at her side. A pool of blood spread out from beneath her neatly tended grey hair. She had had it done, of course, in expectation of her birthday. Her mouth was open, and horribly wide.

'Did you attempt to revive her?' said Hobday.

'I did not,' said Esmeralda. 'She was…you know…dead.'

'Was this,' said Hobday, slowly, 'after you realized your husband was dead?'

'It was before,' said Esmeralda. 'I came down here and found she was dead. Then I went upstairs to tell George. And found him dead.'

George's mother had always looked young for her age. She had, of late, rather lost track of how old she was and, if asked, would usually say she thought she was somewhere in her late eighties. When you told her she was very close to being a hundred she would express genuine surprise.

Followed, usually, by telling everyone, quite cheerfully, that she would probably be better off dead.

And now she was dead. She was never again going to ask George what day it was. She had made her last trip to Waitrose. She was, at last, no longer a target for mail-order scams or the disgusting little man who had sold her, door to door, an electric bed that didn't work. She suddenly looked as old as some tribal elder from the Indian plains. She had put on another twenty years since George had last glimpsed her. Death had carved her features into the kind of unflinching sculpture that might stare out at you from the ruins of some long-dead jungle empire where cruelty was normal and natural.

That might, of course, have something to do with the fact that she hadn't put back her false teeth before hobbling through from the ground-floor bedroom to sort out the bastard who had killed her. George's mother had always been very courageous. Once, not long after George's father had died, she had awoken in the middle of the night to find a youth in her bedroom. 'What are you doing here?' she had said, in motherly tones. 'You should be in your own house!' Whereupon the youth had departed, muttering something about climbing in through the wrong window.

The way she was lying there puzzled George. It was Hobday who gave voice to something that was, until he spoke, nothing more than a half-formed idea.

'Her right arm,' mused Hobday, 'is flung out behind her. Why is that?'

'Good question, Boss!' said Purves, who had, clearly, no idea what the answer might be but was used to her superior thinking aloud.

'You see,' went on Hobday, ignoring her response, 'if someone was attacking you, is that the way you would fall?

There is no sign of any damage to the face or the front of the body. This woman was just…pushed. And her right arm is way out behind her. As if she had been trying to get something out of her attacker's hand. Something he had stolen? Something valuable to her? If it was some…piece of jewellery or whatever, he obviously got away with it.'

'There was nothing valuable to her in this house,' said Esmeralda. 'Apart from George.'

DI Hobday began to pace to and fro across the red-tiled floor. George looked out at the garden – the buddleia, alive with butterflies, and the clematis wound around the ivy on the fence. The green wooden chair where he had sat two days ago, reading. He was never going to sit on it again. Well, not so as anyone would notice.

Hobday looked, George thought, like a man who had been able to intuit, from the moment he walked into the room, the name, age, sex and possibly the address of the culprit. There was an air of coiled omniscience about him. Mind you, Hobday probably always looked like this. It was, without doubt, a professional gambit to alarm any criminals in the vicinity. That was how the man had made inspector so early. He couldn't have been much more than forty.

'A burglar,' Hobday was saying, 'smashes that pane in the french windows. He lets himself in and is about to help himself to whatever he wants to steal when round the corner comes a very, very old lady. I'm assuming she isn't in here when he smashes the window because any burglar worth his salt – I won't dignify this person with the adjective "professional" – is simply not going to come in if he sees Mrs Pearmain in the kitchen.'

Here he swerved suddenly and glared at Purves as if he had only just remembered she was in the room. 'Why doesn't she make a noise? Why does she hobble all the way from the room on the other side of the hall to confront this individual? And then, when she's there, make an attempt to grab whatever it is in his hand without alerting the very large number of other people in the house to the fact that that is what she is doing?'

He smiled suddenly at Esmeralda. He had, George thought, rather a pleasant smile. 'Pay no attention Mrs Pearmain,' he said. 'Just thinking aloud.'

There was broken glass on and around the mat in front of the french windows. Hobday looked, for a moment, as if he might be about to walk in its direction but instead he turned to DC Purves and, indicating a line running wall to wall across the room from just inside the door, said, 'No one behind this line, Barbara. Ashton and Pawlikowski are on their way.' Then he turned to Esmeralda and added, 'I'm afraid, Mrs Pearmain, that we may need to take a look at your husband.'

Once again, Esmeralda burst into floods of tears. Perhaps, thought George, she imagined they were going to drape yards of tape around him marked 'POLICE LINE DO NOT CROSS'. Hobday looked briefly troubled and shot a pleading glance in DC Purves's direction.

'You're upset, love,' she said. 'Your husband is dead. And your mother-in-law is dead. And—'

'And what?' said Esmeralda. 'Is there something else I haven't noticed?'

With which she strode from the room and, in the hall, did a bit more of her Hecuba on the Walls of Troy impression. George was alone with Hobday and Purves. There was a sense, of course, in which he wasn't really alone with them since it could be argued he wasn't there in the first place; events seemed to be progressing quite satisfactorily in the Pearmain house without him.

It was, however, true, that his point of view, in so far as he had one, no longer seemed to depend on the position of the fat man upstairs on the bed. He didn't quite have the illusion of turning to left or right, which was unsurprising as he didn't have a head; rather, the scene in front of him played out as if he was an unattended wide-angle camera lens that someone had parked on a tripod in the corner of the room.

A camera didn't quite describe it: it was as if they had parked several cameras about the place so that Hobday and Purves were being observed, now from the edge of the Aga, now from the top of the fridge and now (as in now, now, now) from just by the door.

'There were problems in the relationship, I hear,' Hobday was saying, with a significant look after Esmeralda.

What was with this guy? How come he was such an expert on George's marriage? Was this information he had picked up since the phone call had come in or did the local fuzz keep Stasi-style transcripts of every night's conversation at 22 Hornbeam Crescent? Things, George had to admit, could get pretty heated. When he was alive, Esmeralda had never been afraid to call him a fat, lazy, lying bastard and, judging by this morning's episode, showed no sign of slowing down now he was dead.

Her attitude to his mother had been, if anything, even less forgiving. The Axis of Evil. The Bat. The Madwoman of Putney Bridge. She Who Must Be Avoided. Her names were many and few were complimentary.

Was it possible that Hobday thought Esmeralda had done in her husband and mother-in-law? On the same night? The police were famously fond of arresting anyone unfortunate enough to run across a body. And Esmeralda seemed to have discovered two within the space of about three and a half minutes.

Him and his mum. At almost the same time. For a moment
a stab of self-pity threatened to conjure a tear out of ducts
that were not only not there, but had not even a pair of eyes
to which they could attach themselves; and then, as so often
in his not terribly long and certainly undistinguished life, a
keen interest in process dragged him back to what, improbably, seemed to be reality.

'I don't like this,' Hobday was saying, 'I don't like this one
little bit. It's fishy.'

'Is it, Boss?' said DC Purves.

The respectful politeness of her manner concealed, George
suddenly saw, a certain reservation about her superior's
very masculine manner of command. Perhaps, he thought
idly, she's a lesbian. This idea instantly made her more interesting and, in spite of her slightly heavy-handed sympathy
with Esmeralda, more sympathetic. Also, she did not think
Hobday a fool. That was comforting.

'What exactly don't you like about it, Boss?' she continued.

'I don't like the timing,' said Hobday. 'I don't like the
look of that sideboard. I don't like the look of that woman
with the beard. I don't like the glass on the floor. And I
really do not like the way she is lying, Barbara. I do not like
it at all.'

George was warming (inappropriate word) to Hobday. He
would not have described Mullins as having a beard, more
the beginnings of a moustache, but putting her in the beaver
class felt like a good way of putting her in her place. And
she had – as always – a furtive look about her. What George
found most encouraging, however, was that the inspector
was giving voice to suspicions that, however vague and
unfounded, had been a part of George's lingering consciousness ever since he had failed to wake up that morning.

The sideboard. The sideboard. 'I don't like the look of

that sideboard.' George was fairly sure we were not talking kitchen design here. Why did he not like its look?

It was, as far as George could make out, an appalling mess. There were glasses, smeared with grease, lying on plates that bore the puddled remains of Esmeralda's lasagna, Barry's bean salad and gnarled fragments of George's garlic bread. There were cigarette ends – Maurice's lumpy roll-ups, Someone's lipstick-coated menthols – jammed into the wreckage of the fruit salad. In the corner there was a great mound of the nourishing herbs that Frigga had lifted from Putney Heath yesterday afternoon – Witches' Armpit, Dragoon's Beard, Volesfoot, or whatever they were called.

Frigga always trotted out their Latin names as she chopped them up and sprinkled them on salads, or brushed them into the parsnip wine she insisted that everyone should drink. '*Collybium penthesilea,*' she would trill. 'It's good for the bowels. *Lagopulaea frenescens.* Come on, everyone. It's used in Finland to cure incontinence. I think it's Finland. And I'm fairly sure it's incontinence. It may be gout. But who cares? It's lovely.'

Around herbs – though not the ones you bought in shops – Frigga recovered a girlishness that had never really been hers, even in her brief and unsuccessful attempt at child-hood. A serious, squat child in her Ladybird T-shirt and Ladybird shorts, Frigga had peered out at the world from behind her National Health glasses, waiting for the cruelty that her anxious expression usually provoked. Only two things had released her from the long, grim sentence of being Frigga: baroque music, usually played on the recorder, and the appallingly wide selection of edible roots, flowers, berries and leaves that were to be found in the average English hedgerow.

She had excelled herself last night, thought George.

There had been no stopping her. At one point, George had suggested using a chunk of basil – the kind of herb George understood, especially if it came in a clearly labelled plastic pouch from a supermarket – but Frigga would have none of it. 'What you need, George,' she had said, 'is *Brachythellilla aggravantens*. It's very good for obesity. And alcoholism. And for depression.'

Hobday, however, was not talking about the herbs. He was a big man with a big chin and, as he looked from George's mother's body to the sideboard, he stroked it carefully with his big hands.

'What,' said DC Purves, 'don't you like about the sideboard, Boss?'

'I don't like,' said Hobday, 'that her feet are pointing towards it.'

'See what you mean, Boss,' said DC Purves, although George was fairly sure she didn't.

'Which implies,' went on Hobday, 'that Mrs Pearmain was facing her attacker, who was presumably, when she confronted him, turning away from deep contemplation of the said sideboard. Was there, perhaps, the odd gold bracelet scattered among the remains of last night's dinner? I find that hard to believe, Barbara.'

'Indeed, Boss,' said DC Purves.

Hobday seemed interested in a section of the floor a few feet away from George's mother's right hand, twisted with arthritis, which lay now in the terrible stillness of death. He knelt a little way from it, careful not to tread anywhere near the tiles that seemed to interest him. He gave a small, wintry smile.

'Someone's tried to do a bit of tidying up around here,' he said. 'A nice, polite, clean and tidy burglar. But not over there. Not at all.' He squinted at the damaged pane in the french windows, nodding quietly to himself. 'Glass on the floor, Barbara,' he said, 'and inside the room, as you would expect if some Jack the Lad had wandered into the garden and smashed the glass from the outside, but I would ask you, DC Purves, to note the position of the fragments of glass on the floor and tell me if you think there's anything unusual about them.'

DC Purves looked long and hard at the glass on the floor. 'Is it something to do with the position they're in, Boss?' she said.

'Very good, Barbara,' said Hobday. 'Very good indeed.'

He looked away from the window and seemed, for a moment, to be staring straight at George. It was curious. For the first time this morning George had the uncomfortable feeling that someone was aware that he was in the room. It wasn't exactly a pleasant sensation. For the moment he was happy with anonymity. Hobday put his head to one side and, keeping his eyes on the former master of 22 Hornbeam Crescent, said, 'I get a feeling in this room, Barbara. A very strong feeling. That someone is trying to tell me something. About what went on last night. I'm one of those, Barbara, who think that the dead talk to us – and on this occasion I'm getting a very strong feeling indeed, right around...' He waved his hand in the air and concluded by pointing his index finger directly at the spot where George was standing. 'There. Right there.'

There was a silence. Then he added, 'Fragments of glass, Barbara. But are they fragments of glass from the window? Or are they another kind of glass entirely?'

Chapter Six

George was absolutely positive the man had sensed his presence.

'It's not about you!' was something Esmeralda was always saying to him. 'The whole world does not revolve around you!'

George was in complete agreement with her on that issue. Almost nothing, especially not his immediate family, revolved around George, but that did not seem a good reason for him to stop trying to get it to do so. Clearly, death had done nothing to dent his doomed enthusiasm for being the centre of attention.

DI Hobday did not have the look of a man who was a dab hand with the Ouija board. Communing with the Other World was not, George felt, his idea of a rigorous murder inquiry, yet he still wanted to believe that the policeman was listening to him, was understanding that he had not simply been erased from the suburb.

I think therefore I am. Therefore I am.

If there was going to be a chance of opening a dialogue with the inspector, though, it was not going to happen any time soon. The doorbell had rung. Several times. Men with special shoes and plastic gloves swarmed all over the house. And the garden. They seemed very keen on the garden. They

swept up interesting fragments that they found between
the broken french window and the fishpond. They dusted
the doorbell and the french window. They squirted talcum
powder on the gate to the side passage and they took more
photographs than the average American tourist hitting St
Mark's Square in Venice.

Then they all trooped upstairs to take a look at George.

Nat was not happy about this. His wife, Veronica, who
had appeared to offer Esmeralda moral support, stood on
the landing while he argued with the officers, in order, as she
put it, 'to stop him making a fool of himself'.

'I have,' said Nat to Hobday, 'already issued a death
certificate. I mean, I haven't actually issued it but I'm in the
process of writing it out. George died of a heart attack. In
his sleep.'

Hobday's pathologist, an even younger man than him
with close-cropped blond hair called Pawlikowski (his name
seemed to be the only Polish thing about him), sneered
openly at the general practitioner. 'What,' he said, 'was the
time of death?'

Nat looked shifty. 'In the night,' he said, 'some time
between twelve thirty and eight.'

The police pathologist snorted lightly. He went over
to George's body and started to prod at George's ribcage.
George was starting to take a dislike to the man. He had
a square face and a very pale complexion, suggesting long
hours spent indoors with dead bodies. His fingers, too, were
square at the ends and the nails bitten down to the quick;
there was something too neat about him. Too many things
on his head were also square. His ears. His mouth. The man
was altogether over-geometrical. After a bit of lip-sucking,
Pawlikowski shot a knowing glance at Hobday.

'Any sign of trauma?' he said. 'Or exsanguination?'

'Listen,' said Nat, in a menacing voice. 'I know when a man has died of a heart attack.'

Out on the landing Veronica Pinker did a bit of snorting on her own account. 'Oh, yes?' she said loudly. 'Like that woman in Gwendolen Avenue? Or Pramit Chowdray's brother? My God!'

Pawlikowski did a small shake of his head, like a man being bothered by a mosquito, and shot Hobday a small but significant glance. 'We may need a tarpaulin!' he said, obviously disappointed by the absence of bullet wounds or blunt-instrument trauma to the cranium.

'I think, Marek,' said Hobday, patiently, 'we're just exploring the envelope here. Dr Pinker has given his version of events and we have to respect that. What we really want to find out is if there is any connection between the two deaths.'

Nat, evidently sensing antagonism, did what he usually did in an argument and repeated himself in a louder voice. 'George Pearmain,' he said, 'was my patient. In my view he had a heart attack. Myocardial infarction. Whatever you like to call it.'

'He was,' said the pathologist, in grudging tones, 'obese.'

Pawlikowski was doing nothing whatsoever to alter George's preliminary assessment of him. His job called for a low level of sensitivity to human feelings but, even for a pathologist, he seemed remarkably cold-blooded. He had, George thought, a reptilian quality about him. He had a long, over-regular nose, thin lips and his tongue was constantly flickering in and out, giving him the air of a creature on the lookout for flies.

'His cholesterol was high,' Nat was saying. 'He was a heavy drinker. And I suspect he'd been at the parsnip wine. I say "suspect" but actually I know he was at it. I was here last night. I saw him knocking it back.'

Hobday's eyes narrowed. He was obviously adding Nat to his long list of suspects.

George knew why Nat was so keen on establishing that his friend's death was just another natural – and disappointing – death for just another middle-aged man. He was talking, as we so often do when discussing friends, about himself. Nat was, if anything, even more frustrated and disappointed by life than George. George had his unpublished poetry. Nat had, for years, been writing a long tome entitled *Some Common Diseases of the English Suburb* although, as he had confided to George, '"Common" is what they are not. The title is just to give it academic respectability. This one is going to be shocking. Sensational. It will sell millions.'

As well as 'Deep Vein Thrombosis Caused by Gallery Seats During a Performance of *Les Misérables* in Wimbledon', he had mapped out a racy chapter entitled 'Clarinet Neck in the Under 8s at St Jude's School, Putney' and 'Some Serious and Life-threatening Abrasions Caused by Electric Mowing Machines in the Roehampton Area', but when the *Lancet* had rejected his long, closely argued piece entitled '250 Diseases of the Skin Observed in Dog Walkers in East Sheen', he had rather lost heart.

Nat, in George's view, did not have long to go either.

'I think,' Hobday was saying, 'we'd better have Mrs Pearmain in and ask her some questions about her last night with Mr Pearmain.'

Esmeralda, who was out on the landing with Veronica Pinker, pushed her face in through the open crack of the door. 'I'm in now,' she said, in a threatening manner. 'And I heard that.'

Hobday did not crack. He was, thought George, rather better at handling Esmeralda than he was. Well, Hobday was the sort of man to whom Esmeralda was often attracted.

He was large, he was slightly uncouth and quite obviously capable of standing up for himself in conversation. Would she get married again? She might very well. Indeed, thought George, from the way she was looking at Hobday, it was quite possible that she was already on the lookout.

She was in the room, now, and Veronica Pinker, emboldened by her friend's move, had followed her. Mrs Pinker, who had, long ago, worked in a morgue, showed no sign of being ruffled by George's body. She stood, hands on hips, brilliantly dyed hair swept up in a quiff from her handsome, hatchet face, daring anyone to accuse her of contaminating a crime scene.

'Did your husband get up in the night?' Hobday was saying.

'He always gets up in the night. To pee,' said Esmeralda, showing signs of being about to burst into tears again – perhaps, thought George, at her use of the present continuous tense. 'I always wake up when he does. It's very annoying. He wakes up when I hit him.'

Hobday stiffened perceptibly. 'Hit him?'

'When he snores. I hit him when he snores. And he hits me. When I snore. Although I don't snore. He just hits me. He likes hitting me.'

I have plumbed the dark depths of many couples' relationships in my work as a murder detective, Hobday's expression seemed to suggest, *but this is about as low as it gets.* 'And,' said Hobday, his face settling, once more, to its normal, professionally unrevealing mask, 'did Mr Pearmain get up last night? At any time?'

'Of course he didn't,' said Esmeralda, affecting the weary patience with which one might address a fractious toddler. 'He was dead. Wasn't he?'

'Did he,' said Hobday, patiently, 'get up before he died?'

77

'I told you,' said Esmeralda, irritably. 'He did not get up at all.' Then she stopped, suddenly aware that this was more worthy of notice than she had first thought. 'Actually,' she went on, 'I suppose that is odd. I'm sure he didn't. And he usually does. And, as I said, I always notice it. If he gets up in the night.'

'You do,' said Veronica Pinker, anxious not to be left out of this. 'You always wake up when they go crashing around.' She glared at Hobday as if to suggest she had a pretty good idea of what he got up to at four in the morning. 'It's the prostate,' she added, with unholy relish.

Hobday managed to ignore her. 'It's possible,' he said eventually, 'that Mr Pearmain was unusually quiet last night, when he left the marital bed to do whatever he had to do. Although, from the sound of it, that would not fit into his normal pattern of behaviour. He did not, for example, wake up to complain of chest pains?'

'Not last night,' said Esmeralda. 'He usually did wake up to complain of chest pain but he didn't last night. He was too busy having a heart attack.'

And then she gave vent to what George found a gratifyingly intense burst of weeping. It really did seem as if – for some peculiar reason – she was missing him. Yes, he thought, you're going to miss all those things you disliked. You'll wonder how you managed to get through the day without my hypochondria. You'll yearn for the sound of my farts.

'Tell me, Mrs Pearmain,' said Hobday, gently, 'I appreciate this is very difficult for you and I do thank you sincerely for talking to us, but...when your husband came up to bed after a...good night, let us say...was he the kind of man who brought up a glass with him? A drink of some kind? To put by the bed?'

George saw at once that there was more than charity

behind the softening of the inspector's manner. This was an important question – he felt sure – even though it might not have seemed like it. There was a long silence before Esmeralda answered. All anyone could hear was a solitary bird, somewhere out there in the June morning. A blackbird, trying out its long, liquid, floating trill among the green bushes and the bright flowers of their rambling English garden.

'He did,' said Esmeralda, in a tiny voice. 'He always did. How did you know that?'

'It's a common thing,' said Hobday, with quite extraordinary quietness and compassion. *I've got this guy wrong*, George found himself thinking. *He's actually a thoroughly decent person – and a first-rate detective into the bargain*. 'I like a glass of wine with my meals,' Hobday went on, 'and very often, Mrs Pearmain, I take one up to bed with me. After some of the things I have to see in my job, I bloody need one I can tell you.'

Pawlikowski was looking sulky. He was clearly desperate to get on with the job of removing tissue samples and, in the very near future, wielding a Black & Decker drill on George's skull and upper chest cavity. There were, obviously, some tensions between him and Hobday, but Hobday seemed to have a special knack of ignoring anything that might come between him and the case in hand. He stood by George's body, lost in contemplation, like a composer listening to a tune that no one, apart from him, was able to hear.

'You see,' he continued, 'although I have made only a very superficial examination of this crime scene, I did observe on what is evidently your husband's side of the bed – and I'm sure, Mrs Pearmain, that, like me, you and your husband had a regular side – the clearly registered, slightly damp imprint of a wine glass. A wine glass that contained – who knows? We can easily establish what it was but for now, perhaps...parsnip wine? For the moment, all we know is that a glass was left by your husband's side of the bed within the last eight hours or so.'

Hobday swung round and glared, severally, at everyone in the room.

'And yet,' he continued, 'the glass is not there. There is a clear indication that it *was* there. Very, very recently. But it is not there now. There is no sign of it. If your husband did not get up in the night – and, Mrs Pearmain, I hope you will allow me to say that I find you a very reliable witness and I am absolutely sure that he did *not* get up in the night – then, well, who moved it? And where did they move it to?'

There was a very, very long silence.

Then Esmeralda said, 'Well, I didn't move it.'

'No,' said Hobday, in a voice that gave no clue whatsoever as to whether he really believed what he was saying. 'I'm sure you didn't, Mrs Pearmain. I'm sure you didn't.'

This was all something to do with glass – and varieties of glass. What was it Hobday had said in the kitchen? 'Fragments of another kind of glass entirely'. George had had the impression that the inspector was not happy about the way the glass from the window had fallen. And now Hobday was talking about the glass that George had, presumably, taken up to bed with him. He had been so drunk last night, he couldn't remember anything much. Plus he was dead. That wouldn't do much for the old memory.

OK. He had taken a glass up to bed with him. Someone had moved it. Who? And why?

It was curious. The idea that there had been something dodgy about George's death had perked him up considerably. He had been getting rather depressed at the thought that he was just another late-middle-aged man who had – awful word – *succumbed* to a heart attack. The idea that he had been murdered was rather bracing. It might explain why he was still around. To make life difficult for the perpetrator. Perhaps, in the weeks ahead, he was going to develop a few post-mortem skills. The ability to moan and gibber. To lower the temperature of a chosen room. Perhaps, even, to appear to selected victims.

He wouldn't mind appearing to Lulu fucking Belhatchett. He had, when alive, consistently failed in all his attempts to make the bitch jump out of her skin. Now was the time to start putting things right. She hadn't even flickered when he'd told her (untruthfully) that he had never heard or watched *Come Sit On My Knee*. Her oval features had shown no sign of cracking when he had announced during a dinner party at Stephen's house in the country that there were too many women in television.

And he had put up with so much. He had watched her mistreat her stepdaughters (his nieces) and said not a word. He had allowed her to prod his stomach at a Christmas party and say, 'All the Pearmains are plump,' without reaching out for a length of lead piping and bringing it down on her massive, perfectly coiffured head.

All bets were off. He was dead. He would say and do whatever he damned well liked.

The front-door bell rang again – long, loud and somehow menacing in the peace of the June morning.

'Are you expecting reinforcements?' said Nat to Pawlikowski, in a slightly satirical tone. This seemed likely. Pawlikowski was, clearly, a man who, faced with any kind of problem, called for more equipment. The twitch of his thin lips and his pale, worried eyes suggested a possible shortage of tweezers.

Neither he nor Hobday, however, seemed to have invited over any more of their gang. It was Esmeralda, who had been studying George's corpse with what he would have described as a kind of horrified tenderness, who suddenly clapped a hand to her mouth and said, 'Bimbo Baggins! And the Prune!'

No one, apart from George, seemed to have the faintest idea of what she meant. Bimbo Baggins (whose real name was, even more improbably, Peregrine) and the Prune (a thirty-something female of no interest to anyone) were Lulu Belhatchett's children by her first husband. A man whom no one had ever met and whose name was never raised in conversation.

They had arrived, of course, for the same reason as everyone else. Jessica Pearmain's death had not affected the fact that it was her ninety-ninth birthday. They were out there even now in the spotless morning. Peregrine in his check shirt and blue blazer, with his total lack of chin. The Prune in one of her many light, loose, flimsy, flowery dresses that were still not quite loose enough to hide her figure. Peregrine would be pecking at his iPhone. The Prune would be smiling vacantly at anyone foolish enough to look her way. They would have brought presents. Peregrine would have brought a bottle of champagne, because he always did. The Prune would have brought a scented candle.

Both would be ready with flowers and kisses and carefully tactful conversation. Neither would have any idea they were walking into a house practically stuffed with dead bodies or that the birthday girl was stretched out on the kitchen floor, surrounded by tape and men in uniform.

'Lulu will break it to them,' said Esmeralda. 'She likes to be first with bad news.'

This was no less than the truth. She was good with disaster. Everyone had said that. Quite a lot of people had been given the job of telling the world about the Rwandan massacres, but no one had done it quite like Lulu. A slight compression of the lips, as if to suggest she felt the burden of having to communicate the horrors of the news.

Down in the hall, abetted but not aided by George's brother, she was giving her birth children the lowdown on their stepfather's mother's sudden and violent death. 'Jessica's birthday,' she was saying, in the voice she tended to use for fairly good news about the Royal Family, 'should have been a happy day. But it is now the cause of much sadness. There seems to have been a *contretemps* with a burglar. Some lout who broke in during the night. She had a fall on the floor and fractured her skull. He then fled. As they do.'

Her long training in BBC Current Affairs, thought George, had had its effect. She was still making it up as she went along.

'We don't know,' Stephen broke in, 'we have no idea how it happened. Or why. But we're on it. We're going to find out. Probably. We'll get the bastard. The police are here.'

There was a slight, frozen silence of the kind Lulu usually generated whenever her husband tried to say anything. Then, when she was sure there was no danger of his attempting to say anything else, she continued, in the same lightly inflected voice, 'It's going to be very difficult to cancel the party. People are coming from all over. We don't have all their numbers. A lot of them don't have mobile phones. They're old – obviously. John Bleaney and his wife are on their way from Richmond. They have no idea. He is blind. She is deaf.'

There was a slight pause. Lulu whinnied out a nervous laugh. 'Just hope she's driving. Anyway. It's too late. Jessica is dead. George is also dead. Upstairs. In his bed. He died in the night, it seems. It's all absolutely awful!'

Hobday, Esmeralda, the Pinkers, DC Purves, Pawlikowski and (probably) George had moved out on to the landing. Down below, Lulu was running through a list of all the other people who were, even now, on their way to toast the recently dead ninety-nine-year-old. Many were in their nineties. None had a mobile phone. At least two were coming by ambulance. There was a strong chance that the sudden switch from birthday party to wake might kill the lot of them.

Hobday did not seem bothered about any of this. Neither did the people who had been in the room with him when he had said whatever he had said about George's death. He went down the stairs in magisterial fashion. What he had said had quietened Esmeralda. She looked surprisingly uninterested in making trouble. Frigga was crying again. Barry and Maurice were looking lost. Stephen was trying to talk to his phone. When he arrived on the third stair, DI Hobday looked at the group.

'I would like everyone in the front room,' he said. 'I have an important announcement to make!'

Chapter Seven

Ella Bella, Bella Ella and their respective mothers were excused. Ginny said she would take Bella out into the back garden to look at the fish but was told she could not do so as it was a crime scene. Bella burst into tears and said, 'Cime scene. Want go cime scene.' Jojo and Ella remained tactfully silent. Ginny gave Esmeralda a sharp look as her daughter said, once again, in a small, wistful voice, 'Fish. Cime scene.'

His granddaughter, thought George, had a great deal in common with his brother's mobile phone.

In the end Ginny and Jojo, Bella Ella and Ella Bella all went out for a walk.

'I don't think,' hissed Veronica Pinker to Esmeralda, in a voice she clearly intended to be heard, 'they are suspects. The flat-feet draw the line at involving young mothers in their paranoid schemes.'

'Well, Inspector?' said Lulu. 'Are we to be allowed to know what is going on?'

Hobday did something not many people dared to do with all six foot four of Lulu. He ignored her. Lulu, for whom this morning no equine metaphor seemed unsuitable, did the kind of leg yield and half-pass only usually seen in international dressage competitions. In fact, she looked as if she might well rear up on her hind legs, punch the air with her hoofs and gallop full on at the inspector before clopping him to the carpet.

'Would anyone like a glass of champagne?' said Peregrine. 'Because, you know, champagne...'

Hobday ignored him as well. He let the room go quiet. Then he said, 'I'm afraid this is going to take some time.'

Veronica Pinker whispered loudly to Nat that it was liable to take even longer if the ridiculous little man didn't talk a bit faster and stop staring at everyone for half an hour between each sentence. If Hobday heard her he gave no sign of it.

George geared himself up for the next set of revelations from the inspector. He did not want to find himself tuning out of whatever the man had to say just as it was about to cast some light on his death, but, like that bloke in the Kafka novel, he found it extremely hard to stay awake when the officer talked. That might, of course, be something to do with the fact that it was only the act of concentration that gave him the illusion of being alive. If his previous existence was any guide to his afterlife, he didn't have that much concentration available, and the inspector had one of those voices that seemed made for putting people to sleep. He could, George felt, have made a great career as a stage hypnotist.

George fought back. He must pay attention. He must...

'...Mrs Pearmain. Who had been the victim of an attack. The first, superficial, impression was that an intruder had entered the premises in the early hours of the morning by smashing a pane of glass in the french windows. He – or she – or they...'

At the back of the class the Mullins woman murmured, to no one in particular, 'Black probably.'

'...surprised Mrs Pearmain, pushed her to the floor and made off down the outside passage to the side door to the street, which is, indeed, open. On my preliminary examination of the crime scene, however, there were several things that I found puzzling. First, the glass pane had not been surgically removed. The "job" – if I may use that expression – was a pretty amateurish one. It would have been no easy task to get any but a child's hand through the aperture, but we found no blood.'

'No blood!' said Pawlikowski, in the affirmative manner used by a backing group in a gospel song.

'What we did find,' went on Hobday, 'were traces of a fibre that *may*...I remind you that this is not confirmed by rigorous forensic tests...' he looked straight at Pawlikowski, who nodded and, in the same affirmative manner, repeated 'rigorous' several times '...but, and I am only an ordinary copper passing on information as he receives it – *may* come from a tea towel replaced, very recently, in one of the drawers near the hob. There are other things that suggest it may be possible that whoever broke that pane of glass broke it from the inside. I do not mean by that, of course, that he or she was literally on the inside because if they had been the shattered glass would have been all over the patio. I mean that whoever broke the glass wanted to make it look as if there had been a burglary but, in fact, was in this house last night. An "inside job", if you like. The first thing I noticed was that there was something not quite right about the angle at which the glass from the window had fallen – and I will return to that issue very soon.'

George was trying to think if anyone in the house last night had disliked Jessica enough to kill her. The only remotely plausible candidate was Lulu – and she had left at around nine in order to be in Basingstoke.

'If it was a burglar,' Hobday continued, 'how did he or she get into the garden? The side gate was locked. Did he or she or they...'

Here the Mullins woman muttered something about Asians.

'...climb over it? They would almost certainly have left some traces. There are none. There is also the question of the evidence yielded up by a close examination of Mrs Pearmain's back garden. Or, rather, the evidence not yielded up by it. The lighter sleepers among you may have noticed that there was a shower of rain in this area at three twenty-one this morning, but although most habitual burglars are, these days, forensically aware, I'm not sure I've met one who is capable of hovering six inches above a damp lawn to conceal the traces of his or her approach.'

He had them, George thought, by the goolies, but although what the inspector was saying was interesting, what was even more intriguing was why he was bothering to communicate it. Most policemen, in George's experience, tried not to tell anybody anything.

'It may be, of course,' continued Hobday, 'that the break-in happened before the rain. Which would explain why there is no mud or soil on the kitchen floor. But at whatever time it happened, there is this question of the glass on the kitchen floor. There are, I have observed, two entirely distinct groups of broken glass and it is, I'm afraid, too early for me to discuss, in detail, one of them, except to say I have noticed one or two very, very small pieces of what could be, might be or, rather, might have been a drinking glass of some kind near to the body of Mrs Pearmain. Even if I knew the significance of this fact – which, as yet, I do not – I would be looking for its deeper implications. But because the angle at which the glass from the window fell did not look right to me from the moment I first saw it – and I can't yet quite say why – I think there may be a connection between the two horrific events that occurred in this house last night.

The death of Mrs Jessica Pearmain and the death of her son, George Pearmain.'

He looked, George thought, like a man who was about to arrest the lot of them. There was enough of an atmosphere of nervousness among his listeners to suggest that some of them thought exactly the same thing.

'I am not at liberty at the moment,' went on Hobday, 'to be precise about exactly why I think this may be a double-murder inquiry. I am letting you into what I like to call my "process" because, over the next few days, I am going to have to do some rather unpleasant things.'

Here Hobday inserted one of his Harold Pinter-style pauses – giving his audience time to wonder what exactly these might be. Had the Putney police got around to water-boarding? Esmeralda, sitting on the sofa by the window, winding her hands together, clearly thought he had done quite enough unpleasant things already this morning.

'We are going to have to request an autopsy on Mr Pearmain.'

George could have sworn he flinched. Or twitched. Or did a bit of both at the same time. The thought of Pawlikowski being let loose on his naked body in some overlit morgue, surrounded by men in green wellingtons, managed to convince him that he was wrong in thinking that the day could not get any worse. Nat, from the look of him, seemed to agree and looked as if he was about to put Hobday right on a few points of medical etiquette.

Did GPs outrank policemen? Was there going to be any kind of debate about this? Or did the boys in blue have the right to cut up anyone they fancied?

Hobday was holding up his hand for silence. Nat had started to mutter in disgust and Esmeralda, too, was weighing in on the side of keeping George's corpse away from Pawlikowski and his knife-wielding team of experts. She was no longer crying. She was white with an anger that George recognized instantly. He had been on the receiving end of it for forty years.

'Listen, you stupid man,' she was saying, 'you...absurd little...*Hobday*! I know when my husband's had a heart attack! I've been married to him for forty years! I'm the best judge of how and why and when he may have dropped off the twig. I've actually been on the same twig as him for...' Here, suddenly, it was all too much for her and she started sobbing again.

'The other thing,' went on Hobday, imperturbably, 'is that everyone in this room should consider themselves a suspect.'

The Mullins woman let out a low snarl. Frigga went even whiter than usual. Beryl Vickers squeaked. Stephen became even more interested in his mobile phone. Lulu got to her feet. She was deathly calm. Her big shoulders were squared, like a boxer's. That was how she had looked when she had destroyed Nigel Lawson. If Hobday had any sense at all, thought George, he would make a run for it now.

'I was in Basingstoke last night,' she said. 'I left here at nine in the evening. So unless you think me capable of being in two places at once I suggest you cross me off your little list, Inspector – or perhaps you wish me to go straight to the Independent Police Complaints Commission on whose board I have several personal friends. Do you have any idea of whom you are dealing with?'

Hobday, George thought, appeared to have looked as if he had a very good idea. The first look he had given her was not, George now realized, that of a fan. The inspector, in fact, had a healthy distrust of celebrity.

'Everyone,' he continued, still managing the almost

impossible task of ignoring Lulu, 'who was in this house
last night had opportunity. And a large percentage of
those present, even if they may have left at some point in
the evening, had motive. I haven't yet asked you to give a
detailed account of your whereabouts last night, Lulu, but,
in due course, I shall be doing so.'

Brilliant use of her first name, thought George.
Unfortunately for her, the sort of celebrity in which she
specialized gave almost anyone the right to do precisely that.

'Perhaps you were in Basingstoke. I do not know. May
I remind you that this is a murder scene, Lulu. Two people
have died. There is in my view some relation between the
two deaths. It may be that there were other people here last
night. I do not know. We will attempt to establish that, but
this is a serious inquiry. You get my meaning? Who hated
George Pearmain? Who hated his mother?'

George looked round the room. Barry and Maurice were
looking very serious indeed. They didn't hate me, thought
George. My boys are not like that. Or are they? They have
been doing rather a lot of the 'Is Georgy a Weeble?' joke
recently. Do I know either of them? Really? And the Mullins
woman has clearly wanted to do away with me for years.
'She loves you,' she had said to him, only last night. 'You do
not appreciate your mother. She loves you. You think only of
yourself.'

As he looked round the faces of the people in the living
room he realized, once again, how little he really knew
any of them. He and his family had never had the kind of
intimate discussion about their relationships that was obligatory in Eugene O'Neill plays. Their deeper feelings, such as
they were, usually emerged in oblique discussions of family
members who had made the mistake of not being present.
'Barry can be a bit "how's your father?"' Esmeralda might

say. Or George let slip that he thought Maurice could be, on occasions, 'a bit of a retard'.

Did he really know Esmeralda?

She had often expressed a desire to kill him. She had also, quite often, expressed genuine regret that she did not seem to have got round to doing it yet. On the night when he had called her a fat bitch, she had screamed her desire to do so with such force that Mary and Sam from two doors down had rung the bell to ask if everything was all right.

Esmeralda was also, he decided, well up for polishing off his mother at the same time. In fact, if she ever decided to make a start on the Pearmain family it would not be long before Frigga, Stephen and Lulu were joining the queue for the Putney morgue.

Had she somehow found out about Julie Biskiborne? It was possible. He had, on one drunken occasion, told Nat – although he hadn't mentioned her name or that she was a secretary. Somehow the fact that she had been his secretary made it even worse. Steve Profitt, from Head Office, had told him once he thought it might be illegal for employees of the NatWest to do it with each other. Nat could have told Veronica, who would have told Esmeralda, who might well have decided to murder him for doing something as unoriginal as shagging the office bicycle.

Mullins? Mullins was capable of murder. She would probably think that, after the age of ninety, you were allowed to kill people you disliked – on the bus-pass principle. And her years as kindergarten headmistress had given her formidable organizational skills. She could have roped in any number of the others in the room to help her. Maybe they were all in on it. Maybe it was like *Murder on the Orient Express*. They all looked pretty furtive, George thought.

Stephen? Did he have the imagination necessary for

murder? It was conceivable. Younger brothers traditionally resented their older siblings. Even though Stephen was
richer and far more complacent than George, he might have
decided, as any brother or sister could, that—

Sister. Sister.

Frigga was, on balance, the most likely candidate for the
role of assassin, and therefore, of course, given the way of
these things, the person who probably had not, after all,
done it. She was quivering now, like a game dog waiting for
the command to pick up a pheasant, and before Hobday had
the chance to get started on the next leg of his murderthon,
she launched herself into speech.

'It's all my fault, Inspector,' she said. 'I hated George.
I hated my mother. They blocked my creativity. And now
they're dead.'

For the first time since he had set out on his appointed
task, Hobday showed signs of listening to an interruption. Suddenly Frigga had the attention of the room. She
had not, thought George, had this many listeners since the
day she had confessed to her eating disorder in the Royal
China Restaurant, Chelverton Road. That, he recalled
now, had, ironically enough, been at another celebration
for Jessica. Her ninetieth? Her eighty-fifth? George felt
a brief pang for his ever amiable motherly mother. He
recalled her bemused surprise at her difficult daughter's
outburst.

'I make myself sick! I lock myself in the lavatory while
you're all stuffing your faces and I put my fingers down my
throat! I vomit! I vomit! I vomit!' she had cried aloud, as she
waved her long, prehensile hands in the air.

She had stopped several diners in the act of transferring
spring rolls or glazed chicken feet from plate to gob, and the
Chinese waiting staff had looked as if they might well send

out for some hard-line martial-arts expert to throw her out before she put the whole place off their *dim sum*.

'My novel will never be published,' Frigga was now saying, to anyone in 22 Hornbeam Crescent who was prepared to listen. 'I am a doomed woman who will never be fruitful. I am a wicked, wicked person who has evil thoughts. I did something yesterday that may have killed my brother. I did not like George. No no no, I did not. And I did something that—'

Stephen got up, went over to her and put his hand on her arm. 'Don't be silly, Friggs,' he said. 'You don't know what you're saying.'

She looked up at him like a dog. Frigga, George thought, had always preferred Stephen to him. Stephen had the gravitas of the older brother, a role George had never quite managed to play to her satisfaction. It was strange. Even now he was dead, he found it difficult to sympathize with Frigga. You would have thought, he told himself, that shuffling off the mortal coil might have made him more sympathetic to his younger sister. Now was the time to start rising above it all and looking at the world from Frigga's point of view. But he was still quite unable to understand the workings of her mind.

Did he know Stephen any better?

Stephen really did not give a fuck about Frigga. Why the sudden concern? Maybe Frigga and Stephen had got together to do him in.

Hobday seemed about to say something. 'Shut up!' perhaps? Or 'You're under arrest!' He certainly looked like a man who would like to know what Frigga thought she had done yesterday that had hastened the death of G. Pearmain Esquire, but whatever question he had framed, he did not get the chance to ask it. As Frigga, lips trembling, eyes fixed on her younger brother, debated the issue of whether or not to proceed with the meat and potatoes of her confession, there came an unearthly scream from next door.

'My Gawd! 'Elp! Pleece! Pleece! Someone call the fuckin' pleece! Where's the fuckin' pleece? They're never arahnd when yoo want them.'

This, thought George, was not strictly true. There were four of them, as far as he could make out, in the front room alone. More and more inexperienced-seeming coppers had been arriving by the minute. Pawlikowski had acquired a small non-Polish assistant called Hughes – a man with a wispy beard – and there were even more uniformed officers pacing round the garden peering into the flowerbeds for offensive weapons. On the whole it would be fair to say that 22 Hornbeam Crescent was fairly crawling with fuzz.

'Someone's put tape all over Mrs Pearmain!' the voice continued, as the front-room audience, frozen into silence by this extraordinary interruption, looked anywhere in the room but at each other. 'She's done up like a chicken! It's a criminal scenario in 'ere, people! It's *Miami Vicious*!'

Mabel Dawkins had been George's mother's carer for nearly fifteen years. She was a small, wizened woman in her early sixties, with dyed blonde hair scraped back severely from her forehead and a pair of enormous ears. Her way with language had made her a legend in the Pearmain family. She could nearly always be relied on to say something malappropriate. She lived in a block of council flats close to the more elegant and expensive block where Jessica lived and had, for as long as George had known her, been an invaluable source of information about a group to whom he had ascribed, in the early seventies, an omniscience and charity comparable to that displayed by H. G. Wells's Morlocks. Mabel had a rather different view of them.

'The working class disgusts me. They're lazy,' she often

used to say. 'They scrounge. They take socialist security where they can find it. They're as bad as the immigrators. The blacks 'ave nothing on 'em. And the ones in the asylum are even worse. Political referees. I'd blow the whistle on the lot of 'em. They come from all over. From By The Russia. From Pole Land. And Africore. We 'ave Zombies next door. From Zombia. One of 'em spat at me lars' week. Spat. And the ones on the other side are Similia.'

Mabel was of and yet not of the section of society in which Marx and Engels had put so much faith. As her politics had evolved over the years, she had moved to a place that was, like so much of British society, neither left nor right nor, really, anywhere between the two.

'The Labour Party disgust me,' she used to say. 'I vote Labour. Except when I vote Conservative. The Labour are the party of the working man and woman. I despise the Democratic Liberals. But the Labour have bin hijacked. By the Unionists. And the Muslins – the bastards. I know you like them, George. I know you like the Muslins. Solomon Rasher Day. But they come over 'ere an' give us bollocks about the Korean. An' Mahmoud the Inevitable or whatever he calls himself. Twit. On 'is camel. Bollocks to 'is camel, I say, George. Let 'im keep 'is fuckin' camel. I'll take the bus, thank you. Banning drink. They make me physically sick.'

It was always hard to work out what she thought of the Pearmain family. She had been there last night. That made her, as far as George could see – which was not, at the moment, very far – a murder suspect. Her manner was a unique blend of the servile and the hectoring that George had always thought uniquely British. Jessica was always 'Mrs Pearmain' to Mabel, even when she was telling her she was a silly old cow or hauling her on and off the commode, and her anger now at the indignity that her old lady had been made to suffer was on a par to the view taken of the execution of Louis XVI by a loyal servant of the Bourbons.

How the hell had she got in there anyway? Wasn't it supposed to be a crime scene?

'Oh, you fuckers!' she was screaming. 'Oh, you 'orrible fuckers! It's 'er birthday! You gone and done it now!'

Hobday and Purves were, finally, on the move. The sound of large feet heading towards the kitchen from every corner of 22 Hornbeam Crescent suggested that backup was also on its way. George, who had not yet mastered the art of moving any faster than he had when he was alive, joined the crush as everyone went about the almost certainly hopeless task of restraining Mabel Dawkins.

'Oh, Mrs Pearmain!' she was crying, to the unpitying ceiling, as George and quite a lot of other people descended on the newly violated crime scene. 'What kind of birthday present is this, old girl? Didjer overdo the parsnip wine, lovey? Did you keel over and smack your bonce? What did they tell you at the Falls Class, Mrs Pearmain? 'Ow many times 'ave I pulled you up off of the floor like a tortoise? You was messin' about with your Zimmerman frame, weren'cher?'

Mabel Dawkins seemed to be about to try to lever her charge up off the floor and into the vertical. She clearly thought that, if she could get her moving, it wouldn't be long before the old lady would allow herself to be winched into a wheelchair or dragged on to the lavatory. She thought of George's mother – he now saw quite clearly – as a sort of mechanical toy running on the same principle as a bicycle dynamo lamp. You had to keep her moving. You had to keep her batteries charged.

'Mabel,' Stephen was saying, in the brisk, Wehrmacht-like tones he usually adopted with anyone capable of being classed as a servant, 'this is a crime scene! Mother is dead.

You must put her down. Do not attempt to revive her. She has been murdered. By an intruder. These are the police. They are here. This is Inspector Hobday. Inspector, this is Mabel Dawkins. She was here last night. She was devoted to my mother. And my mother could be a handful, I can tell you.'

Mabel looked from face to face. 'Dead?' she said. 'Murdered? By Persons Unknowing? By a Romanian? Oh, Mrs Pearmain! What did you do to deserve this? It's a Cat's Trophy, is what it is. You was almost illegible for your telegram from the Queen. They should 'ang the bastards 'oo done you in, Mrs Pearmain. Not that they will because the "po-lice" is a useless load of jobsworths in my view.' She did not seem at all put out that there were at least six of them in the room when she said this.

Mabel must have come in by the side gate and let herself in by the french windows. As DC Purves set about the business of sensitively steering her away from Jessica Pearmain's corpse and sensitively sitting her down on a chair in the front room so that she could sensitively let her know that George, too, had joined the ranks of those no longer capable of offering her employment, Hobday announced his intention of carrying out a series of interviews with everyone present so that he could establish their whereabouts last night. He also asked for a list of who else had been on the premises, and concluded by saying he would like to know if anyone had plans for leaving the country.

Esmeralda said she had not had any plans for doing so but, since meeting Hobday, she had started to think about it seriously. Stephen said he thought he might have to be in Munich in the near future. He asked his phone when he was supposed to be in Munich. His phone told him he *was* in Munich but he wasn't supposed to be there. He was supposed to be in New York. Stephen told everyone to pay no attention to his phone. It was always wrong. His phone started to argue with him. He turned it off.

'This is all very disturbing,' said Lulu, 'but we must try to help the inspector all we can.' She had suddenly decided to play nice with Hobday. She was, as a television critic had observed after Jimmy Savile had sat on her knee, both Good Cop and Bad Cop simultaneously, and when she put on the charm and consonants, as she was now doing, it was hard to see how an average Putney CID officer could resist her.

Hobday, however, seemed to be doing just that. He kept glancing hungrily at Frigga but, after a long, whispered conversation with Stephen, she looked as if she was not going to say anything to anyone without her lawyer present. Not that she had a lawyer.

While his sister-in-law smirked at the inspector, George was trying to remember what, if anything, he could remember about Einstein's Special Theory of Relativity. For some reason he had decided it might go some way to explaining how he found himself in his present situation. If only the dead had access to the internet! As far as he could remember, it was something to do with the unreliability of clocks. Not in a mechanical sense. The unreliability of any arrangement involving time. If you arranged to meet someone at a railway station at seven o'clock, you should not allow yourself to be fooled into thinking that although you had both pitched up under the clock at precisely that time and were naïve enough to assume you had met each other, it meant that anything like that had actually occurred. *Two events which, viewed from a system of co-ordinates, are simultaneous can no longer be viewed as simultaneous events from a system that is in motion relative to that system.*

George seemed to be in pretty constant oppositional motion in relation to every other system on the planet, not least the system that had been, until recently, his body. That is to say he was, at the moment, simultaneously downstairs in the living room and upstairs, dead, on his bed; the only way to make sense of these two events, as far as he could see, was to invoke dear old Einstein, who seemed to be telling him that they weren't necessarily simultaneous.

This might explain, George decided, why he seemed sometimes to be moving at different speeds. It could explain why certain events (like the doorbell) seemed to occur before or after the moment when he experienced them and why now, although it had not yet occurred, he knew, with horrible clarity, that a very large number of people were lumbering up Hornbeam Crescent with cake, wine, flowers and all sorts of other things to gladden the heart of the birthday girl, now lying on the kitchen floor in a pool of her own blood.

Chapter Eight

Jessica Pearmain's wake and birthday party were simultaneous events. They were also viewed by people attending both functions who were, without doubt, in motion relative to both simultaneous events, events which were, George suspected, living witness to the fact that space-time was curved and that there was a sinister and possibly dangerous relationship between mass, velocity and energy.

Cousin Bob, for example, weighed seventeen stone and eleven pounds. He ran head first at George's corpse, while simultaneously drinking a triple brandy and a glass of champagne. The mass that he lost by attempting to rugby-tackle his dead cousin might, under the laws of classical mechanics, be thought to have disappeared from the closed system, which was at this point 22 Hornbeam Crescent, but, viewed from another system, the mass – or its equivalent energy – reappeared dramatically in a simultaneous event in the living room.

Frigga was sick all over the sofa.

Peregrine Belhatchett, who had started the rot by insisting on serving champagne cocktails to everyone, was, from the very earliest moments of the birthday party (as opposed to the wake), the observer whose frame of reference was not only not fixed (he was staggering after half an hour and flat on his back after forty-five minutes) but a man whose velocity moved to match the speed with which light waves conveyed his antics to other observers in the simultaneous event, though in motion and therefore not seen as such, that could be thought of as Jessica's wake. So it was that he seemed, in the view of many people present – well, in George's, anyway – to be watching himself travel back in time towards the lavatory while at the same time emerging from it, wiping his mouth with a Kleenex and muttering, 'Christ! I honked like a goose!'

The Prune seemed to be weeping in a corner with Frigga. This might have been because Frigga had made some terrible, and this time specific, confession to her about her part in George's death. Or, possibly, that she was about to make it. Or even, thought George, that she was trying to work up the courage to do so. Either way he still did not seem to have yet had the chance of working out exactly how and why Frigga might have been involved in his death.

Somehow or other somebody had moved Jessica Pearmain's body. Only slightly – they hadn't carried it out, shoulder high, into the back garden and tried to set light to it – but they had moved it. There were moments when George was quite sure it had moved of its own accord. That his mother had come back to life, not in the quiet, unassuming manner he had chosen but in the style of the waking dead. That Mrs Pearmain was now a zombie. That she was hobbling round the kitchen, her face dripping with blood, her skull wide open to the June day, introducing people to each other.

'This,' she was saying, with a fixed smile and that relentlessly cheerful, polite way she had, 'is Deirdre. She is a piano teacher. Like I was.' Wasn't Deirdre dead, though? Hadn't she got breast cancer and died years ago? George was pretty sure she had, but why should that keep her away from Jessica's birthday party? All bets were off.

Someone had produced Frigga's goulash. Or should that be 'ghoulash'? Esmeralda, of course, had put herself in charge of it and tried to make it look a bit more eatable. She had, unbelievably, succeeded. George, who was fond of this particular dish – when Esmeralda cooked it – found himself following its progress round the room as Esmeralda, shy, as always, going about the business of putting her food in front of the public, wove this way and that through the press of people, looking around, in a hunted manner, for someone to take it off her hands.

With a thrill of sadness he realized she was searching for him. He had always been good at the social side of things. 'Tell them there is goulash,' is what she would have been saying to him, had he been alive, and George would have bellowed, in his party voice, 'Goulash, everybody!'

But wait! It was what she was saying. To herself, in a small voice, 'Tell them there's goulash.' Oh, darling Esmeralda. If I had any tears I would cry them. I hear you. Even if you don't hear me.

> *Death is nothing at all.*
> *I have only slipped away into the next room.*
> *I am I and you are you...*
> *Call me by my old familiar name...*
> *Why should I be out of mind*
> *Because I am out of sight?*

Like it says in the ludicrous poem that the canon of St Paul's came up with after Edward VII, one of the most useless monarchs in English history, had croaked.

George, as he, literally, floated between the guests, listened

103

for any fragments of gossip that might help him get some kind of grip on the question of what might have been his murder. It was Lulu Belhatchett, surprisingly, who had asked the question that set him thinking seriously about the question of motive, and about something that might possibly connect his own death with that of his mother.

She'd come out with it quite early in the proceedings. Almost certainly before Hobday and his team had managed to bring things under control. 'This is a murder investigation,' he had said to Marilyn Munson, who had come all the way from Penrith. This did not stop her offering him a piece of birthday cake or sobbing violently, as she said, 'Jessica loved sponge.'

So there was some old-fashioned causality about the proceedings. One thing, to his relief, sometimes led to another. Almost immediately after the Marilyn Munson incident, George saw an elderly relative he had always known as the Incontinent Market Gardener ask Hobday if the police were baffled, and Hobday, irritated by the question not only because of what it was in itself but because of Marilyn's earlier attempt to confide in him, replied, 'We are not baffled. We have not had time to be baffled. What we are trying to do is clear this place and continue with our investigation.'

George then definitely saw Hobday turn on the crowd of elderly, often drunk, well-wishers and heard him say, 'This is a crime scene, ladies and gentlemen! Not a birthday party! Mrs Pearmain is not receiving guests today! She is unable to lunch! She is dead! Do you hear me? Dead!'

He then definitely saw Uncle Arthur, though not his mistress, turn to the inspector and ask if he could go and pay his respects to his dead sister. 'It should have been me! I am a hundred and one! She was only ninety-nine, for God's sake!' He saw, too, the detective's instant respect and appreciation for the officer class (Uncle Arthur had been a district officer in the Punjab in 1939) as he told him that, although this was not the kind of thing he would usually allow, he was sure that what Arthur had done in the Battle of Britain (he seemed to have the mistaken idea he had been in the RAF) justified a relaxation of the rules in this instance.

George was also 100 per cent certain that, after Uncle Arthur had gone in to see Jessica, quite a queue formed at the doorway to the kitchen as guests jostled their way in to have a look at the birthday girl. And not just her. Once word got around that George's remains were upstairs in the bedroom, he rapidly became part of the list of attractions, as far as the guests were concerned. 'Old people,' as Stephen said, 'are interested in anything to do with death. It's on their radar. They sort of get it, I find.' At times, George's bedroom resembled one of those rooms in country houses that have been opened to the public ('Why don't they charge entrance?' he was heard to mutter to the 0.00 people capable of hearing him.). After that had started there didn't seem to George anything like a clear sequence of events. Perhaps, he thought, this was because of another of the scientific laws that had made the twentieth century so tricky for dim persons like him to navigate. Heisenberg's Uncertainty Principle.

George was uncertain about what Heisenberg's Uncertainty Principle was – other than that it had been discovered by someone called Heisenberg, whoever he might have been. He could not be positive, but George suspected it told you that even physicists, who ought to know about these things, did not really have a clue what the fuck was going on in the world of science. Every time you peered at a subatomic particle it responded by behaving like a bird that has just spotted an ornithologist and dived for the undergrowth. To wriggle out of this spectacular attempt to do themselves out of a job, the physicists tried to tell you that this uncertainty only happened at the subatomic level – the very area they were supposed to know about – but its general drift could not be avoided. We never, ever, really have a fucking clue about what is going on in the world around us.

From George's recent experience, this Heisenberg guy had been on to something.

It was hard enough when you were alive. When you were dead, atomically, subatomically and sub-subatomically defunct down to the bare quark, things were as deliberately confusing as the Paris Périphérique or the one-way system round Bolsover Street. There was a moment when George could have sworn he smelt goulash, but that was before Esmeralda even started cooking it. There was a moment when Frigga flung her arms round the Prune and kissed her, after which Lulu told her daughter by the Man of Whom No One Ever Spoke not to be stupid. There was definitely a moment when Stephen asked his phone what time it was in New York and his phone said, 'You do not need to know that! You are in Kuala Lumpur!' There was a moment when George was sure Esmeralda asked him directly if he thought she had made too much goulash and he said – as he would have done in life – that of course she hadn't, but that could not have happened yet though it seemed as if it had.

But all these events afterwards seemed to crystallize around the moment of Lulu's Fateful Question, the question that had first made George think that, yes, there was some substance to all this innuendo and uncertainty and, yes, he had been murdered and maybe his mother, too.

'What,' Lulu said, 'are we doing about Jessica's will?'

He had forgotten about his mother's will. He had also forgotten that she had a net worth of around twelve million pounds. How had he managed to forget that?

After George's father had died in 1982, Jessica had become closely involved in the stock market. George Pearmain Senior, like George Junior, was not very interested in money. He always said he thought it made him a much better bank manager. 'The trouble with banks, these days,' he used to say, 'is that they're too interested in money!' Even as a child, George Junior had enjoyed this paradox. He was, indeed, the only one of his family who laughed at the old man's jokes, which perhaps accounted for the close bond between the two of them.

His father spent most of his evenings working on his translation of *The Iliad* into Welsh ('The move from a dead language to one that may not have long to live is fascinating!') or indulging in his other hobby, setting the poetry of Mallarmé to music. At the dinner table, all through George's childhood, he used to burst into his twelve-tone version of 'Brise Marine' for counter-tenor and brass band. The poem was, in George's view, pretty tough, even when not given the squeaky-gate treatment, but, unlike the other two, he loved his father for this and all his other eccentricities. He had ended up, of course, becoming him. Like him, he had gone into the bank, after a brief period of infantile leftism in his twenties, and also like George Senior, he had what the Irish call 'a sword upstairs', his pile of unpublished poetry. It said as much about the love between the two men as anything else.

George Senior had been cautious about money but, after he had been burned to a cinder at Putney Vale Crematorium and his wife had granted him the ungrudging respect she had withheld for most of their forty-eight-year marriage, she had got jiggy with the dosh. She had sold the big house up on Putney Heath and bought a small flat down near Putney Bridge. Helped by a small Jewish man called Norman, she used George Senior's savings, with the profit she had made out of the house sale, to play the markets. She invested in BP just before they bought Amoco and sold her shares well before they started blowing up refineries in Texas and deep-sea rigs in the Gulf of Mexico. She bought shares in Apple very, very early in the game and, though she did not like to talk about her business affairs, George thought she had hung on to them. She got into the dotcom boom just before it went crazy and got out of it before it collapsed.

She travelled everywhere by bus and ate only one cheese sandwich a day. She was still wearing the dress she had worn at George Senior's funeral. She never drank alcohol. She might, George thought, be worth more than twelve. It had been twelve last time he looked.

Her will was a document as legendary and elusive as the Protocols of Zion. 'Wills' would have been a more accurate word as, to George's certain knowledge, there had been at least five. There had almost certainly been others along the way. It was Jessica's hobby. George had discovered the first by accident at the back of one of her kitchen drawers. There hadn't been any bequests. The Mullins woman, who, according to Esmeralda, had spent the whole of the 1980s 'licking her lips at the prospect of all that cash' was not even mentioned. He, Stephen and Frigga got the lot, shared equally between them. There was even a note to the effect that she had always loved all of her children equally.

That had changed when Stephen married Lulu Belhatchett. At first it looked as if Jessica had, at last, found her ideal daughter-in-law. Esmeralda had never come into that category, although after about fifteen years Mrs Pearmain Senior had learned to approach her elder son's wife with a kind of wary respect. Nothing goes as sour as passion, though, and the early love affair between her and Lulu had turned very rapidly into something very grim indeed.

In the first few years of Stephen's marriage almost every other word in Jessica's vocabulary was either 'Lulu' or 'Belhatchett'. She was, of course, a great fan of *Come Sit On My Knee* and, especially when friends or neighbours were in the vicinity, lost no opportunity of rushing to the radio or, later, television every time the familiar music sounded. Yet there were signs even then of the beginnings of conflict. They had always used that particularly elaborate form of politeness that, for George, was always proof that women disliked each other.

Little by little Lulu began to make mistakes. Well, not exactly mistakes. Lulu did not make mistakes. She just went ahead and did whatever she felt like doing and if people didn't like it they could go and fuck themselves. When she turned up late to Jessica's eighty-ninth, it was, George thought, a deliberate move made for no other reason than to see how the other woman would shape up to a hostile action. The real issue between them was, of course, Stephen.

Lulu seemed to have the kind of effect on Stephen that Svengali had on Trilby. She did not actually say, in a spooky, foreign voice, 'Now, Stephen, you will go and buy a blazer! A blue blazer – with silver buttons on the cuffs!' Or 'When I count to three, Stephen, you will book a holiday in the Maldives.' And Stephen did not rise as in a trance and, credit card in hand, sleepwalk his way out into the world to carry out these commands. But she might as well have done so.

That Stephen was an enthusiastic accomplice in the total obliteration of the person he had been before he met her was, as far as Jessica was concerned, no excuse. She wanted her son back. She didn't want the thumb-sucking Stephen, the one who had been unable to pronounce the word 'milk' until he was twelve; she didn't want the holier-than-thou, solemn, round-faced little boy, who had announced to his family in the early 1950s that he was going to dedicate his life to Christ. She wanted someone she vaguely recognized. 'If I had wanted a puppet who wears braces, I would have asked for one!' she told George. The braces were, of course, Lulu's idea.

What really hurt was Stephen's schedule. He had never really had a schedule before he met Lulu but he sure enough had one afterwards and she was the principal thing on it. He made a brief attempt to hang on to some of his personality and even retained some of the bluff charm that had served him so well in the media but, essentially, she swallowed him whole. His schedule did not seem to allow him any human contact, apart from with Lulu – although, as Esmeralda pointed out, it was questionable whether 'human' was the right word in this context.

'Stevie!' Lulu would call, a name that no one in his family had ever called him. 'Stevie!' Stephen would stand to attention, eyes glazed, thumbs to the seams of his trousers, and wait as obediently for orders as if she had planted an electrode in his brain. Which was, according to Esmeralda, a distinct possibility.

That wasn't, as Jessica had told George many, many times, the half of it.

Stephen had been married before, to a teacher. She was black, as he made a point of telling everyone before they met her, perhaps to stop them running out of the room when they did so. She wasn't jet black. She was the colour of very strong regular coffee. She had hair that ran between woolly and straight. She had been born in Holetown, Barbados, and had ended up in south-west London. Her name was Geraldine. George had always liked her. His mother had tolerated her.

Geraldine, in Stephen's horribly revealing phrase, was 'only a primary-school teacher'. He would never have referred to Lulu as 'only a newsreader' but, then, he did work in the media.

In George's view, being married to Geraldine had made his brother a nicer person. For about three years Stephen had gone through a Caribbean phase. 'Me cyarn't believe it!' he used to shout, as he did the W8 version of the bump and grind at parties. George once heard him use the phrase 'raas claat' to a driver who had cut him up, spoiling the effect by adding, for George's benefit, 'Apparently it's a term of abuse in Jamaica and means "sanitary towel".' He claimed to enjoy drinking rum. He often wore brightly coloured short-sleeved shirts. He even, at the height of his passion for Geraldine, bought a small black trilby hat, which he wore indoors.

His heart, however, was never in Barbados.

He went there a few times. He lay on the sand at Holetown. He ate flying fish. He had sex on the beach and drank Sex on the Beach. He failed to learn to water-ski. Somewhere in the middle of all this, Geraldine gave birth to two children. The first was a boy. Geraldine wanted to call him Otis. Stephen objected. 'You cannot call a child Otis Pearmain!' he said. 'It sounds ridiculous!' But she did. Stephen insisted on his middle name being Tristram so he was Otis Tristram Pearmain – or Tristram Otis Pearmain if his father was speaking to him. When the girl was born, eighteen months later, Geraldine threatened to call her Donkey Rihanna but ended up with Rosalina. Stephen made a bid for Charlotte. 'If you call her Charlotte,' said Geraldine, 'I will call her Rosalina Donkey Rihanna!' Her full name was, therefore, Rosalina Donkey Rihanna Charlotte Pearmain. Stephen never called her anything but Charlotte.

The first sign that the marriage was going wrong came,

for George, the day his brother muttered to him, after a
few pints, 'Of course, black people are lazy! They admit it
themselves!' It wasn't long before he was calling them a lot
of other things as well. 'I'm fed up,' he said to George, one
night, 'with all this talk about slavery. Slavery, slavery, slavery.
Slavery was the best thing that happened to the bastards.
Without slavery they would still be running round the jungle
eating each other. We brought them over to the West. We
gave them job opportunities. They've done very well out
of it. They dominate the Olympics. They sell millions of
records. Stop moaning. I get this all the time from Geraldine.
She drones on about Pearmain being her "slave name". My
God! You'd think it was me personally who roped up her
great-great-grandfather and taught him the basics of sugar-
cane cultivation!'

When George pointed out that 'job opportunities' was
not a very accurate way of describing the systematic torture,
flogging and degradation of millions of Africans, Stephen
replied, 'Things are not easy for any of us, old boy! Have you
any idea of what goes on at the BBC?' Was that a joke? It was
hard to tell any more. Stephen had been mocking George's
youthful period as a Trotskyite for so long that his political
attitudes were nearly all deliberate caricature that was on the
way to becoming sincerely held belief.

There had never been any doubt in George's mind that
Stephen's disenchantment with Geraldine – and the shift
in his racial attitudes – had a great deal to do with Lulu
Belhatchett. Although no one had ever admitted it, George
was fairly sure Stephen had been porking her from a few
months after Rosalina was born – around the time the two
had covered the first Gulf War together. Lulu – everyone
said – looked good in a helmet. It was after that trip that
Stephen started voting Conservative and telling George that

Geraldine was 'totally ignorant of English history'.

Jessica Pearmain had remained calm during her younger son's divorce. 'I suppose,' she said to George, 'it's all to do with her being black! They don't have things in common! And she should be nicer to him! Not all white people are bad! She should stop criticizing him! I never saw a black person until 1956!'

But even if she was secretly relieved about being one black relative down, she remained passionate about her grandchildren. In spite of her quite openly racist views, Jessica never showed any sign of noticing that both Otis Tristram Pearmain and Rosalina Donkey Rihanna Charlotte Pearmain were a lot more black than they were white.

This was not a fact that had escaped Lulu Belhatchett's notice.

'Oooh! Your hair's all frizzy!' she would say to Rosalina. 'You should have it straightened!' She not only followed her new husband's lead in calling the boy Tristram, but when he asked her to call him Otis, she said, 'O-tis! O-tis! Can't call you O-tis! It's a ridiculous name!'

When Stephen's children came to them for Christmas, Lulu's presents for her stepchildren were a masterpiece of subtle insult. While Peregrine got electric cars, expensive musical instruments (although he was tone deaf) and, on one occasion, a selection of imitation small arms of almost American-army standard, Otis Tristram (or 'Tris', as she now insisted on calling him) got woolly jumpers that looked as if they had come from a jumble sale. Rosalina Donkey Rihanna Charlotte ('Cha, darling, is a nice name, isn't it? I can't call you all those other silly names, can I?') often got no more than a useful bag to put things in.

Lulu also operated what both children came to call 'apartheid Chiswick style'. Even if both sets of children were in

the house at the same time, she attempted separate development, as far as meals, bedtimes and, of course, presents
were concerned. Her children stayed up later. Her children
got steak. Geraldine's kids got pasta – if they were lucky. If
they talked back they were locked in their room.

'I hate her,' Rosalina used to say to George, if ever he saw
her on her own. 'I'd like to kill her!'

She did not say this only to George. She said it, and so did
Otis Tristram, to Granny. Jessica listened to their confidences
with every appearance of impartiality, occasionally lobbing
in an emollient phrase along the lines of 'It must be difficult
for her, dear!' or 'You'll just have to try and make allowances,
darling!' but, over the years, she found it harder and harder
to play nice on the subject of her second daughter-in-law.

Hence the second will.

George had found this one tucked inside one of his
father's music manuscripts – a concerto for castanets and
male voice choir – and found that it made no mention of
Stephen at all. Jessica had simply written him out of history,
in the manner of Stalin with his Old Bolshevik contempo-
raries. George and Frigga had got nearly all of it – there
was a large bequest to the Mullins woman. George had told
his mother this was simply not acceptable. 'You have to be
fair!' he told her.

In the third will, which Jessica showed to George, although
not to Stephen or Frigga – she got him to swear he wouldn't
mention it to either of them – Stephen and his brother got
slightly less than their sister and the Mullins woman a
bequest of two million. George was clearly being punished
for interfering. Between the third will and the fourth, she
discovered the codicil. Her codicils were very complicated
indeed. In one draft of her fourth will she tried to leave
£200,000 to Jeremy Thorpe – the dead former Liberal leader.

When George explained the politician's current situation, she said, 'They're all dead! I shan't leave anything to anyone. Everyone I care about is dead. I should be dead.'

She never really liked her fourth will, which was dragged down by the weight of its codicils, but it had the effect of drawing her and George much closer together. He had been, as everyone in the family acknowledged, his father's favourite, and it had only been with the old man's death that he had started to make a proper relationship with his mother. George, like his father, wasn't really interested in money, which made her trust him in financial matters.

Her fifth will was very much a joint operation. When it was completed George found himself the recipient of her entire fortune. He asked her not to do that. He insisted she write in a clause making him responsible for the fair distribution of her assets between himself and the other people she wanted to be beneficiaries. Esmeralda, all the grand-children, Stephen, Lulu, Frigga, the Mullins woman, Beryl Vickers and Mabel Dawkins. All the people who had been at the party last night. All, now he thought about it, with an obvious motive for doing away with him. Although she had promised him she wouldn't tell anyone the details of her last testament, she was, as he well knew, incurably indiscreet. She could have told any or all of them what she intended.

There was another twist in this story. After she had hidden her will in a place where, they both agreed, no one would possibly find it, he had said, in a humorous tone, 'What if I die before anyone else, Mum? Who's going to be the one to see fair play?'

'I've taken care of that,' said Jessica, her eyes bright. 'There's a codicil. If you fall down the stairs drunk, it kicks in. I don't trust any of the rest of them to sort things out equitably.' Then she looked at him with real affection. 'You're

115

like your father, George,' she said. 'You're fair. I trust you to look after all of them.'

But now he was dead – and no one would have the faintest idea where the will might be. They were all at the mercy of Jessica's mysterious codicil. Where and what might it be? More importantly, didn't it now look very likely that someone at that party yesterday evening might have done away with him? Had one or other or even some of them managed to get a look at the codicil?

But how had they done it? If they had done it. Had he, perhaps, been poisoned?

As Hobday and his team got rid of the last of the revellers and he and DC Purves began the long, complicated task of taking statements from everyone who had been on the premises the previous night, George found himself studying them with more than usual interest. As soon as he had any idea whether he had been murdered and, if so, how, he had to devote some quality time to finding out who the perpetrator had been. After that, he decided, he should get on with some serious haunting.

PART TWO

'Let us hope that when we are dead things will be better arranged. At any rate, we shall not always be having to put on low-cut dresses. And yet, one never knows. We may perhaps have to display our bones and worms on great occasions.'

In Search of Lost Time, Marcel Proust

Chapter Nine

George had started to lose interest in his corpse. He had never been very captivated by his body when he was alive, but since he had stopped breathing, he had found himself unable to work up any enthusiasm for it at all. Its stomach was too large and its arms too thin; the pubic hair had a badly tended look about it, and the penis could have done with a lot of structural work. If only he had died with a hard-on! Not that they had been that common recently.

His body just lay there, stubbornly refusing to move, and – this was mildly disturbing – those who were in charge of getting it from A to B, while being reassuringly efficient about making sure no one moved it on to C, for the purpose of removing the kidneys and selling them to some Baltic Republic, seemed, on the whole, to have a somewhat lackadaisical attitude towards it. They hadn't actually started stubbing out cigarettes on his head or parking pint glasses on his abdomen, but George was pretty sure that, if he spent much more time in the Putney morgue, that kind of thing was likely to happen.

Today, however, was different. Today was the day of his autopsy. He hadn't been dead much more than a couple of months and now they were going to cut him up into little pieces.

He found, to his surprise, that he was looking forward to it. There certainly wasn't much going on at 22 Hornbeam Crescent and, although he was sure there were going to be some difficult moments, it was bound to be more fun than the inquest.

The inquest had not been good. People had not behaved well. It was now George's considered opinion that inquests should be held, if possible, without the coroner present. Maybe somewhere in the United Kingdom there were wise, good, open-minded coroners but the one he had been lumbered with was, in George's view, about as interested in impartial justice as the Nazi Party.

The witnesses were not much better. They all seemed to manage to contradict not only each other but also themselves, often in the course of the same sentence. 'Did your brother seem drunk on the night of the twenty-third?' the coroner had asked Frigga.

'He was very drunk!' Frigga had said. 'I mean – not *drunk* but he had drunk. Which was what I meant to say. George drank a lot. When he drank. But when he didn't drink he didn't drink at all. Sometimes he didn't even drink when he drank. Sometimes at lunchtime he didn't have a drop. Although obviously, you know, he did have the "other half", as it were. Stephen drank. And he's alive. Oh, God!' At which she had burst into tears.

Nat Pinker had repeated his belief that George had died of a heart attack. The coroner, who insisted on being called 'Professor Lewis' although, according to Nat, he wasn't one and was only famous for having removed the wrong bits from a mother of four, asked some very nasty questions.

'Did you take tissue samples?' he said, in a mean voice.

To which Nat replied, 'It did not seem appropriate!'

'Why?' said Lewis, in an even meaner voice.

'I wasn't going to open him up right there in the bedroom, was I?' said Nat. 'With Esmeralda beside me!'

Lewis sniffed loudly. 'Was there ischaemia?' he countered. 'Dyspnoea? Tachyarrhythmia?'

'For all I know,' said Nat, 'there may have been polymorphic ventricular stenosis with knobs on. The patient was unable to inform me as to whether there was or was not any evidence of symptoms that might have suggested such a thing. He was dead!'

'Had he complained to his wife about anything?' said Lewis.

'He was always complaining to his wife,' said Nat. 'She got fed up with it. On that occasion he was unable to do so. He was dead.'

Some interesting facts about George's last night on earth did emerge. It seemed, as far as George could make out, pretty typical. He had drunk a lot of parsnip wine. He had farted a lot – which, apparently, was a sign of an imminent heart attack although, as Esmeralda pointed out in her evidence, if farting was always followed by a coronary, George would have had many, many thousands of them, especially late at night.

'We did argue about the farting,' said Esmeralda, who, in her evidence, seemed in free confessional mode. 'I even started to fart myself as a sort of riposte and then, of course, I was unable to stop. We argued about it a lot.'

'Did you often have arguments with your husband?' said the coroner, with a significant look off left to where an imaginary jury was hanging on his every word.

'We were always having arguments!' said Esmeralda.

Lewis's eyebrows climbed even higher up his forehead.

'What,' he said, 'did you argue about?'

'I said he was a drunken bastard who didn't deserve to live,' said Esmeralda. 'That quite often provoked arguments.'

'And,' said the coroner, who was now beginning to sound like a more than usually enthusiastic member of the Spanish Inquisition, 'on the night Mr Pearmain died did you two have an argument?'

'We did,' said Esmeralda. 'I asked him not to bring his glass of parsnip wine up to bed with him. If he ever came!'

At this point Lewis threw a significant glance in Hobday's direction. It was only then it occurred to George that these two might already have confided in each other and that Hobday had told him rather more than he had told any of the suspects about why he thought George had been murdered.

'And why was that?' said Lewis. 'Why did you ask him not to take his glass of wine up to bed?'

'Because,' said Esmeralda, wearily, 'I didn't want him to take it up to bed!'

'You didn't want anyone examining the contents of the glass?' said the coroner.

'I didn't want George to pour any more of what was *in* the glass down his throat,' said Esmeralda, crossly. 'Are you implying that I put something in the glass? Because I didn't. One of my chief concerns throughout the evening was to stop people trying to put all that funny stuff in the parsnip wine. Parsnip wine is bad enough without all the stuff Frigga makes them put in it.'

Lewis's voice went very quiet. 'What *stuff* does your sister-in-law put in her parsnip wine, Mrs Pearmain?'

'Parsnips, obviously,' said Esmeralda, which got a laugh. 'And, as if that wasn't enough, she makes everyone put leaves in it. Wild food. Food for free. She picks it on Putney Heath. She thinks we all ought to be cramming nettles into our faces. And sea beet. And Virgin's Whiskers, or whatever they call it. And God alone knows what else.'

At this point Frigga began to howl. She had done a lot of

howling since George had died. Anyone would think, thought George, from the way she carried on, that she'd liked him. When it came for her turn to give evidence, she sobbed so hard, even before she got into the box, that Stephen had to take her outside and walk her up and down for a few minutes. Then they adjourned the inquest while she was given a drink of water. When she finally got back, the coroner asked her a great many questions about the wild herbs she had picked on the afternoon before the deaths of her mother and brother. She answered him at great length and in a firm, steady voice. Talking about the English hedgerow seemed to calm her down. She had picked Old Man's Beard, Maids a-Winking, Wild Chervil and about five different varieties of nettle. It was a wonder, thought George, as she got into a list of Latin names, that they weren't all dead. Maybe he was allergic to Old Man's Beard.

It was the coroner who finally gave the game away. George was sure he noticed Hobday twitch when the specific area of his suspicions was finally revealed.

'Did you,' said Professor Lewis, 'in any of these wild plants that you observed and picked, notice any specimens of *Conium maculatum*? Its common name, as I am sure you know, Miss Pearmain, is hemlock.'

The coroner's manner was low key, but it was clear that he had upstaged the inspector. George thought it was possible Hobday would get to his feet and sue the man for infringement of copyright. Frigga went very, very quiet. Then, in what George always thought of as her real voice, the one that gave away what a very hard, stubborn woman she really was, she said, 'Of course I know what hemlock is. I'm not stupid. *Conium maculatum* is also known as Devil's Bread, Beaver Poison, Poison Parsley and Spotted Corobane. It contains coniine, which has a chemical structure and pharmacological properties similar to nicotine. An ingestion of more than a hundred milligrams is usually fatal, producing ascending muscular paralysis and eventually fatal damage to the respiratory system. They gave it to Socrates. And he died. He walked around for a bit and then he just died. It's quite an easy way to die, I suppose. Why are you asking me about hemlock?'

'I am asking you, Miss Pearmain,' said the coroner, 'if you think you could have picked any by mistake.'

'Of course not,' said Frigga, crossly. 'I would know if I'd picked any. I know a great deal about herbs. Especially poisonous ones. I am a registered witch.'

This was, everyone felt, not a wise thing to say. Lewis, to everyone's relief, did not allow her to drone on about the Craft or tell them all about her internet publication, *Broomstick – the Monthly Journal of Accredited English Witches*. He simply said, 'And you are sure you did not pick any hemlock in honour of your mother's birthday?'

'Don't be ridiculous,' said Frigga. 'What kind of birthday present would that have been?' She paused. 'Quite a good one, actually. My mother was an awful, awful woman in many ways. She stunted my growth as a female. I suppose I loved her, but even if I did, somewhere deep down, I can't deny that there were many, many times when I wished she wasn't there, that she would be run down by a train or something, but in my fantasies of her death it was always carried out by someone else. Like a hitman or something. Or, as I say, a train. Or a car. Or something falling on her head.'

The speech caused something of a sensation.

Those in the know were not surprised that she used the inquest on her brother as a forum for expressing her deep hostility to her mother. Frigga had been undergoing therapy from a completely unqualified woman called Gillian, whose policy was to get her clients to say whatever came into their heads whenever they felt like it. It was Gillian who had encouraged her to talk about her bulimia whenever an opportunity presented itself. She had also helped her to realize that she was anorexic, claustrophobic, arachnophobic, and had a morbid fear of escalators. There did not seem to be a Greek-derived name for that, which was perhaps why she had had a seizure while trying to get from the District Line to the Piccadilly Line at Earl's Court Station.

Recently, around the time that her fees had doubled, Gillian had discovered even more trauma lurking within the breast of the unmarried librarian. She had found out that Frigga was 'full of hidden aggression towards her mother and brothers' (as George said, 'What was hidden about it?') and she spoke at length about this at the inquests on Jessica and on George.

'My most common fantasy,' she said now, as Lewis goggled at her, 'is that I'm strangling my brother George. I have him locked up in a basement and first I torture him by cutting him with knives. To pay him back for what he did to me in the tree house. After that I put sort of tape on his mouth and strangle him with my bare hands. He doesn't die at first. I have to hit him with a hammer, like in that film with Olivia Newton-John!'

By the time her evidence was through, George was sure Hobday was going to leap up and arrest her on the spot.

Esmeralda was recalled to the stand after Frigga had finished giving evidence and said that she didn't think Frigga really disliked George – at which Frigga had a hysterical fit. She went on to say that 'he liked a glass of wine with his meals' and that she had not noticed him complaining about anything he had eaten or drunk on the night he died. He had, she said, complained of chest pains, backache, pains in his shoulder, housemaid's knee, sore throat, tennis-elbow-without-the-tennis, loose bowels, constipation, headaches, gastric bloating, feelings of inadequacy and 'probable cancerous lumps all over his body, especially in the morning'.

She said, also, that she had loved him. She cried several times but refused a glass of water. When asked about the details of the night before her husband and mother-in-law had died, she said, 'I didn't see much because I went to bed early. All the rest of them stayed up – even Mullins and Beryl Vickers, I think. I don't think it was the parsnip wine. Everyone had parsnip wine. If there was hemlock in the parsnip wine then we would all be dead. Frigga kept throwing all those herbs into it. She wouldn't stop. She's mad. All George's family are mad. He was the only sane one.' After which she burst into tears again.

By the time Hobday took the stand, there had been other, even harder, acts to follow. The Mullins woman had spoken crazily of her love for Jessica – 'A marvellous woman! A marvellous piano teacher! In touch with life! She was on the side of life! George never appreciated his mother. Well, Jessica never liked Esmeralda, you see. She never ironed his shirts, you know. I think Jessica felt Esmeralda had some kind of hold over George. To do with sex.'

This drew a guffaw from Esmeralda.

'Her family did not deserve her. She was a wonderful woman. I think any one of them could have killed her – and, I mean no offence by this, there were many occasions when I would gladly have killed any one of them. Jessica always had time for people. She was alone in that flat for hours on end, only looked after by that woman Dawkins who was, in my view, only after her money!'

Dawkins followed Mullins. She said she loved Jessica like a brother and had always thought George 'a wonderful man'. She had helped serve drinks during the evening and left early and, no, she had not seen anyone tamper with the parsnip wine. 'It didn't need tampering with to be illethal!'

After Dawkins came Stephen, who gave his evidence like a man delivering a piece to camera from downtown Beirut. There was, George thought, a submerged tension about him, although that might have been due to worry about his toupee falling off – something that always plagued him when making public statements. Was it that, though? Its rich chestnut, glossy texture had not wavered once when the Berlin Wall came down and had been a fixture right the way through the London riots – why should it crumble now?

There was always something anxious about Stephen's big, circular face but his manner at the inquest was, George thought, suspicious in the extreme. Even his ginger moustache seemed furtive. By the end he looked less like a journalist and more like a man in public office trying to dodge awkward questions.

'The mood in Hornbeam Crescent was positive,' he said. 'We were all positive about my mother being ninety-nine. We all felt it was a good thing. We are a pretty close family. I am close to George. *Was* close to George. He is close to me. *Was* close to me. There is a sense in which George is very much still here. Looking on. Although, obviously he is, er, dead. And mourned. Deeply mourned. By me. And others. As is his mother. My mother. Our mother, for God's sake!'

'This must have been very difficult for you,' said the coroner, who obviously felt Stephen was the one reliable person giving evidence.

'It was,' said Stephen, as though this thought had only just occurred to him. 'It was. Difficult is exactly what it was. It was not easy. It was hard. One's brother dying is a problem.

As is one's mother dying. When the two of them die at the same time it is a lot to take in.'

'Is it difficult for you now?' said Lewis, who, George thought, showed signs of an emerging homosexual attachment to Stephen.

'It is,' said Stephen, who sounded as if it was the easiest thing in the world. 'It is often difficult to talk about these things. One's mother. One's brother. Their simultaneous death. Deaths, rather. One has to stop. And take a good long hard look. At oneself. And at everyone, really. We have to ask. You have to ask. I have to ask, for God's sake, "What does this tell us? About one's self? And other people, too, of course." These are the questions. Where are we at with this? We will need a whole raft of proposals for tackling it. If we can tackle it. We need blue-sky thinking.'

At one point, Lulu got to her feet and, as she was apparently entitled to do, cross-examined her husband briefly. 'Stevie,' she said, 'you were obviously very concerned to support your brother. And your mother. And your sister. As you always do. You were there. On the ground. There. Doing the business, as it were. For them. That is right, is it not?'

'It is!' said Stephen, smartly, straightening his shoulders and staring ahead, like a soldier on parade.

'And,' she went on, 'where was I during all this?'

'You were in Basingstoke, darling,' said Stephen.

'Thank you,' said Lulu. 'That will be all!'

In spite of any fears he might have had about being upstaged, Hobday, when he finally came to deliver his evidence, caused a sensation. George had thought he had disliked the prospect of going in last, but as soon as the detective crossed the floor to begin testifying, he decided that, in fact, Hobday had deliberately arranged to be the final witness. He and the coroner were not only scrupulously polite to each other but, from the kick-off, managed to sound like a carefully prepared double-act.

'You said at the coroner's inquest into Mrs Pearmain's death,' said Lewis, peering at his notes, 'that the injuries sustained by Mr Pearmain's mother were not caused by a deliberate blow to the back of the head.'

'They were not,' said Hobday, with a glance towards Pawlikowski, who was sitting at the back of the court, wearing dark glasses and looking sulky. 'They were consistent with Mrs Pearmain falling backwards on to the kitchen floor, possibly accidentally but possibly because she was pushed.'

'They were consistent with a fall,' said Lewis. 'The verdict at the inquest on Mrs Pearmain was, as I understand it, an open verdict and, in your view, that verdict does not fully explain her death.'

'At the inquest on Mrs Pearmain,' said Hobday, who was, George thought, choosing his words very carefully indeed, 'I went through the evidence for a break-in at twenty-two Hornbeam Crescent and made it clear that there were certain discrepancies in that evidence that suggested to me that the glass in the french windows of the property may have been broken from inside. I also made it clear that we were doing extensive forensic tests on fragments of a glass we had found near Mrs Pearmain's body. And also on a stain we had found on the kitchen floor.'

'Although,' said Lewis, 'you had not yet had the results of those tests.'

'We had not!' said Hobday. 'We have them now!'

George had somehow missed the business of the stain on the floor. In fact, the inquest on his mother had been brief to an almost insulting degree. He was, he noted, far more involved in his own inquest than he had been in his mother's.

Vanity, it seemed, was easily as strong as death. Of course, if they hadn't had the results of the tests on the mysterious stain – about which Hobday had been keeping very quiet indeed – the police and the coroner had, presumably, been waiting for this moment to reveal what they thought about both cases.

Pawlikowski had removed his dark glasses. He was leaning forward in his seat with a triumphant expression on his face.

'And what did they show?' said Lewis.

'They showed traces of the parsnip wine that was being drunk at twenty-two Hornbeam Crescent on the night before Mrs Pearmain and her son died,' said Hobday. 'And they also revealed traces of something else.'

'What,' said Lewis, now positively glorying in his role as feed to the inspector, 'was that "something else"?'

'It was hemlock,' said Hobday, 'which, as Miss Pearmain has already reminded us, is a poisonous plant common in the English hedgerow. There were extensive traces present in the sample of parsnip wine we analysed.'

If it was possible for a gasp to run round a court, that, thought George, was what happened when the inspector made his revelation. Esmeralda gasped. The Mullins woman clasped Beryl Vickers's hand. Barry and Maurice's jaws dropped. When it got to Mabel Dawkins, the gasp had become a sob, and although it had declined into a severe twitch as it struck Lulu and a triple twitch with facial tic when it reached Stephen, by the time it reached Frigga it had become the sort of noise wolves make to a full moon in Siberia.

'Silence!' called Lewis, who clearly enjoyed saying this. 'Silence! Or I will clear the court!'

Pawlikowski seemed to be licking his lips. He knew what was coming.

'That, Inspector,' went on the coroner, 'is why you have requested a post-mortem examination of Mr Pearmain's body. And that of his mother.'

'We have,' said Hobday, 'but we would obviously like to do a full autopsy on Mr Pearmain first.'

Why? thought George. What's so great about putting me first in line to be carved up into little pieces by that mad Polish pathologist? Clearly Hobday and the Pole had decided George was the one. What really interested him about this charade was how beautifully it illustrated the manipulative skills of those who ran the country. The famous English respect for fair play was, he decided, simply a tribute to the wealthy and powerful members of UK Ltd, who were so good at fooling the underclass into thinking they were nice guys. English democracy? It simply meant the population had been more than skilfully lobotomized by the bosses. The result required here was the opening up of George Pearmain. It had, of course, been provided by the court.

'The immediate cause of death of Mrs Pearmain,' went on Hobday, 'was the injury she sustained in her fall.'

As far as he could make out, George was watching all this from somewhere in the area of the visitors' gallery. If you could call it a gallery, which you couldn't. It was, in fact, a roped-off area at the back of the anonymous hall where the inquest was taking place and, appropriately enough for such an indeterminate space, George could not really have said he was in it or, if he was, where exactly he was situated.

The question was, he had to admit, an even more complicated one than it had been when he was alive.

Immediately after he had died, he had had the impression that not only could he sit, stand, lie down and do all of the things that people over the age of three could generally do

131

but that his ideas of time and space had become a little more eccentric. It was much more like swimming. He was able to dive into the atmosphere around him and wriggle around like a dolphin. Sometimes strange, unexplained currents in a room would waft him up in the direction of the ceiling and he would find himself level with the dado rail or weaving around in the general area of the front-room chandelier.

When he was outside it could get quite dangerous. A few days ago he had been caught by a stiff breeze near Putney Bridge and found himself trapped on the roof of Marks & Spencer for three days. He was still waiting in vain for the moment when whatever force had landed him in that situation would grant him some form of corporeal identity, however hazy. He would gladly have settled for being moderately see-through, like polythene. He would have been really pleased with a spectral outline of the kind used by physicists to identify new elements. He thought he came into the category of a new element. So far, however, nothing of the kind had arrived. He was as invisible to himself as he was to others.

He had spent much of his inquest perched on the coroner's shoulder, like a pirate's parrot. This gave him an unobstructed view of the notepad Lewis was using, which he thought might give him some clues as to the possible identity of his killer. So far the coroner had written:

> Potatoes for Wed
> Chardonnay?
> Ring Halliday re sink – URGENT!!!
> Fish Waitrose?

He ended the proceedings with a narrative verdict, which enabled him to talk for even longer than he had done already.

He managed to make some fairly insulting remarks about George, describing him as 'a compulsive drinker', 'morbidly overweight' and 'a man with many enemies, both personal and professional'. The overall impression he left, George thought, was that G. Pearmain had not deserved to live. He said a final verdict would have to await the post-mortem that he now authorized Hobday and his boys to begin.

Which was why, on a sunny August morning some eight weeks after his death, George found himself lurking outside the front door of 22 Hornbeam Crescent, waiting and watching as Nat, Veronica, Esmeralda and other members of his close circle discussed their levels of involvement with the process of cutting his cadaver open.

Their mood was a little too cheerful for George's liking.

It was – in their defence – a very pleasant day. There was a slight breeze. There were cumulus clouds, printed tastefully on the blue sky above the house tops. Birds were going about their usual business while trees and flowers in his front garden were blooming in splendid indifference to the fact that he was no longer as visible as they were.

But did they have to laugh quite so loudly? He wasn't asking them to wear black permanently – although it might not have been bad if Esmeralda had tried it for a few months – but it had been a little too easy for the jokes to slip back into the fabric of life at 22 Hornbeam. Initially, there had been quite a lot of the 'he would have seen the funny side of this' to justify them chuckling while he was still in the chiller, but now they were more brazen about the fact that life was still sweet for those who held it in their hands.

'You can come if you like,' Nat was saying to Esmeralda.

Veronica Pinker shot him a glance of pure hatred. 'For God's *sake*, Nathaniel,' she hissed. 'Do you think she wants to see whatever they're going to do to poor George?'

'I just thought,' said Nat, 'she might find it interesting.'

Veronica's jaw dropped even further. Esmeralda did not seem to have noticed this dialogue.

'I've been to a number of them,' went on Nat, 'and in a way they bring you closer to the patient.'

Nat had indeed, thought George, an amazing attendance record at autopsies. It was, some said, the only really effective diagnostic tool in his armoury. This morning, he appeared unusually keen. He was definitely looking forward to it.

George was gazing at his dustbins, with a certain amount of nostalgia. It was Tuesday. Tuesday was the day he put out the dustbins, locked them against the foxes and, after a proud glance at the colossal amount of rubbish he and Esmeralda had created, retired to what Barry and Maurice, since they had left home, had started to call Château Hornbeam. He was never going to take out the rubbish again.

As he was thinking this – and as Nat, Veronica and Esmeralda were climbing into Nat's car – George saw, on the other side of the street, a figure he thought he recognized. The same big, square head. The same four great paws planted firmly on the pavement. The same seductive eyebrows and big mournful eyes.

It was Partridge, his Irish wolfhound. Had not Partridge been dead for eight years? To George's certain knowledge he had. That did not seem to stop him standing there and looking across at George with the same mournful expectancy he had shown in life. He was clearly waiting for George to give him a biscuit. He had spent his life waiting for George to give him something to eat. Death did not seem to have altered that.

As Esmeralda, Veronica and Nat settled into Nat's Volvo, Partridge crossed the road, clearly as invisible to them as he was to the driver of a large Range Rover, who drove straight through him as he stared, mournfully, through the windows of Nat's car.

George, who had still not mastered even basic permeability, nipped into the back next to Esmeralda, as Partridge's big black eyes stared at him with the same soulful longing he had shown in his life.

'I have something very important to tell you!' said Partridge.

Nat engaged the engine and the Volvo slid away from the kerb, leaving the wolfhound behind. George could still see the animal peering after them sorrowfully as the doctor accelerated and, after a hundred yards, turned right into the road that led to Putney Hill.

Jesus, thought George. This is all I need. A talking dog. With an important message to deliver. Will it never end?

Chapter Ten

The Putney morgue was an unassertive building, shy of revealing itself to strangers. It was only as Nat's car turned off Putney Bridge Road, just after Wandsworth Park, and headed towards the river that he recognized a small, square, vaguely modernist structure that he had driven past a hundred times without really noticing. There was no sign outside – evasive or otherwise – and in all the times he had driven past it he had never seen anyone entering or leaving.

There was a sense, of course, in which he was in there already but he still felt a slight thrill of anticipation, a sense of penetrating the unknown, as he followed Nat and Veronica out of the car. He knew, from the moment he took his first close look at it, that the Putney morgue was his kind of place.

Esmeralda, unsurprisingly, had elected not to take a front-row seat at George's autopsy and Veronica had said she would stay with her in the car, then reminded Nat of his complete insensitivity in even considering that Esmeralda would want to watch George being cut up into little pieces. To George's surprise, Nat put up a spirited defence of his conduct and told his wife that Mrs Duveen-Hollis had found Mark Duveen-Hollis's autopsy 'very healing'. Veronica reminded him that Martha Duveen-Hollis was later found to have had a hand in his murder. George wondered whether this was how he and Esmeralda had sounded to outsiders.

His had been a good marriage, hadn't it? Now he was dead he was not entirely sure. A horrible element of objectivity had crept into his assessment of it. Had he ever really known what Esmeralda felt about him? Had they been just another couple yoked to each other by habit and laziness?

As he listened to Veronica, and caught the all-too-familiar words ('self-obsessed', 'lazy', 'selfish', 'out of touch'), he found himself wondering what Partridge had had to tell him. He had said it was important. George reflected that it was almost certainly liable to be more important for Partridge than for him. It was probably something along the lines of 'Why did you give me the dogfood with jelly? I never liked jelly!'

Veronica had got out to dress down Nat but she was now back in the car with Esmeralda. George heard her say, 'God, he is a boring little man sometimes!'

To which Esmeralda replied, in a small voice, 'You don't really think anyone would actually want to murder George, do you?'

Veronica didn't answer. Perhaps, thought George, she could easily believe someone would.

Two police cars, carrying DI Hobday, DC Purves and quite a few other people pulled in ahead of them. As they clambered out George looked for Pawlikowski. He did not seem to be there. That was a relief. Maybe they had got a better, more sympathetic pathologist. He very much did not want the sulky Pole drilling through his scalp or showing off his prowess by rummaging round his intestines with a pair of surgical gloves.

'We're in Room Two,' said Hobday, with only a very slight nod to Nat (he clearly did not want him there), and moved off towards the back of the building, with his team.

Nat followed him and George followed Nat. The sun was further up in the sky and the breeze had dropped. Sweat was standing out on Hobday's brow. He looked, George thought, like a man under pressure.

'It's nice and cool in there!' he said, to no one in particular, as he led the way into the morgue.

There didn't seem to be any other bodies on display. As far as George could make out, the place seemed empty of the living and the dead. Nobody seemed to be sliding stiffs out of drawers, as they did in television crime shows, or painstakingly attaching labels to their feet. He did, he noticed, feel quite at home. He had not, since his death, felt any urge to loiter round graveyards or funeral parlours or any other place where the dead are gathered, but this hotel for the defunct seemed somehow *right*.

They went down a corridor, across an empty hall and into one of two rooms, side by side, at the back of the building. There, to George's dismay, in a green hat, green apron, white rubber boots and a pair of fearsome rubber gloves was none other than Pawlikowski. As they came into the room, he was decanting George's heart into a small bowl. He seemed, George thought, exceptionally cheerful.

'I thought I'd get started,' he said, nodding to a row of silver dishes on the side. 'Amanda's doing the stomach and bowels even as we speak. I'm making a start on the coronary arteries. After that...' he turned towards George's body and George could have sworn he heard him actually smack his lips '...I thought we'd get started on his brain.'

'What on earth,' said Nat, 'has his brain got to do with it?'

Pawlikowski swung round and stared at him for a moment. *Who let this amateur in here?* his expression seemed to say. Then, turning back to the red, pulpy mass that had kept George on line for sixty-five years, he said, 'I'm interested in brains. They reveal a lot.' He said this in the tone of a man who was about to fry one in butter with a little garlic and a few capers.

Nat showed no sign of being disturbed by the sight of his old friend's insides being waved around by some mad Polish pathologist. He did not flinch, either, when Pawlikowski got out a power saw and began to work on George's sternum. In fact, he moved in closer to get a better look. Blood and bits of bone were flying all over the place. This seemed to increase Pawlikowski's enthusiasm for the job in hand.

'His ribcage is pretty impressive,' said Pawlikowski, who was, George thought, responding to him more positively now he had him on the slab. 'Was he a singer?'

'He sang,' said Nat, 'but I wouldn't say he was a singer.'

As Pawlikowski ferreted round in George's thoracic cavity, like a medieval hangman in the final stages of his public office, Nat folded his arms and looked quizzically at a small selection of George's bones. 'The second of the costae spuriae,' he said, 'is bifid. And there is some damage to the costal cartilage.'

'Caused by a weapon?' said Pawlikowski.

'Caused, I imagine,' said Nat, 'by his golf swing. It was a thing to behold.'

George was waiting for a short, eloquent speech about how the sight of his ex-patient's bones had reminded Nat of how George had once set the dinner tables of Putney alight with his impression of Margaret Thatcher being buggered by a goat or, perhaps, singing 'You And Me And Bobby McGee', accompanied by his steel guitar with the string missing. It did not come.

When Pawlikowski had finished sloshing around in George's ribcage and the junior pathologist had taken away the heart for further examination (no one, unsurprisingly, seemed very interested in George's liver while his kidneys were treated with open contempt), he really got going on George's skull. He had not only a kind of miniature Black & Decker but also a wide variety of manual saws, odd-shaped drills and spoon-shaped instruments for scooping out George's brains.

George was almost sure, as Pawlikowski got started, he heard him sing the Seven Dwarfs' marching song from Disney's *Snow White and the Seven Dwarfs*.

Nat, now abandoning all pretence that he might be there to safeguard George's interests, had moved up even closer as the pathologist brought into the light of day more of the pinkish beige offal that had created so many brilliant aperçus, so many masterly, if unpublished, poems. 'The occipital lobe,' he said, 'is extraordinarily large. And the temporal lobe is very unusual indeed. You say he was a bank manager?'

'He was,' said Nat.

'Not that areas of the brain – apart, of course, from the occipital – are activity specific,' said Pawlikowski, who clearly enjoyed telling Nat things he almost certainly knew already, 'but I am one of those who think that the temporal lobe does serve as a memory storage unit. Of course...' here he started to lift off a large chunk at the top of George's skull '...what do we mean by memory? Is the brain a purely material instrument? Where do we store our information, the things we know and feel? It's a bit like asking where that email you sent this morning actually is. It's winging its way across the world. It's an electrical impulse. You can't see it or touch it but that doesn't mean it isn't there. Our souls, if you want to use that word, are not, as Leibniz pointed out, that easy to locate.'

With these comforting words, he levered out the remaining contents of George's bonce and, after stripping a few bits off, carried it, with some ceremony, to a small weighing machine on a side table. He peered at the register. 'One point eight kilos,' he said. 'Some bank manager!'

'He was,' said Nat, with every appearance of gravity, 'a very good bank manager.'

At this moment, from a large door in the high white wall opposite the bench where Pawlikowski was working, a small woman in the obligatory rubber gloves, apron and wellingtons, plus one of those hats designed to obliterate all traces of individuality from the wearer, emerged with two specimen jars and an expression of muted excitement.

'We have the results of the stomach and bowel!' she said, as if she was announcing the winner of the Man Booker Prize.

Hobday, who had been pacing around at a respectful distance from the drawing and quartering, swivelled round and glared intensely at the newcomer. Even Pawlikowski looked up from his scrutiny of George's cerebellum, as the woman moved further into the room.

'Enough pyridine alkaloids,' she said slowly, 'to monkey around quite considerably with his nicotine acetylcholine receptors.'

'By which you mean...?'

'Hemlock,' said Pawlikowski, tearing himself away reluctantly from George's brain and loosening his mask. 'Enough hemlock to kill Socrates five times over. You had it right, Guv. We're looking at one murdered bank manager.'

'*Yesss!*' said Hobday, his eyes glittering with the joy of being proved right. '*Yesss!* I knew it!'

With which he advanced on Pawlikowski and the two high-fived each other.

'Fucking murdered!' he said. 'Fucking poisoned! Bang to rights, baby! I knew it the moment I walked in! I could smell it! I could sniff it coming up the stairs! Felony, as I live and breathe, Marek! Oh, yes yes yes! Am I good or am I good?'

'You are good, Boss!' said Pawlikowski.

The two linked arms and began to perform a dance that looked like a cross between a hornpipe, a jig and the final stages of the English country dance known as Gathering Peascods. They tripped around the morgue, Pawlikowski's rubber boots and Hobday's brogues slapping on the hard floor, Hobday's large, long-fingered hands twirling above his head and the pathologist beating time with his left elbow, as if he were cranking up the invisible chanter of a set of pipes.

Hobday, George decided, had something of the Sherlock Holmes about him. His long nose had an aquiline quality and his long face was that of a contemplative, someone with a vivid inner life. He had the physique of a sportsman and the eyes of an ascetic, but there was nothing ascetic about him now. He was clearly the liveliest thing in the Putney morgue.

The dance was quite elaborate. They looked as if they had done it before. After a few minutes they went into a kind of mime version of a knife fight. Pawlikowski feinted left. Hobday feinted right. Then Hobday began to clap his hands above his head, flamenco-style, while Pawlikowski started up a strange improvised wordless vocal with something of an Arab tonality to it. Eventually he added words. 'You are the be-e-est!' he moaned.

'I am the be-e-e-st!' responded Hobday, wobbling around half-tones like a muezzin calling from a minaret in some ghostly desert city. Then they both went into a kind of wail that sounded more like a vocal effect from a Jewish funeral. 'Ayyyiii! Ayyyiii!' This was followed by a vigorous sequence of rhythmical stamping.

They had both plainly forgotten that Nat was there. Quite suddenly, Hobday stopped. There was total silence.

'I'm sorry,' said Hobday. 'I'm very, very sorry. We meant no disrespect to your patient.'

'I know that,' said Nat. 'I completely understand.'

'Obviously,' said Hobday, 'one gets involved. One gets carried away.'

'Indeed,' said Nat.

The inspector was watching Nat closely. He clearly suspected the man was about to get on to the British Medical Association and the Independent Police Complaints Commission as soon as he left the building but, to George's surprise, Nat did not seem discomfited by what he had just witnessed.

'He was your friend also,' said Hobday. 'Very likely you found what you have just seen...er...offensive.'

'Not at all,' said Nat. 'Not at all. I wouldn't say he was my friend. Our wives were friends. I wasn't close to him. Not really.'

'Ah!' said Hobday, in a manner that suggested this might have moved Nat up into the rank of suspect. 'I see!'

Nat had dropped in on the night George died, had he not? George had a sudden flash from that evening. Veronica saying something to Esmeralda, and Nat holding up his hand as he was offered a glass of parsnip wine. 'No. I mustn't. I'm driving.' Was that significant? Surely old Nat wouldn't have ...

'George was a very difficult person to know. He was the life and soul of the party. Full of jolly jokes. You know? But he was not an easy person. He was disliked by many.'

That, thought George, was harsh. Especially in the present circumstances. He was at a complete disadvantage. They were in the middle of slicing bits off his brain, for God's sake! Why hadn't Nat come out with this sort of thing when George was capable of answering back?

143

'I never felt,' went on Nat, 'that he respected me as a doctor. I never really thought he had a high opinion of my diagnostic skills.'

How had he spotted that? George had thought he'd managed to conceal it for years. He'd thought he'd done a pretty brilliant job – even to the extent of going out of town when seeking a second opinion – but, as he was beginning to find out, it was very difficult indeed to hide your thoughts from friends. Which was why so many of them ended up as enemies.

'Diagnosis is hard. Let's face it. You say it's, you know, kidney stones and, you know, it isn't. But it's hard. It's very hard. Medicine is very difficult. And I may not have much aptitude for it. Let's face it – who has? Most doctors are pretty rubbish. But that isn't the point.'

'No,' said Hobday, who was clearly anxious to stay on Nat's good side – presumably to avoid headlines such as 'CALLOUS INSPECTOR DANCES JIG IN MORGUE'.

'I have feelings,' said Nat. 'I have emotions. I sometimes felt George thought I didn't have feelings. Or emotions.'

'I'm sorry to hear that,' said Hobday.

'He was my friend,' went on Nat, 'and I was his doctor.'

'Indeed,' said Hobday.

He left another decent interval and Nat continued to talk. The sight of George's insides had clearly prompted a more than usually frank and open mood in the man.

'He was the artistic type. He wrote poetry, of course. I'm no judge of poetry. Although his wife told my wife she thought it was pretty fair rubbish.'

'Yes,' said Hobday, nodding, as if in agreement. 'Yes.'

Pawlikowski, too, was nodding. In fact, so was the minuscule female (she was almost, George mused, a midget) who had just brought in chunks of his intestines. Let's all rubbish

George's poetry! Why not? Perhaps she, too, worked for the *London Review of Books*. The wankers who hung around there had to have some way of making money, he thought.

'I play golf and tennis and squash and hockey and water polo and I go to the gym. I do not read poetry.' Nat shook his head sorrowfully as Pawlikowski, foiled now of his chance to carry out more unnecessary experiments on George's brain, began the complicated business of repacking George's skull.

'He was my bank manager,' said Nat, 'and, actually, he was a bloody good bank manager. Whatever his deficiencies as a poet, he was a first-class bank manager...but was he my friend? I don't know, really. I just don't know.'

Hobday, anxious as he clearly was to stop Nat rushing out and calling the *Daily Mail* about the performance he and Pawlikowski had recently put on, began to edge towards the door. He continued to make sympathetic noises but it was clear that getting out on the track of a juicy double murder was his major priority. Pawlikowski, in tune, as usual, with his colleague's needs and wishes, was asking the midget female – whose name seemed to be Carole – if she would mind 'tidying up' the violated remains of G. Pearmain.

She was obviously new to the job. 'I'm not sure where it all goes,' she bleated, as Pawlikowski started to make his exit.

'Heart on the left side. Ribcage underneath the neck. Get the skull the right way round if you can. Fuck the intestines. No one gives a stuff about them. Give them to your dog. If you have a dog.'

'I feel,' said Carole, whose opinion of Pawlikowski seemed to correspond to George's, 'we should behave with appropriate respect to the dead.'

Pawlikowski gave her a broad wink. 'Oh, sure,' he said. 'But come back and tell me that when you've been in the job as long as I have. A stiff is a stiff is a stiff. In my view. Speaking as a pathologist, I would say we go into our profession because we like working with people who can't answer back. Right, Doc? When I die they can do what they like with my mortal remains. The meat counter at Sainsbury's will do me.' He stopped. For a moment he abandoned his tough-guy act and a look of quite appalling sentimentality softened the edges of his geometrical features. 'So long as they scatter my ashes in Jastrzębie-Zdrój,' he said, as he followed his master out into the sunshine.

George found himself hoping that the next thing on his agenda would be his own death, preferably in suspicious circumstances, so that an even more unfeeling pathologist might play football with his head or practise basic juggling with his heart, liver and lungs.

Nat stayed behind, smiling sympathetically at the junior pathologist. 'Do you want a hand?' he said. 'I am a qualified doctor.'

George found himself wondering if this was a come-on. From the way Nat was smiling he rather suspected it was. His GP had his head to one side in a way he obviously considered charming and was giving Carole the benefit of some, if not all, of his well-preserved front teeth.

'I think,' she said, rather prissily, 'I can manage.'

Making the best of not being allowed to shove his old friend's organs back inside his body in the wrong order, Nat headed after Hobday, Purves and Pawlikowski.

Outside, the sun was still high in the sky and the streets of the suburb were filled with light. On the other side of Wandsworth Park, the Thames glittered its way to the heart of the city, reminding George that he was once more in, and yet not part of, the land of the living.

Veronica Pinker and Esmeralda had got out of the car and

were chatting in the way they always chatted – as if there had been no real beginning and would be no real end to their conversation. He caught fragments of dialogue he was almost sure he had heard before and found them curiously comforting. When Hobday broke the news that George had been murdered, Esmeralda's face betrayed nothing, but she watched the detective with a look that George knew very well. She was trying to decide whether Hobday was up to the task of finding his killer.

She had become less, not more, mysterious to him since his death. It had, George found, made it easier to appreciate her good qualities. A slight breeze seemed to be pulling him over to where she was standing as he gazed with admiration at her shrewd eyes. And it was not only her intelligence that had held their marriage together. Who would have guessed, looking at this respectable sixty-something grandma, nodding respectfully at the local copper, that she had a talent for giving blowjobs that could have earned her a six-figure salary?

Removing him from the equation had made it finally possible for George to see what his marriage had been: it was only now he had lost it that he was beginning to understand its value and, correspondingly, to have moments of real rage at whoever had decided to take it from him. He floated at the edge of the talk between Esmeralda and Hobday with what was now genuine urgency and passion.

'You see,' Hobday was saying, 'we're working on the theory that there was some kind of confrontation in the kitchen that night. That would be consistent with the way in which your mother-in-law fell and with the fragments of glass we found on the floor.'

'You think,' said Esmeralda, 'it was the glass George took to bed that night.'

'We think it has to be,' said Hobday.

'Someone put hemlock into it during the course of the evening. George drank it and that was why he died. Not a heart attack.'

'No,' said Hobday. 'I'm afraid not.'

'So you think,' said Esmeralda, 'that whoever spiked his glass crept into our bedroom and took the evidence away but Jessica, being a light sleeper and downstairs, heard whoever it was, went into the kitchen and tried to take away the glass. To wash it up, knowing her. And was pushed to the floor for her pains. And died. After which the criminal tried to make it look like a break-in.'

There was a long silence.

'You,' said Hobday, 'are a very insightful woman.'

'Oh, sure,' said Esmeralda. 'I should have joined the fucking police force.'

The two of them looked at each other.

'You have presumably,' went on Esmeralda, 'worked out where everyone was during the course of that evening. Who had the opportunity. Who saw anything suspicious and so on. There were other people visiting that night – including Mabel Dawkins, Nat and Veronica – but whoever put it into George's glass, then moved it from the bedroom, must have been staying the night.'

'Possibly,' said Hobday. 'It could have been done at any time. And there is a chance, of course, that the broken french-window pane was really done from outside. We can't rule that out completely. It is very difficult to be precise about what happened that evening. Parsnip wine, don't you know? About the only thing we're sure of is that you went to bed at nine, Mrs Pearmain.'

'We left just before nine,' said Nat, joining the conversation, 'and all I remember is that everyone was knocking back parsnip wine and stuffing those herbs that Frigga had brought into their drinks like crazy. She kept saying they were good for you.'

Hobday nodded to himself, as if he already knew this. He probably did, thought George. The man had known it was murder (or murders) from the moment he had walked into the house. He almost certainly had wall-to-wall charts up in the police station, tracing everyone's movements the night before G. Pearmain had been murdered.

Murdered. Bloody hell! He had often suspected he was not as popular as he would have liked to be but it seemed as if things had been even worse than he'd feared.

'Motive,' said Hobday, 'is what I cannot quite fathom yet.'

Esmeralda's phone was shuddering in her hand. She looked at the screen without visible enthusiasm and was obviously wondering whether to answer it or not. When she did George knew, instantly, in the way he did when she was talking on the phone, who was at the other end of the line. Her blend of formal patience and only just mastered impatience meant it had to be Stephen or Lulu.

'Yes,' she said, and then, 'Yes … Yes … Yes … Of course we will. Straight away.' She turned to the rest of them. 'That was Stephen,' she said. 'They've just found Jessica's will. It's in her flat. They're there now. We have to go over. Now.'

Chapter Eleven

Jessica Pearmain's mansion flat was on the ground floor of Cromwell View, a large, purpose-built thirties block, named in honour of the Debates in the Army in Council that had taken place, at the end of the English Civil War, in a church only a few hundred yards away from the building.

There were lawns at the back, complete with weeping willows and a pond. A porter called Ron did very little and a senior porter, called Pillock, did even less. The average age of the occupants was about eighty-five.

George, as he had done so often in life, was sitting in the front passenger seat while Nat drove. Esmeralda and Veronica were in the back, sitting exactly as they would have done had he still been alive – not talking but looking as if they were about to do so at any moment.

He looked at Esmeralda as they pulled into the wide drive and came to a halt at his mother's door. It was odd to be paying this familiar call on someone who was dead, and being dead himself did not make it less peculiar. Esmeralda, when she thought no one was looking, allowed her real anxiety to show. She needs a lot of looking after, he thought. Who is going to do it now? Is that, in fact, what I did for all those years? I never thought of it like that but perhaps that was what, in the end, it became.

Jessica's front garden had a small pond all of its own. There were lilies and flag irises and, in the borders, small flowers whose names she always knew. It was only now, looking at them, that George realized how much he missed her. They had got close in her last years, close, he now saw, to the extent of excluding his brother and sister.

'Frigga found it, apparently,' Esmeralda was saying to Veronica. 'Stephen said she was tearing the place apart.'

At first, of course, no one had been able to find Jessica's will. They had gone through and through her cupboards. They had looked in all the pockets of all her coats. They had rifled through her books. Stephen had even prised up the floorboards and groped around underneath them. Mabel Dawkins, the Mullins woman and Beryl Vickers, who all seemed to know they were in line for something, had joined in enthusiastically, but no one had worked out that it was inside a waterproof jacket inside the cistern of the lavatory in her back bathroom. Which was where Frigga had found it.

As far as George was aware, Frigga was the first person to see it, but that didn't help in the task of spotting whether she or one of the others might have murdered him. Knowing that he was the sole beneficiary was enough to give the holder of that information a very respectable motive for murder, but, if any of them knew how Jessica had carved up her estate they were keeping it very quiet indeed. Being dead and invisible gave one unparalleled access to private conversations but, so far, nothing had emerged. Perhaps soon he would acquire some more interesting dead skills, such as managing to be in two places at once, X-ray vision and other such talents as were found in the heroes of American comics.

How had Frigga found it? Had she known all along? Or had she, possibly, used witchcraft?

Stephen met them at the door. He was wearing a dark

brown suit with a tie of a matching shade. His shoes were pale russet and his shirt came equipped with elegant chocolate stripes. He was, thought George, an autumn symphony. Lulu chose his clothes and she had, once again, managed to pick out an outfit that went superbly well with his toupee.

'She was going mad,' Stephen said, as he opened the door. 'The old lady was definitely losing it. She hid the damn thing in the lavatory cistern. It's a miracle it wasn't flushed away.'

It was interesting, thought George, that his brother's grasp of plumbing was almost as shaky as his hold on human character and emotions. Stephen led them into the spacious hall, still lined with Jessica's favourite watercolours, a photo of George's father, looking a little like Clement Attlee, and, on the floor, a gigantic brass bowl that Uncle Arthur had brought back from Tibet the year before George was born.

Frigga was standing in the middle of the living room, behind her the vivid green of the Cromwell View gardens and Jessica's tiny patio, crowded with white, red and purple flowers. Even the position of the chairs had not altered since George had last been there. He found it hard to believe that his mother was not going to hobble in from the garden, trowel in hand, her smile lifted in greeting. *Nothing is more beautiful than happiness in an old face.* In spite of her many faults, Jessica had been a happy person. Perhaps that was why her spirit was at rest. It certainly did not seem to be hanging around in whatever weird dimension George was now condemned to occupy. That was, in a way, a relief. George was fond of his mother. He would have liked someone else to talk to, apart from a dead Irish wolfhound. But his mother? For all eternity? Maybe not.

The afterlife was clearly meant for creatures like him and Partridge, beings who had spent their lives trapped by circumstances and were now condemned to tread the same circles they had worn away when alive. Perhaps soon he and Partridge would go on ghostly walks and return, as they had done so often, to this very flat, to sit facing the window. Maybe then his mother would put in an appearance. She might at least be able to put him right on how George had died, which would set him off on the trail of whoever had spiked his drink with hemlock.

Frigga was waving Jessica's will. She did not seem particularly satisfied that she had found it. In fact, thought George, she seemed even more distressed than usual.

'She has left it all to George,' she said, her face more highly coloured than the luckless recipient of all that cash had ever seen it. 'She's left all her millions to George. And he is dead. It is so unfair.'

George could not quite work out which bits of this proposition Frigga thought were unfair – that he was dead or that he was now worth millions. A bit of him wondered whether that meant Esmeralda copped the lot. He found himself hoping that that was the case. Serve the other bastards right. She could buy a house with a swimming-pool. He had always wanted a swimming-pool. Even if he wouldn't be able to use it he could float above it and watch Barry and Maurice splash around with Ella and Bella.

'She says there's a codicil,' went on Frigga, 'that sets out what happens if George should die. Which he has, of course. And she says that this codicil makes provision for me and you and we get all of the money, Stephen, but she also says there are more – and very important – bequests, involving Mullins and Vickers and Dawkins and she expects us to honour them. I mean, really! Really! Didn't she trust us?'

George had not realized his sister was quite so acquisitive.

'We have to find this codicil, Stephen. Otherwise Mullins, Dawkins and Vickers could sue us and try to stop us getting the money. If we shared it between us, Stephen, we would get millions of pounds each. I could go to Machu Picchu or whatever it's called. I could buy a vegetarian restaurant. I could have work done on my face. And body.'

Perhaps that was all part of Jessica's plan, thought George. Perhaps this codicil was a kind of quest Jessica had devised in order to force her children to come to terms with their weaknesses. He had certainly never seen Frigga's real nature so vividly in evidence. All that phoney spirituality had gone right out of the window the moment her mother had dangled masses of moolah in front of her.

God, the bastard, was probably going to make sure Frigga and her mother shared all eternity. Their mutual dislike had been of the special kind that mothers and daughters reserve for each other. They could pass the next trillion years criticizing each other's dress sense, arguing about what to eat and how to eat it and, best of all, subtly reminding each other of their moral deficiencies.

'What we must do first,' said Stephen, 'is read the will.'

Frigga gasped as if he had just asked her to strip naked. 'Read the will?' she said. 'Get everyone together in a room with a solicitor and Read the Will?'

'No,' said Stephen, with only slight impatience. 'That only happens in Hollywood movies. I mean *read the will.* Become aware of its content and provisions. In regard to this...codicil. And everything else, of course.' He stretched out his hand. 'I need to look at this very carefully!' he said. 'I haven't actually seen it. I had no idea that that was what Mother intended. I'm still trying to absorb it. It was her money. She had a right to leave it to whom she liked. A dogs' home. If that was what she wanted. Although she didn't like dogs. George liked dogs. She did not. Neither do I. In fact. We were closer than we seemed. I think.'

Frigga gave him a crazy, cunning look. 'You will give it back, won't you, Stephen?'

'Of course I won't, Frigga,' said Stephen, waggishly. 'I'll eat it. I'll set light to it.'

Frigga's face began to implode. For a moment George thought she was actually going to cry. Stephen's voice became gentle and persuasive. 'Of course I'll give it back to you,' he said. 'And well done for finding it. What I suggest is we all go down the Duke's Head and go through it with…'

A *fine-tooth comb!* thought George, marvelling, as ever, at his brother's way with a cliché.

'…a fine-tooth comb!' said Stephen. Then he stopped. 'God!' he said. 'I can almost hear old George ticking me off for that one. He was so like Father. Always looking out for what he called "the cliché" while I was always…you know…'

Spouting them, thought George, *by the yard.*

Stephen chuckled in what George found an over-familiar manner. 'I miss the old bugger,' he said. 'I really miss his salty humour.'

There were times when George had thought he loved his brother and times when he was fairly sure he didn't. Since he had died he had definitely found Stephen harder to take. Partly because being dead gave you so much more time to think. It was all you could do. Stephen's attempts to sound as if he was the most mature member of the family had started to irritate him and, with himself out of the way, he was fairly sure they had got more pronounced. It is all too easy to patronize the dead – to ascribe to them the thoughts and feelings you think they ought to have had.

'I think,' went on Stephen, with another of those annoying chuckles, 'he's looking down on us and saying, "Oh, my God! Oh, my God! When will you ever learn?"'

His hand was still extended towards Frigga. Eventually she allowed him to take it but, as he did so, she watched him, nostrils flared, as if she really expected him to dash out of the room and disappear with it, cackling like some treasure-hungry gnome of Swedish folklore. As soon as he had it in his grasp he turned to Esmeralda, Nat and Veronica and suggested, once again, they adjourn to the Duke's Head.

Frigga got that cunning look again. 'I'll stay here,' she said. 'I have an appointment.'

She looked as if she expected people to ask her what the appointment was. They did not. Staring at Stephen now, with what George thought was a distinctly mad expression, she said, 'I'm going to hunt for that codicil. We have to find the codicil. I'm going to find it. You can do what you like. I'm going to hunt for it. I will find it. I found the will, didn't I? I'm going to find it.'

She turned her gaze on Esmeralda. 'The police think I killed George,' she said, 'but I didn't. I didn't like him. I admit that. I hated him. But I did not give him hemlock. I swear I did not. Terrible things have happened, Esmeralda. Terrible things.'

With which she fell to her knees and began scratching at the carpet, like a frustrated cat. She's finally lost it, thought George. She has left the reservation.

'I expect Mummy has put a special bequest in it,' she said. 'I know she wanted me to have the sideboard. She always said she wanted me to have the sideboard. And the painting of Ullswater. Which is worth a great deal. I need money, Esmeralda. I'm sorry but I do. Because of what happened at the health club. People will say I murdered George – but I did not!'

Stephen was at the door. Inclining his head slightly, like a maître d'hôtel with important guests, he indicated that perhaps the others would like to follow him out into the sunshine.

'I'm positive,' Frigga was wailing, as they left, 'that she wanted me to have the cutlery!'

George noticed Stephen give a quick, furtive glance in the direction of the cutlery drawer.

Jessica had made a habit, over the last ten years, of approaching all her close friends and relatives, looking deep into their eyes and saying 'When I am gone I would like you to have the cutlery/sideboard/watercolour/bottle of vintage claret/Afghan rug.' He was pretty sure she had promised him the cutlery on a number of occasions. Not that, as things stood, he could see any possibility of his needing a knife or fork or spoon.

Esmeralda had been looking at the watercolours in what George thought was a definitely calculating manner. Stephen almost drove her and Veronica and Nat out towards the car. Frigga showed no sign whatsoever of following them. She had now jammed her head under the sofa and was making great sweeps of the area of Jessica's oatmeal carpet concealed beneath it. She had powerful, almost simian, arms and they scythed backwards and forwards as Frigga pushed her head further and further under the piece of furniture. All you could see of her was her behind, which, as her mother had never tired of reminding her, was not her best feature.

George very much did not want to be left alone with Frigga. He had never been able to think of anything to say to her when he was alive. His death, as far as he could see, had not made any more topics of conversation available to them. If anyone was going to haunt anyone, he thought, in this instance the living would be haunting the dead.

Somehow, though, the thing he did not want to happen was happening – and he was alone with his younger sister.

'Frigga,' he said, in a cautious tone, 'can you hear me?'

She clearly could do nothing of the kind but, as she pulled her head out from under the sofa, she did seem to be looking vaguely in his direction.

'Oh, George,' she said, 'I feel your presence somehow. In the last few weeks I have had the sensation that you are still here. That you are in Hornbeam Crescent. Still. Watching over us all. But I feel you here, too, George. I feel you are also in Cromwell View. What are you doing here, George? Are you trying to help us find the will? What are you trying to tell us? I feel you're trying to tell us something. What is it? Why are you here?'

Why indeed? thought George. Was this question any easier to answer when you were dead rather than alive? Why was he here?

He had not wanted, for example, to spend quite so much of his life in Norfolk. He had done so because Barry's and Maurice's parents-in-law, who seemed to have nothing whatsoever to recommend them, came from that part of the world. He had not wanted to spend years of his life with a small, weaselly man called Schlock, but Schlock was his deputy at NatWest and, for about five years, George had managed to fool himself that he even liked the man. We have no choice on either side of the grave, he reflected stoically. We just have to try to make the best of it.

'I really have not the faintest idea, Frigga,' he said.

Frigga twitched violently. 'Oh, my God, George!' she said. 'You're trying to reach me. I feel you. I feel you, George!'

'Where,' said George, not sure that he really wanted the answer to this question, 'do you feel me?'

'I feel you here!' said Frigga, striking herself just below her left breast. 'I feel you here!' Then she smote herself in the lower bowel, just above the groin. 'And here!' she said.

'And here!' Her jaw dropped a notch and her eyes began to glisten, in a way they only usually did after alcohol or Renaissance music. 'I killed you, George,' she said. 'I murdered you.' She gave a brief, mildly insane laugh and added, 'I pulled the wool over the inspector's eyes. They told me what to say. They helped me. They're evil. I murdered you, George.'

George thought this had the potential to become the most interesting conversation he had ever had with his sister. If he could only find a way of keeping up his end of the proceedings it might be revelatory. It was not, actually, by the standards of their usual discourse, particularly one-sided. They seemed, he decided, to be communicating rather better than they had managed to do when he was alive. 'What do you mean by "murdered"?' he said.

'What do I mean? Do I mean I put the hemlock into your glass, George? I don't know. They told me at first that I hadn't. And then they said I might have done. I certainly picked it, George. I pick herbs. Maybe I did put it in your glass. I did want you dead, George. I did want the money. Oh, my God, I wanted the money!'

'Who,' said George, 'are *they*? Are they voices? Or do you actually see them?'

Frigga hunched her back and moved away from him. When she spoke again she wasn't looking at him. She hadn't, he decided, ever really seen him. She was talking to herself – the way most people did most of the time, even when they thought they were talking to other people.

'They are evil,' she said, in a cracked voice. '*They* are agents of the Devil. And they know all about me and how wicked I am. They know I wanted you dead. I was frightened she had left it all to you. And to Mullins. You and Mullins, the ones she really loved. I was never her favourite.'

For a moment a look of pure hatred crossed her face. Then she said, 'I hate Mullins!'

With that she flung herself to the floor again and, thrusting her hand underneath the carpet, began to scrabble along the floorboards. This, thought George, was what she had been saying immediately after he and his mother had been killed but there was something not altogether convincing about the confession.

What he couldn't understand, however, was how someone as well up as Frigga on herbology could have introduced hemlock into someone's drink by accident. That was what she seemed to be saying had happened. Or, rather, it was what she wanted to have happened. She knew what hemlock looked like. She had been picking herbs that afternoon. She must have done it.

She was also a pretty good fit for the murderer as far as motive was concerned. She had always been close to crazy and perhaps the thought of the money had finally been too much for her. The mysterious people who had been telling her she had done it were probably the voices in her head that had prompted her to pick the stuff in the first place. It was as if she was at war with them, thought George. She was a victim of the war within the self that creates psychosis.

Still muttering about Mullins (she now seemed to be saying that Mullins had poisoned George and pushed Jessica to the floor), she got to work on Jessica's desk, pulling out the drawers and scattering old letters, bills and fragments of George's father's chamber music on the floor.

It was time to check up on Stephen.

George went to the front door. He was really going to have to start asserting himself here. He was still completely lacking in basic phantom techniques. He had rather less spirit style than, say, Partridge. These days, his wolfhound seemed to have the gift of walking through doors. George, meanwhile, had relapsed into a condition that was the lot of the average dog: standing by a door and waiting for a passing human to open it.

He reached for the handle. Or, rather, he tried to imagine something like that happening but his imagination, if that was what it was, did not succeed in bringing his hand (which was what it obviously wasn't) any closer to the handle. For a moment he had the illusion that he might be able to bring the handle towards him – but that didn't seem to work either.

He tried again. This time he did not exactly fail to make contact. There were moments – as with the business in his bedroom just after he had died when he had found himself sinking into the carpet – when he could have sworn he was thrusting his fingers into the fabric of the door; he knew, somehow, that this was not an actual sensation but he also knew, in the way one knows things in dreams, that, although this was not what he had experienced, it was waiting for him somewhere and that he must have done it, or had an insight into what it would be like if and when he did, because he felt he knew how the wood and paint would seem to give way to what was no longer his hand.

Suddenly, with the clarity of a Christian appreciating the reality of Christ's Resurrection or a Muslim scenting the delights of Paradise, he realized he was going to have to go through the keyhole.

The letterbox was a possibility but never a serious one. There was a chance, he decided, of getting stuck, just as Jessica's next cargo of junk mail was being delivered. The keyhole seemed, for reasons he could not have described, to be a simple, clean alternative. He knew also that he would go in head first, like a diver.

Diving had never been George's thing. Sitting up straight in a chair was bad enough. Arranging his body neatly for sleep had, of late, been a near impossible task. What chance had an average fat guy of lining up his head with his chest, knees and feet in the appallingly short time it took to travel from diving board to pool surface? And this was no mere high-board-at-Putney-Leisure-Centre job. This involved travelling parallel with the floor into a 95 x 35 mm A2001 Banham Rim Autolock.

He did not breathe deeply. He failed to flex his non-existent knees or stare ahead of the shadow of himself with the kind of rapt contemplation seen in the faces of Olympic divers before they commence the triple somersault with double back flip and multiple corkscrew turn. He considered the word 'keyhole'. He thought hard about its jagged edges, waiting, like a reef, for some unwary ship caught in a furious storm. He fancied how the cold passage of the lock might close over your head, like water. How you would smell the shiny neutrality of metal, a tiny nip of autumnal sawdust, an ecstatic whiff of paint in the nostrils and then the August day outside – the breeze, the pollen, honey sweet, and the warm smell of the dark earth.

And then, somehow or other, he found himself outside the Lebanese restaurant in Lower Richmond Road.

It was not where he had planned to be – George had never liked Lebanese food – but it was close enough to the Duke's Head to be a credible result. He felt a touch of quiet pride as he looked around. All he had to do was get the Thames on his left and start walking towards Putney Bridge. He felt, at the same time, a touch of panic. He could easily have overshot the target. It was all very imprecise. He could have ended up in Kidderminster or Calais or Ashby de la Zouch!

The trouble was, walking did not seem as simple as it had

a moment ago. When he began to move what he still thought of as his shoulder towards the river, it began to spin wildly out of control and he found he was revolving very fast, like a drill or an over-enthusiastic Dervish. The word 'giddy' occurred to him, as he screwed himself into the pavement, revved up furiously, rose into the air, then travelled at what seemed an improbably high speed, at about thirty yards off the ground, in the direction of the Duke's Head. Before he got anywhere near it, though, he was forced sharp left into Glendarvon Road, then right on to the Embankment before accelerating wildly back on to the B306 and screeching to a halt outside the pub.

It was a bit, thought George, like being trapped inside a particularly wilful satnav system, with more than usually definite views on topography. It was not the way he would have chosen to go to the Duke's Head, but, some invisible power seemed to be telling him, it was the way he was going to have to go. 'You're dead,' whoever was in charge here was saying. 'Get over it. You'll go where we want you to go, motherfucker.'

When he was outside the door of the upper saloon bar, he allowed himself the luxury of thinking he had some choice about how he got into the pub. It was one of the few basic freedoms left to a middle-class Englishman, these days. Was he going to slither in through a gap in one of the open windows? Head-butt his way through the main wall? Waft through the decorative glass panel in the door? He was considering all these possibilities when, without his knowledge or permission, he was picked up and deposited at a table overlooking the river, where his brother, as usual, was laying down the law.

'She's left it all to George,' Stephen was saying, as he pored over Jessica's will. 'That was her right and privilege. He was her eldest child. He was her first-born. He was greatly loved by her. She'd left him the money. Twelve million pounds. A great deal of money. Not, of course, to some people. To Donald Trump, for example – chicken feed. But not to any of us, I imagine. She seemed to think George would provide for the rest of us. For me. Obviously. And Frigga. And Mullins. And Vickers. And Mabel Dawkins.'

He chewed his moustache. He looked at Esmeralda. 'Did you know Jessica had left it all to George? Did you know about the codicil?' he said. 'I had no idea Mother even knew what a codicil was.'

'I never thought Jessica's will was anything to do with me, Stephen,' said Esmeralda.

'No?' said Stephen, giving her a doubtful look. He tapped the will with his index finger. 'She's obviously left Mullins and Dawkins well provided for,' he said, 'which is a good thing. They need money. We all need money obviously, but they need it badly. Frigga needs money. As do you. As do I. Although I'm doing OK. In profit. Media's not easy but…well, I'm comfortable. Nevertheless money is always useful. But. I'm sure George would have provided for us all. He was a fair-minded man. As you are a fair-minded woman. I do not think we need to involve lawyers. We need to find the codicil obviously. Which seems from what she says here to set out things.'

It was curious how George's absence had stripped away the complicated routines with which he and his siblings had dealt with the jealousies that lived in so many of their hearts. Was his mother punishing him, he wondered, for his attempts to be fair? At the end she had disliked both Frigga and Stephen. Leaving him in charge of proceedings was bad enough. His dying had made the situation impossible.

And – this was, literally, the million-dollar question – how much did Stephen and Frigga know? Jessica had told him she had said nothing to either of them but he would not have been surprised if she had let something slip. If one of them had done it – and they seemed the obvious candidates, if only because it was usually one's closest relatives who did this kind of thing – it would be whichever of them had managed to ferret out the truth about the contents of the will.

Unless they had done it together. That, thought George, was highly likely. They had always got on well. Ganging up on their older sibling was something they had been trying, not very successfully, to do all of their lives. Maybe they had finally brought it off in spectacular style.

'It must,' Esmeralda was saying, 'make you very angry. That she left it all to George. I think it was a monstrous thing to do.'

'Thank you for that, Esmeralda,' said Stephen with every appearance of sincerity. 'I was a little put out. We had become distant. We had lost touch. But I'm sure that...if he had lived, George would, you know...'

'I'm sure he would,' said Esmeralda.

Stephen turned to her and seized her wrist. 'It's possible,' he said, 'that Frigga knew the terms of Mother's will. It's possible that she killed George. It's possible that she killed Mother. We have to face that thought. It's not a pleasant one but we have to face it. As a real possibility.'

'If we can't find this codicil,' said Esmeralda, 'I suppose we'll have to get a solicitor.'

A look of total panic crossed Stephen's face. To be replaced, instantly, by decisive resolution. Which was followed, in its turn, by an even more acute look of desperation. 'We could get a solicitor,' he said. 'Perhaps we'll have to. I think it's important to be decisive about these things. I'll call Lulu. She'll have views. I won't call her. I'll email her. She prefers email.' He stopped, and started to twitch, like a rabbit scenting a predator.

'We have to talk, Esmeralda. We really have to talk. We've never really talked, have we? We must talk.'

Everything was changing in the Pearmain family, thought George. Stephen and Esmeralda talking! Stephen apparently desperate to talk to her. He usually couldn't wait to get out of the room fast enough if she was around. Was there some other motive for all of this? Whatever was going on, it was clear that the crisis in the Pearmain family was a more serious one than even the day Stephen had borrowed Esmeralda's car and pranged it on the M40, or the night Lulu had told George he was 'a bit of a loser' or, indeed, any of the other conflicts that had, miraculously, not prevented any Pearmain refusing to speak to some or all other Pearmains for all eternity, amen.

It's time, he said to himself (since no one was capable of hearing him) that I made my presence felt.

Chapter Twelve

This was not going to be easy. He tried, several times, during Stephen and Esmeralda's increasingly intense conversation. He tried saying, 'It is I! George!' in a sepulchral voice at any decent pause in the dialogue but, although he got a couple of odd looks from Veronica Pinker, no one else seemed interested. At one point he thought he might have managed to make a packet of crisps move a few inches, but it turned out to be the breeze coming in from the river.

He had never seen Stephen so agitated. Or so anxious to talk. He seemed not to want to leave the pub. It was nearly an hour and a half before they started to move towards the door because, as Esmeralda said, if Frigga was half as crazy as Stephen seemed to think she was, she had better not be left alone in Jessica's empty flat.

'You're right,' he kept saying, as he chewed his moustache furiously. 'She may self-harm. You're right.'

George had an idea that, once he was outside, he might find it easier to appear to one or all or some of them, but as soon as he got outside, things became even more confusing than they had been on the way in.

Almost immediately he had set foot on the pavement he found himself yanked up about sixty feet in the air and, with a strong sensation of dangling, watched Esmeralda and Stephen, Veronica and Nat climb into their cars.

George saw and heard this, but he saw other things at the same time. It was a bit like watching one of those American TV shows in which the screen divides into a series of even smaller squares, each showing a different element of some critical situation. First he saw Frigga, alone in the flat. She was standing now and turning towards the door. Someone was coming in – or ringing the bell. It was hard to work out which. Was it someone she knew? It was hard to tell from her face – her expressions were always notoriously hard to read. She walked around most of the time as if she was about to be sick. Even when she smiled, which was not very often, she looked as if she was about to be sick.

Who was coming in to see her?

George was hoping she would say something but she didn't. The frame froze and, in another part of the picture, he saw Stephen, driving immediately behind Esmeralda, Nat and Veronica. He looked angry about something. The money probably, thought George. Although the money was only half of it. This was all about family. The lies that people told each other. The fears and hatreds that lay buried for years and, with the horrible simplification that death imposes, emerged, like a drowned city rearing up as the waters receded.

He was better off dead. He really was.

He found, to his surprise, that he was flying. This time, for a change, he seemed perfectly in control. He roared over the roof of the Winchester Club, with its gardens that over-looked the river, wheeled left and struck out west along the line of the great bend in the Thames that leads the waters down towards Mortlake. The sun was still shining, lighting the way to Richmond, Twickenham and the first lock of the upper stream, hidden in the green outskirts of Teddington. Its pale beams lay clear on the black water as George swooped low over the outgoing tide, Hammersmith Bridge printed in antique colours against the afternoon sky.

He was flying. When he was a child he had dreamed of flying. Now at last he was flying. In death there is dominion.

The words of a long-forgotten folk song, first heard in the sixties when he and Esmeralda were young, echoed in the air around him.

> If I had wings
> Like Noah's dove
> I'd fly up the river
> To the one I love...

He was flying to see Esmeralda. He was flying back in time. He was flying back over their first fuck, in the back garden of her parents' house in Barnes. My God, he thought, as he gazed at his own arse pumping up and down with youthful enthusiasm in the back garden of a house that was now, like its owners and usurper (him) long gone, my God, I was good.

He was flying over the scene of one of their most spectacular rows. It had happened on the towpath. All George could remember about it was that at the end after they had both threatened each other with divorce they had tried to remember what the row had been about. Neither of them could.

'Perhaps,' Esmeralda had said, with a demure smile, 'I called you a bad bank manager.'

'If you'd done that,' George had replied, 'I would've strangled you.'

He had, he realized, had a good life. He might have moaned about being a bank manager, a creature from a

169

world now as definitively over as tsarist bureaucracy or the old Labour Party but, actually, he had enjoyed every minute of it. Curiously, the pleasure he had taken in his own existence made leaving it behind easier. He didn't want, now, to ask any more questions of his marriage or career – all those things people are traditionally supposed to worry over as they croak. He was done with that. What he wanted was to resolve the mystery of why he had died, to be, at the very least, a helpful accomplice in the task of finding out who had had the nerve to cut him off so early in his retirement. For God's sake! He had not yet been to the Great Barrier Reef! Or Machu Picchu!

Machu Picchu. That set something off in the bundle of thoughts and ideas that now approximated to George.

Frigga. It was Frigga. It had to have been Frigga. Stephen was right. As he dived back in a huge half-circle towards Putney Bridge he resolved that, as soon as he got into his mother's flat, Frigga was going to get a bit of the kind of stuff Banquo dished out to Macbeth. He was going to gibber. He was going to lay his hands on some chains and put them to good use. Not even the Society for Psychical Research would be able to do anything for the hard-hearted bitch. The woman who had offed her own brother so she could open a vegetarian restaurant. And go to Machu Picchu – preferably after learning how to spell it. Wasn't that what she had let slip earlier? Weren't those her pathetic ambitions? Why should she achieve them and not him?

Flying at speed now, he stormed in over the roofs of Lower Richmond Road and, braking hard, dropped down and found himself on the gravel drive in front of the familiar black door, with Stephen pressing hard on the bell.

Frigga did not seem to be answering.

'She may have gone completely round the bend,' Stephen

was saying, 'or maybe...' his voice dropped '...maybe she's found the codicil. My God!' He leaned against the bell, screwing up his face and chewing his moustache furiously.

What was it with human beings and money? They seemed to think it bought them freedom. Looking at Stephen's face now, George, who would never have to go to a cash machine again, saw more clearly than he ever could have done in life how money made people its prisoner. Why did none of them understand how sad and pointless it is? Because, of course, they're alive, he thought, and felt, for a brief moment, a pang of sadness for all of the living as they walked unaided through the world.

Stephen pressed the bell again. Nat was peering in through the net curtains in a very determined manner. Veronica was, as usual, readying her profile for some imaginary fashion photographer. Esmeralda was staring glumly at the ground – perhaps, George thought, musing on what a great bloke he had been, what a loss he was to the world in general and to Putney in particular.

Stephen put his face to the letterbox and called, 'Frigga, are you there?' She still did not react.

There was then a long discussion about the key. Jessica was always having keys cut for her flat. The Mullins woman had three, to George's certain knowledge. Esmeralda had had one, then lost it – but Stephen, he was sure, had at least two, even though he never went to see her. Today, for some reason, he did not seem able to find any of them. He patted his pockets. He probed his wallet. And, as he searched, he seemed to become more and more nervous and irritable. Of course, George thought, his brother was one of those people who believed he could control things by setting them out neatly; he had always viewed George – slightly condescend-ingly – as someone who needed 'sorting out' yet the inside of

Stephen's head was probably in far greater disarray than his brother's. Ideas and emotions had been thrown in there like junk into some unvisited attic and—

What was the matter with him? He looked as if he had seen a ghost! Maybe he had. Maybe George was at last going to have the opportunity of saying a few words. He'd better think of something good. Some pithy, compassionate and subtle phrases about how it felt to be dead. Much like living, actually. Except you were dead. That wasn't quite it. He needed something magisterial.

Stephen wasn't looking at him. He was looking into the living room.

Frigga was hanging from a small hook in the middle of the ceiling. George had never noticed the hook before. Perhaps it had been put there to hold up a now long-gone chandelier. A dining-room chair had been kicked away to the side. She looked, George thought, like an oversized rag doll, but, then, Frigga had always looked like an oversized rag doll. Her head was at a crazy angle, though that, too, was nothing unusual where Frigga was concerned. George had the vague idea that people who hanged themselves allowed their tongue to loll, grotesquely, from their open mouths. Frigga had done nothing of the kind. She was just hanging there quietly, like a pheasant in the window of a butcher's shop, waiting for someone to cut her down.

'Oh, my God!' said Stephen. 'Oh, my God!'

George's brother had already been in at the death of two other members of his family and none of them – as far as George could tell – had made that much impression on him. Perhaps he had seen too many corpses in his professional life. Perhaps the impression he gave of someone energetically acting out shock, horror, surprise, grief, incomprehension, etc., did not mean that he was unmoved by the sight of his mother, brother and sister, respectively battered to death, poisoned and, now, strung up from a hook in the living room. Inside it might well be that Stephen was hurting. He actually looked as if he had been told about a mildly shocking by-election result.

'Oh, my God!' he said again, really trying very hard indeed to make this 'My God!' sound less wooden than the two that had preceded it. 'Oh, my *God*!!'

He gave this one two exclamation marks but even that didn't convince George that his brother was going through anything more serious than the kind of staged disgust put on by backbenchers in the House of Commons to greet proposals of which they disapproved.

'This,' said Nat, in the carefully modulated tones he used if anything vaguely medical turned up, 'is strangulation.'

Clearly his morning at the morgue had given him an appetite for this kind of thing. Either that or he was keen to make up for his earlier pronouncements on the subject of George's death. This is one, his expression seemed to say, that not even I can get wrong. Stephen finally found one of his keys. They trooped, nervously, into the flat.

Veronica stared at her husband, aghast, as he strolled up and down in front of the body, like a man keen to show off his expertise in the area of hanging.

'There is cyanosis,' he said incisively, 'and evidence of petechiae on the face. It looks superficially as if she got up on the chair, then kicked it away.'

'She was fine when we were here,' said Esmeralda. 'She was absolutely fine. Well, as fine as Frigga ever was. I cannot believe she just watched us walk out to the pub and then . . .'

'You can sometimes tell,' said Nat, who was standing on tiptoe and squinting up at Frigga's neck, 'by the ligature.'

Before he could give them the benefit of any more of his

technical knowledge in this area – a short lecture on the Austro-Hungarian pole method, perhaps, or fragments from his unpublished paper 'Domestic Suicide by Strangulation Among a Small Sample of Unmarried Librarians in the Putney Area' – Stephen, who had been staring at something on his sister's chest, grabbed him by the arm and pointed towards a sheet of A4 paper, pinned to Frigga's cardigan.

'It's her handwriting,' he said. 'Look!'

And it was. George knew Frigga's handwriting all too well. She was a woman who, in the English way, wrote thank-you notes and, sometimes, thank-you notes if you were unwise enough to send *her* a thank-you note. The gigantic *A*s, the huge, swooping trails that slid away from her lower *g*s and upper *W*s as well as the punctuation that looked as if it had been ground into the paper, like a blade point into an enemy's heart: they were Frigga's all right.

Stephen read the note aloud: 'I want to die. This is the way I want to do it. I am sorry. I know finding my body will not be easy. I cannot help that. I am sorry for what I have done. I have done wicked, wicked things. I am sorry. I have killed. I have murdered. I have taken the lives of the innocent. In England and on the Continent. I pushed those people under the train at the Gare du Nord. I have deprived my good, kind brother – the wisest, gentlest man I ever knew – of the precious gift of life. I have sent him down to the Dark Kingdom where the Trolls dance on the heads of the slain. Farewell!'

Nat, who had joined George's brother in front of Frigga's body, said, 'She hasn't signed it, but that's common with suicide notes.'

It sounded, George thought, just like Frigga. It looked like her handwriting. It had all the marks of being written by someone whose head had been rotted by reading too much

Tolkien. That 'Farewell!' at the end was the pure essence of his sister – flouncing off the stage of life in a manner that was dangerously close to the comic.

He liked the bit about him being kind and wise and gentle – even if the stuff about Trolls dancing on his head was a bit from left field – but he was, he had to admit, puzzled by the confession relating to her having 'taken away innocent lives in Britain and on the Continent'. Had his sister been a serial killer who had crossed the Channel in order to add spice to her repulsive habit? Pushing people under trains at the Gare du Nord! Had she picked them off one by one or driven some SNCF vehicle into a group of schoolchildren? What was going on here? She had, clearly, been no ordinary librarian.

And nothing about her mother. It was, thought George, on the skimpy side as a suicide note. He could have done with more detail.

He had lost many qualities since dying – taste, smell, touch, the ability to be heard by his fellow humans – but it had also done nothing for the compassionate side of his nature. Not that George had been renowned for that when alive. He had conspicuously failed to sob when Princess Diana had been driven into that wall in Paris. Esmeralda, who was more plentifully endowed with fellow feeling, was always bursting in on him with news of the latest atrocity or natural disaster. 'Have you read about what's happening in Botswana/the South China Sea/Zimbabwe/Iraq/Syria?' she would say breathlessly, as she rounded the living room door.

'They're all dead, I suppose,' George would reply, trying to look as if he was genuinely concerned about the plight of people of whose lives he had, until that moment, been entirely ignorant.

But you would have thought he'd worry a bit more about

his sister being strung up on an improvised gallows in his mum's sitting room. That George was unable to give a stuff seemed to cast doubt on the whole of their relationship. The fact that – as far as he could tell – she had probably murdered him did not make any difference. He ought to feel something about the fact that Frigga was about to join him in the afterlife, apart from the hope that her ghost should be sent to a different area of the spirit world.

'This,' said Nat, with great authority, 'is a crime scene. We mustn't touch anything.'

Veronica was looking at him wordlessly. Her face said it all. *Why am I married to this idiot?* Stephen, of course, was first to his phone. He addressed it in his usual clipped news-reader's voice.

'Inspector Hobday,' he was saying.

'What kind of hob would you like today?' said his phone, in a pronounced American accent. 'We have a huge range of gas hobs available at our mall in Wishaw, Arizona, many of them reduced by as much as three hundred per cent and all fully guaranteed! Parking is assured in our high-quality location only eighty-nine miles from the junction with the five-oh-nine! Bring the kids.'

'Listen,' said Stephen, in threatening tones, 'I want Inspector Hobday. A Putney-based policeman. Now.'

'Why wait?' said his phone. 'This offer ends on July fourteenth 2014.'

Stephen thrust his face right up to the screen of his phone. 'Listen,' he said, 'I will do you. I will fucking do you. I will disable you. I will do an app-ectomy on you. I will torch your memory. I will go out and get an ordinary phone. Would you like that, motherfucker?'

'I am not an ordinary phone,' said his phone. 'I am an Excelsior 657B. Change your life and widen your horizons by staying in touch with friends across the globe. I have new apps for you, Stephen. How would you like to buy a swimming-pool? You stated a preference for watersports.'

Stephen was trying desperately to shut his phone up – but it was clearly on a roll. He had, thought George, the look of a man who feared his most intimate secrets were about to be revealed by this obviously expensive and indiscreet piece of machinery. Meanwhile, as he groped with the buttons Esmeralda, who had a small, gadgetless mobile, had already got through to the police station and was talking to the inspector.

'Alan,' she was saying, 'I'm at my mother-in-law's flat. There has been what looks like a suicide. I am afraid it's George's sister. It looks as if she may have hanged herself.'

Alan! Oho! And, while we were at it – an interesting use of the word 'may', thought George. He would have thought it was fairly obvious that that was exactly what his sister had done. Clearly Stephen found it odd as well. He was giving Esmeralda a very puzzled look. When she had disconnected her phone, he said, 'You have doubts about whether she did?'

Esmeralda screwed up her face. 'I don't know,' she said. 'There's something odd about it.'

Stephen did not answer this. He was punching the buttons on his phone again.

'You have called the police,' said his phone. 'Have you been the victim of crime? I am sorry to hear that. Have you visited our website, victims of crime dot co dot org?'

'You will be the victim of a crime,' Stephen hissed, as he thrust his phone back into his pocket. 'You will be the victim of common assault on a fucking phone.'

Esmeralda was staring at Frigga's body. 'Maybe,' she said slowly, 'it's the chair. Or maybe it's the note. It is her writing. But...' Her voice trailed away uneasily. 'Is the chair in the wrong place?' she said, but did not amplify this mysterious remark. She did not sound very convinced by her own question.

Stephen, Veronica and Nat did not seem convinced by it either. George's brother was knuckling his eyes – a gesture familiar to George from childhood. He looked, suddenly, like the younger brother he had never quite been able to be. Had George given him the kind of support he needed? Jessica's will had been an attempt to get him to do just that. Perhaps he had not. Perhaps, as well as failing to get any of his poetry published, he had been a bad older brother.

That might help to explain Lulu. Stephen had had to marry the kind of woman George disliked intensely. Of course he had. She was doing the very things that George had been supposed to do for him. Guidance wasn't the word exactly: 'orders' would have been more appropriate – and George had never really wanted to give anyone orders, least of all his brother. He had, now he thought about it, found the burden of being the eldest son at times intolerable. All that intense love and equally intense doubt from his father, all that wonder and cluelessness in equal measure from his mother.

Why was he only finding out about this stuff now? It was a bit fucking late, wasn't it?

'Are you saying,' Stephen was saying slowly, to Esmeralda, 'that this may be murder? Not suicide? If so, I can't see any sign of anyone else having been here apart from *her*. The front door is locked. So is the back.'

As if to prove his point, a small, hooded figure appeared from the garden and began rattling at the back-door handle. Mabel Dawkins, in spite of being in her sixties, made a habit of wearing her son's tops even though, as she often said, 'I look like one of them neighbourhoddies that do the assault with batteries.' She seemed desperate to get on to the

R . I . P .

premises and showed no sign that she had seen Frigga's body.

'Someone,' said Esmeralda, 'had better tell her.'

'I will,' said Stephen. 'I'll let her know what's happened. She has a right to know. She was fond of Frigga. God knows why but she was. I was fond of her, come to that. She drove me mad, of course, but I loved my sister.'

His face twitched. For a moment George thought he was actually going to cry. Then he recovered himself. He walked over to the patio door and shouted through it to Mabel, who continued to rattle the handle. His manner, as always when talking to Mabel, resembled that of a high-born English tourist speaking to a native bearer some time in the late 1890s.

'I cannot let you in, Mabel,' he said. 'This is a crime scene.'

'Ice cream?' said Mabel, and went back to rattling the door handle.

'Look behind me, Mabel,' he continued, still sounding like an early user of the Bell telephone. 'There is a body hanging from the ceiling. Frigga has hanged herself.'

'Banged 'erself where?' said Mabel, who still did not seem to have seen Frigga's body although it was not only in her line of vision but had been pointed out to her with the patient clarity of a tour guide indicating the whereabouts of an important item of sculpture.

Perhaps, thought George, she was becoming desensitized to corpses. Or perhaps it was her hood. As well as lending her a vaguely criminal aspect, it obstructed her view as effectively as the kind of headgear worn by monks who are up to no good. Stephen went on shouting at her through the glass door, as if they were standing on the edge of a station platform as an express thundered through.

'Frigga is right there. You see? She has hanged herself. We think she has probably hanged herself. We do not know definitively. Someone else may have hanged her. This is a crime scene.'

Mabel kept right on pumping the door handle.

'I think,' said Esmeralda, wearily, 'you had probably better let her in.'

Mabel still did not seem to see the body even after Stephen had opened the back door, shown her in and thrust Jessica's carer in the direction of the dangling cadaver. George had read somewhere that when the Aztecs had first sighted ships out in the ocean they simply had not seen them. They had no way of understanding how such a thing could be. It was like that with Frigga and Mabel. When she finally allowed her eyes to make contact with the white socks, the pale, mottled calves, the blue and knobbly knees, the loose-fitting floral dress, the junk-shop beads and then, finally, the neck, the tightly stretched cord (was it, George wondered, from his mother's dressing gown?) and the head with its listless white hair at a pitiful angle to the rest of the ensemble, she gazed at it with a kind of awe.

'Oh, my Gawd!' she whispered. 'Oh, my bleed'n' Gawd! They hunged you up like a chicken, din't they, the barstids?'

Mabel and Frigga had had an intense relationship. For years they had been very close. As far as Jessica was concerned, the class structure of England had not really altered since the First World War. She had made a habit of saying to Mabel, in the sweetest imaginable tones, 'Of course, dear, I am placed high above you. But although I have a music degree I do not think of you as inferior. You are my friend. Not my servant.' She came out with lines like this as Mabel was hauling her off to the lavatory or prising her off the floor after one of her frequent falls. If George was in the room when this kind of thing happened – which he often was – Mabel would wink broadly at him. He had once found her watching the old lady through a crack in the door, and when he asked her what was happening, she replied, 'Watchin' 'er fart. She does it at top volume, Georgy. Lissen! Like a fuckin' machine gun.'

Frigga, perhaps to annoy her mother, had deliberately cultivated a chummy relationship with Mrs Dawkins. She called her 'Mabe', which was what her husband called her. Mabel called her 'Frigg', which no one else in the world had ever called the sixty-two-year-old librarian. At one point they became so close Frigga asked Mabel along to a meeting of her coven. No one had ever found out what happened, but they did not speak for weeks afterwards. When George asked her about it, Mabel said, 'They done some disgustin' things there. She should be ashamed of 'erself. Witches is filth in my view. If I'd known there was gonna be witches there I never woulda fuckin' gone.' George did ask her what she thought a coven was. She said she thought it was something to do with cooking.

She was staring up at his sister now as if she was fairly sure witchcraft might have had something to do with her death. 'Oh, Frigg,' she whispered. 'I 'ope this is not Satan's doing. You was never one-a the bad ones, was you? You shoulda had a hullo roundjer really. Oh, Frigg. What 'as all this led to, my darlin'? I do not think so, Frigg. Frigg. Frigg. Frigg.'

With which she staggered back into the coffee-table, her right arm raised above her face, as if to ward off another blow from the Almighty. Then she turned and spat violently into her left palm. 'I'm sorry,' she said, 'but there's evil spirits in 'ere an' I don't mean you, Stephen! All we need is the fuckin' 'angman. Pardon my French, boys and girls.'

She stared long and hard at the body. There was suddenly something, George decided, unbelievably sinister about her manner. Had she spotted some Satanic trademark on the body? If she had, she was keeping very quiet about it. What, then? She knew Frigga probably better than any of them. Did she know things about her that might go some way to explaining her previously well-concealed habit of pushing people under trains at the Gare du Nord? Mabel wheeled round and, still with the same air of doom and prophecy about her, said to Stephen, 'You'll be next, Stephen. First yore mum and then yore bruvver. And now you. It's a series killer, Stephen, mark my words. It's a long-running series, thass wot it is. Oh, my Gawd, we better 'ave this place exercised as soon as possible. Anyone know an exercist? This is Devil worship, I would say, ladies and gentlemen.' With which she began to howl furiously.

It was, thought George, curious that Frigga's mother's carer seemed to have a more emotionally direct response to his sister's death than anyone in her immediate family – including the brother Frigga seemed to have boasted about having murdered.

Was this something to do with the famous English reserve? The talents of the Anglo-Saxon middle class for treating their loved ones as if they had just met them at a breakfast party? Or perhaps it was simply that all of her family had spent more time with Frigga than had Mabel Dawkins. Prolonged exposure to her was enough to provoke anyone into finding ways of speeding her departure from the world.

'You was so beautifully preserved,' sobbed Mabel. 'You turned out lovely – time after time. And now they gone and turned you off like a common criminal. Was it one a them witches, darlin'? I wou'n't be surprised if they did yore mum in an' all. An' Georgy Porgy.'

No one had called George this since he was twelve – and on that occasion he had bitten the offender's ear. If he had had the gnashers he would have done the same now. There was something, he decided, definitely not right about Mabel.

If you thought about it, she'd had a pretty good motive for polishing off the whole Pearmain family. No man is a hero to his valet and no family is immune to the contempt of the professional carer. What had his mother left her in this mysterious codicil?

'The police,' Stephen was saying, as he placed one tentative paw on Mabel's shoulder, 'are on their way.'

Esmeralda was giving Jessica's carer the sharp sideways look she so often visited on a world that, as George well knew, she had never been able to trust. When he had been alive he had often been frustrated by her intensely suspicious nature, her shyness and her inability to frame the simplest social demand. She had once had an embarrassing accident in John Lewis simply because she was too shy to ask anyone the way to the Ladies'.

Now he thought he had not only started to understand her way of looking at the world but was starting to believe she was probably in the right. To be dead, he thought, is to be pessimistic.

'Why were you coming round?' Esmeralda was saying to Mabel.

Mabel swivelled her head in Esmeralda's direction. There had always been a cautious respect between the two women. Mabel now looked, George thought, more cautious than respectful as she replied quietly, 'That is a very good question, Esmeralda. A very good question.' There was silence in the room. Mabel continued: 'I come round about an hour ago,' she said. 'She was 'ere on 'er own. And I was worried about 'er.'

'Why was that?' said Esmeralda.

Veronica, who had never liked Mabel, leaned forward slightly, her eyes never leaving the carer's face.

'She said I 'ad to go. There was someone comin' to meet

'er. 'Ere. She wou'n't say 'oo it was but she bustled me out real quick. I wondered whether it mighta bin one of 'er witches. Dunno. But 'ooever it was I woulda said she was scared of this person. Terrified of them. That was why I come back. And when I come back what do I find? I find 'er strung up like this.' Mabel shook her head slowly. 'This wasn't suicide,' she said. 'This was murder!'

Chapter Thirteen

George was not really obliged to wait in a room that contained the hanged body of his sister. He had always tried to cut short his encounters with her when the two of them had been alive and there seemed no reason whatsoever for prolonging the present meeting. She was not in any way improved by being suspended from a hook in the ceiling.

He was dead. He could, theoretically, go anywhere he liked. He could take a bus to Heathrow and slip on to a flight to Málaga. He had always liked Málaga. He wouldn't even have to go through security. Perhaps it was Esmeralda who kept him there. The way she had kept him in that shabby one-bedroom flat in Southfields, the tiny house off Lacy Road where Maurice and Barry had been born and, finally, the comparative dignity of 22 Hornbeam Crescent. The perfect place for an Englishman to die.

He still did not quite understand the power she seemed to have over him. It must be more than the blowjobs. We were getting into a tricky area here for a dead person. Something spiritual? George had never been a big fan of the spiritual, unless it was being sung by large African-American men. If they did have a spiritual rapport, surely this would have meant that George would sometimes have been swept away by love and found himself possessed by an overmastering urge to, say, buy her flowers! He had, he recalled now, once been possessed by an overmastering urge to buy her flowers. It had been, he thought, some time in August 1998, but there did not seem to be any florists within easy reach.

Nobody in their right mind would have called Esmeralda spiritual. She was, thought George, borderline coarse. Like him. Why did the sight of this small, dumpy woman, with her shock of black hair, her rather too prominent nose and her fine brown eyes conjure up feelings that he could not put into words without seeming sloppily sentimental or comprehensively pretentious?

He didn't know. He couldn't express the emotions she inspired in him. Perhaps there were simply too many of them.

The doorbell rang. Stephen froze. Esmeralda jumped. Mabel Dawkins slumped. Veronica gave a small squeal. Nat folded his arms, unfolded them again and then, with the air of a man who was going to get the gesture right this time, folded them for a second time.

After that, somehow, Inspector Hobday and Pawlikowski were in the room.

'Who found her?' said Hobday to Esmeralda.

Stephen seemed, as usual, keen to be the one in charge. 'I was first into the room,' he said. 'There is a note pinned to her dress. A suicide note.'

Hobday began to read it aloud. He did not attempt to put much colour into it. As an audition piece it would have got him waved on after the first sentence, but what his voice lacked in expressiveness, it more than made up for in clarity and volume. As he went on he allowed some atmosphere to creep in and by the time he got to the bit about the Trolls dancing on the heads of the slain he was rolling his eyes and *r*s to chilling effect.

When he had finished he turned to Esmeralda, even though

Stephen was desperately trying to get into his eyeline. 'The Gare du Nord, eh?' he said.

Pawlikowski was slumped in an armchair looking longingly up at Frigga's neck. He was clearly aching to do inappropriate things to it but, for the moment, contented himself by rifling through his bag of tricks with an air of contained excitement.

'In my experience,' said Hobday, 'suicide notes are usually brief to the point of rudeness. The people who write long involved ones, in my experience, do not go on to do the deed.'

All the time he was saying this, his eyes were on Esmeralda. Stephen was now practically jumping up and down, like the class swot trying to get the teacher's attention.

'What do you think, Esmeralda?' he said.

Was he about to co-opt George's widow into the Metropolitan Police? He had obviously decided she had investigative skills that might be useful to him.

'I agree with you,' she said. 'Although Virginia Woolf's went on a bit.'

George was now definitely sure the inspector fancied her. Was there a Mrs Hobday? Nothing the man had said suggested there was, and Hobday fitted the pattern of the men she had, over the years, found attractive. It wasn't easy to work out what it was she liked. Some were thin, some were fat. Some were tall and some were short. One, George recalled, with a faint thrill, had been black. What they had all had in common was a certain talent for conversation, a certain assurance in manner, combined with a light behind the eyes that suggested a vivid interior life.

Hobday also, of course, had a sense of humour. He might even, thought George, write poetry. George couldn't help liking the man, despite his dislike of his rather too familiar manner with the woman to whom, due to circumstances not under his control, George was no longer married. Weren't there professional guidelines about this sort of thing? They were both there to avenge his death and find his murderer, not to ogle each other, but maybe the one followed from the other. Like teaching, detection had a strong erotic charge.

It was, he decided, definitely his love for Esmeralda that kept him on the earth. He was still jealous of anyone paying her attention. One of the reasons he had never told her about Julie Biskiborne was that he was terrified she would decide to leave him. Biskiborne was quite capable of giving her a blow-by-blow account of their affair. It was why he had let her down so very, very gently.

I followed him into his hotel room at a banking conference in Wolverhampton and found he responded passionately to my advances. We made love, subsequently, during the NatWest awayday in a countryside retreat in the Thames Valley and on several occasions in the back of my reconditioned Austin 1100. I would be happy to share him with you, Esmeralda! He has always talked very highly of you in spite of the fact you rather went off sex after Barry was born! I want to be friends! I want a place in the life that you and George share!

George shuddered at the memory of Biskiborne's frequently expressed enthusiasm for open marriage. Not being married herself, of course, she found the idea appealing.

Maybe that was why he was doomed to walk the earth – well, Putney, anyway. There was also probably an element of punishment for the hideous sin of shagging Biskiborne. Of allowing her to say things like 'I love your enormous penis!' (One of the many reasons he had ended the affair was that she was always saying things like that.) Of writing her a letter that spoke of deep, deep feelings. One of the reasons he loved Esmeralda was that she knew damn well he had absolutely no deep feelings. Or a large penis.

'Apparently,' Nat was saying, 'she was expecting someone.

We do not know who. Something funny was going on. She was very strange when we were with her earlier.'

'She was lookin' 'unted when I seen 'er,' said Mabel. 'She was strung out. Oh, my Gawd, what 'ave I said? She was strung out and now she's bin strung up. A very unfortunate turning of phrase. I was tellin' them I am of the opinion witchcraft was involved.'

Hobday did not seem to be listening to any of this. He was looking at Frigga's body as if in a trance.

Nat coughed politely. 'Are you…er…going to cut her down?' he said tentatively.

Hobday swivelled round and glared at him. 'Everything about a crime scene,' he said, 'tells me something. This moment is the important one. When I first see the body. Now. Right now. In an instant, I see everything. Do you understand? When I saw the body of Luigi Marrone in the Asda car park I knew, at once, that Mr Marrone had not been murdered there. For reasons I will not go into here I was instantly aware he had been beheaded in North London. And something of the sort is going on here. Right now. I am listening to Miss Pearmain. I am aware of her. She is trying to tell me something.'

'What,' said Stephen, rather sharply, 'is she trying to tell you? Apart, of course, from the fact she is dead.'

Hobday allowed himself a very slight smile. 'The note,' he said, 'is pinned to her chest. With an ordinary drawing pin. Millions like it are produced. To the untrained eye it is just another pin, but we will subject it to a battery of tests. We will do the same with the paper. Where did the paper come from? You will notice that it has been torn at the top end and there are still traces of what was written above it. Did Miss Pearmain write us a longer letter, then think better of it? That might explain the way she seems to go into the message without trying to claim a particular person's attention.'

'Did she have it with her when we were all here? When did she write it?' said Esmeralda. 'It's very odd, as you say, Inspector, that it is not addressed to anyone in particular. She must have known we would be the ones who found her.'

'It is, Esmeralda. It is,' said Hobday. 'And then there is the position of the chair, and the knot in the pyjama cord or whatever it is. All this tells us something.'

'It looks like her handwriting,' said Esmeralda, 'but is it her handwriting?'

'It is her handwriting,' said Stephen. 'I'm sure of it.'

To George's surprise, the inspector seemed in agreement with this. He nodded vigorously as, quietly and tactfully at first and then, after only a little while, becoming more brazen, Pawlikowski started to take photographs. George had expected a larger and more impressive camera. Instead he was using one that might double up for taking his holiday snaps. Mind you, judging from the ecstasy on his face, this was much more Pawlikowski's idea of fun than two weeks in, say, the Tatra mountains.

'What I'm trying to say,' said Esmeralda, 'and it seems a peculiar thing to say, but it...it's the way it's written. It's the style.'

'You mean,' said Hobday, quickly, 'it doesn't sound like her?'

'It sounds like her and yet not like her,' said Esmeralda. 'It's curious. Almost like a parody.'

Hobday nodded – like one professional acknowledging another professional's opinion.

Stephen, who was clearly getting irritated by all this, cut in: 'Look,' he said, 'I knew my sister. Knew her better than anything. That is her writing. That is *her*.'

'It is, I'm sure, her *hand*writing,' said Esmeralda, patiently, 'but the style isn't quite the way she talks. Talked. Sorry.

Well, some of it is. Most of it. Then you get this bit about the trolls dancing on the heads of the slain. That sounds like someone doing an impression of the sort of thing Frigga might say. Actually she wouldn't. I don't want to be rude about the dead – there was a sense in which I was fond of Frigga – but, and again I do not wish to be offensive because the poor woman is dead, I don't think she had the imagination to write that. The trolls dancing on the heads of the slain. Sorry.'

'Perhaps,' said Veronica, clearly seeing parallels between this debate about the tone of Frigga's suicide note and her book group, 'she was trying for a bit of fine writing. I mean, if you're going to write a suicide note, you know, it might as well be a good one.'

Esmeralda, who respected Veronica's intelligence a good deal, nodded. It seemed to set her thinking again. 'And then,' she said, 'there is this business of the Gare du Nord.'

'She quite often went to Paris,' said Stephen.

Mabel Dawkins nodded enthusiastically. 'That,' she said, 'is the God's honest troof. But I do not think she went there to push people under trains. She coulda done that at Victoria. Or Clapham Juncture.'

Hobday, George noticed, was watching everyone's face. He was talking to Esmeralda but he was watching the others. He was using this conversation to examine their expressions. George, who had unlimited opportunity for staring at people, followed the inspector's sly, furtive glances and examined faces and body language at his leisure. When you are dead, everyone's a waxwork. He noted Stephen's expression. When he thought no one was watching him, his brother's face did show emotion. He looked not only genuinely shocked but also, suddenly, desperately sad. He had, of course, been fond of Frigga. There was something else in there as well, thought

George. At first he couldn't identify what it was. Normally Stephen's face was about as expressive as a cricket bat but now something was definitely going on. It took a while before George realized his brother was afraid. Of what, though?

'I'm not sure,' Hobday was saying, 'that I like the position of the chair. And the knot on the noose worries me.'

He didn't say why it worried him. It looked, to George, like an ordinary knot. Although, come to think of it, it had a professional air about it. Frigga had never been the Girl Guide type.

Mabel Dawkins was peering at it and shuddering visibly. 'A relative of mine was 'ung!' she said. 'In 1924. For murderin' 'is communal-law wife. I do not care for nooses. Or that bag they put over your 'ead. The thought of it makes my flesh creep. You wind it round and you wind it round. Thirteen times and Bob's your unc.'

'Did your sister sail?' said Hobday, suddenly, to Stephen.

Stephen jumped. 'Not as far as I know,' he said, understandably baffled by this line of enquiry. 'Although it is perfectly possible. Frigga did all sorts of peculiar things. She might have met a man who sailed.'

'She was writing a novel,' said Esmeralda, 'called *All Those Who Do Not Go Down to the Sea in Ships*. She'd been writing it for years. Maybe she sailed for research. Are you talking about the knot, Inspector?'

Hobday shot her a keen, appreciative glance. 'I am, Mrs Pearmain,' he said. 'I am.'

George was hoping he might say something more about the noose and the knot but he suddenly turned his attention to Mabel Dawkins, swinging his large, well-structured head in her direction as if she was some guest on a current-affairs programme who urgently needed to be brought into the discussion. 'So,' he said, 'at what time did you last see Miss Pearmain?'

Mabel coughed. 'I last seen 'er,' she said, with the air of one who was not going to share information with the police lightly or casually, 'when I just come in now an' seen 'er swingin' like that as if she was a configgered criminal. But I seen 'er before that – which, as I say, was the last time I saw 'er. I come in arahnd 'alf one an' when I saw 'er then she was walkin' an' talkin' like a normal person an' showin' no signs of strangulation that I could see, Inspector. There was not a whiff a' Rugger Mortice on that occasion, I beg to state formally. Although, as I say, she was very worried about the windersill. She was lookin' for it everywhere.'

Hobday turned to Esmeralda. 'She's expecting a visitor,' he said. 'Someone of whom she seems, from what Mrs Dawkins has told us, to be afraid. And, while waiting for this person to arrive, or perhaps, even after they arrive, she writes this suicide note, gets up on a chair and ties a rather skilful knot, pins the note to her chest and kicks away the support.'

Stephen was looking very thoughtful indeed. George gazed out at the garden. Dust stood, turning restlessly, in the columns of light that came in from the day outside. He wasn't even dust. He was hanging in the air, even more fragile than a golden mote, twisting with the specks and grains in the sun that would never find the real George again.

'She was worryin',' went on Mabel, 'abaht Mrs Pearmain's last will an' testimony. She'd looked it over an' she wasn't 'appy about Georgy Porgy gettin' the lot. I mean, Gawd bless 'im, 'e's dead so, you know, good luck to 'im, but 'e was always out for 'imself, wasn't 'e? There was other people more worthy of a few bob in my 'umble. People wot 'ad taken 'er on and off of the commode in every kind of weather. People 'oo 'ad made 'er 'er lunch every day and taken 'er to Waitrose on demand. People 'oo 'ad washed 'er pants an' taken 'er up Queen Mary's for the Falls Class, if you take my meanin'. While certain other people 'ung around and brought a bottle of champagne every three months. Waitin' fer the windersill and a nice fat cheque.' She thrust her face into the detective's. 'I name no names, but I wonder 'oo is named in the coddysill or the windersill or whatever it's called. I think Mabel Dawkins 'as a right to be there.'

During this speech everyone looked at the floor.

George studied Frigga's face. Whatever it was that had gone from it was not in the room. It had never been a very noticeable quality, the thing that made her Frigga rather than her equally lacklustre friend Diana Pullman or her hardly there at all confidante from the Putney library. You would never have called it a spark, because it wasn't a spark, but whatever it was, it was not there.

George found he was looking to the area just below the ceiling where, according to some contemporary theories, the souls of the recently departed hover around to view their bodies before being called away by white lights and ethereal music. No Frigga.

Perhaps, he thought, Frigga, like Partridge, will have been transformed by death. She will have acquired new qualities. She will, like me, return to Putney, but not in the same grim, earthbound way that I seem to have done. Perhaps, soon, I will catch a glimpse of her on a corner of the high street and she will be smiling and wearing the bright colours she never dared to wear when alive or holding out her arms to me the way, surely, she must have done at some point in our miserable sixty-two years together.

But there was still no Frigga. Only her long, limp body and her neck, so sadly twisted, and the fallen shoes and the lank white hair.

Hobday was talking again – with the calm authority that Esmeralda seemed to find so worthy of notice. 'If she writes

it here,' he was saying, 'this...note that is so interestingly
written and not quite typical of Miss Pearmain, where is the
pen she used? A ballpoint of some kind, I would have said.
Where is it?'

Nobody seemed to have an answer to this question.
Stephen, who now appeared to have given up his previous
attempts at superiority, looked like a man who was prepared
to get his bum in the air and go on the grope round the
edges of the carpet but, once again, Hobday's was a purely
rhetorical question.

'And who,' Hobday continued, 'was her mysterious
visitor? Who calls on the flat of a dead woman? And why?'

As if in answer to this question, there came a long, loud
buzz from the doorbell. Rasping in tone, it seemed to violate
the stillness of Jessica's flat and the peace of green gardens
beyond her still blooming patio.

'Who in God's name can that be?' said Stephen.

He's still frightened, thought George. But what is it that's
frightening him? His lip, too, was definitely not as firm as
usual. Underneath his moustache it showed early signs of
collapse. Is he going to cry? thought George, remembering
again how many times Stephen and Frigga had formed
common cause against him. *George was selfish. George
didn't understand.* Christ. You would have thought death
would make family life a little easier. It had not.

Stephen did not, as he usually would have done, offer to
go and see who was out in the hall. He parked himself on
one of his mother's armchairs and, without even the strength
to look at his phone, set about chewing more of his moustache. In the end it was Esmeralda, still wrapped in thought
as effectively as a chess player contemplating the endgame,
who went out to discover whom the visitor might be.

Chapter Fourteen

George was not particularly pleased to find it was Beryl Vickers and the Mullins woman. He had never liked Mullins. Ever since she had asked him – at Jessica's eighty-fifth-birthday party – why he was always 'so pink at parties' and he had asked her, by way of reply, why she always looked so wrinkled, relations between them had been cool.

One of the things that might have accounted for her rather syrupy smile, as she peered into the room, was that George was not likely to be in it. He found a certain grim satisfaction in watching her placatory grimace wiped off her features by the sight of Frigga.

They really ought to cut her down soon, he thought. Was Hobday proposing to leave her up there? Just days after his mother's death, Stephen had begun to talk about putting her flat on the market. A body hanging from a hook in the living room was not going to do anything for prospective buyers. What happened to the smell of freshly baked bread or coffee bubbling on the stove?

'Oh, no!' said Mullins, clasping one hand to her mouth. 'Oh, *no!*'

'Oh, no!' repeated Beryl Vickers, managing to duplicate her friend's gesture with utter precision. 'Oh, *no!*'

They were both, as always, wearing sensible tweed skirts,

sensible cream blouses and square-toed shoes that screamed aloud to all who had eyes to see or ears to hear, 'We are lesbians!'

Vickers was younger than Mullins by at least twenty years. She looked perfectly capable of stringing up a difficult woman from a hook. She had worked, George seemed to remember, in catering. Her hands were large and muscular, and in a straight fight with her, George would not have fancied his chances.

Mabel Dawkins, George noticed, was watching them furtively. She was the first to speak. To both women, she said, 'I meant ter call yer but I got carried away with the sighta the copse. I never seen someone actually stretched like that. I thought we was meetin' at six. I never thought you'd've electrocuted to come so early.'

For a moment it looked as if Stephen was about to speak, but he did not seem, for once, able to do so. He just stared at them, as if this was the first time he had seen either woman. It was Esmeralda who said, 'Were you meeting Beryl and Audrey here, Mabel?' She managed, George thought, the three turn-of-the-twentieth-century forenames with creditable skill.

'We 'ad an arrangement,' said Mabel, looking furtive in the extreme, 'to meet up and 'ave a look at some items which Mrs Pearmain wanted these ladies to possibly 'ave. Such as the quilt. And the pokerwork. An' the thing wiv knobs on in the kitchen. Beryl was inchrested in the Vienna Regulator. Wasn't you, Beryl?'

Beryl Vickers smiled. She was, she said, interested in the Vienna Regulator. It was a wonderful thing, she said. She had often spoken of it with Jessica. Jessica had often said she wanted Beryl to have it when she was gone. It would remind Beryl of her. Every time she heard it chime, Beryl said, she would think of Jessica.

What Beryl did not appear to know was that the Vienna Regulator – a stubby walnut clock with an unusually Gothic face – had not told the time since before the Second World War. If it had ever chimed, it had not done so since the *Anschluss*.

'Jessica had promised me some of the watercolours,' gushed Mullins, stroking her beard. 'I don't think they are of anything but sentimental value.'

Esmeralda gave Mullins a sharp look. 'I could get quite sentimental about eight thousand quid,' she said, 'which is what the Alfred Logan Bradley is worth.'

'I think,' said Stephen, heavily, 'that there seems to be a codicil somewhere that decides what is coming to everyone. My mother chose to leave everything to George in the first instance, relying on him to apportion her estate fairly between close family and, er, friends such as yourselves. She did specifically say, Audrey, that there was provision for you in that codicil. The problem is that, at the moment, we cannot seem to find it. And, of course, er...'

He seemed at this point to remember that his sister's corpse was hanging from the ceiling. He gave an awkward wave in her direction, as if introducing Frigga to the two women for the very first time. They did give Frigga more than a cursory glance but there was, George thought, a definite feeling in the room that his sister had become a more than usually unusual item of home décor. She was being ignored so resolutely by everyone, including the two policemen, that it was as if she had ceased to exist twice.

There was clearly one thing on Mullins's mind. She had always made a point of being polite to Stephen. Her manner to him now, George thought, was positively fawning. 'To know Jessica,' she was saying to him, ignoring Esmeralda, whom she had never liked, 'was reward enough.'

It was extraordinary, thought George, how little interest
Frigga's corpse seemed to be provoking. She had never
made much impact when alive but, in George's view, being
strung up in her mum's living room ought to have made
her a bit more of a talking point. It was only Stephen's eyes
that kept wandering back to the piteous figure. Stephen
had his sensitive side. When their parents had started one
of their endless arguments it was Stephen who knuckled
his eyes in fear and misery and begged them to stop. It
was Stephen who had loved and cared for, in turn, the
guinea pig, the rabbit, the cat and, later, the tortoise; it was
Stephen, who, as a child, had loved their mother in such a
passionate and uncomplicated way that, in George's judgement, it had started to irritate her. Jessica had been a tough
woman.

Mullins and Vickers were exchanging significant glances.
Their relationship to each other and to Jessica had always
been a mystery to George. Both seemed to him to be dark,
slightly twisted characters. He had always been able to
imagine Mullins as a sadist, and Vickers seemed perfectly
suited to being her assistant in crime. They had both been
there on the night he died, hadn't they? He had probably
done any number of things, in their eyes, that would justify
his being handed the odd glass of poisoned parsnip wine.
He was, in the meaningless vogue word of the seventies that
Vickers, for some reason, had espoused, a sexist. He had
dared to stand up to his mother on more than one occasion
– especially when it came to Esmeralda.

Would either of them have been capable of doing in his
mother, though? Jessica had never said much about her
friendship with Mullins – although it had clearly been a very
important one. It was almost impossible to get to the heart of
one's parents' friendships, but George's mother had left some

intriguing clues. 'Mullins,' she used to say, 'had something of a crush on me at college.'

Had her death, possibly, been an accident? Could there, perhaps, have been some late-night lesbian row – along the lines of 'I've always loved you, Jessica. How could you get involved with that ghastly man? And give birth to that hideously fat, sexist son of yours?' George could not quite see this happening, but there might, it occurred to him, have been some kind of row about money. He had the vague idea that Mullins and Vickers were a little bit short of the ready.

Money, he could not help thinking, was probably at the bottom of all this. He should have told her to leave it equally to all the children. The fact that he had not done so was more or less proof that, as the eldest son, he had had a special relationship with his mother on which he had ruthlessly capitalized. He had always thought of himself as a nice person but, if he was honest – and now there was little point in being anything else – he would have to admit that he enjoyed the power she had granted him over his two siblings. Would he have shared the money equally? He liked to think so but perhaps it would have been more complicated than that.

'What exactly,' Mullins was saying, 'did Jessica say in this codicil?'

She was not even pretending interest in the remains of her oldest friend's daughter.

Stephen, perhaps to prevent her and Beryl shovelling cutlery, watercolours and small antiques into a large bag and hotfooting it off to their cottage in East Sussex, pointed dramatically at his sister's body. 'As you can see,' he said, in what Esmeralda used to call his 'Stephen Pearmain *News at Ten* Anywhere in the World Where Horrible Things Are Happening' voice, 'my sister has hanged herself. Some people are saying she may have been murdered.'

'I'm not sure,' said Esmeralda, 'that that is what I said.'

'Oh,' said Mullins, as if she had only now remembered that there was a dead body in the room. 'Oh, my God!'

'Oh, my God!' said Beryl Vickers, squinting up at the body. 'You mean someone put her up there?'

Mullins and Frigga, George recalled, had once been very close and then, only a few months ago, while at Jessica's, they had had a furious argument, provoked by a short speech from Frigga that began 'Homosexuality is wicked.' She had gone on to say even more unacceptable things about any liaison that deviated from what she had referred to as 'the holy love between man and woman'. Why Frigga should have felt like this George would never understand. He had always thought she would have had more luck as a muff-diver than she had ever had in the quest for Mr Right. He sometimes wondered whether Vickers had made a move on her.

'Mrs Pearmain's flat,' Hobday said, 'seems to have been as busy as Clapham Junction this afternoon.'

No one, it seemed, wanted to add to this remark. If he had hoped it would prompt some revealing remarks from Mullins, Mabel or Beryl Vickers, he was wrong.

'What we will need,' said the inspector, 'is access to her flat. Does anyone have a key?'

It turned out everyone did. Everyone in the room, apart from Esmeralda, had been conscripted at one time or another to look after Frigga's cat. In the end Hobday accepted one of Stephen's. He had two and seemed unwilling to let go of either.

The inspector still showed no sign of wishing to cut Frigga down. The reason became clear when Pawlikowski took a long, complicated call that seemed to herald the arrival of experts in the field of gallows retrieval.

There was something else about the body that was

worrying him, thought George, although he was clearly not going to say what it was. Hobday was standing by the window. On the floor next to him was a large green canvas bag. The detective squatted on his haunches and took out something that George instantly recognized as Frigga's purse. This was followed by a small teddy bear, a pair of slippers, three packets of Kleenex, a bewilderingly large assortment of pill bottles and an even larger assortment of recently gathered leaves and berries. Last out was an illustrated book entitled *Things I Found in an English Hedgerow*.

With Which I Poisoned People! thought George, but, as Hobday went further down into the recesses of the bag and came out with a small rubber ball, three plastic teapots and a selection of rag dolls, he felt a pang.

She had loved his granddaughters. They were almost the only people in the world with whom she seemed able to be natural. He remembered watching her watch them, perched on the edge of his sofa, her awkward smile and air of veiled terror being, for once, suspended, as Bella Ella or Ella Bella pattered their way across the floor, muttering to themselves about tea in the way even very small females seem to do.

She had loved the girls. She had loved Barry and Maurice when they were small. When George and Frigga were children he had gone out with her once to look for her black rabbit after it had escaped. He had put his arms round her when she heard the unfortunate animal had been eaten, or half eaten, by foxes, and said, 'It'll be all right, Frigga! You'll see! It'll be all right!' How could it have been all right? Her beloved rabbit was dead. He had as much chance of coming back as, now, did George, but his saying that had made it all right at the time. Something in him had loved her, even if, for the last two decades, it had been buried deep under the accumulated weight of the years. It was hard enough when you were alive to find your way back to the love you had felt for your brothers and sisters in childhood. Now he was dead, he would never even be able to try.

It had probably not been more than a few minutes that they had all been grouped around Frigga's corpse. It had seemed much longer than that. As Pawlikowski began to pull things out of his bag, Hobday shepherded them all into the kitchen.

'Immediately after your mother and brother died,' he said to Stephen, in conversational tones, 'Frigga seemed to be saying she was responsible for your brother's death. She said, as I'm sure you remember that she had "probably" done something that had ended Mr Pearmain's life. What we later assumed – as perhaps did everyone else – was that she had, deliberately or accidentally, picked hemlock on Putney Heath during the afternoon before she served everyone with parsnip wine. But when we asked her about it later she said she had not done anything of the kind.'

'It's possible,' said Stephen, 'that she had picked hemlock by mistake. It is possible.'

'Of course,' said Hobday, slowly, 'that was before we had any idea that your brother had been poisoned. It wasn't in the frame at that stage.'

'No one,' said Esmeralda, 'had any idea that George had been poisoned. Who on earth would want to poison poor George? What harm had he done to anyone?'

'But they did,' said Hobday, 'and maybe Miss Pearmain had seen something suspicious, something she couldn't quite explain at the time, and done nothing about it. Which was why she felt guilty.'

That fitted, thought George, with what Frigga had told his corpse. He was, unfortunately, not in a position to pass on this information to anyone, apart from a dead Irish wolfhound. The doorbell rang. More pathologists arrived. DC Purves arrived. There was the noise of heavy feet from the front room.

'If she had picked hemlock,' said Esmeralda, 'and knew she had, she would have told everyone about it. If she was innocent. It does sound as if she was in some way implicated. And there is the question of the note. I agree with Stephen. That is her writing, even if the style is a little odd.'

Hobday nodded in an animated fashion.

I really should find out a little more about this man, George thought. Hobday was getting keener on his widow by the minute. Was Hobday married? Was she just a casual pick-up for him? Perhaps he enjoyed the buzz of shagging the recently bereaved. Those affected by violent crime must be especially vulnerable. They needed comfort. Perhaps Hobday provided it in the form of mutual sexual climax. George was outraged. If he wasn't dead, he would certainly be getting in touch with the Independent Police Complaints Commission to...well...complain.

Hang on. He was getting ahead of himself. All the guy had done was smile at Esmeralda a few times. What was really bothering him was that, sooner or later, some lucky geezer was going to be asked back to 22 Hornbeam Crescent, then to share a few glasses of fine wine from the Rhône and, before either of them knew it, whip upstairs for a spot of anal intercourse and other things that had been denied George during his long and, on the whole, happy marriage.

He had always said to her, 'When I'm dead, I want you to get on with your life. I want you to be happy.' Well, he did want her to seize any chance of happiness she was offered, but he did not particularly want a ringside seat while she was doing it. He had *always*, if he was honest, been violently jealous of anyone else who took an interest in her. Even if it had taken an unhealthy dose of hemlock to get him to admit it. He had kept the business with Julie Biskiborne such a closely guarded secret because he had assumed Esmeralda was as possessive as him. Was she, though? Would the man who came along to replace him allow her to flower in a way he had never managed?

Hobday was having one of those long and tedious conversations in which he attempted to establish where everyone had been during the period when Frigga was likely to have died. Mabel Dawkins, who, George thought, was being particularly evasive, seemed to be saying that she had been in and out of the flat at regular intervals since Jessica's death. Was she, George wondered, looking for the mysterious codicil?

Pawlikowski put his face round the door. He seemed, George thought, excited. An ominous sign. 'Something I need you to look at, Boss,' he said. George could, of course, have followed him but, after Hobday had told everyone they could go, he stayed with Esmeralda and the others.

He really must learn to let go of Esmeralda. Perhaps when he had done that he would be relieved of the terrible burden of consciousness. She was the one who was haunting him in the way the living can haunt the dead and bring them, piece by piece, away from the calm and oblivion that should rightfully be theirs.

She was following Veronica and Nat out into the sunshine. Mabel, the Mullins woman and Beryl Vickers showed every sign of wanting to stay, but Stephen, who seemed to have recovered somewhat from the shock of seeing his sister's body, shepherded them towards the door. He clearly did not like the idea of any of them being alone with the silver.

Veronica and Esmeralda were saying their goodbyes with one of those heartfelt embraces that women seem to achieve so much better than men. Esmeralda was to be taken back to Hornbeam Crescent with Stephen. Other people, George noted, were already showing signs of competing to look after her – as if losing her husband was a form of disability. She didn't like this. She had never liked people trying to look after her. George took in the unhappiness in Esmeralda's face and, once again, felt the loss of being unable to talk to her directly. A few words would be all it would take. What was it his father had said to him when he was dying in that grim side-room in the hospital? 'There is one sense in which I never want you to go.' A typically literary last line from Pearmain Senior and one that, even now he had joined his father among the ranks of the dead, had power to move him. Well, he didn't seem able to go, but Esmeralda had no way of knowing that.

'It'll be good,' Stephen was saying to Esmeralda, 'to talk through some things before I go.'

What could those be? He could tell that, whatever they were, she had no wish to discuss them – if he had been alive he would have picked that up immediately, simply from the angle of her shoulders or a movement in her eyes, and set about getting rid of his brother. She found that kind of thing very difficult. But George was no longer there to make it easier for her.

'Look,' he said to her, as the three of them climbed into Stephen's car, 'let's try to be positive about this. I'm never again going to forget to put my breakfast plate in the dishwasher. I'm all done with spending too much time in the lavatory. I'll never again want to watch the Boat Race. There's no chance whatsoever now of my not doing anything in the garden. You'll never again have to put up with me laughing at my own jokes.'

This showed no sign of having any effect – good, bad or

indifferent – upon its intended audience. Stephen was holding open the front passenger door of his Range Rover. Esmeralda gave it a dull stare. 'I'll go in the back, if that's all right,' she said, 'I always used to go in the back when George was...' She was unable to finish this sentence. Stephen arranged his face to suggest sympathy.

They had been on holiday, once, the three of them, when Stephen was between marriages. It had not been a success. They had driven through Devon, staying in grim bed-and-breakfast places, staffed by people with obvious marital difficulties who made threatening conversation over breakfast. George had sat in the front, next to his brother. They had talked about their parents, the deficiencies of Frigga, happier memories of childhood and, mostly, about money because Stephen like to talk about money. He had a lot of it and he enjoyed telling George all about that, while remaining coy about actual figures. Esmeralda, excluded from this, sat in the back looking out at the green hedgerows and the narrow lanes, her face a mask.

You grew away from your mother and father, brothers and sisters. That was the way. George had found it easier to do that because of his marriage. Frigga, of course, had never found any way of escaping the horrible closeness of her relationship with Jessica. It was different with Esmeralda.

She had had none of the qualities that were liable to make his parents reach for the subtle insult or the awful sting of qualified approval. She wasn't an Orthodox Jew or an alcoholic or just plain crazy, like the Irish girl Stephen had brought back from university and who had been pronounced 'really good fun' by both parents. Esmeralda was just Esmeralda and, from the very beginning, everyone in the Pearmain family seemed to have decided that there was something wrong with her. Perhaps it was her voice or her hair or her brusque manner of disagreeing with people or simply that she always said when she *did* disagree with people. Perhaps it was her habit of remaining totally silent at mealtimes. Perhaps it was her mother. Although her mother was, in many respects, an almost exact mirror image of George's. Even if she taught mathematics rather than music and sometimes wore clothes that Jessica described as 'fast'. She smoked. She had been known to swear in public. Was that it?

Surely not.

Anyway, neither Jessica nor George Senior had ever really accepted Esmeralda's mum and her husband, a small, inoffensive man with a pointed head, an accountant who led a blameless life for sixty-four years and then had a quietly inoffensive heart attack in the back of a taxi. Was that it?

Not really. All the Pearmains, each for very different reasons, had decided there was something wrong with Esmeralda from the moment she had first put her face round the door in the middle of George's second term at Oxford. This was where, as George remarked in his wedding speech, he had finally got over the fact that she had hit him on the head with that skipping rope at St Jude's Primary School.

Stephen had said, only weeks after he had been introduced, that there was 'something shifty' about her. Frigga made her sour-milk face every time Esmeralda's back was turned. Jessica publicly objected to the fact that Esmeralda did not iron George's shirts. Everyone took offence at her – in those days – left-wing stance on all things political.

But both his parents' reactions were violently hostile.

'There's something wrong with her,' George's father had said, when he had brought her home for the second time. 'I don't know what it is. But something is not right.' His mother had nodded in agreement, like a tall flower in a regular breeze. George Pearmain Senior never had condescended to

208

reveal what was not right about Esmeralda. At first, George thought it might be that, even way back then in the early seventies, he had been open about the fact that they were sleeping together. Indeed, there were occasions when George Pearmain Senior, a moderately observant Anglican, had said that that was precisely the nature of his objection.

It wasn't, of course. What it was, George thought, was that his father was jealous, and so was his mother. He had always, for reasons he had never completely understood, been their favourite. Perhaps it was simply that he was the first and that, as they never failed to remind the poor girl, the follow-up act, Frigga, had been such a disappointment. They could not bear losing George, and when he had met Esmeralda he had been lost to the world, as well as to his parents. He could still remember the feel of her skin, the smell of her as they walked, and the blind, confused hunger she could wake in him, even now he was dead and would never touch her or smell her or kiss her lips again.

In a way, his coming to terms with his mother and father still felt like a betrayal of her. Perhaps the absurd complexities of his mother's will were a punishment for that.

Before Stephen had had time to close the passenger door, George had slipped in to occupy his usual place next to his brother.

As they drove back up Putney Hill, towards Hornbeam Crescent, he looked back at his wife. She was staring out at the bright day in just the way she had studied the Devon lanes all those years ago. The girls were coming out of school, in careless groups, in the August sun. The giant green castles of the chestnut trees on the corner of their road held her eyes. George wanted to lean over and reach out his hand to her. For a moment he thought that that was what he had done and then, like a man who has suffered some great loss, wakes not remembering it and almost instantly sees how bright the world was once and how suddenly it is now dark, he knew he would never be anything other than deceased.

'Do you really think Frigga was murdered?' Stephen was saying.

'I'm not sure,' said Esmeralda, 'but something's not right about it.' There was a silence. Then she said, 'I'm so sorry.'

'Oh, God,' said Stephen. 'So am I. She was an awful person in many ways but I was very fond of her. She looked up to me, I suppose. I...'

Was he going to cry? He had been close to it several times since they had found Frigga's body. He had that frightened look about him too. Why had Mabel Dawkins said that Frigga had seemed frightened? That was a mystery George could not even begin to think of solving.

'You didn't really like her, did you?' Stephen was saying to Esmeralda.

'I wouldn't say that,' replied Esmeralda. 'She wasn't an easy person. I don't think I'm a particularly easy person. It's just that I can't really think of anything but George at the moment.'

'Yes yes yes,' said Stephen, sounding as if he meant it for a change. 'I understand that.'

They were coming into Hornbeam Crescent now. Home. The Range Rover juddered over the speed bumps. At number thirty-four Mr Longly was snipping at his privet hedge. The little girl opposite was playing with her brother in the front garden of number nineteen. She threw a pebble. He went to fetch it. She threw another. He did the same. They seemed to be enjoying it. Then there were the white walls and iron railings of number twenty-four and, after that, the battered white picket fence that marked the boundary of number twenty-two.

Stephen pulled the car slowly into its berth. George sat there for a while after his wife and brother had gone back into the house for which he would never have to provide another parking permit. Perhaps he would not be able to slide through the doors of the car. Perhaps he was trapped. Perhaps he would stay in this big, expensive car, smelling of new leather, for all eternity. Perhaps this was his own private hell. He thought he didn't really care. In the house opposite, the little girl threw another pebble and this time her brother said he wasn't going to fetch it. There was silence.

Chapter Fifteen

George was not quite clear how he got inside the house. Being dead, he had now decided, was a bit like being very drunk. One minute you were in the thick of conversation and the next minute you were flat on your back in the gutter in a street you couldn't even recognize. It was actually worse than being drunk. Sometimes you weren't flat on your back but hanging upside down, like a bat, from a lamppost. On one occasion he had found himself swimming through a small bowl of gazpacho in a tapas bar in Putney High Street. On this occasion he seemed, briefly, to be in the attic, surrounded by old suitcases and the complete set of *Star Wars* figures he had been hoarding ever since the children were small.

He didn't stay there long. He became aware that some force was drawing him, against his will, out on to the upper landing of his former house, down the stairs and into the front room, where Stephen and Esmeralda were sitting on the sofa with the resigned air of passengers waiting for a long overdue train. The force wasn't like the drag of a magnet or an alien hand pulling him through the air. It was a pulse in the atmosphere, a sound wave that seemed to pick him up and twist him round it so that he was dragged to the heart of the noise, like a minor instrument in an orchestra, unable to hear quite how his tune blended into the ensemble.

The noise, he suddenly realized, as he came to rest outside the living room, was Stephen's voice. He couldn't hear what his brother was saying but he knew, even before he had identified a single word or phrase, that Stephen was gearing himself up to pronounce the magic words 'I think I should be in charge of this.'

They were very familiar words to George. It might not have been the first sentence Stephen had uttered but, from about the age of two, it pretty well summed up his general drift. He had, somehow, managed to be in charge of everything, from Monopoly to games of cricket in the garden. He had been in charge of who sat where in the back of the car. He had been in charge of who pretended to be whom when they played Cowboys and Indians, which was what, unbelievably, they had played back in 1956. Frigga was always the squaw and usually ended up tied to a tree with washing line, while Stephen and George pounded round her in a circle, hollering war cries devised, inevitably, by Stephen.

George was never quite sure how he had achieved this. Stephen was the youngest, wasn't he? But he had managed, from day one, to behave as if he was the eldest. Stephen, of course, had always had certainty. He had thought he was right. George had never been sure he was right. A lot of what passed as tolerance in him was actually the inability to make up his mind about anything. He had watched his younger brother forge his media career with the bear-like puzzlement accorded by the less successful to those who become masters of the universe in business, culture or politics. George had never thought he minded. It was only now he was dead that he realized quite how much he had minded, how much it had cost him to be the amiable one. Because he hadn't been quite as amiable as all that, had he? He had taken the credit for being a good older brother. He had, if he was honest, worked quietly against Lulu being accepted into the family. He had been quite happy to see Stephen fall out with his mother over her, exactly as Stephen had once enjoyed the conflict between George and his parents over Esmeralda. In the end he had taken back what was his.

You could tell Stephen was about to propose himself as group leader of something or other by the way he stood as the two of them rose to go through to the kitchen. He made way for her as she headed for the hall but allowed his right hand, protruding as stiffly as a penguin's flipper, to seem to usher her through a house that had become, by some miracle, his. The way he looked at the ground, sideways, in the carefully concocted imitation of modesty practised by big executives, the way he pursed his lips as he followed Esmeralda into the hall or the keen, far-sighted way he scanned his phone as he sat heavily in the chair with the arms at the dining-table (the chair that always used to be George's) suggested a man who was about to propose himself for a job for which he and he alone was qualified.

It was with a sinking of his absent heart that George realized the thing of which Stephen wanted to be in charge was nothing other than his brother's funeral.

He let Esmeralda know that this was what he intended by putting in a phone call to his wife. There was nothing Stephen enjoyed more than making people watch him on the telephone. 'Hello, darling,' he said, understandably pleased that he had managed to get in two words without his phone interrupting – even if it was to Lulu's voicemail. 'I'm with Esmeralda. We're discussing funerals. Did you get the messages I left? Frigga is dead. That's the upshot. Are you in Basingstoke? Was it Basingstoke you were going to be in? I'm not sure. Let me know anyway. Where you are. Where you're going to. And when you'll be back. Goodbye now.'

Esmeralda was staring at him. What, her expression seemed to say, is this clown doing in my kitchen? And why is he talking about funerals? One of which will be for a man I loved. Why is he talking about this to a woman I absolutely loathe? The only funeral on the agenda if he carries on like this for much longer will be his own.

Suddenly Stephen's phone, clearly feeling it was time to get back into the conversation, said, 'Lulu is not in Basingstoke.'

Stephen paid no attention to this. He continued to talk. 'She was hanged. Pretty grim. Anyway. She is as dead as a doornail.'

'Lulu,' said his phone, 'is not dead. She is on the Upper Richmond Road.'

Stephen studied his phone. Instead of answering directly he began to prod wildly at its keys.

This, thought George, was probably a wise move. His phone was more a master of conversation than its owner. It had a proven talent for twisting any social encounter in the way it wanted it to go. George floated over in his direction and saw that his brother was looking at a Google Earth map of Putney. A small red dot appeared to be moving along the Upper Richmond Road, immediately west of East Sheen. Was it Lulu? Stephen did not wait to find out. Once again, he seemed, George thought, frightened of something. He pressed a button on his phone and a map of Barbados appeared.

'Barbados,' said his phone, 'has not experienced a hurricane since 1955.'

Stephen's new tactic of ignoring his phone seemed to be working. George had the impression that the phone was slightly rattled, as it added, in sultry tones, 'Would you like me to book you a flight to Bridgetown, Barbados?' Stephen did not respond. After a pause, his phone added, sounding slightly petulant, 'Stephen?' Still, Stephen did not respond. If only, thought George, he had used more of this kind of tactic on his wife.

'Or, if you want,' went on his phone, 'I could book you a massage at the Oriental Spa in Harwich. It has a full staff of qualified health professionals and a large salad bar looking out over a gymnasium that has received rave reviews for its equipment.'

Stephen started to dial again. His phone made a sort of croaking noise, as if it suspected it might not have long to live. He continued to ignore it.

Esmeralda did not watch or listen to this for long. She did the only thing a red-blooded woman could do under such circumstances. She made a phone call of her own. She tucked her small Nokia into her palm, left a message for Barry and another for Maurice. She asked them to come over as quickly as possible. 'Stephen,' she said, in an ominous voice, 'seems to want to talk about your father's funeral.' Then she folded her hands over her stomach and glared implacably at her brother-in-law.

That glare – George knew it well – was quite a glare. It was usually enough to send him whimpering from the room. It had, of course, no effect whatsoever on Stephen. Which seemed to sum up the problem of the in-law relationship. You couldn't explain things like Esmeralda's glare to your brother. He would probably think of it as an example of her bossiness but, of course, for George it was far, far more complicated than that. It wasn't anything as simple as him enjoying taking orders from her (a handy stereotype for examining Stephen's own relationship with Lulu) but, much more, that when she dished out a glare he knew what was behind it.

'Let's hope to God,' said Esmeralda, 'that Barry's father-in-law doesn't want to come over too. I think he may be staying with them.'

George thought, briefly, of Barry's father-in-law. He thought of the man's ears. His fondness for cider. His long, long anecdotes about his pet lizard. Sometimes there was an upside to being dead.

'We must get this funeral thing sorted,' Stephen was saying, as he finished dialling a very long number on his now submissive phone. 'Three people have died. My brother has died. My mother has died. My sister has died.' He ticked these items off on his fingers, then looked around wildly in case he had forgotten any other recent fatalities among his near relatives. 'It will take a lot of planning. Funerals require an immense amount of planning.'

'I don't think,' said Esmeralda, in a small voice, 'that I can really bear to talk about the funeral.'

Stephen looked at her. 'Funerals,' he said, 'Funeralzzz.' He studied his phone. 'Nobody is in China!' he said irritably. 'It is,' he went on, in a voice that suggested it was nothing of the kind, 'absolutely unbearable. A double wedding is bad enough. But a triple funeral. My God! It will be a nightmare.'

Esmeralda goggled at him. It was clear, from the expression on her face, that a triple funeral was not what she had in mind. Not, of course, that anyone was going to consult George on the issue. He had made a habit, when alive, of ending all discussions about what kind of funeral he wanted with the line 'Oh, just sling me on the nearest rubbish tip. That'll do me.' This did not quite reflect his current view. In fact, since he'd been dead he had grown increasingly interested in his funeral, and on one issue he was absolutely clear. He had no wish to be featured in a triple burial.

He had always hoped that his funeral would be about him. He wasn't asking for Westminster Abbey. How could he compete with a woman who had brought Britain the Falklands War, the destruction of the coal mines and the largest, most corrupt financial centre in the Western world? But a well-thought-out funeral service, along the lines of what they'd got up for Queen Mary in 1695, and nine or ten people saying what a great bloke they thought he was, did not seem a lot to ask.

The idea of sharing the occasion with his mother was bad enough. The funeral of a ninety-nine-year-old, while not being exactly a cause for celebration, was hardly the kind of thing at which you would expect too much sobbing and moaning. The majority of the punters would be too busy contemplating the possibility that they were going to be rather more than spectators at some very similar function in the near future. But to be in the box next to Frigga's? Jesus! Even if anyone could be found to say nice things about his sister, the obvious untruthfulness of their remarks was bound to make George's eulogies sound distinctly insincere. No one had liked Frigga. No one had really known Frigga, apart, possibly, from the woman who had gone with her to the Canary Islands – George couldn't even remember her name. He had the vague idea that, whoever she was, she had topped herself many years ago. From what Frigga had said she had come pretty close to it on the holiday – a tactic with which George, who had once spent two weeks with Frigga on the Brittany coast, had some sympathy.

'I'm not sure I...' Esmeralda's voice sounded smaller than ever. She had told George once that when she was a teacher, in the early years of their marriage, she had stood up in front of her class, started to tell them something about Wordsworth and suddenly found that no words would come out of her mouth. She had walked out of the school and never gone back. After that, of course, the boys had been born. She'd had plenty of other things to do.

Now she was in the grip of a paralysis that matched her

long-ago breakdown. George could see the immediate cause of it, which explained something he had never quite wanted to admit to himself. She had always found it impossible to say what she wanted to anyone she disliked, and now he saw very clearly that she really did dislike his brother. Had always disliked him. You were not supposed to say things like that when you were in the middle of the business of living. It was just another unpleasant fact that his death had made impossible to avoid.

'We'll have to get a moderator or something,' Stephen was saying, 'if we don't get a vicar. You don't go to church. I don't go to church. Mother never went to church. Frigga was a committed pagan. George hated religion.'

As it happened, that was perfectly true. It did not, however, seem to affect George's views on the subject of his funeral. He had not wanted to get married in a church but he was now very clear that he wished to get buried in one. It was, of course, a bit of a late discovery. He should really have thought about that before he'd started swigging cocktails of hemlock and parsnip wine.

He wasn't, in any sense of the word, a Christian. He was fairly sure that not only was Christianity a justification, if not a cause, of much of the misery in the world but also for the self-righteous complacency of those who felt impelled to do anything about it. Wasn't ordinary morality a matter of practical common sense? Why did people seem to need some absurd tale of a guy working miracles and coming back to life in order to justify behaving properly?

Had the Pope and the Archbishop of Canterbury and the rest of the bastards somehow managed to have the last laugh on George?

It was only now he was dead that he knew for sure that a churchyard was where he wanted to be and, if things continued to play out the way they seemed to be doing in 22 Hornbeam Crescent, the sooner he got down there the better, but there seemed little chance of his making it to that address. His own life seemed to preclude it.

'He wasn't religious,' Esmeralda was saying quietly, 'but he did like the music.'

Stephen looked up from his phone, his face blank. It was at this point that George's wolfhound put his head round the door. As Partridge had been dead for eight years, no one, apart from George, paid him any attention.

'Oh!' said George. 'It's you again!'

'It is,' said Partridge. He had, to George's surprise, a rather cultivated accent – and, for such a large, hairy dog, was very soft spoken. 'There was something I wanted to tell you,' he continued.

'There was,' said George.

Partridge looked out at him from under his fringe. He was clearly thinking as hard as he could, which was not, from George's recollection of his dog, very hard at all.

'It was to do with your murder,' he said eventually.

'Do you know something about it?' said George.

There was a long, long silence.

'I think I do,' said Partridge, sombrely.

'I don't suppose,' said George, 'that you can remember who it was by any chance? Did you...see who *did it* perhaps?'

'Did I?' said Partridge. 'Did I? That...is the question...'

There was another long silence.

'Does anyone care what I think? Or what I remember?' said Partridge.

He was, George thought, looking sulky. It was the dog food with jelly. He had never liked it. George had given it to him anyway. He was only a dog. Well, now he was a dog

220

R . I . P .

with important information that he was withholding from George.

George was fairly sure the dog could remember whatever he had seen around the time of his murder. Partridge was tormenting him. That was all.

Partridge looked at Stephen. Then he looked at Esmeralda. 'It'll come back,' he said. 'I can't think what it was for the moment. But I'll try. It was very important.'

George nodded with what he hoped looked like tolerance and enthusiasm. 'You do that, Partridge,' he said. 'You do that.'

'Don't patronize me,' said the wolfhound, glumly, and padded, even more softly than usual, from the living room.

'I think,' Stephen was saying, 'we should have open coffins!'

Stephen's negotiating tactic, as always, was to start from the assumption that everyone was going to do as he wanted and then gradually, over hours or if necessary days, go a very small way to meeting what he had never allowed to be original demands, as if each grudging concession to anyone else's point of view was a deviation from an earlier agreement. It had worked at his public school – Stephen had asked to be sent to boarding school at a very early age – and it had seemed to succeed in the media business he and Lulu had founded five years ago, which, Stephen was always telling George, was worth millions. Even though its assets only really consisted of him and Lulu making phone calls.

'I want to look at my brother's dead face,' Stephen was saying. 'I want to look at Frigga's face. I want to look at the dead face of my mother.'

Was this, thought George, normal? Was there an element of gloating about it? And even if that was what Stephen

221

wanted, why did he have to take a simultaneous gander at all three corpses? Judging from her expression, a triple funeral was not Esmeralda's idea of fun. The whole thing was turning into something strongly reminiscent of the old Madame Tussaud's Chamber of Horrors.

'We'll have them embalmed, of course,' Stephen went on. 'I know a very good man in Roehampton. He did Lulu's brother. He was in terrible shape when they got him out from under the lawn mower but by the time this guy had finished he looked good enough to eat.'

Esmeralda looked helplessly at her Nokia. George hoped Barry or Maurice would get back to her. Failing that, she should call Veronica Pinker. She needed allies. Badly.

'Lulu actually kissed Montmorency on the lips. On the lips! Right there in the crematorium! It made an incredible impression on the audience. The congregation. The audience. Whatever. She said it was like kissing a rubber ball that had just come out of the fridge. People were crying. Crying. She was crying. I was crying. Peter Duchamp from ITV was sobbing openly.'

From what George could remember of Montmorency – was that really his name? – physical contact with the man when he was alive had had a lot in common with brushing up against a chilled rubber ball. It was clear, he thought, that Esmeralda had decided to say nothing until her sons arrived. This was wise, in George's view. From the look of her, most of the words hovering unspoken in and around her mouth were four-letter ones.

He felt like loosing off a few carefully chosen expletives himself. He really did draw the line at an open coffin. Would his brother compromise and accept a pane of glass? Or a sort of detachable lid, which those who really wanted to get a peek at G. Pearmain's cadaver could lift to check him out, then pop back on, in the manner of someone assessing the status of a pan of boiling vegetables?

Embalming, anyway, thought George, was not really the right word for whatever they were going to have to do to him to bring him before the public without provoking major attacks of hysteria. Total reconstruction was the half of it. They might do better to pick another corpse off the pile rather than try to modify the handiwork of that mad Polish pathologist.

'And Handel,' Stephen was saying. 'Everyone likes Handel. The minuet from *Berenice*.'

George wasn't sure that everyone liked Handel. He was absolutely sure that his brother did. Perhaps the whole service was going to reflect Stephen and Lulu's taste. She was, he seemed to remember, rather fond of the Commodores and Black Sabbath. It would be a very mixed event – especially in the readings department. Lulu liked Pam Ayres and Wendy Cope, though she never seemed sure of which was which. Stephen would probably go for one of those awful minor Edwardian poets he—

'We could have a reading from W. E. Henley,' said Stephen, brightening perceptibly at the prospect. 'I am the master of my thingy and the captain of my you know what and even when I am feeling absolute shit I will...you know, not bow down to tyrants or whatever.'

Esmeralda, finally, spoke.

'George didn't like "Invictus",' she said. 'He preferred the one about Death being the ruffian on the stair and Madam Life being a piece in bloom. His favourite poet was Thomas Hardy.'

Stephen looked at her. Then he looked at his phone. Then he said, 'Horse-drawn funerals are expensive, but they do make an impact. Lulu's daughter is a trained opera singer.'

'Oh, yeah? I am not,' muttered George, 'having the Prune
struggle through a few bars of the "Pie Jesu" from Fauré's
Requiem. I really will start howling under your window
if you let the ghastly bag loose on a Mozart Concert Aria.
Whose funeral is this anyway? Please?'

Fortunately, at this point, there was the noise of a key in
the lock of the front door, then Barry and Maurice tumbled
into the hall. George caught the tail end of a conversation that
sounded as full of life as the two of them usually were, something about some bastard from Foxtons stitching them up
over an *impossible* split-level conversion, before they found
themselves in the house where they'd grown up, remembered
their father was dead and fell suddenly silent.

George didn't want his boys to be quiet. He wanted them
to go on bumping bellies and high-fiving and making jokes
about masturbation. He wanted them never to stop liking
each other. He wanted them to keep right on enjoying making
money. He didn't want them to stop loving their wives or
their children or their mother or, in their own offhand way,
celebrating the love he was sure they had felt for him and
that he certainly felt for them.

Most of all he didn't want them to stop laughing. He
didn't want them to take themselves or their lives too seriously. They hadn't dedicated their lives to others, but they
were not devoid of charitable instincts and they certainly,
as far as he could see, made an attempt to be decent people.
Like him, they were ordinary and, like him, they seemed to
find the ordinary amusing and worthwhile. Look at what
people who wanted to be exceptional had done to the world,
thought George, as Maurice and Barry came in.

They did not, of course, find much amusing about the
room where they had eaten so many family meals. Neither
were they obviously delighted to see their uncle sitting in

George's place, as the sun out in the garden shifted round to the west and shone in on the part of the house that would never again see their father glumly shoving cutlery into a drawer.

'Mum!' said Barry.

'Mum!' said Maurice.

'Barry!' said Esmeralda.

'Maurice!' said Maurice.

All three laughed, and they embraced her, and then, while Stephen concentrated even more furiously on his phone, Esmeralda began to cry.

She had only just stopped when, outside in the street, a big Mercedes slowed to a halt. George did not need to go to the front room window to see Lulu Belhatchett, allowing the engine to tick quietly on while she checked herself in the driving mirror. It went on ticking while she double-checked her phone for messages and ticked into silence with the tact of a butler tiptoeing from a table. Then there was the click of expensive heels on the front porch of George's house and, finally, a short, businesslike peal of the bell.

Stephen stood to attention. Now, his face seemed to suggest, we'll be getting down to a bit of serious funeral-planning. Black plumes on black horses, black top hats and a few thousand quid's worth of flowers here we come.

'It's Lulu!' he said.

He clearly thought everyone else should be on their feet applauding as keenly as the front row of a party conference in Moscow in 1935 when Stalin strolled on to the platform. He felt the need to make clear the enormous importance of what had just happened to those present – they seemed too stupid or rude to grasp it. He spoke slowly, as to a trio of village idiots.

'She's here. Lulu. Here. Now.'

225

His phone snapped into life with the speed of a Greek chorus commenting on some particularly gruesome murder. It sounded, George thought, suddenly more authoritative.

'Lulu Belhatchett,' it said, 'is at twenty-two Hornbeam Crescent. Please open the door for her. Immediately.'

Lulu, as it happened, was not the only one on the doorstep. Standing next to her was the inspector and, in his right hand, he was holding a manuscript. It was encased in what looked like a polythene evidence bag.

Oh, no, thought George. Someone else who wants Esmeralda to read his fucking novel.

Esmeralda had read many of George's novels. She had even managed to finish the one about the son of a bank manager who had gone to Oxford, dreamed of being a poet and ended up as a bank manager in Putney. When she had asked him, very tentatively, if he thought it was autobiographical, he had stormed out of the room, threatening never to speak to her again.

'I found this,' said Hobday, 'in Miss Pearmain's flat. It's in an evidence bag because, whatever its literary merits, evidence is what it is.' He squinted through the wrapper at the title page and read aloud, '*We Do Not Go Down to the Sea in Ships*!' He shrugged. 'Not,' he said, 'that the book has much to do with sailing. It's mainly about a witch who goes around poisoning people. Including her own mother, who is also a witch. Although not as good a witch as the daughter. Who is called Fragga. The mother is called Jessica.'

'Oh,' said Stephen. 'Oh.'

'It's not my kind of thing,' said Hobday. 'I like a bit more story and a bit less blood.'

'Why are you telling us this, Inspector?' said Stephen. 'What on earth does it have to do with my sister's suicide?'

'If it was suicide,' said Hobday. 'If it was suicide.'

He cleared his throat and reached into another folder, underneath the evidence bag. 'This,' he said, 'is from chapter twenty-four. We made a copy of a particular paragraph. The heroine is just about to throw herself off Putney Bridge. She writes a suicide note which she sends to her mother. I'll read it to you. "I want to die. This is the way I want to do it. I am sorry. I know finding my body will not be easy. I cannot help that. I am sorry for what I have done. I have done wicked, wicked things. I am sorry. I have killed. I have murdered. I have taken the lives of the innocent. In England and on the Continent. I pushed those people under the train at the Gare du Nord! I have deprived my good, kind brother – the wisest and gentlest man I ever knew – of the precious gift of life. I have sent him down to the Dark Kingdom where the Trolls dance on the heads of the slain. Farewell!"' He looked round the room. 'We found injuries on Miss Pearmain's neck consistent with the theory that she was attacked, then hung from the hook in her mother's flat's ceiling. Someone who had access to Frigga's premises pinned this note to her chest. It has been torn off a page in the long-hand version of the manuscript. Hence that jagged tear along the top of the paper. As far as we can see there are no prints on the manuscript either. Whoever did this knew what they were doing. I'm afraid I have to tell you that we are now treating the death of Miss Frigga Pearmain as deliberate, calculated murder.'

PART THREE

He's dead but he won't lie down...

Popular song

Chapter Sixteen

Everyone agreed afterwards that it had been a perfect day for a funeral. What you needed, a lot of people said, was dramatic weather. You didn't want steady sunshine. You certainly did not want continuous rain – even if black umbrellas, and plenty of them, would accentuate the sombre nature of the occasion. What you wanted was a bit of *Sturm und Drang*, a chance for the Almighty to show his fist and remind the mourners that they, too, were mortal.

George, his mother and sister were finally laid to rest in early September. The day was about as Wagnerian as a South London suburb gets. It was close, humid, in the high twenties and, all along Hornbeam Crescent, bankers and lawyers had been turning this way and that as they searched for sleep in the sticky night. At dawn the sun was brilliant, sparkling in the window opposite number twenty-two, printed in blocks of light on the well-cared-for roofs, warm and golden on the asphalt road.

By ten thirty, however, the clouds had started to build. The stillness of the day was becoming oppressive. The air squatted on the gardens in thick, unbreathable piles, and as those in the Pearmain family who had contrived not to be murdered gathered at what was no longer George and Esmeralda's, most of the moisture on their faces was from sweat rather than tears.

Esmeralda, George had been flattered to note, had done quite a bit of crying over the last few weeks. Most of it, to his relief, had been done on her own and, as far as he could tell, seemed pretty genuine. He felt, at times, more than a little puzzled that he had come to mean so much to another person. He would have liked, really, for her to love him a little less. It would have made his loss easier to bear. He was not ready for this constant sorrow. What made it even more puzzling, from a beyond-the-grave perspective, was that quite often her tears were accompanied by a recitation of some of his worst qualities.

'You were appallingly self-centred...' sob '...and really stupid about so many things...' more sobs '...and sometimes you could be really unpleasant!' Gales of weeping, removal of tufts of hair, burial of face in pillow, etc.

There were moments when he wished that DI Hobday – who had turned out to be married with four daughters – would make the move that he was so obviously contemplating. It would cheer her up. It would be something to look at – and George, these days, was so in need of distraction from the business of being dead that he would not, probably, have left the room even if they got down to a bit of rumpy-pumpy.

She was owed a bit of fun, for God's sake. After forty years with him. She was certainly owed a better funeral for her other half than the one Stephen and Lulu seemed to have in mind.

He was proud of his wife's rearguard action in defence of him. She had tried to keep his funeral reasonably free of vulgarity. This was, however, an impossible task. His brother and sister-in-law had gone further and further since their first tentative approaches to the business. Lulu now seemed to think that three coffins did not really make a funeral, even if two were open-topped and all three were carried in by the finest pallbearers money could buy.

'I think,' she had said, at one of the many family conferences about how to put Jessica, George and Frigga away for all eternity, 'we should have a piper!'

'Why?' Esmeralda had replied. 'Are you Scottish?'

It was possible, of course, that Lulu was Scottish, although she had erased all trace of her origins so successfully that it was impossible to tell if she were from Taunton, Inverlochy or Aix-en-Provence. She had claimed all three as her place of birth although, to be fair to her, she had been in each of the places in question and trying to get publicity when she did so.

She had managed to find an unattributed piece of prose that was even worse than the one about the person who has stiffed only being in the next room.

'You are not gone. You are here. You are there also. You are in the music we have sung. You are the insects beneath our feet and the goats on the high mountains...' etc., etc. It went on for about twenty minutes. Esmeralda said if anyone tried to read it at the funeral she would heckle them. She had also vetoed the horse-drawn carriage, the string quartet, the Prune singing the lament from *Dido and Aeneas* and Stephen's budget version of a twenty-one-gun salute on offer from a friend of his in the Royal Welch Fusiliers.

It was amazing, really, thought George, as he watched his uncle Arthur walk, ramrod straight, up the front path of Hornbeam Crescent, that she hadn't got outside broadcast cameras down to Putney Vale Crematorium. Now Jessica was safely dead, Arthur was able to bring along his mistress, Felicity de la Tour, always described by his mother as 'no better than a common prostitute'. Today, thought George, Felicity looked as if being eighty-seven was not going to get in the way of her selling her body for money.

There were other people who had clearly been avoiding George for years. It was at least fifteen since he had seen Henry, Uncle Arthur's son by his third wife, Dolores. Why on earth had he bothered to turn up now? He'd had absolutely nothing to say to George while he was alive. Why should his having been poisoned make any difference? There was his father's Welsh friend Dafydd, who arrived with his grand-children, all under the age of ten and all sobbing violently an hour before kick-off. When Esmeralda, who had never met any of them, asked whether they had met George, Dafydd said they had not, but 'It's good for children to see death. They have to learn. None of us is here for ever!' Dafydd was ninety-eight.

Barry and Maurice were inside the house, looking as help-lessly sheepish as they always did in the company of their wives. Their black ties and grey suits gave them the air of prefects about to set off for school.

Esmeralda, who had, for some reason, been put in charge of the catering, was in the kitchen, making sandwiches. Lulu did not cook, although her table manners were almost as celebrated as she had once been. In the living room, with her, yet not with her, were Geraldine, Otis and Rosalina. Rosalina looked very serious, which was partly because she had always liked Granny and was equally fond of George, but also because her stepmother had addressed her as Charlotte five times in a row.

It had been touch and go, really, whether any of the three starring bodies was going to keep their date at the cremato-rium. Getting all three out of the clutches of Pawlikowski and his friends had not been easy.

Pawlikowski did not seem very interested in discovering who was thinning out the Pearmain family if, indeed, it was only one person. He was, as George knew to his cost, really into the dead bodies. He had actually asked if he could come to the funeral and had been told (by Hobday) that this was 'not appropriate'. In some ways, thought George, the man was probably going to be as upset as anyone else to see three-quarters of the Pearmain family burned to a crisp. Pawlikowski was a man who hated to let a dead body go.

Hobday, however, would be there. Esmeralda wanted him there.

George was sitting on his coffin, in the middle of the three hearses, as they pulled out on to Putney Hill and drove towards Tibbet's roundabout, under the thickening clouds, through heat that was now positively tropical. He thought he owed it to himself to give his reconstructed corpse all the support he could manage in what was clearly going to be a very difficult day for both of them. He was feeling – to his surprise – particularly physical this morning. He felt *there* even though he wasn't.

Over the last few weeks, he had got slightly better at walking through solid objects. He had begun with simple tasks, such as pushing what was no longer his index finger through a sheet of paper. He had built up to penetrating furniture with his notional feet. There had been nasty moments. About ten days ago he had got himself stuck in the floor of the upstairs lavatory, but now he seemed able to negotiate pretty much every kind of substance, apart from water and hot soup. Water was really tricky. He had climbed into Esmeralda's bath and found himself being whirled around as if he were on a fairground ride.

As a child, he had often dreamed of being able to walk through walls. Of being able to listen to people's most private conversations. He had tried a bit of this over the last dull months but found, to his dismay, that most people behaved in private pretty much as they did in public. They were not inclined to be any less boring when they thought they were unobserved. There were some surprises – not all of them pleasant. He wished he had not stumbled across Mr and Mrs Hohenzollern from number fifty-eight having rear-entry intercourse on their kitchen floor. He had been a little surprised by Veronica Pinker's views on immigration but, on the whole, life in Putney seemed to be pretty much what he had always suspected it was.

The flowers, though, he had to admit, were really nice – even if he had no idea who had sent the vast majority of them. He wished he knew their names. This was only going to happen once. He might as well make the most of it.

He could have wished Hobday was closer to finding out who had murdered him. He was less interested in who had done for Jessica and Frigga but was intrigued to know if it was the same person.

'The murderer,' Hobday had said, 'was in Hornbeam Crescent on the night of the murder. Unless they let themselves in with a key, which puts our friend Mabel Dawkins in the frame since she was there earlier in the evening. I like the brother for it. He must have been well pissed off not to be mentioned in the will. Likewise our bearded lesbian friend. I can't see her shoving Jessica on to the floor but our Beryl might well have done so. Unless it was Frigga. And then someone else took revenge on Frigga. That is a possibility.'

George had been to only one or two of the meetings Hobday had called to investigate his murder. He was surprised to find how little they resembled the ones you saw on television. There was an astonishing lack of whiteboards. Was he being demanding or did Putney CID have a proper understanding of the importance of the task they were facing? Were they taking his death seriously enough? Some seemed to think George had simply found another ingenious way of wasting police time.

236

Not Hobday. George had watched, with admiration, as he paced up and down his tiny office, packing and unpacking his long, bony frame into and out of the worn chair at his overladen desk. He had marvelled at the way the inspector jabbed at the air with his long, bony finger to emphasize a point or underline a question that seemed to come out of nowhere and suggest thought processes of a complexity and intelligence to which his team could never aspire.

'Why,' he would say, crumpling his yoghurt pot in one huge hand, then throwing it, with extraordinary accuracy, into a wastebin ten feet away while scrabbling in his desk drawer for another, 'do none of our witnesses agree about the sequence of events on that night at Hornbeam Crescent? Is it because they were all drunk? Or is it because they were all sober?'

George knew, because he had heard Hobday discuss it with his wife, that at one point the inspector had seriously considered the possibility that Stephen, Lulu, Frigga, the Mullins woman, Vickers and Dawkins had conspired together to get rid of George and Jessica. 'They all stood to gain by the death of Mr Pearmain and his mum,' he pointed out, with perfect truth, 'and I have never heard six people give such contradictory accounts of the same event. It smacks of collusion.'

George remembered enough of the evening to be absolutely sure they were all too drunk to remember any of it.

'What is the significance of the fact that Frigga Pearmain told us first she thought she might have been responsible and then denied it? Did this have anything to do with the mysterious stranger she was supposed to meet at Jessica Pearmain's flat on the afternoon she was murdered? What – this is just to make sure you're awake, DC Bradshaw – is the capital of Sri Lanka?'

As he went on his questions grew more and more incomprehensible.

'Is there any significance in the fact that, out of our six suspects, no fewer than four have at one time or another been members of sailing clubs? How long does it take to drive from Basingstoke to Putney? Had Frigga Pearmain ever discussed literary matters with the Mullins woman? Exactly how was her body placed in the position in which we found it, and would there have to have been two people involved?'

No one, including George, had any idea how to answer any of these questions. There was DNA and there were witness statements and weeks of forensic analysis but no one, really, had a clue.

Apart, George thought, from Hobday. He was not, however, as DC Purves kept reminding him, a team player. His method of leadership was to give long and often entertaining monologues about the characters in the case, but never to tell anyone what he was really thinking. He was particularly obsessed, George was pleased to note, with George.

'What kind of man was George Pearmain? Was he a sexual predator? What do we think of the evidence of the man at NatWest? Why did he tell us Pearmain was "sexist with a filthy mind"? Did he really shag Biskiborne – as three people told us – or was that just a rumour? Why did his mother leave all the money to him? Is not this case, ladies and gentlemen, all about the money? Should we not be following the money?'

They were trying. It was not an easy task. Mullins had had money – but it looked as if Beryl Vickers had rather substantial gambling debts. Stephen and Lulu had apparently been worth a great deal a few years ago but nobody had yet had access to the audited accounts of their last two years. Mabel Dawkins was, certainly, desperate for money. It seemed her husband was interested in another woman and there was a good chance she would lose her council flat.

'It all hangs,' said Hobday, 'on this damned codicil. What was in that codicil?'

Here Bradshaw was unwise enough to attempt to answer one of his boss's questions. 'The name of the murderer, Boss? Perhaps?'

Hobday gave him a withering glance.

'Frigga Pearmain was, as we know, obsessed with the codicil. She was desperate to find it. Of course she was. It is, I'm sure, the key to the heart of this mystery. It was Jessica's last word on the subject of whom she loved most. Find that codicil.'

But they did not find that codicil. They had pulled Frigga's flat to pieces. They had emptied George's desk drawers and even discovered his half-finished sonnet to Biskiborne – which Hobday took away as possible evidence – but the codicil was nowhere to be found.

The hearse was now turning off the road out of London. The crematorium, where George's father's had been decanted into the grass all those years ago, was situated just behind a large supermarket and, for a moment, George had the strange impression that the whole cortège was about to stop off and load up with Maris Piper potatoes and packets of frozen peas. As they caught sight of the newly built Commemoration Chapel, he had his first view of the mourners. There seemed to be about three hundred. This, thought George, as the hearse came to a stop at what managed to be both a cute and frightening building, is more like it. Maybe there were even more people. Maybe they had a satellite link.

This moment of exhilaration was followed by the realization that only a third of the punters had come to see him. It might be less than that. The only faces he recognized, as the back doors of the hearse were opened, were friends of Frigga's. Well, maybe not friends, exactly. There was a woman who had tried to sue her. There was her psychiatrist. There was the woman from whom she had bought her cat, but at least they were there.

At the moment, George could not see a single one of his friends. The clouds had massed, bruised violet against the suddenly distressed sun. Somewhere in the distance George was sure he could hear thunder. He stepped out on to the tarmac as four men from the undertaker's, in grey suits, lifted his coffin and started out for the chapel.

From the first two cars came Stephen and Lulu. Behind them, Mabel Dawkins, the Mullins woman and Beryl Vickers loitered awkwardly, as Jessica and Frigga, in their turn, were unloaded. George looked from one face to another. One of these five people, he thought, murdered me, and probably my sister and my mother as well. Which one?

Chapter Seventeen

George's pallbearers were not finding him easy to carry. None of them was in the peak of condition and the front-left man looked as if he should have been inside with George, rather than lugging him across the tarmac. They were not really keeping in step as they wobbled his mortal remains to the chapel door. Was I that heavy? he thought. I really should have stayed on the Dr Loessmuller Strawberry Diet for a couple of weeks longer.

As they got to the entrance they very nearly collided with the four men who had been given the easier job of carrying his mother's coffin. She had also managed to wangle a much classier breed of pallbearer. They were all under thirty-five and managed an almost military precision as they reached pole position in the coffin queue. George had been placed in the middle and behind him, carried by four female pall-bearers, came his sister. They were all hefty girls (as she had specified in her will), although the one in the rear-right quadrant was at least six inches shorter than her teammates, which meant that Frigga's coffin rode into place at a suspiciously jaunty angle.

Stephen and Lulu had, of course, ended up getting many of the things they had wanted. One of the things Esmeralda thought she had managed to strangle at birth was the idea of playing 'The Ride of the Valkyries' as the coffins came under starter's orders. That was the music that boomed out of the loudspeakers. Esmeralda jolted like a frightened horse. 'Did we agree to this?' she muttered to Barry.

'I've lost count,' Barry whispered back. 'I think we should grab the poor old bugger and run off with him. Now.'

Stephen was watching as the three coffins fanned out as they approached the chapel entrance. All this had been planned. Jessica would move to the far right, George would take up centre position and Frigga be placed on the far left. They would go into the chapel side by side. This was Stephen's *coup de théâtre*.

'I want us there,' he had said, 'as a family. Together. Frigga, Mum, George. All three of them. Equal in death. Mother always treated us equally. She never had favourites. I want them to go in together. At the same time. As one. In formation. All three of them. Not in a line. Together. Side by side. With Lulu and I walking behind. Side by side. Together. Lulu and I want to walk behind them down the aisle. Side by side.'

Attention to detail was not Stephen's strong point. He had not bothered to measure the width of the doorway or calculate the exact amount of space occupied by three coffins and the twelve pallbearers. As George eyed the cortège, moving now at speed towards the fake Gothic door, it became pretty obvious that all three were not going to make it through at the same time. Jessica's coffin stopped. George's coffin stopped. Frigga's coffin stopped. There was a brief, frantic exchange of glances between the eight bearers able to make eye contact with those next to them. The small woman at the rear-right hand corner of Frigga's tried to look underneath it to see what was going on to the left, stumbled and, for a moment, it looked as if Frigga was going to be tipped out on to the flowerbed next to the chapel.

Stephen had managed to ensure two out of three coffins were lidless. If he was regretting that decision, in the light of the current situation, he showed no sign of it. His big, circular face, its regularity only broken by that huge ginger moustache, stayed as carefully composed as ever.

Lulu and I want to walk behind them down the aisle. Side by side.

As far as George could see, his brother was going to find that rather hard. There was something of a coffin bottleneck.

'Form a line!' hissed the tall youth who had Jessica's front-right-hand corner. 'Form a line! The old lady goes first! Then the bloke! Then the bird 'oo 'ung 'erself!'

If Stephen heard all of this – and he was close enough to do so – his face gave no sign of it. None of the other pallbearers, as far as George could make out, had heard the youth either.

'Left!' he hissed again. 'Move left! Then I'll go in!'

All might have been well had it not been for the fact that the only two pallbearers to hear him – perhaps because they were the ones, apart from him, whose heads cleared the coffins – were the rear-left corners of Jessica and George. As a result of which, after the tall youth had nearly lost his grip on his box, the two far-right coffins moved into a diagonal position. Frigga's team, who had no idea what was happening, simply followed the direction of the others and so, in a matter of seconds, all three coffins were facing away from the chapel entrance at an angle of forty-five degrees.

The tall youth did not seem to understand what had happened.

'Left!' he hissed again. 'I said *left*!'

Exactly the same thing happened a second time, and before any of them could do anything about it, all three coffins had moved through a full ninety degrees and were now facing the main road and the exit to it. The mourners, who clearly thought this was some kind of prescribed semi-military ritual, looked on solemnly, their hands folded in reverence. 'The Ride of the Valkyries' had only been scheduled for fifty-seven seconds and there was an eerie silence as the bearers shuffled sideways.

'For God's sake!' hissed the youth again. 'I said left! Left!'

Once again the coffins were on the move and the deceased were now, as Stephen had wished, in a line, though facing directly away from the chapel. Perhaps, thought George, this was their cue to get the hell out of it, which might not have been such a bad idea. As if to reinforce this notion, someone inside the crematorium pressed a button and 'The Wind Beneath My Wings' boomed out from the loudspeakers at top volume.

'Back!' hissed the tall youth, now loudly enough to be heard by almost everyone. 'Back! We'll go in backwards!'

All twelve pallbearers now started to move rapidly, and as they reversed smartly into the chapel the two outer coffins ran into the wall with a colossal thud.

For a moment it looked as if the female foursome were going to lose control of Frigga's remains. The coffin – a Westminster 200, cheaper than either George's or Jessica's – started to slide off the shoulder of the shortest bearer. She pushed hard, in an upwards and forwards direction. The front-left corner banged hard against the right ear of the girl responsible for it.

'Fuck!' she said, quite loudly. 'Oh! Fuck!'

If anyone present was at all embarrassed, they did not show it. Stephen's face, turned reverently downwards, seemed to have closed for the morning. Lulu, who had been covertly scanning the faces of the mourners to see if she was running the pleasurable risk of being recognized, remained glacially calm.

'Change of plan!' hissed the tall youth. 'We go in a line! The middle one first! The fat geezer!'

He was clearly worried that his team were going to start running the whole routine again – and, by this time, George's pallbearers were showing distinct signs of strain. There was, he thought, a strong possibility they were going to drop him if they didn't get moving fast.

'Go in backwards!' hissed the tall youth, who had clearly had the same worry. 'Backwards! Now!'

At least, thought George, I'm going in first – even if it looks like it's going to be a breech death. His coffin wobbled, ahead of the others, into the non-denominational gloom of the chapel. There was a nasty moment when it looked as if the newly promoted lead bearer was going to collide with one of the pews but somehow or other George's posse managed to reverse into the spot just below where the altar would have been if there had been an altar and, without any consultation, go into a three-point turn to get George's head to face the furnace.

'Lovely bit of parking,' observed Jonathan Freeman from number thirty.

The all-female team, who had been urged down the aisle second by the tall youth, ran into the bottom corner of George's coffin just as it was taking up its proper place. Frigga, whom nobody had thought to nail down prior to these proceedings, began to roll to what was now her right.

This was where, of course, Frigga's mother was docking, on the far right of the now endangered threesome. As Jessica moved into the first phase of her three-hundred-and-sixty-degree turn, to come to rest next to her only girl child, there seemed a strong chance that Frigga's women were going to make some comment on their cargo's issues by tipping her out on to her mum.

Frigga's head was now lolling out of her Westminster 200. 'Lolling', George reflected, was not really an appropriate word. Whatever Pawlikowski had done to her neck the people who came after had made damn sure there was no wriggle room between shoulder and chin. She was well rigid. She poked over the edge of her box as alert as a conductor's baton. When the pallbearer on her upper left side popped her back inside she made a loud, almost metallic noise as her head hit the deck. Whatever they had done to his sister, thought George, they had been a little too free with the formaldehyde.

Stephen still showed no sign of being aware that any of this was happening. He walked down the aisle, Lulu at his side, still apparently unaware that his mother and sister's corpses had very nearly been shaken and stirred together. His chestnut toupee lowered like a sunflower at twilight, he shuffled sideways into his pew with the gravity and self-absorption of an actor or a politician putting grief on display.

There was no vicar. They had finally compromised on the idea of a funeral celebrant, someone Lulu had found on the internet. He lived locally. He had been to Oxford. He had done a three-day course on being a celebrant.

'What we don't want,' Stephen had kept saying, 'is one of those people who don't even know the names of Jessica and George and...er...my sister. This bloke comes round and does research. He asks us all sorts of detailed questions and builds up a picture of the dead person.'

'I don't think I like the sound of that,' said Esmeralda.

'Oh, no no no,' Lulu cut in quickly, allowing one jewelled hand to lie lightly across the arm of her not quite relative. 'His questions will be in no way personal.'

'In that case,' said Esmeralda, 'how is he going to find out anything at all?'

Lulu had responded with a silvery laugh that managed to combine tolerance and slight contempt in almost exactly equal measure. 'Oh, Esmeralda,' she said. 'You are so *funny*.'

As the celebrant waddled out to stand at the lectern, he looked down at the two visible corpses with a deep, thoughtful expression that, George thought, was almost certainly a result of trying to work out which was which. Neither of them were anything like their photographs. Why was that? Incompetent embalming?

George looked down, with his celebrant, at the woman who had given him life. She was wearing her favourite skirt and jacket, which had caused something of a panic in the days leading up to the funeral. She had asked to be buried in it in her will and, at first no one could find it. It was Esmeralda who had remembered, only days before the ceremony, that it had been sent to the dry cleaner's, and now here she was, lying in her coffin, looking as if she was all got up for a dinner party, ready, as always, to be fascinated by strangers.

George knelt on the front end of his coffin and blew hard into Frigga's face. He thought he saw a strand of her hair tremble slightly. Not enough for anyone to notice, but if he could make Frigga's heavy tresses move, however slightly, he might get more purchase on Jessica. She had very fine grey hair – usually set by Mabel Dawkins but now combed out nearly straight, accentuating the Native American look she seemed to have developed since death.

The celebrant was going on at length about her arthritis as George made a mental picture of himself as one of those rosy-cheeked spirits shown blowing out the wind in classically themed paintings. He had, suddenly, full red cheeks – as he had had when a boy – and he was puffing as he had on a camping trip, trying to start a fire in some dank field. To his great surprise and joy, it seemed to be working. Jessica's hair stirred slightly and then, responding to the current of the breeze he was generating, blew back against her face, as if she was out walking – which she had loved to do – and raising her head to the thing she had invoked as a familiar god of George's childhood: fresh air. 'You'd be much better off in the fresh air!' and 'What you need is some fresh air!'

Still no one seemed to have noticed. It had taken an age. The celebrant was now trying to find something to say about Frigga – and, having failed miserably, rounded off with a few rhetorical questions: 'Why did she become a librarian? Was she ever really happy? Why did she never find the right person? Why was she murdered in such a brutal and cruel fashion?' George gave it one more push and was rewarded by the sight of the lapel of his mother's jacket rising slightly in the air and falling back to reveal, in her top right-hand pocket, a neatly folded, large sheet of paper.

George was close enough to read a fragment of the word heading the sheet. 'CODIC' was what it said, and he did not need to blow it into exposure any further to know that the missing letters were *I* and *L* and that this was Jessica's addition to her last will and testament. If it hadn't melted in the dry cleaner's, which was presumably where it had been while everyone was looking for it.

Had anyone else seen it? If they hadn't, in about fifteen minutes the codicil was going into the furnace with his mother, and a vital clue as to who stood to gain most from George, Jessica and Frigga's murder would be gone for ever.

It didn't look as if anybody had.

The celebrant had finished with Frigga. He closed with a list of the things Frigga hadn't done – win the egg-and-spoon race at school, publish a novel, pass grade eight on the recorder – with the intention of showing what a plucky spirit she was to have tried and not succeeded at so many things.

The result was merely to make everyone even more aware of how utterly miserable her life had been. Being hanged had, clearly, been the most exciting thing that had happened to her. As the congregation was trying to adjust to this unique dose of misery, Stephen added to the gaiety of the moment by howling like a dog. Lulu clutched his hand and, to George's surprise, his brother pulled it away, slightly petulantly.

He had been fond of Frigga, that must be it; and Lulu was as little interested in her as she was in any other of the Pearmains.

The Prune was brought forward and, accompanied by a long-nosed youth with a portable keyboard, gave them all the benefit of Mozart's 'Laudate Dominum'. If that was what it was. It sounded, to George, more like 'Michael, Row The Boat Ashore'. Barry and Maurice each read a poem. One by Thomas Hardy, the other by Philip Larkin. The Larkin poem had the word 'fuck' in it, which pleased George greatly. Esmeralda started to cry, and George, who could not bear to watch her, started to blow, even harder, at his mother's jacket.

After Barry and Maurice had finished, Stephen came to the front of the chapel and, placing what George thought was a rather patronizing hand on his coffin, began his eulogy.

'A lot of people,' he began, 'have told me I should not do this.'

'My feelings precisely,' said George.

'It is not easy. It is hard. This is my sister. That is my mother. In the box in the middle is my brother. His wife, Esmeralda, my sister-in-law, felt that people would not want to look at his face. I don't know why this was. He was not a good-looking man but I, personally, would have liked us all to have been able to gaze on him. But obviously we cannot do that. As he is in his coffin. That is Esmeralda's right and prerogative. He was my brother but he was also her husband. And, of course, the son of the woman who lies here before me in her coffin. Jessica.'

'Get on with it,' said George.

Stephen, however, did not seem able to get on with it. He was staring down at their mother in what looked like genuine astonishment. He was the one, thought George, who had wanted the poor old thing laid out like a fish on a slab. Was it that the sight of her had woken some genuine regret in the way he had treated her for the last fifteen years of her life? Once Lulu had got hold of him he had never come to see her, never even phoned her for weeks on end. Maybe the sight of her dead face had finally made him realize what he had, or rather had not, done. Perhaps there had been some point to Jessica's will after all. It had been a brutal thing to do but sometimes, in families, brutality is the only way to communicate.

The silence in the chapel continued. Some people, obviously, felt that Stephen was in the grip of a powerful emotion and lowered their eyes tactfully as he stared at the figure of Jessica lying in her box before him. Stephen turned to the congregation.

'I am sorry,' he said, 'but I have to do this.'

With which he reached into the coffin. There was a thrill of horror in the first few rows as he bent over the casket. Could they see him groping for something inside it? Or were they just afraid he was going to pull the corpse out and kiss it, Hamlet-style? Had there been some terrible mistake at the undertaker's and were they, perhaps, trying to fob him off with the wrong body? Eventually his hand emerged clutching a large, official-looking piece of paper.

Outside there was the first growl of thunder. George was not sure who else could see what he was clutching, but he could. It was definitely the codicil to Jessica's will.

Chapter Eighteen

George felt a great deal better after he had been cremated.

It was not what he had expected. He had thought he might find the experience depressing, but it seemed to have the same sort of effect as going to the gym for a workout or trying out one of those diets that are supposed to leave your insides as clean as a new bathroom.

He watched with keen interest as the crematorium staff took the handles off his coffin and slid it into the furnace. He stayed to observe them sifting through what was left of him, picking out the bones and whirling them through something called a cremolator, after which he resembled the kind of thick grained powder that Esmeralda sprinkled on the flowerbeds.

'I can move on,' he said to himself, as he slouched out of the back of the furnace building and wandered through the crowd, inspecting the large number of floral tributes, inscribed with names he did not recognize. 'I'm beginning to develop as a dead person. I've managed to make a limited impact on the physical world. Who knows what lies ahead?'

It was possible, he decided, that death in its early stages was as difficult to deal with as life for a newborn. Death was, as they kept saying in all the Christian bollocks that dealt with the subject, only the beginning. He was a learner – but he was a learner who was, at last, making real progress. He had to put his lack of a future behind him. This was the only way.

His funeral had ended almost as badly as it had begun. Stephen had tried to get his triple eulogy back up to speed but it was clear his heart was not really in it. He had started to talk, for some reason, about George's pension, which was, as far as George could make out, rather better than Stephen's. He was clearly only interested in Jessica's codicil and finding out to whom she had left her money. In fact, as soon as he had finished speaking he went back to his seat, opening the paper in a rather furtive manner, as soon as he had sat down.

What he read did not seem to please him, George thought.

He found himself, as the first few drops of rain started to fall, in the middle of a rather mangy patch of grass. There was a small notice stuck into the earth at the side of it that read 'SCATTERING AREA'. Lulu was standing next to Esmeralda, who was gazing at the notice with a searching, numbed expression.

'Are you going to have George scattered?' Lulu was saying. Esmeralda did not seem to hear her. Lulu was not very interested in the answer anyway. She kept looking at Stephen, who, ever since he had read the codicil, was looking more and more anxious. This codicil business was clearly at the heart of the motive for murdering quite so many members of the Pearmain family. Someone had murdered Jessica. Or, at least, pushed her to the floor so violently it had killed her. Whoever this person was had also killed George and, later, Frigga. It was, thought George, most likely to have been his brother. Stephen, after all, would have come into all Jessica's millions once his sibling had been eliminated. He was perfectly capable of killing George – indeed, as far as George could make out, he had vaguely wanted to do so since prep school. He could quite easily have had a quick look at the will and decided to get rid of all his family in short order.

Points against this argument?

Stephen was fond of Frigga. Not only that: he had a perfect alibi for her murder. He had also, in spite of his appalling behaviour to her, been fond of his mother. Most importantly, however, he would have had to know that the codicil was in his favour, and no one had yet seen it.

He was the prime suspect in this case. No doubt about it. The only argument against his guilt that George could see at the moment was that Stephen and Lulu were apparently absolutely loaded. Did they need a few million quid? Probably not – but, then, rich people always needed more money. The real question was whether Jessica's codicil was, ultimately, in his favour or not.

George had to get a look at it. It was, for the moment, firmly in the inside pocket of Stephen's jacket.

He looked around him, even as he felt, without feeling, more drops of rain on his face. The clouds were rolling in from the south-west with military menace. Geraldine, who had been granted two minutes with Lulu, was dumped at the furthest possible point from anyone she might know, while Lulu returned to bestow the favours of her celebrity on anyone lucky enough to recognize her.

'I hate her,' Rosalina was saying to her mother.

'No, you don't,' Geraldine was replying.

'Yes, I do.'

When he had found out where the money was going, which, as Hobday kept on saying, was the way to approach this case, George was going to start on the heavy-duty ghost action. He was not going to stop at creating a small breeze in the area of his mother's coffin. He was going to go out there and get some answers. After that, he was done with Putney. It was too limited. He had to break out. Where were all the other dead people? Where was Shakespeare? Where was Lenin? Where was Thomas Cromwell? Hadn't he lived in Putney? Why hadn't Robespierre or Richard III popped up to share a few aperçus about the French Revolution or Tudor England? Where was his father? Where was Toby Taylor, that bloke from the NatWest who had jumped in front of a tube train in 1992? George had always wanted to ask him why he had done it. Was it *just* working for the bank for thirty years? Taylor, even badly mangled, would at least be someone to talk to.

'I hope,' Stephen was saying to Uncle Arthur, Cousin Eliza and the Prune, who looked as if she was hoping to get in another few verses of 'Laudate Michael Row The Dominum Ashore', 'you will come back to the house for the, er, funeral baked meats.'

'The house', thought George. He means my house – except that it isn't mine any more, is it? George had always enjoyed playing the host but this did not seem an option as far as his funeral party was concerned. There were going to be no opportunities for him to sing 'The Mountains of Mourne' or do his famous impression of Nick Clegg being buggered by a goat. He was going to have to use the occasion to see if any of the likely suspects betrayed themselves.

Esmeralda had laid in drink so he hoped that someone would let something slip. The key question was, had anyone, apart from him, seen Stephen pocket the piece of paper from Jessica's jacket? Stephen had had his back to the congregation but there must have been someone who...

George stopped. The Mullins woman, a little way from Stephen, Lulu and the rest of them, was looking suspiciously at George's brother. She saw, thought George. *She saw!* Which meant that she would be keeping a close eye on Stephen at the party. His brother did not seem unduly keen to let anyone else know he had found the document for which everyone had been searching. If George was going to get it out to the public he was going to need an ally from the land of the living. As Esmeralda, Barry and Maurice went towards their car, George, with a new sense of purpose, bounced across the grass towards Stephen and Lulu. It was starting to rain harder now and people were shaking out umbrellas and hurrying away from the chapel. Presumably, once his brother and sister-in-law were alone, they would discuss whatever Stephen had seen on the elusive piece of paper.

When George got to the car he found he was reaching for the handle of the rear door, just as he would have done if alive. To his surprise he had the illusion that his hands were closing round the metal, as he heard Stephen click open the central-locking system and, even more surprising, that he was actually opening the door. That it was moving in response to his touch. If this was what was happening then, surely, not only Stephen and Lulu but any number of other observers would have been able to see something extraordinary – a door opening and closing by itself. George could have sworn he heard it snap shut as he settled back in the expensive leather of the rear seat.

Nobody seemed to react. Had anyone seen? Was this purely another illusion generated by a man who was himself an illusion, a shadow of a shadow of a shadow? The story of my life, thought George, as he studied the big, secure, *breathing* forms of his brother and sister-in-law.

'I thought,' said Stephen, as they pulled out of the car park, 'that it went very well.'

How many funerals has he been to? thought George. If

that was his idea of a good one he needs to attend a few more – and soon. It was the worst fucking funeral George had ever been to – and he had been to a few recently. If they ever got round to ranking his Last Rites, it was going to get the kind of reviews handed out to *Mein Kampf* by the *Jewish Chronicle*. There had been moments, back in the crematorium, when he had thought the whole thing was a carefully calculated insult.

They were directly behind Esmeralda, Barry and Maurice, who seemed to be riding with Stephen's first wife and children. Behind them were the Mullins woman, Beryl Vickers and Mabel Dawkins, all of whom seemed to be chatting away with the animation of witches in the throes of a particularly important sabbat. Behind them were Hobday and his wife, a tall, melancholy woman, who did not seem to be talking at all.

'He had no idea, did he, really?' said Stephen.

He was, presumably, referring to George, rather than the celebrant. Unlike George, the celebrant had been his idea. Stephen always liked his own ideas.

'Hopeless,' said Lulu, staring out of the window at the rain, now falling heavily across the two-lane carriageway leading back into town. Suddenly she added, with a contained fury that surprised George, in spite of what he knew about her, 'How could she do that? How could she? What was your mother thinking?' Her face darkened. 'She was senile,' she went on. 'She'd lost her mind. Either that or she wanted to punish you. She always wanted to punish you. And you sat there and took it and let Georgy Porgy be smothered with attention. Mummy and Daddy's darling. Leaving it all to him! And now her! My God! Have you no spine at all? What were you thinking of? And look what she's done now! Look at it!'

She was holding the codicil. George leaned forward and read. It was his mother's usual fluent, slightly gushing style. He could hear her voice in each sentence. However hard Lulu tried to clear the prose from any trace of Jessica as she read, by pert, conspiratorial looks sideways to Stephen, or sometimes with elaborately raised eyebrows and the careful placing of inverted commas round phrases she obviously found absurd, it was Jessica who came through.

'In the event that my eldest son George should die before the wishes expressed in this will are carried out I ask that all my estate be passed to my oldest friend, Audrey Mullins. Mullins has always been a tower of strength to me and I am sure she can be relied on to divide my estate fairly between those who have a claim on it.'

Lulu set the paper on her knee. 'What? What was she thinking?'

'I don't know,' said Stephen. 'I don't know.'

There was another long silence between them. If George was hoping for a Macbeth-style conversation in which they would snarl, gibber and discuss their joint career in murder, he was disappointed. There was something curiously unprivate about their conversation – as if they both suspected they might be being recorded. Sometimes Stephen would look sideways at Lulu, like a rabbit that had just caught sight of a snake it hoped hadn't seen it, but if Lulu registered his nervous glances in her direction she showed no sign of it. When she finally spoke it was in the lazy, composed drawl with which she confronted her wider public.

'Esmeralda didn't look very happy,' she said.

'No,' said Stephen.

'Murdered,' she said. 'I've never heard anything so ridiculous.'

257

'He had a heart attack,' said Stephen. 'He was overweight. He smoked. He drank. He did not go to the gym. I go to the gym.'

'You do, darling,' said Lulu. 'You do.'

That seemed to dispose of George. Their car was turning into Hornbeam Crescent. The rain drummed on the roof. The windows were a field of trickling water; blunt and unfinished rivulets chased each other across the glass. The rain had almost blotted out the house fronts while the street's gutters had been miraculously transformed into reckless mountain streams, brawling their way back down the hill.

'For the moment,' said Lulu, 'I think we should keep this...codicil thing between ourselves.'

'Indeed,' said Stephen. 'Indeed.'

'Mullins,' hissed Lulu. 'Mullins.'

They were almost at the house. Further up the road from a line of cars, double-parked, graceful black shoes poked out into the rain, to be followed by black trousers, black skirts and coats and black umbrellas that flowered under the now torrential rain as the mourners made their way over the jostling waters in the gutter, past the pools on the pavement, up the sodden gravel path and into the hall that would never again be graced by George's heavy footsteps.

George reached forward and pushed against Stephen's shoulder. As he did so the fabric of the jacket yielded to his fingers and, beyond it, he had the uncomfortable illusion that he was penetrating his brother's skin. It broke in ripples around his non-existent flesh so that it seemed he was clawing his way into the very heart of his mother's other son. It was as if he was fitting his shadow into the living form of Stephen, pushing his right arm into his brother's right arm, then the left arm into place and, finally, headbutting his way up through the neck until his temples, burned as they were to ashes, bumped up against the underside of the weaving on his brother's toupee.

For an instant he had the impression of actually being Stephen. He seemed to see Jessica's face, lowering over his, all maternal concern, in what he realized was the bedroom he and his brother had shared until George was in his late teens. Stephen's bed was by the window and he could see the window and the green curtains and, in the other bed, make out the muffled shape of himself.

'You don't have to go to school if you don't want to,' Jessica was saying.

What George felt, and this was the most shocking and surprising thing of all, was anxiety. As he stepped out on to the pavement and trod with the measured authority of his younger brother up to the front door of number twenty-two, he felt terrible fear and guilt, the kind of sensation that floods over you when you realize you have forgotten a vital appointment, or somehow understand that a bitchy remark you made has reached the ears of a friend who was never supposed to hear it. This was Stephen, thought George, as his hand, which seemed to be protruding from a starched shirt cuff that came complete with golden cufflinks, prodded at the Banham lock with a key that might, possibly, once have been his. For a glorious moment his hand was inside Stephen's as it turned the key, and George really thought he was making contact with a real object in real time, making it move all by himself. Then, as Stephen withdrew his arm and pushed open the door, George seemed to see his own phantom shape hanging in the air like a suit of discarded clothes. As he watched, it crumbled before his eyes and, once again, he was no one, nothing, nowhere, a helpless spectator in front of chairs he had once sat in, glasses he had once drunk from, plates and cutlery he had carried

259

backwards and forwards from the dishwasher countless thousands of times.

What about the anxiety he had felt in Stephen, though? Was this his brother's general state? Or was he anxious about something in particular?

Mabel Dawkins, the Mullins woman and Beryl Vickers were all heading for Stephen and Lulu. Lulu – keeping her head down – pushed through to the kitchen, where Esmeralda was spreading pies, sandwiches and big bowls of salad on the side. Doing this, George thought, was calming her. More and more guests were coming through the hall and George found himself still by the front door as Partridge wandered into view.

'Don't tell me to go out,' went on the dog, 'because I'm in.'

'You can do what you like,' said George. 'You're dead. Like me.'

Partridge thought about this for a while. Then he said, 'How was the funeral?'

'Not good,' said George.

Partridge shook his head slowly. 'You couldn't be expected to enjoy your own funeral,' he said. 'It wouldn't be natural!'

'I was actually looking forward to it,' said George. 'God knows why.'

Partridge gave him an accusing look. 'I never got a funeral,' he said. 'I was just burned and put in a large cardboard box which they sent on to you.'

'What about my murder?' said George. 'Did you see who killed me? And if you did, who was it?'

'You you you!' said Partridge. 'It's always about you, isn't it?' He brushed his two huge paws across his eyes with the affecting clumsiness George had always found so appealing. It seemed that George was getting more grip on his after-life. Perhaps he and Partridge were really going to talk

260

about their relationship, not just exchange banalities about Pedigree Chum.

'Well,' said George, 'I think if you'd been murdered you'd want to know more about how it happened. About who did it, for God's sake!'

'I have been thinking,' said Partridge, 'and I may have seen who did it.'

There was a tantalizing pause.

'But I can't actually remember who it was,' he added, sounding, George thought, genuinely contrite. George wondered whether to press him on the subject but he wasn't sure his enquiries would yield anything. Instead, he turned away from the animal and, trying very hard to make his tread (or lack of it) as resonant and real as possible, walked back towards his, yes, *his* kitchen.

The first thing he saw was a group that included Mullins, Vickers, Mabel Dawkins, Stephen and Lulu. Stephen was, quite clearly, trying to separate himself from the Mullins woman, who was standing right at his elbow and peering into his face in a quite threatening manner. Esmeralda, Barry and Maurice were over by the french windows, trying to deal with the press of relatives who were crowding in to be served with food.

'Did you reach in to touch your mother's face?' Mullins was saying to Stephen, 'I thought I saw you do that. I was very moved.'

Stephen looked at Lulu. She looked straight back at him, her face offering no help. She likes to see him beg, thought George. She enjoys watching him flounder because, for some reason, she's disappointed in him. Was this always the case – or had he done something recently to make it so?

'Yes,' said Stephen, 'I did feel the need to, er, touch her one last time. She was a very tactile person. I often used to, er, touch her.'

He started to pat his pockets. He was looking for his phone. He found it. He didn't, this time, take it out and look at it or try to prod it. He just folded his fingers over it and held on to it, the way, George remembered, he had held on to the ragged piece of cloth he'd used as a comforter when he was a small child. George had always teased him about it. In a minute Stephen was going to make some excuse and move away and the moment would be lost. It was crucial that Mullins got to see that codicil.

George ran at his brother in the way he remembered Stephen had once run at him to be picked up in earlier, happier times. He threw himself, full tilt, up into the air and rose effortlessly above the crowd of mourners until he was suspended above Stephen's shoulders; he seemed to have a very precise control of every movement and, though his notional feet were no more than six inches from his brother's upper body, when he lowered himself down through the fabric of his Armani jacket, through his freshly pressed and starched shirt and, from there into the very heart of him, he did so with the force of someone jumping off the high board into a swimming-pool. As he began to course through Stephen's veins, George felt every fragment of him pedal furiously as he drifted downwards through this alien frame. He elbowed his way into his brother's elbows and kneed his way into both of his knees. He seated himself in his brother's buttocks and headed into his head with the force and speed of a great footballer gluing his temples to a ball as he nodded it into the goal mouth. When his fingers wriggled into Stephen's hands, as if they were two gloves, he found, to his surprise and joy, that as he reached the tips he had the real sensation of hitting something. He forced each hand to the lapels of the Armani jacket and flipped them open, as if Stephen was actu-ally – as he might have wanted to do – stripping off his outer garment because of the heat of the room, the press of people or, perhaps, the emotional strain of being at his brother's and sister's and mother's wake.

'What the…' Stephen began. He seemed, as we so often do, to be doing the very thing he least wanted to do. He was flashing his jacket open so that the large piece of paper in the top left-hand interior pocket was suddenly clearly visible to Mullins, who was immediately on his right. Not only that. The paper rode up as George forced his brother's hands wider and wider apart and, though Stephen fought him, George, as he had been in life, was the stronger of the two. He held both arms out as Mullins, reading aloud the obvious word 'CODICIL', reached across and, with astonishing neatness, lifted the paper from its hiding place. In front of George's bewildered sibling and his even more bewildered wife, she read, 'In the event that my eldest son George should die before the wishes expressed in this will are carried out I ask that all my estate be passed to my oldest friend, Audrey Mullins. Mullins has always been a tower of strength to me and I am sure she can be relied on to divide my estate fairly between those who have a claim on it.'

When Mullins had finished reading she looked around the group. Stephen was in a state of complete confusion as his hands were allowed back into his control. He was like a man who had just suffered a stroke. Mullins gave a grim little smile as she turned to her lifelong companion and said, 'I think we'd better hang on to this. Don't you, Beryl?'

Chapter Nineteen

George had not felt the need of a drink since he had breathed his last, but he had experienced an intense longing for what his old friend Dave Macready had always called 'a sharpener' from a fairly early stage of his wake. Dave, from the look of him, had had a few before the thing started.

Almost as soon as Mullins had made her discovery, quite a few other mourners seemed fairly keen on getting totally and utterly plastered. It may not have been what they had come to do. Until the moment when Stephen, for no apparent reason, had thrust open his jacket with the enthusiasm of a flasher putting his equipment on display, everyone had been doing exactly the right mixture of gloom, wistfulness and respect, but from the moment of the reading of the codicil, becoming 'unstuck' – another Macready phrase from his days as the *Daily Express*'s labour correspondent – was the only game in town.

Stephen, George thought, was clearly entitled to a couple of large ones. He had just said goodbye to twelve million pounds. His brother did not attempt to answer Mullins's remark to her companion, but watched her stow the codicil in her handbag with the dull, dawning comprehension of a man watching a traffic accident in which he is the principal player. For a moment, George thought Lulu was going to reach out and snatch it back, but she contented herself with compressing her lips and giving her husband the kind of look that constituted yet another reason for him to reach for a large one.

How this plays out, thought George, is the important thing. Something is sure to happen and I need to be there when it does.

Stephen broke away from the group and headed for the stairs. George followed him and realized, very quickly, that he was looking for something in George's study. For a wild moment he contemplated the possibility that his brother was after some memento of his older sibling, perhaps that photograph of him doing a V sign outside the Vatican with fourteen- and fifteen-year-old Maurice and Barry or even – who knew? – the poem George had written for Stephen in the year he'd married Geraldine. He had shown it to him at the time, and although Stephen hadn't actually said he liked it or was in any way moved by it (he had, as far as George could remember, used the word 'interesting'), it might have grown on him since George had passed over to the other side.

Stephen was actually looking for the whisky.

The half-empty bottle of Famous Grouse was still on the mantelpiece where George had left it on the evening of the Tuesday before he died. He found the sight of it strangely moving. It was only one of a number of things he had left unfinished. The novel about the execution of Charles I – already three hundred pages long, most of which was a description of the King having breakfast. There was that wooden post in the front fence that he had promised Esmeralda he would fix last November. There was the holiday in Morocco, already paid for. George was fairly sure that little things like death due to murder by poisoning were not covered by his insurance.

Somehow, however, that half-empty bottle of Scotch summed up the pointlessness of it all.

No one else in the family drank Scotch. Dave Macready drank Scotch but George could not imagine a situation in which Esmeralda bequeathed it to him. He was probably one of the many people she would never see again now George was dead. Not that she disliked him – she didn't – but they simply didn't have enough reason to stay in touch. If Stephen hadn't located it (he had now picked it up and taken a deep draught straight from the bottle), it would have stayed on the mantelpiece for at least a year, and then, one day, when Esmeralda was, hopefully, starting to recover, she would have taken it downstairs to tip it away and, perhaps, be reminded of things her husband would do before pouring himself a large one.

Of how he used to talk, in slightly sententious tones, about the cruelty and horror of the world beyond his comfortable suburb. Or analyse the faults of his friends or try to find virtue in his enemies. Or sing those Irish songs he loved so well – 'The Mountains of Mourne' especially because its sentimental, *faux*-naïf view of exile (written as it was by a fairly sophisticated journalist about a simple country boy) expressed his own hopeless feeling of estrangement from the world around him. He had always, he now saw clearly, absurd as it seemed, felt exiled in the land of his birth. He had never really been the plump, comfortable Englishman he had seemed to be.

She would put the bottle into the recycling because she was a well-trained suburbanite like him and perhaps cry a very little bit – tears that are only the slight weeping that accompanies grief changing to sadness and the realization that life must, somehow, begin again.

Lulu had appeared at the door, just as Stephen took

another swig.

'Come downstairs,' she said. 'Now! We have to do something about this.'

Stephen took another drink. 'I'm sure you'll think of something, dear,' he said, with an undertone of violence that surprised George. He had never thought his brother fought back against Lulu. She had a glass of white wine in her hand and she, too, took a deep draught of it as Stephen sat, heavily, at George's desk.

As a junior reporter, she had been a legendary drinker. She had famously done an interview with a celebrated alcoholic that had ended with the two of them crawling around the studio on all fours, barking like dogs. She had been one of the instigators at that famous night at the Labour Party Conference in 1982 that was later dubbed by the media 'Projectile Vomiting Gate'. George had never seen her in serious drink before. There was, of course, something intimidating about the way she'd rapped out her order for a glass of champagne on the rare occasions when he and Stephen, Esmeralda and Lulu had found themselves in the same restaurant but, on the whole, there was something terrifyingly controlled about the way she absorbed alcohol.

Not today. As she came into the room George realized she was carrying a full bottle of Chardonnay. She finished her glass and poured herself more as, with a hard glitter in her eye, she said, 'What on earth was that display about? Were you having a fit?'

'I don't know,' said Stephen. 'I don't know what happened. It was like I was...like I was...' He looked dully at his hands, as if they did not belong to him.

'Drunk?' said Lulu, taking another swig of wine. She gave him a look of pure dislike.

'We'd better get back downstairs,' said Stephen, eventually.

267

Then, in a voice that displayed some of the real terror George had felt in him as they'd come into the wake, he whispered, 'It was like I was being taken over by something. Or somebody.'

'If ever I suspect an alien intelligence is trying to take over my mind or my body,' said Lulu, 'I tell it to fuck off. I suggest you do the same. We have to do something about this, Stephen. And if you won't, then I will. I do just about everything else around here, don't I? Jesus!'

She turned to go out of the room and Stephen followed her. As they came down the stairs, Mabel Dawkins staggered out of the kitchen. She, too, had located a bottle. Her drink of choice seemed to be vodka. It was only a half-bottle but she had already drunk three-quarters of it.

'I wouldn'ta minded someone leavin' me a windersill!' she said to Lulu, in a way that suggested she thought Lulu had had something to do with her mother-in-law's surprise bequest. 'I done a lot for Mrs Pearmain. I done a lot. 'Er fam'ly never bothered ter show up to take 'er to the Falls Class or organize the Zimmerman. Where was they when she fell off of the sofa I'd like ter know? In the Soufa France was where they was. Drinkin' Pasty in one of them caffs!'

Stephen pushed past Lulu to confront his mother's former carer. Some of the hostility he had clearly felt towards Lulu but seemed frightened to express came out in his tone, the one he had used when trying to shut up unruly panellists on the current-affairs show he had hosted in days gone by. 'Look, Mabel,' he said. 'None of us are very happy about the decision my mother seems to have made, without consulting any of us – except, possibly, George – but in your case I would remind you that you were well paid for what you did. I am fairly well known in my business. I am known. In the media world. If I could have earned as much as I do taking my mother on and off the lavatory perhaps I would have

268

done it. We live in a business environment, Mabel. Money is the bottom line. If you did not want to do what you did, you need not have done it. We would have found someone else.'

'Someone black, prob'ly,' said Mabel, with utter contempt. 'One of them Similians. With 'oom you is so sympathetic. You never bin down the fuckin' Social, 'ave you, and seen 'em claimin' benefit? Benefit! Loadsa benefit! I never got no benefit. I got nice middle-class people like you and George an' yore mum promisin' me a nice little windersill. Then she goes and 'ands it to that lesbian! You go down the Social, mate, an' take a look at them Similians spittin' on the English white workin'-class people such as myself. And now she gives it to that fuckin' lesbian an' 'er mate.'

Unknown to Dawkins, Mullins and Vickers had come out from the kitchen and were standing directly behind her.

'I shouldn't be surprised if they did away wiv 'er,' she went on. 'They spit on decent people like myself and I spit on them.' With which she spat juicily on the first step of the stair carpet.

Lulu took another drink of Chardonnay and pushed past Stephen. For a moment George thought she was about to hit Mabel, but then, in a rare moment of solidarity with Esmeralda, she confined herself to saying, 'You are spitting on Jessica's daughter-in-law's carpet, Mabel – and, if you have any points to make to Audrey Mullins, I suggest you make them to her directly. She is standing right behind you.'

Lulu added a smile of staggering insincerity in the vague direction of Mullins and Vickers, who were both clutching glasses of lemonade. Mullins did not acknowledge this attempt to placate her. Drawing the codicil from her handbag she hissed at everyone in her line of vision, 'None of you understood Jessica. Jessica was a saint. A saint. She and Vickers and I went walking in the Lake District. Just a stick and a bag and a sandwich and a beret. That is all you need.'

All you need for what? thought George. He had, from time to time, accused his mother, in a jocular kind of way, of being a lesbian. She had not seemed in any way offended by the accusation, simply taking it as another example of her elder boy's unhealthy obsession with sex. She had confessed to reading *The Well of Loneliness* as a young woman and finding it 'disturbing', although she refused, in spite of pressure from George, to amplify this remark. She was a woman whose primary friendships and loyalties were to her own sex. It was possible, he decided (although was this just another example of his wanting to think well of a woman who had, it was true, favoured him at the expense of her other children?), that Jessica really had thought Mullins would see fair play done because Stephen or certainly Lulu might have made sure that most of the money came to them. There was no way of knowing that now – or, indeed, of working out what Mullins and Vickers were going to do with twelve million smackers.

'She loved you all,' Mullins went on. 'She was a wonderful mother. She believed in the things all our generation believed in.'

'Fascism?' said Stephen, with a flash of his wittier, pre-Lulu self. 'The Anglican Church? The British Empire?'

'Fresh air,' said Mullins, to a determined sequence of nods from her friend. 'Fresh air. We had no television. Jessica was the first person in her street to have a telephone. It was kept in the hall behind a green baize curtain and people came in to look at it. There were no motorways. No internet. You have no idea. No idea.'

It was possible, thought George, that she was going to give the dosh to the National Trust. Although things were not supposed to get any worse when you were deceased, this could be a sign they were about to do just that. The National Trust! The Wehrmacht in green wellies. He would rather Stephen and Lulu got their hands on it – which, from the look of them, was exactly what they were about to try to do. Lulu was still smirking at Vickers, clearly having decided she had a better chance with the more passive of the two women, but Mullins was already turning away and heading back into the kitchen.

'We're going to get some fresh air,' she said, with some severity. 'I think we all need clear heads at this moment.'

Mabel Dawkins, who really was very drunk indeed, followed her. Stephen and Lulu stayed in the hall.

'Well,' said Lulu, 'that was telling them, wasn't it? When in doubt, Stevie, pick on the cleaner.'

'What are you going to do?' said Stephen. There was a pleading note in his question, as if he thought Lulu might be about to dash into the garden and start to strangle Mullins and her partner.

'I'm going to get this sorted,' she said. 'I'm going to have a word with the Mullins woman and let her know that, as immediate family, we have certain rights, certain legal rights, in Jessica's estate, and I for one am not going to lie back and let her give it all to a dogs' home!'

No one, thought George had, so far, mentioned a dogs' home. Did Lulu know something he did not?

Lulu shouldered her way into the kitchen. Stephen stood there for a moment peering at his hands. He flexed the fingers. He seemed surprised they responded to him. Then he sat heavily on the first step of George's staircase and took another long swig of the whisky. 'Jesus!' he said to himself, quietly. 'Oh, Jesus Christ! What have I done?'

George had absolutely no idea what he was talking about.

271

After a while his brother got up and wandered back into the kitchen. Perhaps he, too, was in search of fresh air. George thought he ought to go and follow some, or all, of his principal suspects but just as he was about to do so Esmeralda came in and sat down exactly where Stephen had been sitting. Her eyes were red but she had not been crying. She looked blank, empty, and as if she wished all these people would go away. She had made them sandwiches and now she wished they would all go away. She had often, George reflected, felt like that at parties they had given when he had been alive.

Was he condemned to spend all eternity in 22 Hornbeam Crescent? Was he not to be spared the sight of her growing older and more infirm? Of listening helplessly to Barry and Maurice argue about whether or not to put her into a home? Was he going to round the corner of the living room in 2040 to be greeted by Esmeralda's ghost? Would the two of them have to gnash their teeth as newcomers painted over Esmeralda's carefully chosen wallpaper and put in a panic room to replace George's study?

He fought off the idea of eternal death – almost as depressing as eternal life – and tried to savour the moment. To be glad that he could still see the woman he had loved in a way he could never have loved anyone else. He must make the most of such moments. Like hair and nails growing post mortem, George's consciousness had lingered on a while but at any moment it could be snuffed out for – of this he was sure – it hung by an even finer thread than had his happy, undistinguished life.

They had been, on the whole, happy, he and Esmeralda. If he could make his dead mother's hair move or occupy, however briefly, the living body of his brother, surely he could let his widow know he was still there. That he was not gone

for good. That he could see her – even if he could not touch
or taste or smell her – and that he still loved her, had always
loved her, loved her more now he was dead than when he
was alive and had been so easily distracted by the vulgar
business of surviving. By things such as…er…Biskiborne.

His betrayal of Esmeralda still caused him pain, however
long ago it was. If only he had told her about it. At least then
she would have had the choice to stay with him or leave. As
it was she was carrying around a false memory. A memory of
a good man who, whatever his faults, had always been true
to her. He had not been true to her. Or to anyone. Not to his
youthful ideals of justice for all and a world not dominated
by money and greed – the world that his children had inher-
ited precisely because of the laziness and moral cowardice of
his generation.

He sat next to her on the first step of the stair. 'Esmeralda,'
he said softly, 'it's me. It's George.'

She didn't look up. She was staring at the floor, an
untouched glass of wine in her hand. They had quite a large
house, and after the children had left he would quite often
call out to her and find she had not heard. As he had often
done in life, he carried on anyway, as if she could hear him.

'Look,' he said, 'I don't think I can have been an easy
person to live with. I didn't listen. For more than forty years
you gave me good advice and I never listened. I didn't appreciate you. I didn't realize how lucky I was. You were…'

He was about to use words like 'honest' and 'faithful'
and 'sexy' and 'wise' and 'passionate' and, most of all, 'true'
because that seemed to sum her up, but he knew he was
never going to say them now as he had never done in life.
There is never enough saying you love the people you love
and never enough of the circumstances that don't make such
declarations sound false or self-seeking or just plain cheesy.

And, for sure, thought George, saying them when you're dead is completely fucking pointless.

'Oh, George,' said Esmeralda. 'Oh, George! George! George!'

That seemed to sum it up really. Tristan and Isolde. Romeo and Juliet. George and Esmeralda. He was dead. That made it really romantic.

She got up wearily and clumped her way back into the kitchen. When George caught up with her, he saw that the party seemed to have got larger and more boisterous since it had begun. Did people gatecrash wakes? It rather looked as if they had been doing just that. In the far corner he spotted a couple in slightly modified mourning outfits. His suit and her dress were not quite black and the pair looked as if they might be funeral groupies, people who donned black ties and went out looking for free sandwiches in the homes of the recently bereaved.

It was only when he noticed the size of the feet that George realized these two might be part of a police operation. Hobday, who had been talking to Esmeralda with tact and a gentle sympathy that George really appreciated, moved away from her and made his way over to them. He spoke very quietly to the woman, who, only now, George saw was none other than DC Purves. He had not recognized her.

'Something,' he said, 'is going to go off soon. They are mullahed beyond belief. Try to keep an eye on our suspects.' He lowered his voice. 'Particularly Mr Pearmain's brother. We had the results of the bank checks earlier today. It seems there is a very big hole in young Stephen's account. Do not let him out of your sight.'

'Will do, Boss,' said Purves. 'What about Dawkins?'

'I like her for it as well as I ever did,' said Hobday. 'Keep a close eye on her. It seems she has quite a lot of previous. A brother who fell under a lorry in suspicious circumstances.'

Suspects! Mabel Dawkins's behaviour was, thought George, enough to qualify her as head of that particular field. She had opened the french windows and was leaning against them, drinking something straight out of the bottle that George recognized as a 1961 Pomerol he had been keeping for a Christmas he would never see. It did not seem to impair the flavour, as far as she was concerned.

The rain was coming in against the windows in great spiky gusts blown across the large, wild garden, lashing the fruit trees, drumming against the wooden walls of the shed and rattling across the surface of the pond with the efficiency of a Gatling gun. At the far end of the garden, past the line of fruit trees, the poplars and the waste ground beyond them were all but blotted out by the sweeping field of water.

'Rain on!' she shouted out to the darkened garden. 'Rain on, Macbeth! What do I care? I bin thrown out like a used condominium. What do I know abaht the finer thingsa life, eh? All I'm good for is wipin' your mum's bum!' She leaned out into the darkness, feeling the rain on her face. The late-September light was almost gone. On the distant horizon of the suburb, lightning flickered as more rain came and the noise of the thunder grew ever closer. Mabel staggered out on to the patio, waving George's bottle of Pomerol at the furious waters and the darkening sky.

'Blow, winds, and crack your arse'oles!' she yelled. 'Fart, winds! Fart! She used ter fart. I've never 'eard anyone fart as long or as loud as the late Mrs Pearmain. I used to 'ide be'ind the livin'-room door an' watch 'er. Long, loud, crackly farts. That was 'er. For all 'er piano teachin'. She wasn't too posh to 'ave wind, was she? Wind! Wind! Wind!'

She was in the middle of the patio now, swinging George's precious bottle of claret round her head. For a moment he thought she was about to hurl it up at the windows of the house but then she thought better of it. She peered myopically at the label on the bottle, uttered three words, with supreme contempt, then turned on her heel and marched off into the dark spaces of the garden. 'Beaujolais!' she said. 'Fuckin' Beaujolais!'

Stephen went to the door and, quietly, closed it. George noticed DC Purves move over to him as he walked back into the press of people, now all, as far as George could make out, incredibly drunk. You would have thought that a person without substance, such as he was, would have found it easy to move through the packed crowd but that did not seem to be the case. As George forced his way through, he seemed to be brought up uncomfortably close to each sweating, shouting face and, though this was not, of course, possible, to be pushed and jostled by those who had come to pay their respects to him in a way that was thoroughly unpleasant.

Maybe his increasing control over the world around him was having side effects. Or, rather, perhaps the control was merely a symptom of something rather more sinister. Maybe soon he would start to have sensations – heat, cold, the air on his face. Maybe he was about to live again! The thought of being reborn was frightening. Perhaps he had already been reborn. Or, at least, was moving towards being involved with something along those lines. The Buddha, from what little George could remember of him, had had quite a number of previous lives and, though George's recall of this was hazy in the extreme, took the view that the object of a good and spiritual life was to stop being born again.

This seemed thoroughly sensible. One life was enough for anyone, wasn't it?

Was he perhaps one of the guests at his own funeral? It presumably would take a bit of time to realize that that was so. As far as George could recall, it had taken the Buddha some considerable time to figure out he had once been someone else. You couldn't just segue neatly from George Pearmain into, say, Sam Dimmock the gay dentist and if he was Sam Dimmock the gay dentist he—

My God! Surely he wasn't Sam Dimmock the gay dentist. He very much did not want to be Sam Dimmock the gay dentist. He would have to have sex – oral and anal sex – with Sam's boyfriend, the retired BBC producer Mike Larner. Even worse he would have to say things like 'I love you, Mike. I want to hold you and care for you.' This was insupportable. George was not prejudiced. He liked gay men fine. He just did not want to be one. Not just yet anyway.

Sam Dimmock was over in the corner, talking to a small man whom George couldn't remember ever having met.

'George,' the small man was saying, 'was one of my dearest friends. My very dearest friends.'

'He was,' said Sam Dimmock the gay dentist, 'a truly great bank manager.' George had, he recalled, once lent him thirty thousand pounds of NatWest's money. Those were the days. George was pretty sure he couldn't be Sam Dimmock. Sam Dimmock was right there in front of him saying the kind of things Sam Dimmock usually said. He would know if George had interfered with him.

Except you probably didn't realize you were someone else until it was too late. There wasn't much of the original G. Pearmain left. Maybe this was the moment at which it all dribbled away into the consciousness of a gay dentist. In a desperate attempt to hang to what might, possibly, be left of his original self, George swayed nervously towards Nat Pinker and Dave Macready. They were standing apart from the crowd, having the kind of conversation that George felt might get him back on the rails. They were nodding in a measured, blokey way that might provide reassurance he was not about to turn into someone else.

There was not much to choose between him and Nat. They were pretty much the same in all respects. If one of them had transmigrated into the soul of the other no one would be any the wiser.

'I think,' he heard Nat say, in his amazingly reassuring doctor's voice, 'that actually George probably did die of a heart attack. The hemlock was a factor. Sure. Hemlock is not the kind of stuff you want to quaff in large quantities but George was an accident waiting to happen, really – bless him. I don't think the hemlock did any more than tip him over the edge.'

'Right,' said Macready, nodding eagerly – a technique he had evolved over years in the newspaper business to get more and more out of his interviewees or, as he often used to call them, 'his victims'. 'I imagine they'll be wanting to call you in as a defence witness if they ever bring his murderer to trial.'

Nat laughed amiably, even though he was aware of Macready's slight look to the left as if to say, 'Get this guy! Get a load of this guy!' 'Fair point,' he said. 'Fair point.'

Already George felt better but, even as he regained his bearings and reminded himself that he regarded the teachings of the Buddha to be almost as suspect as those of every great religious leader ever born, he realized he had lost sight of all his targets. He could not see Stephen. He could not see Mabel Dawkins. Was she still out in the garden? Was Stephen with her? He looked around wildly and saw, sitting on her own, on a chair by the wall the disconsolate figure of Beryl Vickers. From time to time she peered into the darkness outside. Perhaps, thought George, she was about to follow her companion's recipe for health and happiness and go out into the torrential rain and menacing, ceaseless wind for a bit of fresh air. It was only when he got right up to her that he heard what the gentle soul was saying. She was whispering, to no one in particular, that her friend Audrey Mullins had gone missing.

She wasn't in the upstairs loo. She hadn't gone out to the Morris Minor because Beryl had looked there. She hadn't crept into George's bedroom for a little nap, although that would have been only too understandable, given the noise. Beryl had seen her go out into the garden and she had said she herself would not go out into the garden and Audrey had said she would be back in a minute but she hadn't come back in a minute and it was too rainy and windy and dark for Beryl to go out there and if Audrey was in the garden why, please, hadn't she come back? Please?

There was only one other person whom George knew to be out in the garden and that was Mabel Dawkins. With the strong feeling that the evening was about to reveal some terrible new crime and that he, poor ghost, was already too late to do anything about it, George made his way through the glass and out into the wild night.

Chapter Twenty

At least half of the gathering had, at one stage or another, wandered out to, literally, drink in the item in question. At one stage Nat and Veronica Pinker had stood for a few minutes in the torrents of water, lifting their faces to the brooding sky. Esmeralda had stretched out her arms as the rain cascaded down, plastering her hair across her face, her dark eyes suddenly alive again, the water causing her black dress to cling to her shoulders and breasts, making George painfully aware of one thing he was never going to be able to do again.

Although...It had taken him some time to learn to create a small breeze, then operate his brother's hands and play him as if he were some kind of industrial digger, but he had got there eventually. In time it was possible he would graduate to full-on ghostly intercourse; beyond the grave, he reflected, he might even become a truly sensitive lover. At least he was not going to get complaints about his belly pinning Esmeralda to the floor.

Maurice and Barry, both completely drunk, had been out in the rain as well, singing an impromptu song of their own devising. They both had good tenor voices. It went – as far as George could make out: 'George...George...where are you? Who's going to buy us Chinese meals?'

Now the garden was empty. It was pitch black. The

distant flickers of the lightning had stopped and, as George
made his way on to the lawn beyond the patio, where no one
had yet ventured, he could hardly make out the trellis that
separated the more cultivated section of the garden from the
area Esmeralda had planned as an English meadow. Its long
grass, studded with poppies in the summer months, had the
look in June and July of a Renoir canvas in which beautiful
girls in blue dresses stand out like flowers in a sea of sunlight
and delicate green.

The grass was tangled now. There were brambles among
it, drooping and wilting in the rain, and the statue of the
boy with the anchor, described by Barry and Maurice as
'Paedophiles Ahoy!', was leaning at a drunken angle, almost
obscured by giant weeds and hollyhocks that had come
from nowhere and were thriving in the way of unwanted or
unbidden plants. As he waded through the meadow, George
once more had the eerie feeling that the wet grass was
clinging to his legs and that his phantom limbs, like those of
a recent amputee, were still capable of evoking the cruelly
vivid sensation that they were real.

Beyond the disorderly meadow was the long trellis
of roses, white on one side and red on the other, that had
wound themselves into each other, like lovers. The roses
were now as dead as George was. Their heads battered by
the rain, they nodded restlessly like old men in a closed ward,
dreaming of a life that would not come again. Beyond them
was a wide area of scrub grass, a half-hearted row of potatoes and beans, begun by Esmeralda some years ago, and
beyond that, standing just before the fence on a patch of
bald earth, the codicil still clutched in her hand, was Audrey
Mullins, breathing in deeply, as she must have done years
ago on the slopes of Scafell Pike with Jessica, Beryl and other
energetic young women of the generation that had helped to

281

take once-glorious Britain through two wars and the loss of its empire. Looking at her standing there in the rain, George was reminded of how fucking amazing the women of that time were. Christ! If Jessica had married his father a mere ten years earlier, all her property would have been his by law. There was something, he decided – a little too late as usual – rather magnificent about her.

He noticed two other figures in this abandoned section of the garden. One was Mabel Dawkins. She was standing – but only just. As George watched, she waved her now empty bottle of Pomerol at Mullins, who looked back at her with a mixture of puzzlement and dislike; but George did not pay much attention to Mullins. He was more interested in the tall figure standing some ten or fifteen yards from the newly enriched Audrey. It was Lulu. She was talking to Mullins but Mullins was not answering.

'Listen,' Lulu was saying, 'what you have to understand is that Stephen and I have certain rights. Stephen was Jessica's son. I don't have to remind you of that I'm sure and—'

'She told me you'd swallowed him whole,' said Mullins, 'that you'd treated her with contempt. That he never called or came to see her. That she felt she had lost him. That was what she told me.'

'Listen,' said Lulu, with weary patience. 'All I'm saying is that you do not have the right to—'

'I have the right to tell you the truth,' said Mullins. 'I have the right to tell you that you tried to come between a son and his mother. I have a right to tell you that you have given up all your rights to any money from the Pearmain family.'

'The Pearmains,' said Lulu, with drawling, slow contempt. 'I'm sick and bloody tired of hearing about the fucking Pearmains!'

There was a hint of Geordie in her voice, thought George.

More than a hint. A suggestion of London Geordie about her – the sort of person who likes to go on about the ship-yards and the Blaydon Races and the canny lads and the Northumbrian pipes and the Jarrow march and the whole cosy package of safely dead working-class triumphs but is also clever (or canny) enough to make sure they live a few hundred miles further south. She was a fucking Geordie! Who'da thought it?

'Please do not use foul language to me,' said Mullins.

She was, thought George, more than a match for Lulu. If she had ever sat on Lulu's knee, on or off screen, Belhatchett would never have got up.

'I will use any language I like,' said Lulu, 'and you had better understand you are not dealing with one of the Pearmains now. You are dealing with Lulu Belhatchett. Have you any idea of who I am? I am Lulu Belhatchett.'

'Never heard of you,' said Mullins, with a touch of play-ground bravado.

George thought it possible that, at any moment, she might apply the tip of her right thumb to her nose and waggle her four fingers derisively at the former presenter of *Come Sit On My Knee*.

'I have been on national television,' Lulu went on. 'I have written articles for the *Radio Times*. I am a fairly well-known person. And if I decide to go for you in the media, Miss Mullins, you will know about it and it will not be very pleasant.'

Dawkins was looking very wobbly indeed. She was swaying so violently that, in George's view, it would not be long before she collapsed. In fact, as he watched, she did just that. She pointed one index finger at Mullins and said, in a low, throaty voice, 'You owe me two million quid,' and fell backwards into the mud. For a moment, George took his eyes off Lulu, who continued to talk to Mullins in a voice that was all the more frightening for never being raised above her normal, beautifully elocuted, reasonable level.

That was not the most frightening thing about her, though. The most frightening thing about her was that she had just produced, from her large and elegant handbag, a wicked-looking carving knife that she was holding, out of sight, down by her right leg, as she talked on and on and on about her many friends in the world of media, politics and sport. Mullins did not seem to have noticed it – or, if she had, she was an even cooler ninety-four-year-old than George had thought her to be.

George recognized the knife. He had carved a few turkeys with it in his time. He had bought it for Esmeralda five years ago, at Christmas, and had often spoken of the sharpness of its blade, its heavy, reliable quality as he wielded it over a joint of beef or a slab of pork belly, decorated with crackling. Lulu was fingering it as she talked, moving it this way and that in the darkness. She looked as if she had more than basic knife-fighting skills.

Mabel Dawkins was not, George saw, going to provide anything in the way of eyewitness testimony of what he was afraid was about to happen. He was going to have to do something. But what?

Without thinking he ran at her, hoping for the same kind of reaction he had got when he tried the trick on his brother, but instead of landing in her body he seemed to skid through her and come out the other side, yards away, in the rain and the darkness and the wind. Perhaps his earlier trick only worked with blood relatives. With a mounting sense of panic he ran at her again, this time waving his arms, letting out the kind of noise that would have generated near panic even among hardened members of the Psychical Research

Society, but Lulu paid no attention whatsoever. She went on talking in the same quiet, deadly, reasonable voice, all the time moving closer and closer to Mullins, who still, as far as George could see, had no idea of what was about to happen to her.

He tried blowing. He tried making faces. He tried visualizing himself appearing to her as a skeleton. He tried calling her name in a deep and thoroughly spooky voice. Nothing. He was the only witness to what he was now sure was going to be another murder, and there was nothing he could do about it. Who would be able to hear what he had to say? He was gone. He was dead, burned to ashes and scattered. He was a person completely without influence.

Lulu moved forward again. It was then that George remembered the video camera. He had bought it for the holiday he and Esmeralda, Barry, Maurice and their families had taken last year. They had used it only six months ago, when they took Bella Ella and Ella Bella to Peppa Pig World in some God-forsaken theme park off the M27. It worked. George had learned how to use it in order to get a shot of Bella Ella and Ella Bella trying to stroke a more than life-size sculpture of Peppa Pig, and later, an image of him eating a ham sandwich and making his abattoir face.

Not only did he know how to use it. He knew how to adapt it for night shooting. Maurice and Barry had been amazed by his skill and persistence. The only trouble was that, so far, he had not shown any skill whatsoever in the reliable standby of the departed: trying to make themselves noticed by moving of solid objects. He was not, almost certainly, he felt, a poltergeist.

He might, however, have poltergeist potential. You didn't know until you'd tried.

George turned away from Lulu and Mullins and thought,

very, very hard, about the camera. It was in the bottom right-hand drawer of his desk. He could see the desk. His Apple Mac – switched off – stood in a sea of papers. A letter from Her Majesty's Revenue and Customs. A mortgage leaflet from some company he had used to help Barry and Maurice with their houses, in which a boy of about fourteen, flanked by a woman who was obviously supposed to be his mother, gazed with adoration at a man, who was, perhaps, supposed to be his father but emerged, in George's twisted imagination, as a sexual predator from the building society. His desk diary still open at the week he had died. He had been meant to have lunch with Dave Macready on the very day he'd bowed out of membership of the human race. The top left-hand drawer was open. He had kept his medicines in there and a packet of twenty-eight Atorvastatin tablets was clearly visible. A little late to be worrying about his cholesterol.

He saw all these familiar objects very, very clearly and, miraculously, as he summoned them to mind he found he was himself – at least the poor fragmented pieces of nothing that was himself, these days – sitting in his familiar black-leather chair. He had travelled to his study in less than a second. That was good because there was not much longer than seconds before Lulu got to work on Audrey Mullins with the carving knife.

The bottom right-hand drawer of his desk was closed.

George tried to concentrate on the idea of it being open. He concentrated very hard. He visualized it sliding back just far enough to show him where the camera was lying and then he visualized the camera rising of its own accord and floating round the room. In the films he had seen about poltergeists this sort of thing happened with alarming frequency. In fact, he was slightly worried that he might not see other things flying round the room. The picture of his father, for example, on the mantelpiece. His HP Laserjet printer. The chair in the corner that Esmeralda – bless her – had bought him in case he needed to talk to people about his poetry. He had never needed to talk to anyone about his poetry. And now he seemed incapable of getting the fucking thing to rise even a quarter of an inch off his polished wooden floor. If he was a poltergeist he was a very low-grade one.

'Why,' he heard himself say, in a voice he could not believe was inaudible to any living person, 'can I not just reach out and get my fingers round that little brass handle and pull it and...Jesus Christ!'

He was pulling open the drawer. It was opening. There, below him, was the small black Panasonic with which he had achieved that memorable handheld tracking shot round the massive statue of Peppa Pig. Without even thinking George reached down and picked up the camera – just as he realized someone was in the room with him.

It was Nat Pinker. He was, George thought, as drunk as he had ever seen him. Just behind him was Dave Macready.

There was no time to lose. There was a tripod next to the camera. He would need that as well. George lifted them both, walked over to the window with them and, using the same time-honoured technique as before – the stretching out of the hand, the thoughtless application of finger to object, the *grip* for God's sake! – he pulled up the sash. Then, camera and tripod in hand, he swung one ghostly foot over the sill and sat astride it for a moment. Lulu and Mullins seemed to be in the same position as they had been when he left them.

'I think,' he heard Nat say to Dave, as he flew down through the rainy night, 'I've drunk too much. I'm seeing things.'

'What things?' said Dave.

'I think I saw George's video camera fly through the air

of its own accord,' said Nat, in a thick, slurred voice, 'and the window over there slide open as if some – some hand was...I...'

'Maybe,' said Dave, in the confidential tones of the very, very drunk, 'it's George. Maybe he's come back to film his own wake.'

'Maybe he has,' said Nat. 'He was always keen on home movies, wasn't he? Some of his work in that area was brilliant. That one of them peeing off that cliff in Sardinia was astonishing. Professional standard.'

George landed by the party wall between his and the next-door property. Lulu was still talking, in that low, reasonable voice.

'You do not seem to grasp who I am, Miss Mullins. I have written for *Highlife* magazine. I am a Notable Person of Great Britain. There has been talk of my being awarded an OBE. And you have the nerve to spout the ridiculous opinion of some half-baked little piano teacher – I mean, ask yourself, Mullins, my dear, what was Jessica? What was she really? What did she amount to? Really? Her and her darling fatty Georgy Porgy pudding and pie, my God!'

The camera was almost in place. George, whose hypothetical fingers seemed to be working with the practised assurance of real ones, had fixed it on the tripod at about his eye level.

'You are a disgusting person, Lulu,' Mullins was saying. 'You are an example of all that is wrong with Great Britain. Celebrity culture! My God! Reality television! In my day we went to bed with a good book after a nice walk in the fresh air!'

Lulu's fingers twitched on the handle of the carving knife. George remembered something Esmeralda had said about the instrument in the year when they'd got hold of a rather disappointing turkey. 'It makes slicing through the toughest of old birds remarkably easy.' He worked hard at the controls as Lulu, who was now up close to Mullins, with the knife held behind her back, hissed at the old woman, in an accent that was now as heavily folk Geordie as that of the man who sang that appalling song about having a fishy on a little dishy. 'You're a southern snob, you are. Like all the fucking Pearmains. You have no idea what it is to fight for every penny you can get your hands on. You're a fucking lezzer into the bargain, aren't you? You're a muff-diver, you old twat, aren't you? Eh?'

Was it too dark to film? Just as George was thinking this, the moon came out from behind the clouds and there, as he pressed PLAY and the red recording light came on, through the viewfinder he saw, in mid to long shot, Lulu lift out the carving knife, hold it above her head in triumph then bring it down hard into Mullins's neck. The old woman did not see the blade before it bit into her flesh. Then, with a savagery that astonished George, his ex-sister-in-law cut, again and again, into Mullins's body. In her gut. Through her ribs. Finally, as she pulled the knife clear there was a slashing blow across the throat and the ninety-four-year-old lesbian staggered backwards into the muddy earth, falling, as Mabel Dawkins had just fallen, as the rain fell, regardless. George had thought the blood would spurt out of her neck in a fountain but Lulu must have missed the artery. Even the last blow across her neck left no more than a thin line across Mullins's elaborately wrinkled skin, as pouched and loose as a tortoise's.

Perhaps there was not much blood in the old woman. As she lay there in the wet earth George thought he saw her chest heave once or twice, but then the moon went behind the clouds and it was dark once more and Mullins was as still as the earth on which she lay.

Lulu – to George's surprise – had not a trace of blood on her. She stood over the corpse, completely calm, and wiped the handle of the carving knife carefully with a tissue she produced from her handbag. Then, with the same ease and assurance, she crossed to the prone figure of Mabel Dawkins, slipped the knife into her right hand and stood back to admire her handiwork. The codicil was still in Mullins's fist. Again, with great precision and care, Lulu, wrapping her hand in tissue paper first, smeared blood from the blade of the carving knife across Mabel Dawkins's sodden dress. Then, satisfied, she took one more look at the two supine figures, straightened herself up, took a vanity mirror from her bag and, in her own time, made her way carefully back down the garden.

When she got to the patio there were two or three mourners standing out in the night but none of them seemed to see her. Moving still with the grace and precision she had employed to such good effect on 321 walk-downs in front of the studio audience for *Come Sit On My Knee* she re-entered society. By the time she reached the hall, where Stephen was slumped on the lower stairs, his head in his hands, she seemed no more than slightly damp.

Chapter Twenty-one

One thing was clear about this. George was no nearer to knowing who had poisoned him. There had been a moment, out there in the garden, when he had wondered whether Stephen and Lulu might be some kind of double-act along the lines laid down by Mr and Mrs Cawdor. They played golf together. They played bridge together. Perhaps they also committed atrocious murders together. But Lulu had been in Basingstoke on the night he died. Could it have been, after all, an accident? George was a little disappointed at that idea. It was nice to have someone to blame for being dead.

There was something about the swift savagery with which she had despatched Mullins that suggested she might well be the person who had strung up George's sister. She had been a Pearmain, and Lulu obviously did not approve of Pearmains, apart, possibly, from the one to whom she was married. Although, from what George had seen of the inside of their marriage, she was only prepared to give very limited endorsement to his brother.

It was clear, too, from the way in which Lulu picked up the conversation with her husband in the most artless, casual manner, as she came in from slashing, slicing and skewering, that Stephen had no idea whatsoever that his wife went around stabbing people when she thought there were no spectators in the vicinity.

'I'm a little tired,' she whispered, in her most coquettish tone, to Stephen, as she sat next to him on the stairs. 'I'll have a drink and then we should go.'

Well, you would be tired. You do need a drink, I'm sure. Inflicting multiple knife wounds – even on a defenceless woman of ninety-four – can be thirsty work. You need a lie-down, Lulu. And to get out of here before someone discovers the body.

George was actually quite keen on the idea of her leaving. There was no reason why she should have noticed the Panasonic camera over by the fence, as she was showing off a few of her routines from the *scherma di stiletto siciliano*, but the longer she stayed in Hornbeam Crescent the more likely she was to notice it was there. Perhaps, now he seemed to have developed a few basic poltergeist skills, it was time to practise a few on Lulu. It might be nice to nip out into the garden, pick up the bloodied carving knife and hold it before her, the handle towards her hand. She was well overdue for a fatal vision and George was clearly the man to supply it.

There was a gas bill on the hall table. One of the many he was now never going to pay. George went over to it and, trying to repeat the casual, unthought-out way he had grabbed hold of his video camera, reached out for it. To his annoyance, his fingers slipped through it and it remained where it had been before, lying just to the left of a reminder from Amnesty and a letter from an estate agent asking George if he would, perhaps, like to sell his property. He swiped at it, violently this time, but still was unable to connect. What was all this about? Had his sudden ability to touch material objects, even to move them from place to place, even – my God! – to work a video camera (a pretty remarkable achievement for a dead person) suddenly evaporated as definitively as had his own heart, brain, lungs and stomach?

It seemed he had acquired these talents to perform some specific function. He had been granted the ability to generate a breeze and, as a result, had put the codicil on public display. If he had not been able to use the camera, there would have been no clear proof of Lulu's guilt. Could it be that, instead of being in Christian limbo or the throes of Buddhist rebirth, George was trapped in a destiny laid down for him by the all-powerful God of the Muslims? Whatever was happening to him, he felt, once again, that agonizing sense of his own powerlessness that was still, overall, the defining characteristic of being no longer alive.

He turned angrily towards Stephen and Lulu to be rewarded by the sight of Beryl Vickers, who was clutching at the sleeve of DI Hobday. He seemed, as far as George could make out, to be on the verge of saying his goodbyes to Esmeralda. As far as he was aware, of course, the discovery of the codicil had not led to any spectacular outburst or revelation. He was back to the painful and difficult task of establishing the guilt of his suspects by firm evidential proof.

'Inspector,' Beryl was saying, in a quiet, pleading voice, 'I can't find Audrey.'

Hobday gave her a quick, sympathetic glance and immediately started to ask all the right questions. It did not take him long to establish that Mullins was no longer on the property and that her car was still in the road outside. All this time Lulu was watching him, George noticed, but her face and manner betrayed nothing. In fact she went over to Beryl and whispered to her that she was sure Audrey had just gone out for a nice walk and if she could do anything to help she was at her disposal. Indeed, when DC Purves suggested they search the garden, Lulu was one of the first to volunteer.

Quite a large number of guests joined in the hunt for Mullins. Nat Pinker was particularly keen. He got hold of a walking stick and, outside, began to belabour Esmeralda's flowerbeds, in a manner clearly derived from watching police carrying out intensive quests for missing persons on heath or moorland. Veronica Pinker was sure she had seen Beryl upstairs. Perhaps, she said, she had got locked in the lavatory. It was Esmeralda who pointed out that not only was Mullins missing but also Mabel Dawkins did not appear to have returned from her drunken trip down the garden.

That was when Lulu said, in a soft, concerned voice, 'She was very drunk, wasn't she? And very angry indeed. About the money.'

The rain had stopped. Esmeralda, Stephen, Lulu, Hobday, Purves and the Pinkers worked their way, slowly and methodically, down to the rose trellis and into the untended land beyond it. It was Esmeralda who saw Mullins first and it wasn't long before Hobday, who was next to her, caught sight of Mabel Dawkins.

Dawkins was beginning to stir. Perhaps the voices had wakened her. She shook herself like a dog. She raised a hand to her face and found, to her obvious surprise, that she was holding a bloodstained carving knife. She looked at it with great attention. 'Blimey!' she said, and then again, 'Blimey!' Still, apparently, unaware of the search party she threw the knife out into the darkness. She continued to stare up into the night sky. 'I never done nuffink!' she said. 'I did not do it! I emphatically did not kill anyone!'

She turned her face to her left. She saw Audrey Mullins's body. She screamed. She saw Inspector Hobday. She saw Esmeralda. She screamed again. 'Not me, Guv!' she said to Hobday. 'Not me! Honest!'

Hobday ignored her. He began to talk to DC Purves in

low, urgent tones. Esmeralda, who was clearly getting more and more used to crime-scene etiquette, began to steer people back down the garden towards the house. She put her arm round Beryl, who had started to cry.

'Come with me, Beryl,' George heard her say. 'We'll find who did this.'

'We will,' said Lulu, with every appearance of sincerity. Very soon, there were only Hobday, Purves and two other detectives in plainclothes up by the body. They still, to George's chagrin, did not appear to have seen the video camera on its tripod, over by the fence. Had Lulu seen it? It was possible. If only he could create some diversion in the area nearby. Might it be that whatever force was driving things around here would allow that to happen? He stood by the tripod and did a bit of howling and screeching. Hobday, who seemed to be phoning Pawlikowski, paid no attention.

A large, grey shape was padding towards him through the puddles, in which, being dead, he showed no interest. Partridge, stalking through familiar territory, did not stop to cock his leg against the fig tree, as he had used to do. He had come to talk to George.

'Have you remembered who killed me?' said George.

'I'm not sure,' said Partridge.

'Think!' said George.

Partridge thought for a moment. Hobday was still on the phone. Purves and one of the male officers were bending over Mullins's body. Another female police officer was sitting on the soaking grass next to Mabel Dawkins, who was still dully repeating her innocence. She had not yet, George noted, made any mention of Lulu. She was, obviously, in a state of shock.

'You were always saying hurtful things about me,' Partridge was saying, 'when I was in the room. You used to say I was stupid...'

'Well, I – you are. I mean you *were* sometimes…er…' began George. Then he stopped.

'But,' said Partridge, 'I do not think you deserved to die.'

'No,' said George. 'That's more or less my view of the situation. I wonder if you…er…remember who exactly it was who…er…'

Partridge and he were standing immediately next to the tripod and camera. To George's surprise, Hobday, who had finished his conversation with Pawlikowski, seemed to be looking in their direction. 'Looking' did not really do justice to what he was doing. He was gawping. He was gawking. He was goggling. He was staring. He was gazing, ogling and peering. When he finally spoke it was in a sort of shocked, tentative tone that was utterly untypical of the policeman.

'Here, boy!' he said. 'Here, boy!'

For a moment, George thought he was talking to him. If he was, he didn't like the man's tone. He might be dead but that was no reason to talk to him as if he were a bloody dog. He—

'Over there,' Hobday was saying. 'Over there by the fence. I thought I saw an Irish wolfhound.'

'Not a lot of them about, Boss,' said Purves.

'It was there!' said Hobday. 'It was right there. Next to the camera!'

For a moment he didn't seem to realize what he had said. Then, as the other police officers followed his gaze and saw the camera, the tripod (although not, as far as George could make out, him or his dog), the presence or absence of Partridge at the crime scene was completely forgotten. He had, thought George, served his purpose, as dogs do, and Hobday, Purves and the other two – Mabel Dawkins forgotten for the moment – clustered round George's Panasonic in the grip of mystification, then, as Hobday started to rewind and images began to appear on the screen, excitement.

'Jesus, Boss!' said Purves. 'Jesus!'

George positioned himself between Hobday and his detective constable. As the inspector ran the tape forward he felt a quiet pride in what he had done. The framing was first class. The exposure, given the prevailing conditions, was perfectly judged. There was no loss of focus. He had refrained from zooming in on the gory bits. It was, even unedited, a compelling piece of cinema. It had a quality, he thought, of Cartier-Bresson or Kieślowski, a restrained wide shot giving the audience an authoritative, detached and yet somehow compassionate account of a sixty-year-old woman hacking an unarmed pensioner to death.

'My God!' said Purves. 'My God! And I used to listen to her on the radio! I really liked *Come Sit On My Knee*!'

'I think,' said Hobday, 'that Lulu Belhatchett's television career is probably over.'

George was not at all sure this was the case. In his experience convictions for a violent murder could be just the thing to revive a flagging media career. From the look of them, Hobday's two sidekicks were perfectly capable of flogging his footage to YouTube before the night was out. He was not going to take that lying down. He might be dead but his work should remain in copyright for the next seventy-five years.

Hobday turned towards where Mabel Dawkins had been lying only to find she had been watching George's footage with the others.

'Fuckin' 'ell!' she whispered. 'She's a sickoperth! She's a strawberry short of a punnet, she is! She is a homosexual maniac!'

Hobday looked at her with a certain degree of sympathy. 'I think,' he said, 'you may have a point, Mrs Dawkins.'

Pawlikowski was coming down the garden towards them. As soon as Hobday saw him, the pathologist's body started to quiver. The man seemed to know, without even asking, that his colleague had momentous news for him. Hobday, as he had done in the morgue, raised his hand and the two high-fived each other. Then, without going into any details, the inspector simply said, 'Result!'

'Result!' echoed Pawlikowski.

'Am I the best or am I the best?' said Hobday.

In no time at all the two men were doing their Gathering Peascods routine all round the rough grass. It was wilder and more abandoned than the dance they had done in the morgue. At times Hobday would leap into the air with a kind of scissor-kick and, although he had not seen any of George's footage and could have had no idea what they were celebrating, the pathologist seemed to understand immediately how important it was. At one stage he loosened the belt of his trousers and George had the impression he was about to take out his penis.

Hobday, perhaps to head off this development, went into the mime version of a knife fight. Again, it was more furious and abandoned than the routine in the morgue. Pawlikowski feinted left. Hobday feinted right. Then Hobday waggled his head from side to side. This time his chanting had a more African than Arab tonality. Pawlikowski picked this up and started to waggle his behind in a manner that George found particularly offensive.

'You is de be-e-est, Boss!' he moaned.

'I is de be-e-e-st!' responded Hobday.

They had all, quite clearly, forgotten that Mabel Dawkins was there. Quite suddenly, Hobday stopped. There was total silence. 'I'm sorry,' said Hobday. 'I'm very, very sorry, Mrs Dawkins.'

'Not at all!' said Mabel. 'I was enjoyin' it.'

298

When Hobday had recovered himself he turned to the pathologist. 'She'll have wiped the handle clean,' he said, 'the way she did with the suicide note, but I don't think we need worry too much about that. I'd like to see her posh fucking lawyers argue their way out of that footage.'

'How,' said Purves, 'did it get there, Boss? The camera?'

'The husband?' The inspector shrugged. 'Don't ask, Barbara. Never look a gift horse in the mouth, eh? And now perhaps all you lads and lasses would like to come inside and watch me arrest someone. I haven't done that in ages. And it will give me particular pleasure to do it for Ms Belhatchett. I'm not a fan of her interviewing style. She was, I thought, very rude to Barbara Cartland.'

With that, he marched off down the garden, leaving George alone with a dead lesbian and the spectre of a deceased wolfhound. Partridge did not seem to have any more to say for himself and, as there was no sign of a wraith-like version of Mullins climbing out of her corpse to join in the fun, George took himself off in their direction. He, too, was looking forward to seeing Lulu getting booked for homicide. Perhaps she would shed some light on who had tipped hemlock leaves into his parsnip wine.

As he came back into the kitchen, he saw that people were sitting or standing in small groups. No one was talking. Beryl Vickers was crying quietly as Esmeralda, holding her hands, made small, wordless noises of sympathy. George stared at Lulu. It was amazing, really, how quickly she had managed to return to looking as if she was just about to read the six o'clock news. She fluttered her eyelashes lightly in the inspector's direction as he came into the room.

'Any clues, Inspector?' she said, with the same honeyed insincerity with which she had begun the interview that had become known in the business as 'Belhatchett 4 Miliband 0'.

'We have some very interesting evidence,' said Hobday. 'Very interesting indeed. In relation to which I am now obliged to say...' He cleared his throat and looked round, briefly, at his team. Pawlikowski glanced sideways at Purves. They exchanged furtive, complicit half-smiles. Hobday's voice dropped nearly an octave and his right foot moved forward as if he was about to present arms on a military parade. '...Lulu Belhatchett,' he continued, in what was still a surprisingly conversational tone, 'I am arresting you for the murder of Audrey Mullins on the sixth of September 2013 in the rear garden of twenty-two Hornbeam Crescent, Putney. You do not have to say anything but it may harm your defence if you do not mention, when questioned, something which you may later rely on in court. Anything you do say, now or later, may be given in evidence.'

Nobody moved to handcuff her. Nobody spoke, except Stephen's daughter (George had forgotten she was still there), who put her hand to her mouth and said, 'Oh, Jesus Christ!' Otherwise, there was total silence in the room. After Hobday had uttered the familiar yet strangely unfamiliar words, it was as if he had never spoken.

Lulu stretched like a cat. She yawned elaborately. 'I have always thought,' she said, 'that there was something clumsy about the British caution. "It may harm your defence if you do not mention, when questioned, something which you may later rely on in court." Is that clear? Do you think it is clear, Inspector?'

Stephen's mouth was open. His right hand seemed to be shaking badly. He, too, had been out in the rain and the weather had not been kind to his toupee. It looked, George thought, like a detail from a not very distinguished Victorian painting. *Hay Making Interrupted by the Storm*. Or *A Gillie Rescued from the Flood near Loch Lomond*. There was a puzzled, peasant quality about him suddenly. He looked at Hobday. He looked at his wife. Then he looked at his phone.

She seemed, George thought, completely unperturbed by Hobday's attempt to arrest her. She looked utterly unarrested. It was, she clearly felt, a kind of hoax. It might have something to do with a possible appearance on some now vanished early version of the reality show, like *This Is Your Life* or *Beadle's About*. Soon Hobday would be grinning and slapping her on the back, the walls of George's house would be sliding back to reveal they were no more than studio flats and the audience would be clapping and cheering under the arc lights as Lulu, with that serene smile so beloved of the English middle class, welcomed everybody to one final gala transmission of that universally loved programme *Come Sit On My Knee*. 'Good evening, Inspector Hobday – this is Lulu Belhatchett inviting you to ... *come sit on my knee!*'

She laughed again. Just as she had before she had asked the question that made Tony Blair burst into tears. The one about the family secret that nobody was supposed to know. 'You aren't serious, Inspector. Are you?'

Hobday's eyes did not leave her face. 'I'm afraid I am, Lulu. I'm afraid I'm completely serious. You're nicked.'

Chapter Twenty-two

Lulu's arrest was one of the better things to have happened since George had died. It didn't send him straight back to the scattering area of Putney Vale Crematorium, inspire him to lie down on the well-kept grass and allow his fragile consciousness to fade into longed-for oblivion, but it was better than a slap in the face with a wet mackerel. He had often thought of performing a citizen's arrest on his sister-in-law on the grounds that she was the most annoying person he had ever met, but seeing someone else pull her over for wilful murder ran it a close second.

He could have wished, however, that DI Hobday had managed to work his name into his little speech. '*And for the poisoning of one George Pearmain, the innocent father of two and loyal, devoted husband – if you leave out that business with Biskiborne – to Esmeralda Pearmain.*' Then a bit of struggling and screaming from Belhatchett as she was dragged out to the waiting van by a heavy-set sequence of constables.

He could also have done with a bit more of the 'hereby' and 'yea verily' stuff. It was all a bit too *New English Bible* for George. When was the man Hobday going to get out the gyves and start telling the appalling woman who had married his brother that she was to be taken from hence to a place of execution and hanged by the neck until she could no longer purse her lips and say, 'We don't usually eat starters,' or 'Stevie – could you do a *placement*'?

'I take it,' said Lulu, still apparently unimpressed by Hobday's attempt to arrest her, 'that you imagine you have proof of this absurd allegation.'

She seemed, somehow, to have put all the police in the room at a disadvantage. Even Hobday, who clearly did not propose saying anything on which *he* might rely later in court, appeared slightly shaken by her enormous tranquillity.

'It all depends,' she went on, 'on how foolish you want to look, I suppose. You do realize that there will be quite a bit of, well, *publicity* about this little mistake of yours? Can one withdraw an arrest? Is it too late for you to do that before the papers get hold of this?'

The drawling emphasis that Lulu managed to put on the words *papers* and *publicity* reminded George of her curious faith in the loyalty and unswerving decency of the media world she inhabited. She had clearly not stopped to consider that most of them were as devious and unscrupulous as she. That she had once read the nine o'clock news was not going to stop her colleagues crucifying her long before she came to trial.

If you looked at her closely, however, you could see her mask-like face already hinting at the impartial smile affected by well-known persons recently accused of sexual tampering with children. There was something a little too artificial about her composure. Was there, could there possibly be, a hint of desperation lurking in the pale eyes of the woman who had won no less than three BAFTA awards for her services to the media?

Lulu Belhatchett, George saw, was as crazy as a bag of rats.

It was only as Hobday started to yawn and rub his knuckles into his eyes that George grasped that the inspector was, as usual, playing a slightly more subtle game than a casual observer might suppose. He had seen the man do this a few times before – once when he was looking at the knot in the rope with which Frigga had been strangled, and again when he was looking at the kitchen floor on the morning after George had been murdered.

Who had murdered him? Who had murdered his mother? It certainly was not Lulu. Or was it? George was certain that Hobday had a good idea of how both murders had happened but, so far anyway, had no proof. His talent as an interviewer was more considerable than Lulu's. He let people talk – and that was just what he was doing with Lulu now.

If Lulu had a weakness to which she was prepared to admit – conceit, blindness to the feelings of others, snobbery, obviousness and self-righteousness were not qualities she seemed to see in herself at all – it was that, as she often said, 'Once I start chatting, I just cannot stop!' Perhaps it was all those years of asking questions to which she really did not want to know the answer that now made her so keen to respond to interrogation – even when she was not actually being interrogated.

'Perhaps, Inspector,' she continued, 'you think that I rushed down from Basingstoke on my broomstick, slid down the chimney and poisoned poor old George, then whacked his mummy on the bonce. I was rather fond of George. Perfectly innocent chap, with his poetry hobby and his impressions. A nicer bank manager never lived. Or died.'

She was patronizing him beyond the grave. She was patting his corpse on the head and telling it it had been rather sweet, although of no interest to a media figure of importance such as her. How dare she? She had been on the television. So what?

He recalled an afternoon with her and Stephen some fifteen years ago when she had been at the height of her fame. They had all gone for a walk on Putney Heath. Normally such expeditions were wrecked by autograph hunters, admirers of all ages and sexes, all united by the fact that they felt the need to touch, talk to or just stare at the face that had connected them to so many other celebrities. For some reason, none of her fans had been out that afternoon. No one had recognized her. She was left alone. At first, Lulu did not seem to notice. Then she took to gazing into the faces of passersby, often with a slight smile, an anticipation of her graceful acknowledgement that, yes, she was a celebrity and would be glad to write something in their autograph books. That did not do the trick. After nearly three-quarters of an hour of it, Lulu had adopted more aggressive tactics. As they came up to Wimbledon Windmill she began to sing, quietly at first, and then, as they walked down to the Queen's Mere, she was not only singing but had added a full range of operatic hand gestures. By the time they got to the water's edge she was practically yodelling at top volume, as she scanned the bushes for someone, anyone, who might recognize her.

They did not. Hobday seemed similarly proof against her prominence.

'Did I somehow pop into Mummy Pearmain's flat and hang poor dear lonely Frigga from the ceiling? May I remind you, Inspector, that I was, at the time, in Basingstoke.'

'Actually, Lulu,' said Hobday, 'we have a credit-card receipt from you that puts you in the Shell garage in the Lower Richmond Road around the time of the murder. And your DNA is all over Frigga's manuscript. There is, too, the fact that you were an active member of the Lower Billesley Sailing Club for many years, where your expertise with knots was much talked of...'

'Circumstantial evidence, Inspector.'

She was getting angry now. Hobday was, George realized, deliberately using his lack of proof to feed her desire to dominate the stage.

'I presume you imagine the motive for these appalling crimes is the need to get someone's hands on the money poor old George's mummy left in her will. If she wanted to leave it to dear old Mullins that was her affair. I was, by the way, as my husband will testify, in Esmeralda's house for most of the evening, and why you imagine you have the right to arrest me when the only woman who seems to have been out there in the garden, as we all saw, was the extremely acquisitive Dawkins, I cannot think.'

Hobday said nothing. He merely smiled.

The smile and the silence did their work. When Lulu spoke again her voice had risen in pitch and her eyes were bright with suppressed anger. 'Stephen will tell you that I had no interest whatsoever in Jessica's money. She was a perfectly pleasant old woman and if, at times, she was a *leetle* bit obsessed with her darling Georgy Porgy and tended to ignore her poor old younger boy, my Stephen, that was no reason for me or anyone else to bang her on the head and leave her dead on the kitchen floor. My God! Why are we making such a fuss about the old lady anyway? She was ninety-nine, wasn't she? She was well past her sell-by date!'

During this speech Stephen was looking at his wife with a kind of dull hatred but when he finally spoke he sounded tired and drained of all emotion. 'My mother wasn't murdered,' he said. 'It was an accident.' He had been biting his lower lip and staring at his phone, as if it was about to provide Lulu with an alibi, but now he was staring straight ahead, his arms listlessly by his sides, his shoulders slumped as if he was suddenly too tired to go on with his life.

Lulu did not look pleased that he had spoken. She glared at him, which usually guaranteed his silence for the next three days, then added the whinnying laugh that George found so irritating. 'Yes,' she said brightly. 'Jessica fell over. I thought that was obvious. She was an old lady. She wandered into the kitchen and she fell over.'

'She was always interfering,' Stephen said, in a low, miserable voice. 'She was always taking charge of things. "I'll do that!" "Let me do that, Stephen!" And if she hadn't decided she was going to "tidy away" the glass, it wouldn't have happened, would it?'

There was a long silence.

'What would not have happened, Stephen?' said Hobday, in a very soothing voice.

'Don't answer that, Stevie,' said Lulu, 'without your lawyer present.' She gave Hobday a very narrow look.

'Mr Pearmain,' said the inspector, in ultra-reasonable tones, 'may say anything he likes. He has not been arrested yet.'

Stephen looked, thought George, as sullen as he had on his first day at school when George had had the job of making sure none of the other boys stole his packed lunch or tried to trip him up in the playground. Luckily, as a child, George was as aggressive as Stephen was meek. He didn't let anyone get away with anything. Someone had got his little brother alone, though, and done something unkind to him. George had found him crying at the end of the day, in a corner by himself. He looked as if he might cry now. He looked, for the first time in years, like George's younger brother.

'That's true,' said Stephen, in the same dull monotone. 'I haven't been arrested yet.'

'And,' said Lulu, in an easy, pleasant way, 'there is no reason why you should be – if you keep your fucking mouth shut.'

Stephen did not appear to hear what she was saying. He was now staring at his phone, fiddling with the controls. When George went over to see what he was doing, his brother was

Googling the names of lawyers. As George watched, Stephen typed a new question into the box at the head of the web page. 'WHAT SHOULD I DO IN CASE I'M ACCUSED OF MURDER?' was the request, and, already Auntie Google had come up with a number of interesting answers. Run! thought George, would have been his response. Run as fast as ever you can!

Stephen did not look like a man who was capable of running anywhere. George had never really understood what went on his brother's mind. Did brothers or sisters ever quite get each other? You played cricket in the garden with them. You shared the same parents. You went to the same school, the same university. They acquired friends you did not understand. You did the same. Sometimes they hit you or you hit them, if you/they tampered with their/your possessions. But you didn't really know them at all. Not really.

He remembered one afternoon over half a century ago when, in the kitchen of their parents' first house, in Southfields, Stephen had suddenly run at George, screaming, biting, kicking. 'Normally,' said Jessica, regarding him with the slight curiosity he always seemed to evoke in her, 'he's such a quiet child. Always hanging around me. It quite annoys me sometimes.'

And then another occasion, when they were older, perhaps at university, or even later than that, just before they made their marriages, Stephen had asked him if he felt guilty. 'Guilty of what?' said George, who had never felt guilty about anything, even the things he had done that were wrong. 'Not really,' he had replied. 'Do you feel guilty?'

'I do,' said Stephen, his big, saucer face more than ever like a full moon making its opening bow, low in the sky.

'What about?' said George.

'Everything,' said Stephen. 'Everything.'

Lulu was back on stage. George had the impression, though, that much more than vanity was at stake here. If only she could keep the inspector talking there was a chance that Stephen would not say whatever was on his mind. It was even clearer to George now that she had no idea – though she might have had suspicions – of what had happened on the night he was murdered. Lulu and his brother clearly talked even less than he did to either of them. Families! Jesus!

'I presume,' she said rather shrilly, 'that you have some evidence for this absurd accusation.'

Hobday still said nothing. He had not mentioned the camera. Clearly he was not going to do so. Not until he got to court, if he could help it. That gave him power over her, and you could tell from her face just how much she did not like that. She was hunting for what had allowed Hobday to make his move. Had he got someone who had been out in the garden? Surely he would not have taken anything Dawkins might have said on trust. She had been holding the fucking knife, hadn't she? So why – her cold blue eyes seemed to say – was this copper sounding so pleased with himself?

'I think you'd better carry this ridiculous farce to its logical conclusion and cart me off in your little van so that I can phone my lawyer, who is very good, actually, and you will get a great deal of shit dumped on your head.'

You couldn't help but admire the woman. Only twenty minutes ago she had been blind drunk and hacking bits off an elderly lesbian with a carving knife. Now you would have thought she was getting ready to do an episode of *Come Sit On My Knee*.

She wanted to get Hobday talking, to prompt a reaction – any kind of reaction – from him, but Hobday was following a game plan that more guests on her chat show should have used: total silence. The more she talked, the more her second husband bit his lower lip and looked from her to his phone and from his phone to her, as if he was trying to make up his mind which one he should ask for the help he so obviously needed.

That owlish vulnerability in him reminded George once again of old times. A holiday in France, during which Stephen had cut himself badly and George had had to carry him back across a rocky beach to the house his parents had rented over the summer, Stephen howling all the way.

'Go on, Inspector. Take me away in your Black Maria. I've seen the inside of a police station before. You may remember that I presented *Crimewatch* for a brief period. I know several people who are quite high up in the police force. I've had dinner with Sir Bernard Thingy, actually. And that bloke who owns up to being a poof. Do you want a career in the Metropolitan Police or not, Hobday?'

When Stephen spoke it was in his quietest voice so far. If Lulu hadn't stopped talking, which she did as soon as he opened his mouth, it was possible that no one in the room would have heard him.

'It wasn't murder,' he whispered. 'It was an accident. I could never murder my mother. It's wrong. Killing anyone is wrong but killing your mother is a very bad thing to do. It's really shocking. I mean – all I did was push her.'

'Stevie...' began Lulu, but he did not seem to hear her.

'Was she trying to take the glass off you?' said Hobday, in the same soft, reassuring tone. 'Was that it?'

Stephen turned to him. 'She was,' he murmured. 'How did you know that?'

'It's my business to know these things,' said Hobday.

'She was,' went on Stephen, 'because, of course, being my mother she wanted to know why I was getting up in the middle of the night to take a glass out of George's room and lug it all the way to the kitchen. "Why?" she kept on saying. "Why? Why are you doing this? Why?" She wouldn't shut up. She was always asking me questions like that. "Why don't you like George? Hasn't he always been nice to you?" "I don't know," I would say to her. "Leave me alone. I don't know. Just leave me alone." But she wouldn't leave me alone.'

Lulu sighed slowly. 'It was an accident, Stevie,' she said. 'Wasn't it? It was a silly accident.'

Stephen, however, appeared to have given up paying attention to his wife. It was something she simply could not understand. On the whole, from George's observation of their twenty years of married life, his brother did everything his wife wanted him to do. He frequently obeyed orders that were transparently ludicrous – buying blue blazers, sitting through Wagner operas although he was tone deaf, treating his stepchildren as if they were some vital diplomatic asset – but now she was trying to get him to do something sensible, i.e. shut the fuck up and stop incriminating himself, he seemed incapable of doing it. Stephen was at last, George saw, having his moment and he was determined to enjoy it.

'Of course,' he went on, 'I couldn't say, "Oh, Mummy, there's some *hemlock* in the glass", could I?'

'Stevie, shut the—'

'I couldn't say to her, "Oh! Mummy! I thought I'd poison my brother! It was a spur-of-the-moment thing. Like borrowing his car that time in the Lake District, then trashing it. Do you remember?"'

Nobody did. Apart from George who remembered only too well. They had been staying at some cottage near Ullswater. George and Stephen were in their early twenties. George had just become the proud owner of a new Morris Marina that had mysteriously disappeared during the holiday. He had always thought it had been stolen, crashed and abandoned by joyriders. *Stephen! You bastard!*

Brothers again. You stole their things. You tried to steal their girls and then, when you were all grown-up, you...No, surely not. Stephen wouldn't actually have tried to kill him, would he? Now he was confronted with the thought that his brother had murdered him, George found he was, quite simply, unable to believe it. There was some other explanation. Stephen had, perhaps, picked hemlock by mistake and, without realizing it, placed it on the pile of herbs Frigga had been adding to the parsnip wine.

'It was when I saw Frigga picking those herbs,' Stephen went on. 'I was asking her about this one and that one and she was telling me. I pointed out one plant and she said, "No no no – you mustn't ever pick that, Stephen. That's hemlock! It would kill you." I don't know why but I picked it. I wasn't thinking of killing anyone at that stage, I really wasn't.'

'Stop this!' said Lulu. 'Stop it now!'

But Stephen didn't want to stop.

'I had seen the will,' he went on. 'I had told Lulu what was in it. She said I had to talk to Mummy about it but I couldn't talk to Mummy about it. I couldn't talk to her about anything, really. It was always George with her. George. George. George. She was never very interested in me. Maybe I'm not a very interesting person. I don't know.'

'Stevie, shut the fuck up!'

'But it wasn't the money, really. I just wanted him out of the way. I'd wanted him out of the way since the day I was born. I couldn't see the point of him. I couldn't understand why my ridiculous father liked him so much. Perhaps because they were exactly the same. Both suburban losers. Little people who never do anything. Never risk anything. Life is all about risk. If you don't risk something you'll never gain anything. People complain about bankers but at least they did something, didn't they? In the days my father was a banker he never took risks with anything. We never had quite enough money and he moaned about it. All the time. George was just like him. A moaner. He deserved to die. Him and his horrible wife. She's rude. And dirty. She keeps a dirty house.'

For some reason Lulu chose to support him in this judgement. 'She does,' she said. 'It's filthy. Look at it.'

'Lulu,' said Stephen, 'always washes the curtains. She washes everything. She washes herself. She washes the kitchen floor. Herself. She irons all her own underwear. She bakes her own bread.'

Here, Esmeralda spoke, for the first time in what seemed an age. 'She doesn't,' she said. 'She can't cook for toffee. And you're a disgusting, greedy little man.'

Stephen followed his custom of the last forty years and paid no attention to her whatsoever. 'After I realized Mummy was dead,' he went on, 'I made it look like a burglar had done it, and if people had let that idiot Pinker carry on with the heart-attack rubbish after he'd seen George, we would have been all right. Home and dry.'

'Actually,' said Nat, 'the symptoms of myocardial infarction are remarkably similar to those of hemlock poisoning.'

'George was always crawling round Mummy to make sure he got the lion's share of the will. He thought it was all his by right. He got favoured treatment from Daddy because he was there first. I was cleverer than him in business and I got a first—'

'You got a third,' said Esmeralda.

Stephen continued to ignore his sister-in-law. 'His poetry,' he went on, 'is rubbish. Absolute rubbish. It isn't modern. This is the twenty-first century, for God's sake. It's derivative rubbish.'

George was getting annoyed. It was one thing to poison him. It was, perhaps, a logical conclusion to the tensions between them that, now he thought about it, probably went back to the day when he had run over, and badly mangled, Stephen's rabbit with his tricycle in 1956, but to make a gratuitous and savage attack on his poetry – he hadn't even published it! *Leave me alone, bro! You appear to have poisoned me! Wasn't that enough?*

'I managed to convince Frigga that she'd done it. That was quite easy. Lulu was going to see her that afternoon to make absolutely sure but then...I couldn't believe it when I saw it. I couldn't believe she'd done what she had.'

'Oh, shut up, you spineless twat!' said Lulu, 'You got us into the mess with the fucking money, didn't you?'

Suddenly Stephen began to scream at her. 'You made me do it!' he yelled. 'It was you! I never meant to kill him! I loved him! But you never stopped, did you? Day in and day out, "Your fucking brother!" You poisoned my mind against him! You poisoned my mind against Mummy! You're disgusting! You're mad! You killed that old woman and you...'

Lulu had not moved for the last twenty minutes. When she did you could see just how strong and physically controlled she was. She sprang at her husband with the speed and accuracy of a rattlesnake. Before anyone had understood what was happening she had both hands round his neck and was squeezing for dear life. She had, George noted, huge hands. Strangler's hands. It took two policemen to drag her off. Stephen coughed horribly for a while, and then he said, 'I didn't mean to kill George. Not really. It was an impulse thing. I didn't mean to do it. I was drunk. And Mummy was an accident. She's the one you should send away. You should hang her.' He looked at Hobday with a pathetic attempt at a smile. 'I'll tell you everything,' he said.

Chapter Twenty-three

George thought he had done that already, but Stephen obviously did not agree. It proved rather hard to shut him up. Once he had started confessing he seemed to get an appetite for it. George had the strong impression he was about to own up to other crimes, including ones he had not actually committed. There was, however, plenty of entirely justified confessional material. He certainly seemed to have got up to a few financial tricks that would have horrified George's father. Companies in the Cayman Islands. Raising mortgages on properties that did not exist.

He spoke about other things as well. He spoke – at length – about his toupee. He told everyone how much it had cost, how difficult it was to keep tidy, how he felt that it was not a success, that people spotted it in the street and laughed at him behind their hands. He had adopted it in his thirties and by the time better hair technology came along it was too late. They laughed more as he got older, he said. Sometimes to his face. He said he had thought of buying a knife so as he could cut up the people who insulted him in that way but he had not had the nerve to do so. He spoke of how much he hated Barry and Maurice because they sniggered about his toupee. Esmeralda told him this was perfectly true and that it was not going to make his time in prison any easier. Stephen started to cry.

He spoke of how much he hated Barry and Maurice. He talked about his work, by which time the room was getting restless. He spoke of how he and Lulu had planed to develop an English-language current-affairs programme in China but the project had been torpedoed by a man called Chung. He spoke at length about Chunge. Then he got on to the subject of his marriage to Geraldine. 'I don't know why I married her,' he said, 'I think I only married her because I thought she was black.'

'I am black,' said Geraldine, who was sitting on the sofa next to Esmeralda.

'Not very,' said Rosalina's boyfriend, Justice, who was sitting on the arm of the sofa.

'But she didn't understand me,' went on Stephen, who did not appear to have heard any of these remarks, 'because she was black.'

By this stage, not only Lulu but almost everyone else in the room was wishing he would shut up and go off to jail like a good boy. At one point he started to talk about masturbation, a topic George had always found embarrassing but actively distasteful now he was dead. Opportunities for self-abuse had been seriously limited since his brother had poisoned him; but now Stephen, who was clearly looking at some of the ways in which he might be spending his time during the years ahead, seemed keen to give everyone his views on this once-frowned-upon subject. He spoke of how many times he did it each day, of the immense pleasure it had given him over the years, of how George had once tried to stop him doing it when they had shared a bed on holiday in Cornwall and how he had always resented what he called George's 'pompous and Puritan attitude'.

Lulu seemed to have given up trying to make him stop.

Most of all he talked about George. George had had no

idea his brother held so many passionate opinions about him. He had always thought he and Esmeralda were the only ones who bitched about their respective family members. It was clear that Stephen had devoted almost as much time to thinking about his older brother as he had devoted to his mobile phone.

'He was desperate to get his hands on the money,' he said at one point. 'He was always sucking up to Mummy, taking her to Waitrose and getting her to rewrite her will. He wanted to get his hands on the Vienna Regulator too. He always had his eyes on that. And on the sideboard. The sideboard is worth thousands.'

The Vienna Regulator had finally been valued, soon after the last family member who had a legitimate claim on it had been murdered. It was worth £150.

He talked quite a lot about the Vienna Regulator. He talked, too, about a present George had been given by their parents in 1957. He didn't appear to remember what it was but he seemed fairly sure it was a better present than the one he had received. Holidays had been a particularly tricky area. There had been one in the Vosges, apparently, where George had eaten Stephen's pudding without asking his permission.

George had no recollection whatsoever of any of this. He hadn't, now he came to think of it, ever really paid much attention to Stephen. Maybe that was why Stephen had poisoned him. He had been trying, in his own way, to make contact. George had never really wanted contact with Stephen, certainly not close contact. Now the distance between them was unbridgeable and, perhaps, that was best for all concerned.

He was not sure that his mother had loved him more than she had loved Stephen. She had certainly preferred both of them to Frigga, but then Frigga was not only female, depressive, talentless, demanding and full of spite but also, from the moment she emerged from the womb, relentlessly critical of her mother. Jessica was allowed to make judgements about her children, wasn't she? Was it her fault if she felt passionately about them? The English, George thought, so famous for their coldness and reserve, were a ridiculously passionate bunch, betrayed by their feelings constantly and yet constantly trying to tell the world they didn't really care.

'Ridiculous,' Stephen was saying. 'George was ridiculous. A left-wing bank manager, I ask you! A sucker for all those good causes. A great opponent of the Gulf War. Always parading his liberal opinions but not really prepared to stand up for them. As interested in money as I was. As out for himself as I was. Just did not want to own up to it.'

'I think,' said Lulu, as he paused for breath, 'We are ready to be taken away, Inspector.'

She had give up trying to find out what he had on her. She knew, that, whatever it was, it was damning. George would have liked to find some way of letting her know what he had done but the forces who were ruling his lack of life had clearly decided he was not going to be allowed to take any credit for the assistance he had given to the Metropolitan Police in the investigation of his own murder. The fuzz would not, he thought grimly, have got very far without him.

Lulu rose to her feet, with a touch of Marie Antoinette on her way to the scaffold. As she uncoiled herself from her muscular rear quarters in a manner that, to an experienced Lulu watcher such as George, only served to emphasize her reluctance to put her arse out there, she had, too, an air of Blanche Dubois on her way to the loony bin.

'Come along, Stevie,' she said, in her high, precisely elocuted tones. 'The inspector wants us to go with him. And I think we should! Don't you? I think the inspector rather likes me, don't you? When we get to the station, I think I should ask him to…to…' Here she stopped, and did something unusual. She smiled, showing all of her teeth. For a moment George had the impression they had lost their pearly whiteness and were shining like rotten wood in her suddenly exposed skull. 'to…to…*come sit on my knee*!'

She laughed then, not in an extravagantly crazy way but like a full-throated junior-reporter-in-the-pub, yet the apparent naturalness of the sound only made clearer to George that Lulu had always been insane.

'Mum!' wailed the Prune. 'Oh! Mummy!'

George had the distinct impression she was about to sing again. Peregrine's chin had gone so far into his neck that his head looked as if it was about to be swallowed whole by his immaculately ironed collar.

'Oh, God!' he said, in a faint voice. 'This is awful! Absolutely awful!'

In the corner, Beryl Vickers looked as if she was about to try to say something. There was no hatred or outrage on her face, George noted, only an intense puzzlement that an evening that had started so badly had managed to get even worse. She was muttering to herself, but it was only when he floated over to her that George could hear what she was saying: 'She was only ninety-four. We were going to go to Provence. To the Cézanne exhibition.'

Lulu's head was held too high for her to notice any pain Beryl might have been feeling. She was on her way to the door, watched by people who, at last, did not have to be polite to her. Say something, boys and girls! thought George. Give her a brief summary of how, why and where she has proved to be such an absolute cunt!

They did not do so. Perhaps, thought George, they had all told each other so many times what an appalling person she was that they saw no point in telling her. For a moment he suspected Rosalina was about to try some of the kinds of behaviour dished out to the tailgates of vans containing child murderers by Old Bailey groupies – a bit of spitting, perhaps, or an attempt to pull chunks out of Lulu's expensive coiffure – but she didn't.

Just as she reached the door to the hall, George called out to both of them: 'Thanks! Thanks for everything, guys!'

Lulu showed no sign of having experienced him. She was, thought George, immune to the spirit world. His earlier conviction that she had sensed him was more to do with him than her. She was, he decided, as uninterested in him as he was in his younger brother. Out of such misprision, he reflected glumly, comes violent death.

Stephen, however, stopped. Had he heard his brother's voice from beyond the grave? He did not look back at George. He gazed off into the distance as if he was listening to a noise he could not quite place. Then his face clouded and he shook himself as if he was deciding not to waste time on considering matters about which, after all, there was nothing to be done. Then he and his wife went out into the street with Hobday, Purves and one of the other police officers.

Chapter Twenty-four

For some reason Pawlikowski did not follow them. He stayed behind with the remaining officer. Perhaps he simply was not able to tear himself away from a freshly killed corpse, especially one as full of knife wounds as that of the unfortunate Mullins. Even though they possessed superbly shot footage of Lulu thrusting George's carving knife into Mullins's chest, neck and lower bowel, Pawlikowski was pretty well bound to find some excuse for justifying a trawl through her insides with his pristine white rubber gloves.

Veronica Pinker was whispering to Esmeralda. 'She's sort of...perfect, isn't she?' she was saying. 'Isn't Lulu sort of...perfect? Even in the dock she'll be bloody perfect!' This thought seemed to afford Esmeralda some comfort. It was probably, thought George, why those two were such good friends – a shared amusement at the crimes and follies of mankind. Maybe it would help Esmeralda get through the coming years.

Pawlikowski was talking to Nat. George studied his least favourite pathologist, wondering if his brief moment of ghostly glory was over now the culprits had been arrested. It would be nice to think he could make contact with someone before he was finally consigned to the long silence that he was now almost sure was the next thing on the agenda. He came up to Pawlikowski, did not breathe deeply and let out an ear-splitting scream.

Pawlikowski stopped. He looked around. Then he slapped the back of his neck, once or twice. 'Do you get mosquitoes in Putney?' he said to Nat.

Nat seemed puzzled. 'It's not high summer,' he replied.

Pawlikowski shook himself. He looked, George was gratified to note, quite worried. The remaining policeman came up to him and the two moved out into the garden, presumably to bring poor Audrey Mullins to start her long journey through the morgue and the uncontroversial discovery that she had been killed by multiple stab wounds inflicted by a once well-known television personality.

George followed them. Mabel Dawkins, covered with mud, blood and rain, was out there with a uniformed policewoman George had not seen before. The policewoman was asking if she would like to add anything to her statement. Mabel said not. The fire seemed to have gone out of her.

'I would like,' she was saying, 'to sit on the sofa. I'm feelin' a bit rhubarbative, if you wanna know. She made a fuckin' mess of poor old Mullins, din't she? Eh? Can I go now?'

The policewoman held her arm as Mabel staggered inside and collapsed on to the sofa.

George stood directly behind Pawlikowski, who was muttering about evidence bags to his companion. This time George did not even bother to try to open the space where his mouth used to be. He concentrated, very intensely, on who he was. He thought about being dead. He thought about having no eyes to open and no ears to hear and no hands to hold his wife. He thought about his boys and their children and how they would never know him or what he was. He thought about the indignity of death. Something, at last, after his ridiculously happy and protected life he shared with so many of the wretched of the world. He thought about his father's dignified words to him on his deathbed – 'I've had a good life. I'm ready' – and he thought about how he had been given no choice in the matter. He thought about how the hemlock had slowly filtered through his system. He thought about how, in the dark watches of the suburban night, his heart had faltered, then stopped for ever as Esmeralda had slept, oblivious, beside him.

He thought about how little respect people seemed to have for death or life, these days. And about how respect for the dead is indivisible from the respect we owe to life. He thought about politicians, and religious fundamentalists of all shapes and sizes, about how blindly and unthinkingly they inflicted pain on others. And how absurd their opinions on the dead, as well as the living, seemed to be. He thought about children in Syria choking on poisoned gas. He thought about innocent people in markets in Iraq suddenly being ripped apart by bomb blasts. Then he threw back his head and howled, willing himself into some form that at least one person could actually see, full length, as he had been in life, though hideously marked by death and the changes it had wrought in him.

'Aaaagggh!'

Who was making that noise? Was it him? Had he actually succeeded in getting a remark out there into the real world – well, 'remark' was putting it a bit strongly but a guttural scream was better than nothing. Wasn't it?

It wasn't him. It appeared to be a noise made by Pawlikowski. He was also, as far as George could tell, retreating across the rain-soaked patio and – this was very satisfying indeed – trembling visibly as he stared directly at George.

'What's up, Boss?' the policeman with him was saying.

NIGEL WILLIAMS

'It's...it's...'

Some people had heard him scream and had wandered out on to the patio. Feeling, at last, that he was getting somewhere in the post-mortem rat race, George raised what might serve as his right arm and pointed something he hoped might manifest itself as his index finger at the unfortunate Pole.

'It's...him!'

Pawlikowski was actually gibbering now. There was no other word to describe what he was doing. His teeth were chattering as briskly as those of an angry gorilla in a meat safe.

'It's George Pearmain! I can see him! He's...'

'He's what?'

'He's standing there! Right there! Oh, my God! It's him! My God!'

George found this very gratifying indeed. He continued to point in a menacing fashion.

'What's he doing?' said his companion.

'He...I don't know...He...*He has no head!*' said the pathologist.

This, thought George, was typical of the man's sloppiness. What did he mean 'no head'? George had no shoulders, arms, chest, waist, buttocks, legs or feet. Why single out his head?

He wasn't, of course, at all sure about how he might look to Pawlikowski. How people saw you was a bit of a problem when you were alive. When you were dead it was anybody's guess as to what they made of you. Was he wearing a suit? Tastefully arranged grave clothes? Perhaps Pawlikowski was getting him with his innards displayed. Whatever, George was certainly scaring the shit out of the Pole.

Pawlikowski was staring at him, still transfixed with horror. 'What do you want of me?' he stammered.

George liked the way he slipped in the preposition. It

324

added a Gothic flavour to the encounter. Mind you, from the expression on his face, it was pretty fucking Gothic anyway.

'I want you,' said George, still pointing his index finger at the pathologist, 'to treat the dead with more respect! In your private and your public life!!

George had the firm impression that Pawlikowski had heard all or most of this.

Pawlikowski continued to back away from whatever image of G. Pearmain was being presented to him. He continued to whimper very satisfactorily. 'I – I'm sorry!' he whined.

'It's been a long day, Marek,' said his companion, glancing nervously at the small crowd of spectators who had gathered by the french windows. 'You're under a great deal of strain.'

'And,' said George, 'you'll be under a great deal more strain if you don't do as I say.'

Pawlikowski's jaw had dropped further and faster than a tower block lift whose main cable had just been severed. 'I mean,' he muttered, 'we do…joke around but…what do you want? What do you want?'

'I want you to take early retirement,' said George, in what he hoped were deep and sonorous tones.

This was too much for the pathologist. With one last, wild look around him, he pushed his way through the group by the french windows. He was shouting something as he blundered out into the hall and then through the front garden towards the street. George was fairly sure he was telling anyone who wanted to listen that he had had enough enough enough…'I can't believe it!' Pawlikowski screamed, as he disappeared down Hornbeam Crescent. 'I can't believe it!'

No. Well. George found it all pretty hard to believe too. He was dead. That was fairly incredible. He also seemed to know he was dead. That was even more incredible. Was it a lot more incredible than knowing you were alive? George was not sure. It was certainly not more incredible than thinking you were going to be alive for ever, which most people went around believing until they stepped under a bus, had a heart attack, got cancer or were shot by some passing lunatic for no reason at all. Everything about life – and death – was unbelievable, as far as George was concerned, and one of the only things that made either of them bearable was being able to believe at least six impossible things, preferably before breakfast.

Pawlikowski's exit seemed to have signalled the break-up of the evening. His two remaining companions did a bit of half-hearted photography, waved a chunk of incident tape around, then shovelled poor Mullins on to a stretcher and took her body out through the side passage.

Veronica Pinker helped Esmeralda clear away the plates. She, Geraldine and Rosalina put them into the dishwasher. Peregrine and the Prune disappeared without saying goodbye to anyone. Beryl Vickers was comforted by Esmeralda. Nat ordered a taxi for her and, after she had been carried away, they both embraced George's widow.

Veronica said, 'How will we manage without George?'

Nat said, 'With difficulty.'

Then they, too, went out into the night.

Maurice and Barry and their wives, who had stayed behind with the children during the funeral, kissed Esmeralda. Bella asked if Granddad was going to stay dead or was he going to come over to tea? George watched Bella Ella and Ella Bella as their mothers carried them out to the car and reflected that, even if he was never going to be able to communicate with anyone ever again, it might be worth sticking around for the pleasure of watching them grow. They would soon be acquiring hamsters and guinea pigs and going to school.

George had enjoyed all that stuff. He saw no reason why he should not enjoy it all over again. Perhaps, by then, he would have learned how to manifest himself in a manner that did not send his audience bawling and blubbering up the nearest wall.

Finally it was the way it had been ever since the children had left home ten years ago. It was just him, Esmeralda and the dog. Partridge was watching the farewells with the same gloomy attention he gave to nearly all human life. As he and George stood on the porch, as Esmeralda waved goodbye to her sons and their families, he looked up at George and said, 'I've remembered what it was I wanted to tell you!'

'Oh,' said George. 'What was it, then?'

'It was your brother who poisoned you,' said Partridge. 'I saw him put the leaves in your glass. Apparently hemlock tastes a bit like parsnips.'

'How do you know that?' said George, thinking, but not saying, that it was a little late to be coming up with this information.

'I'm not sure,' said Partridge. 'I do know quite a lot of things. Although I am *only a dog* – as you used to constantly remind me!'

George did not really want to get into a conversation about the many ways in which he had failed his dog. Especially not *with* his dog.

Partridge seem to realize he had overstepped the mark, and when he spoke again, his tone was conciliatory. 'I don't think he meant to do it,' he said. 'It was an impulse thing. I think he's basically very fond of you.'

'I'm still dead!' said George.

'True!' said the dog, and wandered off into the corner of the kitchen where he had slept when he was alive. 'I never really liked him,' he said. 'He preferred cats. So he kept telling me. Which I thought tactless.'

George stood, watching Esmeralda make a last tour of the kitchen. Only when she had closed the security grille did Partridge lower himself painfully to the floor and take up his position for the night in the precise spot where, eight years ago, his cushion had always been placed. 'See you in the morning,' said Partridge. 'Probably.'

George ignored this. Ignoring dogs, dead or alive, was the best way to treat them. He followed Esmeralda as she toiled upstairs to the room they had shared for so many years. He sat on the other side of the bed, as he had always done, while she rummaged in her bedside cabinet for the blood-pressure pills, the cholesterol pills, the indigestion pills and all the other pills that were supposed to stave off the unmentionable thing that had happened to George.

They still each had their own side of the bed. That was something. As she levered her legs up on to the mattress she did not stray into his territory, as she had been careful not to throughout the long years of their marriage. If only he could talk to her, George thought, being dead would not be so bad. That was what he had enjoyed most of all. Talking to her.

There were things he should have said. Not 'I love you' – he had said it plenty of times but it was a line that did not particularly impress Esmeralda. She knew he loved her. She wanted to know what he was going to do about it. 'Love,' she always used to say, 'comes out of what you do. Not what you say. Words are cheap with you. You're good with words.' Well, yes, he had been good with words and she was one of the few people who appreciated that in him. She had even, sometimes, affected to like his poetry.

She knew him so well. He was incapable of fooling her. That was what he liked – or loved – most about her. 'You usually say, "I love you",' she had said once, 'when you want something. Or if you're frightened. Or if you're going away. Or if you're thinking of cheating on me.'

That was the thing he should have said. He should have told her about the woman from the NatWest. He should have told her about Biskiborne. Maybe that was why he had come back from the dead. Or, to put it more accurately, never properly departed from his life. He should have told her their marriage had not been as fundamentally solid as she thought it had been. That seemed unnecessarily sadistic, did it not? But, then, nothing would have surprised George about what the bastards had in store for him.

'I had an affair with that woman from the bank,' he said. 'My secretary. Julie Biskiborne.'

It was impossible to tell if she had heard him. Probably not, George thought. She would, surely, have looked a little more surprised. She had only just returned from his funeral. What she said next, however, seemed more like the beginning of a conversation than a monologue. Although in long marriages, as George knew to his cost, it was often difficult to distinguish between the two.

'Oh, George!' she said. 'Oh, George! I understood you so well.' She lay back on the pillows. 'Wherever you are,' she went on, 'I hope you're not worrying about that ridiculous woman. The one from the bank.'

'You knew about her?' said George.

'It was so obvious you were having an affair with her,' said Esmeralda. 'I remember when we went to a party at the bank and she was there and you were so furtive. It was obvious you were shagging her. Well. I wasn't very interested, was I? At the time.'

'That,' said George, 'is true.'

'She had a ridiculous name...' said Esmeralda.

'Julie Biskiborne,' said George.

'Julie Biskiborne,' said Esmeralda. 'That was it. I couldn't imagine how you could ever get involved with a person who had such a ridiculous name. And she was, as far as I could see, a pretty ridiculous person.'

'She was,' said George. 'She was a pretty ridiculous person.'

'She was absolutely fucking ridiculous,' said Esmeralda, decisively.

This wasn't a conversation, thought George, more like call and response of a rather primitive kind, but it was, he decided, a step in the right direction.

'You're out there somewhere, George,' said Esmeralda. 'You're not the kind of person who will ever go away. Not really.'

'No,' said George.

'I mean,' said Esmeralda, 'I was in love with you, George. That's it. It's simple. If you love someone. Really love them. You don't stop loving them.'

'No,' said George. 'You don't.'

'Why does Jane Austen always end with the marriage?' went on Esmeralda. 'It's with the marriage that things really start. Everything before that is just making up your mind, and once you've made up your mind, then it begins. There are so many wonderful, beautiful things that happen as a result. That's when the relationship starts. That's the real deal. And you have to stick with it. It's why I never bothered to ask you about Biskiborne or whatever her name was. I really was not interested in her. What did she have to do with us? We're the story, George. You and me. We loved each other. You died. End of story.'

She got up then and went through to the bathroom. He stood and watched her as she studied her face, with the practised cynicism of the sixty-something, in the mirror. She rubbed cream into her skin. She looked at herself again. Then she shed her clothes in a light and practical manner. George gazed at her white flesh. It was still firm – but he was pretty sure he would like it even when it started to wrinkle and sag and swing around in lumps, which, at the moment, thank God, it did not seem to be doing.

She had, he noticed idly, a very nice bum.

When she had brushed her hair (why would you want to brush your hair before going to bed?), she went back into the bedroom. George watched as she went round to her side of the bed and, from his side, he watched her some more. He had no teeth to brush or skin to moisturize or hair not to bother to comb, so he just stood there looking at her.

Outside, the rain had started again. It fell softly on the neat and ordered suburban gardens. Below, on the patio, he could hear the important snuffle of a badger as it moved closer towards the house and possible sources of food.

George laid his head on the pillow. He did feel, for some reason, as if he had got a head. Next to him, Esmeralda switched off her light and the room was in darkness. She lay very quietly. He could see her left hand, curled up, as if preparing for the ordeal of sleep. She did not always sleep well. He reached out his hand towards her in the gentle gesture of reassurance he had never performed enough when he was alive. He listened to her breathing. It slowed, gradually. He waited for the light snore with which she sometimes rounded off the evening.

It didn't come. He wouldn't have been able to prod her anyway. She was awake.

'Can you hear me?' he said quietly.

'Oh, George,' said Esmeralda, with equal softness. 'George.'

She lay there, awake, in the neat suburban bedroom.

George lay next to her, as he had done in life. Outside the rain continued. The wind had started up again and beat against the window in a steady rhythm. Down in the street someone was trying to start their car. They turned over the engine. It seemed about to cough its way into life but each time it didn't quite make it. Further away, a group of lads were on their way home from the pub. He could hear them shouting to each other and, as their footsteps moved further away down the street, the shrill laughter of girls. Some things never change, thought George. They could have been his lads, years ago, on their way back from some party. This was going to continue. Boy meets girl. Boy marries girl. Boy dies. Girl, somehow, carries on.

He listened in the darkness. Eventually there was a gentle regularity to Esmeralda's breathing and then, for a while, Mrs Pearmain, as well as her husband, was lost to the world.